PC TEAM III

*Action-Adventure Stories
of a Police K-9 Team
in Latin America*

A Novel

Allen Coryell

Copyright © 2012 by Allen K. Coryell
E-Book
All Rights Reserved

This paperback edition 2020
ISBN: 978-1-7345092-2-9
All Rights Reserved

Published by:
Digital Novels, LLC

Allen Coryell was raised in Burbank, California. Professionally Dr. Coryell (with an Ed.D. degree) was an educator, teaching Spanish for nine years and serving as a high school principal for 25 years. He now has time to devote to his profession as a writer of action-adventure fiction. Having spent a total of six years in Bolivia, Brazil, Colombia, México, Panamá, Perú, Portugal, and Spain, the author brings a definite ring of truth to his novels of international intrigue.

This novel is a work of fiction. Names of places, incidents, persons or characters living or dead, organizations, associations, groups, events, or locales are products of the author's imagination or are used fictitiously.

Any resemblance to places, incidents, persons or characters living or dead, organizations, associations, groups, or to actual events or locales is entirely coincidental.

All rights are reserved. No part of this book may be reproduced or transmitted in any form or by any means, electronic or mechanical, including photocopying, or by any information storage and retrieval system, without the written permission from the author or as authorized by Amazon.com's Kindle Direct Publishing or KDP.

Credits
Our thanks to cover designer:
Matthew Morse
Graphic Design
HeyMatthew.com

Chapter 1

The telephone rings at the desk of Susana Castillo, secretary of the Police K-9 School in La Vista, Yuñeco. She answers it.

"Berto, it's for you," she says into the intercom.

Captain Roberto "Berto" Castillo, Superintendent of the School and Susana's husband, picks up his phone.

"Hey there, this is Captain Berto Castillo."

Berto listens, "Berto, this is Chief Tony Camargo in Neblina. We've got a problem, and I think only you can help us."

"Okay, Chief, what's the problem?"

"As you know, we're on the western side of the Andes, and we have two main caves in our foothills. Actually, they're probably just one long cave with two entrances about five miles apart. Four days ago, five boys, age 12 through 14, decided to do some exploring going into the south entrance of the cave.

"We have a Search and Rescue Team with a sub-unit that specializes in cave rescues. They were in the cave for three days with their equipment and rescued four of the boys. The boys all have the same message that the fifth boy, Marco Espinosa, wandered off someplace and sometime. The others don't know where or when. Our SAR team members came out of the cave exhausted. We were wondering if you could send a K-9 team over here at our expense by airplane, to try to get the scent cone of this boy and find him. Any chance of some help? We're stymied."

"Sure Chief. I'll check with my Chief, Luis Medina, and see how he feels about it. I'll take the assignment myself if you can get me to the entrance of the cave."

"How are your horseback riding skills?"

"They'll do."

"Okay, if you can get approval from your Chief, have your secretary book a flight for you and your German Shepherd dog from La Vista to Neblina at our expense. We can start getting prepared. Have your secretary let us know when you expect to arrive."

"Will do. Now you'll need to pick up a 50-pound bag of the most expensive dog food you can find. That's based on my obtaining approval from my Chief. Have you got a paper and pen there?"

"Sure, go ahead."

"Okay, I'll need a pocket radio on your frequencies, a large canteen of water for Franz and me. Franz, that's my dog. Also, if your kitchen staff could prepare us some high energy but light weight food, that'd be great. I'll have to assume that Franz and I may have to stay in the cave two nights. That'll give your people some idea of the food we'll need. Also, a bag with a strap to easily carry the food would be nice. What's the temperature in the cave?"

"It's a comfortable 61 degrees year-round."

"Well, Franz is dressed accordingly, but I should have a jacket. He'll keep me warn at night."

"That's a good deal, a walking blanket."

"We'll try to get out of here today. I'd like to get over there, have a good dinner, and a good night's rest. Where should I stay?"

"I'll pick you up at the airport. We'd love to have you stay at our house, but it's full of so many grandkids right now that you wouldn't get any rest. There's a nice motel right across the street from the police station. You could meet us at 8:00 a.m. tomorrow morning in the rear parking lot. We also have the stables there. They'll have a good horse saddled for you at that time. A couple wranglers will ride up with you and bring your horse back. There's a permanent base camp at the entrance to the cave. Some members of my Search and Rescue Team are there with Sr. and Sra. Espinosa, the parents of the boy still in the cave.

"When you finish your work in the cave, they'll radio for your horse. They keep some good hot food going at the base camp, so you'll find a great meal waiting for you. I'd better let you go so your secretary can get started on the plane tickets. Thanks Captain. We were at the end of our ropes here."

"That reminds me, can you have a strong but light weight rope waiting for me."

"The SAR team has lots of different kinds of ropes standing by."

"Good, we'll be in touch, Chief."

"Thanks Berto."

They both ring off.

Berto quickly phones his own Chief, Luis Medina, and secures permission to take his K-9 German Shepherd dog with him out of the area on a mission of mercy.

Afterwards, he yells out, "Susaaaaanaaaaaana."

Susana comes running into his office with note pad in hand.

"Yes, Berto, what's the word?"

"I need tickets for me and Franz on the first plane out to Neblina. Return flight not known at this time. That's tickets for two so there's no hassle."

"Will you have any trouble getting Franz on the plane?"

"I'd better not. I'll be in uniform with my captain's bars and my 9 mm semi-automatic pistol in plain view. They've got a lost boy in a cave, four days now. He wandered off from a group of five boys. The other four have been rescued by the local Search and Rescue Team, the SAR team. The boy's name is Marco Espinosa in case you want to follow it on the news. They need me and Franz. Horses will take us up to the cave tomorrow morning. The temperature in the cave is 61 degrees all the time so don't worry about our freezing to death."

Susana replies, "Okay, I'll go check now."

She returns to her office, picks up the phone, and calls the local travel bureau explaining the problem. In a few minutes she finishes with, "Charge the tickets to the Neblina Police Department."

Returning to Berto's office, she says, "All is taken care of. The flight leaves in two hours with lunch served on the plane. It's a short flight, but the Sudamérica Air flight crew is well experienced in getting everyone a lunch in a short time. Also, the receptionist said that service dogs are allowed on the plane all the time. Is Franz a service dog?"

"He sure is, and I could get you a whole lot of people who would swear to that fact."

Changing gears in his role, Berto takes his wife, Susana, in his arms, "You'll be all right Dear?"

"Yes, Berto. The boys are both getting older now. As you know, Bobbie is 18, just having graduated from high school. And Miguel is 15. They can really take care of themselves, do dinner dishes, and help with the housework. This leaves me lots of time to take care of the baby. The lady next door is a gem, and takes care of little Elizabeth during the day as if she were her own.

"And by the way husband of mine, have you decided on what name you're going to call Elizabeth yet? Is it Lizzy or is it Beth?"

"Which do you prefer?" asks Berto.

Susana responds, "You know which I prefer, Elizabeth. It's much more refined."

"Okay, Elizabeth it is then. Hey, I'd better get home and packed. And that includes my helmet and jacket. I'd appreciate your phoning Chief Tony Camargo in Neblina. He'll meet me at the airport if he knows what flight I'm taking to Neblina."

"Sure Boss."

She kisses him goodbye and tells him to take care of himself. Then she hands him a plastic bag of fresh treats for Franz. She knows that positive reinforcement is a basic principle in teaching dogs and fresh treats given at appropriate times are just the reinforcement needed.

Later Berto parks his Police K-9 Car in a spot reserved for police cars at the airport. Getting Franz and his gear from the rear of the car, Berto attaches the dog's leash and off they go for this short flight to Neblina. If it weren't for the highway over the Andes Mountains, Berto would just as soon drive to Neblina. However, a flight is much preferable to the highway with its many twists and turns and ever-present road construction.

Later as Berto and Franz enter the plane, the flight attendant puts them in the front seat with two towels having been spread on the seat where Franz will sit. Berto places his gear under the seats, and buckles them both in.

The plane wastes no time as it is soon heading out to the runway. After making its turn, the place accelerates down the runway. Soon it leans back and heads for the skies.

Franz is a bit nervous.

"Good dog, Franz," says Berto as he strokes his head and back. When the plane reaches its cruising altitude, the noise from the engines diminishes somewhat which helps Franz relax.

Berto and Franz are served their meal first. The flight attendant brings Berto his tray. He has a ham and cheese sandwich, chips, a fruit cup, and a lemonade.

He thinks, *There's just about enough time to eat such a tasty meal. I wonder what they'll bring for Franz.*

The flight attendant returns with a tray for Franz. It has plastic plates with some cooked ground meat on one plate, a cooked hot dog cut up as well in small pieces on another plate, a plastic bowl of cold water, and a plate of dog food if he has room left over for such food.

Berto thinks, *Good, lots of protein. He'll need that for tomorrow's workout in the cave.*

A short while later, and just about one minute after the flight attendants picked up the trays, the light goes on to fasten seat belts. The plane is preparing to land at Neblina.

#

Berto and Franz are the first ones off the plane since their seats were at the front. Neblina Police Chief Tony Camargo greets them in the terminal. Berto has only one small bag and his helmet so he doesn't need to go to the carousel for luggage.

Chief Camargo leads the way outside the building to where he parked his police car. They get in, and Chief Camargo gives Berto some more orientation while driving to the motel across from the local police department.

The Chief hands Berto the plastic key to his room which has already been arranged.

"As you can see Berto, there's a nice coffee shop attached to the motel. I'll pick you up tomorrow morning about 7:55 a.m. Will that be okay?"

"Sure, Chief, we'll be ready."

"Good, the horses will also be ready in the rear of the parking lot. I'll stay behind and be in touch with you by radio. The wranglers will escort you to the cave where your equipment is waiting."

"Thanks Chief. I'll see you in the morning."

Berto leaves the car, closes the front door, opens the rear door, and says, "Let's go Franz." The dog immediately jumps out of the car and joins Berto at his left side.

Taking his small bag from the rear of the car, Berto looks at Chief Camargo and says, "Goodbye Chief," and off he walks with Franz staying close to him.

As they walk into their motel room, Franz has to inspect every corner and piece of furniture. Berto drops his bag on the bed and phones his wife.

"Hi Susana, I'm in my room now. The motel is right across from the police department. It's called the Neblina Motel. Very unique, huh?"

Susana responds, "Yes, Honey. How are you and Franz?"

"We're doing just fine. They even had a special meal on the plane for Franz, hamburger, hot dog, water, and dog food."

"Wow, he sure is spoiled."

"We're kind of tired now. I think I'll watch some television, go have a bite to eat, and then hit the sack."

"When will you phone again Berto?"

"I'm not sure. Tomorrow morning will be rather hectic. I think the media will track us pretty well. Just keep your TV news on. You'll probably see some pictures of me and Franz entering the cave."

"Okay Honey take care and be careful. Don't let Franz fall down any hole in that cave."

"I won't Dear. See you later."

"Goodbye."

They both ring off.

Berto turns on the television while Franz takes a nap.

#

The next morning at 7:50 a.m., Berto and Franz are waiting in front of the motel for Chief Camargo to pick them up. Berto is dressed in coveralls. He carries attached to his belt an extra flashlight, a small waterproof container for matches, and a small first-aid kit. He wears a helmet on his head to protect him in case he falls. He also has on a jacket for warmth in the cave.

The Chief drives up stopping in front of Berto and Franz. They quickly get into the car which leaves immediately for the rear of the police station.

The Chief parks his car near the corrals where the department keeps several horses and burros. Since the boundaries of the City of Neblina go right up to the crest of the Andes Mountains, a large, mountainous and foothill section belongs to the city for law enforcement and other purposes, hence the occasional need for horses and burros.

One of the wranglers says to Berto, "Hey Berto, you'd better bring your dog here so I can put leather pads on his feet. The country up to the cave is rather rough on the paws of dogs if they're unprotected."

"Thanks guys. Come on Franz. Take side."

Franz steps to the left side of Berto as they walk into the shed that the wranglers use for storage and tools needed in their trade.

"Berto, can your dog jump up to this counter so we can easily put these pads on his feet?"

"This dog can do anything."

"Franz," says Berto as he places his hand twice on the counter.

Franz jumps to the top of the counter and lies down in a perfect position for the wranglers.

The thick leather pads fit the paws of Franz perfectly. The tops have elastic sewed in which keeps the pads tight on Franz's paws.

When the task is finished, Berto says, "Franz, there."

Franz jumps to the ground and immediately notices that his paws are different. He licks at the leather and looks up at Berto who says, "Good dog, Franz," while giving him his special treats and rubbing his back.

The wranglers are impressed with the dog and his reaction to orders from Berto with one wrangler saying,

"Berto, that's quite a dog you've got there. Would you sell him?"

"Sure, any time."

"What's the price?"

"He's comes cheap, only ten million dollars."

The wranglers laugh.

#

Later that morning Berto and the wranglers arrive at the base camp. Franz enjoyed his new "shoes" as he followed along at the left side of Berto's horse.

Sr. and Sra. Espinosa greet them as they tie up their horses.

Sr. Espinosa says, "Captain, we can't thank you enough for coming here from La Vista with Franz in an attempt to find our boy, Marco. He's only 13 years old, and I'm sure he's as scared as can be by now."

Berto looks around and sees the ever-present TV crew that is filming him and the Espinosas.

Sr. Espinosa says, "Here are several items of clothing used recently by Marco that have not yet been washed per instructions from Chief Camargo. We've kept them protected in Marco's pillowcase."

Berto takes the clothing and says, "Well, that's a good way to protect the scent. I'll have to remember that one. Thanks very much. Now we'd better get going."

A member of the SAR team comes up to Berto and says, "Captain, we would appreciate your attaching this spool of wire to your belt just before you go into the cave. You will notice that the wire is wrapped with white insulation. It has three purposes. First in case you become lost, you can retrace your steps easily with this wire. Second, if you fall down a hole and can't get out, we can follow the wire in and find you. And third, there is a clip on your small radio. Obviously when you get into the cave, your radio transmissions can no longer be heard. But if you will snap the radio clip on this wire, you can hear our messages and can also transmit to us if you need to."

Berto says gratefully, "Thanks for all your help and consideration for me and for Franz. Now let me have a chair please, and I'll give Franz a strong whiff of these clothes. He should be able to pick up Marco's scent cone at some place in the cave. We'll follow it when he does, and hopefully bring you back a young man who should be very hungry and tired. Usually these caves have healthy water trickling through them at various places or pools of good water. Therefore, I imagine that Marco isn't thirsty."

Berto sits down on a folding chair given to him. He says, "Let's go Franz."

Franz walks over to Berto who immediately starts placing various pieces of clothing in front of his nose. Franz sniffs deeply many times and starts to get excited. He knows the game of hide and seek is about to start and all his senses will be tested. Berto tucks one of the boy's shirts into a plastic bag with a zipper on top so he won't personally contaminate the shirt's odor. Then he puts the bag into the pocket of his jacket in case he needs to give Franz a fresh whiff of the boy's odor.

Berto stands up. As he does so, a member of the SAR team gives him a flashlight. Berto reads on the side that it is a "Special LED Flashlight."

As he starts to walk toward the entrance to the cave, Berto ties the spool of white wire to his belt. A member of the SAR Team takes the end of the wire and ties it to a steel bar sticking out of the ground with a sign marking the entrance to the cave. He ties several knots in it.

Then Berto stops and says, "Hey, where's my rope?"

A SAR team member comes forward and asks, "How much rope do you want?"

"Fifty feet with knots tied every two feet or so."

"No problem. Much of our rope comes just that way."

The SAR Team member goes to the shed and returns with a piece of rope rolled up to fit over someone's shoulder.

As he hands it to Berto, Berto replies, "Thanks, this is light weight but strong. That's great."

Putting the rope over his shoulder, Berto heads again for the entrance to the cave.

Once inside the cave, Berto turns on the new flashlight. While it is relatively small and lightweight, it emits a powerful beam of light.

Berto opens the plastic bag and pushes the shirt into Franz's face and says, "Franz, go-after."

Franz puts his nose up high in the air as he seeks to find the scent cone of the missing boy. Berto concludes that he can't find it. He decides they'll have to move farther into the cave.

Walking slowly with the flashlight showing the way, Berto with Franz at his left side moves farther and farther into the cave letting the spool of wire continually unwind.

Berto stops to look around. He has not had much experience in caves. He turns off his flashlight. It is pitch black with no light coming from any source.

Berto says, "Franz, cálmate, cálmate." The dog relaxes and lies down. Berto turns his flashlight back on and kneels by Franz saying, "Good dog Franz. Here's a tasty bite."

The dog takes the morsel from Berto's hand and eats it down quickly. "Good dog Franz."

After looking around for a minute or so and using the flashlight to follow the wire back from whence he came, Berto feels a little better.

He decides to yell, "**Maaarco. Maaarco.**"

He then listens carefully and watches Franz's ears to see if the dog with his super-sensitive ears picks up any sound in response to his yelling.

"**Maaarco. Maaarco.**"

Berto talks to his dog, "Well Franz, I guess the boy can't hear us yet. And you haven't found his scent cone yet either, so we need to move farther into the cave. Take side."

Franz goes to Berto's left side and the two of them continue to walk farther into the depths of the cave. Berto notices some side branches in the cave.

He thinks, *Oh no, what horrible places for a young boy to go exploring.*

"Whoa Franz."

They stop walking as Berto takes the boy's shirt from the plastic bag again and pushes it into Franz's nose. The dog takes another big whiff of the shirt. He then puts his nose high into the air and moves it back and forth and in circles.

Then he starts tugging at his leash. Berto recognizes this as a positive sign. The dog has found the scent cone of the boy. Berto moves along behind Franz keeping his flashlight in front of the dog so he won't fall into any hole or trip on anything. Occasionally, Franz barks and wants to run faster as he keeps his nose moving back and forth high in front of him.

Berto thinks, T*his has got to be one of the easiest trailings that Franz has ever done. This branch of the cave may never have had another human being in it before. It can't be contaminated with lots of scent cones.*

The dog pulls stronger and stronger on the leash.

Berto says, "Franz, whoa."

As the dog stops, Berto yells loudly, "**Marco Espinosa**." The sound echoes throughout the various branches of the cave.

The dog's ears perk up. He hears something. Berto strains to hear it too.

The faint sound comes back to him, "I'm here. At the bottom of this shaft."

"Franz, go-after."

Franz takes off at a faster pace which is rather dangerous in the cave. Berto struggles to hold him back, but he wants to run.

"Franz, whoa." The dog stops and holds still and quiet.

The sound is louder now, "I'm here, at the bottom of this shaft."

Berto shines his flashlight around and sees a hole in their pathway directly 20 feet ahead. Remembering his commitment to his faithful dog to protect him in dangerous situations, Berto calls his dog back by saying, "Franz, Take side." The dog returns to Berto's left side.

"Good dog Franz." He gives him some tasty treats from his pocket.

Berto moves ahead slowly keeping Franz close beside him as they approach the hole in the pathway. Finally they reach the hole. Berto shines his flashlight down the hole and sees a small boy about 30 feet below.

"Hey Marco, how are you doing?"

"Not very good. When I fell in here, I really hit my head hard on a rock. I think I lost a lot of blood. I was knocked out for a while. Also, I think both my legs are broken. I'm pretty weak."

"How are you doing for water?"

"I've had none since I fell in here."

"Okay, the first thing I'm going to do is lower my canteen to you on the end of a rope. Untie it and start drinking, but slowly, okay?"

"Okay. That sounds wonderful."

With Franz standing stiff at his side, Berto lowers the canteen tied on the end of the rope.

"I've got it."

The boy unties the rope and starts to drink from the canteen. "Oh boy, does this ever taste good."

"How about food. Have you had anything to eat?"

"No. What's your name?"

"I'm a police officer Captain from La Vista with my K-9 dog who found your scent trail. My name is Berto. Your mom and dad are at the entrance of the cave and gave my dog, Franz, a good whiff of some of your clothing. That's how he found you."

"Do you have any food with you?"

"Yes. I'll lower some food in a bag on the end of the rope."

Pulling up the rope, Berto ties his bag of food to the rope and lowers it to Marco. He feels that it is more important right now to help the boy regain some strength with water and food before he tries to get him out of the hole in the cave.

Marco tries to yell up to Berto, but his voice is getting weaker instead of stronger. Berto knows that he is unaware of how much blood the boy has lost. He decides he'd better move quickly and get the boy out of the hole, out of the cave, and to a hospital.

"Marco, untie the rope from the bag, and I'll tell you how to tie it around your body so I can pull you out of the hole."

"Okay, Berto." His voice is even weaker now. Berto begins to panic a bit.

"Are you ready to tie the rope around you?"

"Yes, Ber--."

Un oh, I'd better move fast.

"Take the rope and put it around your chest and under your arms."

"Yes, Ber--."

"Now tie a knot in front of your chest. Make sure the knot doesn't slip. But even if it does, I can get you out of there before any problem develops."

"Yes, B----."

The boy faints to the ground before he can get the rope tied around him. He has collapsed completely and is unable to communicate with Berto.

"Franz, we've got a problem here." He pulls the rope up. "We need to find a place where I can tie this rope and let myself down to where the boy is. Find something solid where I can tie this rope. Go Franz."

Berto is too fearful to let Franz loose from his leash. He lets the dog lead him as they seek something in the close vicinity where they can secure the rope. But Berto doesn't want to lose Franz into any hole or to have him encounter any other danger.

"Whoa, look at that. It looks like some miners have been here. I was wrong. This place has had some other scent cones over the years. There's a piece of steel sticking up from the ground. Let's hope it is still strong."

Berto ties the rope around the piece of steel and pulls on the rope. It holds tightly and is close to the hole where the boy fell. It also points straight up from the hole, so the knot won't slip off it.

Berto checks his knot on the piece of steel and makes two more swings around the piece of steel tying another knot. He knows he will have only one chance at this effort.

"Let's go Franz." The dog stands by Berto and the piece of steel. Berto drops the handle of the leash over the top of the piece of steel. It falls to the knot and remains there. Berto pulls on it. It too is strong, and Berto figures that the dog is safe here and will not be in jeopardy at this location.

"Franz, sit, sit."

The dog understands and follows the command and remains in a sitting position.

"Good dog, Franz, good dog." Berto rubs his back and gives him some treats.

"Franz, remain." This is the command that Franz must obey as he has always done in the past. His life may depend on it.

With Franz taken care of, Berto walks back to the hole with the rope which he drops into the hole. He then starts to lower himself into the hole, hand over hand.

He thinks, *Will my hands be strong enough to lower me to the ground and lift me and then the boy out of the hole?*

Eventually Berto feels the ground under his feet.

"Marco, are you all right?"

The boy whispers softly, "Not very good, I think."

Berto feels the boy's pulse on his wrist. It is weak. He then checks his neck for his pulse. It too is weak, but he can feel it. He lowers his ear to the boy's chest to see if he can hear or feel his heart beating. He can, barely.

Is it possible that I got this close only to find the boy almost dead? It can't be. I'd better get him out of here as soon as possible.

Berto takes the end of the rope and ties a knot around the boy's chest. "Marco, is that too tight?"

"No Berto."

"Good, now I'm going to climb out of the hole and then I'll pull you up out of the hole."

Berto knows that under stress such as this, a person's strength and adrenaline are increased. He takes hold of the rope and remembers his days in high school when all the male students had to do the rope climb. He was very good at it. Hand over hand he goes, up the rope without any hesitation. Once he reaches the top, he climbs out of the hole.

He immediately starts to pull the boy out of the hole as well. Fortunately, the boy is small and light weight. Berto pulls him up easily. When he has the boy on the ground at his feet, he unties the knot. He stops for a minute to catch his breath shinning the flashlight around while doing so.

"Marco, we'll be out of here soon and get you to a hospital."

"That sounds good, Berto."

Feeling strong again, Berto puts the boy over his right shoulder and holds him there with his right hand. The boy grimaces from the pain caused by the two broken legs.

Berto leaves the rope exactly where he tied it in case *some other person needs it.*

Removing the handle of the leash from the steel pole, Berto ties it around his belt. "Take side, Franz."

The dog starts to move walking at Berto's side. As they walk, Berto feels the white wire through his left hand. He knows that this is the road to salvation as far as he is concerned.

Eventually, an exhausted Berto, an injured Marco, and a valiant Franz, find their way out of the cave.

The parents rush over as Berto falls to the ground, being careful not to hurt the young boy. Berto is exhausted. Sra. Espinosa sits on the ground and takes her son in her arms. She holds him close and kisses his face.

A doctor is immediately at their side. He checks the boy for vital signs. After several minutes of this, he tells the parents, "The boy is dead."

Berto breaks into tears, "No, no, it can't be. He was alive when I started bringing him out of the cave."

Both parents put their arms around Berto. Sra. Espinosa kisses him several times on the cheek.

Sr. Espinosa says, "At least we have our boy back with us and not lost someplace in that horrible cave. Where did you find him Berto?"

"He had fallen down a 30-foot hole in one of the branches of the cave. He was alive when I found him. He said when he fell he hit his head on a rock and lost a lot of blood. He also felt he broke both his legs."

Berto starts to sob again.

Sr. Espinosa says, "Dear, no more questions for Berto. He and Franz have done a wonderful thing for us. We'll never forget it. I couldn't live with the idea that Marco was lost someplace in that cave. He is not lost, he is found. We can bury him properly and always know where his body is."

"Yes, Dear. I'm sorry. I was just hoping that he could be found alive."

"The Lord did not will it. He has taken him to himself. He was too good for this world with all its evils. A person as righteous as our little Marco does not have to fight his way through 60 or 70 years on this earth."

The EMTs from the SAR put the boy's body on a stretcher and carry him away. The parents accompany them.

#

Berto and the wranglers return to the police station on horseback with Franz enjoying his leather socks.

As they are removing the saddles from the horses, Chief Camargo comes over to Berto who is still in a state of shock and exhausted.

The Chief says, "Well, Berto, I've learned one thing. If we had a K-9 unit ourselves, this boy could have been recovered a day or two earlier, alive. I thought with a Search and Rescue Team and a sub-unit of cavers, we were in good shape. But nothing can replace a trailing dog like your Franz. When do you start your next unit of instruction at the K-9 school?"

"In a few weeks, Chief."

"What's the fee?"

"Well the first fee is the largest one. The cost of a German Shepherd dog, already trained at a K-9 school in Europe that trains their pups in English, is $12,000.00. And then there's the cost of the schooling in La Vista, housing, food, staff, about $3,000.00 with retraining every month, at $500.00. Oh yes, it's expensive, but it's not nearly as dear as a young boy's life."

"I agree Berto. Is your school always full of trainees?"

"Yes, but we can fit in another easily. The handlers must be fully certified and experienced police officers, male or female. Oh and by the way, I didn't mention the K-9 vehicle. Yes, these dogs need their own special air-conditioned car with everything heavy duty so the car can be left running with its light bar on, its radio on, and its air conditioning on so the back part of the vehicle stays under 74 degrees. With the huge investment made in the dog in the first place for purchase and training, the vehicle is essential. The dogs live with their handlers' families. Usually there are some teen-age boys or girls who love to run with them. They have to be kept in great condition since they could be asked to run to the top of the mountains tomorrow, along with their handler. There is an extra stipend for the handler due to the many extra hours required to keep such a dog and another extra amount, not taxable, for dog food, visits to the vet, etc."

"Berto I don't care about the cost. Your efforts today are enough for me to give this a maximum effort. Our Police Commission meets tonight. Are you and Franz up to a short presentation on the subject? I assume you won't be going home until tomorrow."

"Sure Chief, if I can help this evening, I'd be glad to do it. I take my dog to meetings all the time. The people love him."

"That's a great idea. Our commission would enjoy seeing him. He's such a great example of what a German Shepherd trailing dog can do."

"What time?"

"Eight thirty on the dot."

"Okay, since the distance is so short, I'll walk across the street and be there at 8:30 p.m."

#

And exactly at 8:30 p.m. Berto, with Franz at his side, walks through the main door to the large multipurpose room used this evening for the meeting of the police commission. As soon as he takes a seat, the Chairman announces that all should stand for the salute to the flag.

Once that is taken care of, everyone sits down, and the meeting is underway. The Chairman asks that the minutes of the previous meeting be read and approved. Another member has a question on the wording of a motion. Once that is corrected, everyone seems to be in favor of the minutes as corrected. The vote is taken, and the minutes are approved.

Next, the Chairman reviews the agenda for the evening.

Under new business, Chief Tony Camargo says he would like to take a few minutes on Search and Rescue. The agenda is approved with that one addition.

Votes are taken on a series of items all at the same time, "the Consent Agenda." Berto can see that this board moves right along. Finally they get to new business. Chief Camargo walks to the podium and takes the microphone.

He reviews the tragic events of the past few days with a young boy 13 years of age dying after being rescued from a fall into a hole in the main cave in the mountains. He does not give the name of the boy. His parents are in the audience.

The Chief explains that their Search and Rescue Team has a sub-unit trained as cavers, but when a person gets lost in the cave and is alone, the sub-unit cannot find him. A dog that is trained to follow the scent of a person can do that.

The Chairman says, "I suspect this is the reason we have in our group tonight a beautiful German Shepherd dog alongside a police officer from another jurisdiction. Chief, do you want him to speak now?"

"Yes, Mr. Chairman. Let me introduce to you the Superintendent of the K-9 School in La Vista. His name is Captain Roberto Castillo. We all call him 'Berto' for short."

Everyone laughs.

The Chairman says, "Captain, we are pleased to have you here with your dog this evening. Please take the podium and share with us what we need to know about K-9 dogs."

"Thank you Mr. Chairman," says Berto as he walks up to the podium with Franz at his side.

"You may know about the attempt to rescue a young boy this morning. I was asked to fly over from La Vista to give your Search and Rescue Team some help. I brought my highly trained German Shepherd dog, Franz, with me. He is a member of my family. My teen-age boys love him and exercise him daily."

"The problem this morning is that I didn't get to the young man in time. I had to fly over yesterday in preparation for the search today. That extra day cost the young man his life, I'm certain of it. When I found him at the bottom of a 30-foot hole, he could barely speak and was dying from lack of water and food and loss of blood. I sent my canteen down to him on the end of a rope as well as some pieces of food.

"But that didn't do it. I then went into the hole and tied the rope around his chest and under his arms. After lifting him out of the hole, I carried him out of the cave. When I arrived back at the entrance, a doctor rushed forward to take his vital signs. It was then that I learned that he was dead." (Berto chokes up and can barely utter the words.)

"Pardon me for losing it. This business is rather emotionally difficult sometimes. I'll try to continue. My regular job is as the superintendent of the K-9 School in La Vista. This is the only K-9 School in the country, so we train police officers and German Shepherd dogs for all the police jurisdictions in the country. These dogs are very expensive. They all come from Europe and are trained there starting when they are pups. After some 18 months, they are sent to police departments here in Yuñeco. The cost is about $12,000.00. Then they come to our K-9 School for final training with their handlers who are fully authorized police officers from various police jurisdictions in the country. For a department to have a K-9 Team, a special police car is needed, with heavy duty everything, such as air conditioning, battery, light bar, radio, etc.

"Now I am not here to cause any fiscal problems. Your Chief asked me to say a word about these marvelous dogs since I had to wait over anyway for my flight home tomorrow. These dogs are trained to trail scents in the air, called scent cones. Give one of these dogs a whiff of clothing of a lost person or an escaped prisoner, and the dog thinks it's hide and go seek. He loves the game. They are also trained to go into a darkened building and find a criminal. That's the hardest mission they do that affects us handlers. To lose a wonderful German Shepherd dog to a bullet from a criminal's pistol is like losing a member of the family."

The Chairman says, "Captain, if I may interrupt at this time. Chief what do you estimate the total cost of having one of these dogs with us for a year?"

"Remember the first year is the most expensive," the Chief says, "since we would have to buy the dog and the K-9 Police Car. That expense would not be repeated for a number of years. I would estimate the first year as follows:"

The Chairman says, "Madame Finance Executive, please write these numbers down as the Chief reads them off."

"Yes, Mr. Chairman, I was ready to do that."

Another laugh comes from the audience.

Chief Tony Camargo continues, "I estimate as follows: cost of the dog, $12,000; K-9 Police Car, $25,000; Training at the K-9 School with a repeat session one afternoon per month, $3,000; Special stipend for the police K-9 officer, since it takes a lot of time to keep a large German Shepherd dog in shape, $3,000; Food and visits to the vet regularly, $2,500; Transportation from Europe, $2,500; Miscellaneous, $2,000." The Chief sits down.

The Chairman says, "Madam Finance Executive. What's the total of those numbers?"

She responds, "It's a nice even round number which the Chief seems to always come up with. It's $50,000.00."

Everyone laughs.

The Chairman continues, "How much money do we have in our undistributed reserves?"

"One hundred sixty thousand dollars."

A person in the audience raises her hand and is recognize by the Chairman.

"If I might say a word at this time. It was my son who was brought from the cave to us, dead this morning."

Tears start flooding down her cheeks.

"No one could have done more that Captain Berto Castillo. He didn't have to come here. He did it out of the kindness of his heart and his love for little children. He went into that cave alone with Franz his wonderful German Shepherd dog. He could have lost his own life or that of his dog. My husband and I will always be grateful for his bringing out of that cave the body of our son. We can bury him properly and not have to spend the rest of our lives wondering where his body is lying.

"It's just possible, if the Neblina Police Department had a dog as well trained as Franz, our son might have been rescued yesterday, alive. Now I don't want to dictate the agenda for this meeting, but I would appreciate your taking a few minutes to have Captain Castillo take Franz up to the stage and let each one of you rub his back and talk to him." She sits down.

The Chairman says, "That's a good idea. Let's take a break and ask Captain Castillo to bring Franz up here and let us get to know him."

The commission members stand up and stretch a bit.

Berto says, "Franz, Take side." The two police comrades walk side by side up to the stage where the commission members crowd around Franz. They all pet him and talk with him.

The Chairman says, "Berto, have him show off a bit."

Berto responds, "I'll have him do a few things. Stand back just a little bit please." The Commission members do as requested.

"Franz, loud."

The dog barks. Everyone laughs.

Berto then has the dog react to several commands that he gives him. Everyone is impressed as Berto explains each instruction just before giving it to the dog.

A commission member asks, "Berto, what command do you give the dog when you want him to attack some criminal?"

Everyone is surprised that such a question was asked. They're not sure how Berto will respond.

Berto says, "I really wouldn't want to say that command in this group. Franz is liable to attack someone."

Everyone agrees with Berto's decision.

"Franz, let's go."

The dog walks over to Berto who gives him a treat. "Good dog, Franz, good dog."

Everyone notices the treat given to Franz. A young college student says, "Look, there's positive reinforcement."

After some additional instructions to the dog, Berto says, "That's enough, you've got lots to do with your agenda this evening."

Everyone claps for the presentation.

Sr. and Sra. Espinosa have come up to the stage to watch the presentation. She approaches Berto and gives him a big hug and kiss on both cheeks with tears running down her face. All the Commission members see this act of appreciation for Captain Castillo.

After everyone has taken a chair, the Commission Chairman says, "The meeting is back in order."

One female member asks to be recognized and says, "Mr. Chairman, I move that we authorize the expenditure of not to exceed $50,000.00 for the items listed by Chief Camargo so that this police department will have a Police K-9 Team available for emergencies of whatever sort."

Another member says, "I second the motion."

The Chairman asks, "Is there any discussion on this item?"

No one speaks.

"Okay, we'll vote on the motion. All those in favor of the motion to authorize the expenditure of not to exceed $50,000.00 for a Police K-9 Team, please raise your hand."

All members of the Commission raise their hands.

"Anyone opposed to the motion, please raise your hand."

No hands go into the air.

"The motion passes unanimously. Thank you members. I see some hot coffee, cold lemonade, and cookies over there. Let's take a short break for sustenance."

Everyone laughs and stands for refreshments. Those in the audience crowd around Berto and Franz. They all want to pet the great dog.

Chief Camargo approaches Berto and says, "Thanks Berto, your presence here tonight made a big difference. I assume you'll be available by phone to walk me through this purchasing of a German Shepherd dog, signing him up for training at your K-9 School and so on."

"Of course, Chief. That's my job. The more K-9 Teams we have in the country the better. I don't remember, were you at the recent convention in La Vista for Chiefs of Police?"

"No, I wasn't, other obligations."

"Well, you missed a great sight. We had 19 K-9 Teams from around the country checking for explosives having been planted in the hotel by the Cartel de la Selva Tropical."

"Did the dogs find any explosives?"

"They sure did, dynamite and hand grenades. They saved a lot of lives in that hotel."

"Great, I'd better get ready for the meeting again. I suppose you'll be leaving now."

"Yes, Chief, I'll get a taxi in the morning to get to the airport. See you later."

"Okay Berto and thanks a lot for your help."

#

After an uneventful flight from Neblina to La Vista the following day, Berto and Franz get out of the taxi that took them from the airport to their home in La Vista. Paying the cabbie, Berto says, "Take side" and off he walks with his faithful dog at his left side.

As they arrive at the front door, it is mysteriously opened by Berto's wife, Susana.

"Who's waiting for us inside the doorway?"

"It's a big bad wolf waiting for you to come home finally."

Berto growls and Franz follows the pattern of his master, "We're coming to get you."

Franz bares his teeth and lets out a growl that would scare anyone. The big bad wolf decides to run to the kitchen.

Berto laughs, "Hey you chicken. I thought you were the big bad wolf."

Susana then runs to the front room where Berto grabs her and wrestles her to the floor. Franz sees the fun everyone is having so he jumps on top of them both. He is still growling which scares Susana.

Berto says, "Honey, don't be afraid of him. He's just having fun like we are. He's probably thirsty as well."

"Okay, let's get some water for this thirsty pal of ours."

They both go to the kitchen where Susana pours a bowl of water which she puts on the floor for the dog. Franz attacks the water taking big slurps with his tongue throwing the water to the back of his mouth.

Chapter 2

The next Monday, Berto and Franz report for duty at the Police K-9 School. After placing Franz in his corner bed, Berto checks with his second-in-command, Lt. Neto Ramírez, about the happenings while he was gone to Neblina.

The Lieutenant reports that everything went well, and the training of the handlers moved ahead per the schedule.

Berto asks how plans are coming for graduation of the class of handlers and their dogs on Friday. Lt. Ramírez reports that everything is in good shape per the schedule and that a rehearsal was held last Friday.

#

Meanwhile at the headquarters of the Cartel de la Selva Tropical, what's left of the leadership is holding a meeting in the usual location in the shack. There is a void in the leadership caused by the two disastrous Bazooka shots by Captain Roberto Castillo into the car holding most of the top Cartel leadership.

Today's discussion centers around the best method to take out Berto. The son of Anaconda, who was the previous leader, appears to be leading the meeting after the death of his father. He has been called "Junior" for many years. This is not a term of derision but one suggesting that his father was the top man in the Cartel.

After discussion about the various methods possible to kill Captain Castillo, Junior says, "Let's vote on these ideas."

"Just a moment please," says the man among them known as El Catalán. He is considered the most intelligent of them all.

"Junior, there's another option besides eliminating Captain Berto Castillo. We could discredit him. And if that doesn't work, we'll just do an old-fashioned hit on his family."

Several ask what "discredit" means.

El Catalán responds, "We could deposit money in a bank in his name equal in amount to the value of a drug bust. In other words, we could tie him in with illicit drugs, cocaine for example. In this way, he would be discredited and no police agency in the world would want him. It would destroy him and his way of making a living. He would be indicted by a Grand Jury for these illegal activities and would have to go through a trial. The newspapers would have a field day, and so on. He would undoubtedly get some jail time, maybe in the amount of many years."

Continuing, El Catalán says, "We could tie him in with some murders committed in the drug trade. He would be discredited to the highest degree. Now, I know this takes some organization, setting up bank accounts with his correct signature, and so on. It would also take some time. But in the end, it would be so sweet. And we would be through with him forever. He'd have a hard time living in any prison in South America. There are probably several inmates in every prison who'd like to do away with him. The judge may even send him to a prison in Europe where Yuñeco has a mutual agreement to handle this problem of prisoners who need to be incarcerated elsewhere."

One of the Cartel members says, "I'll never be able to understand when El Catalán speaks. Incarcerated, what's that? A car that's rated."

The other Cartel members laugh.

El Catalán says, "It's not a car that's rated. It's incarcerated. You're mixing homophones"

"See what I mean. There he goes again talking about home phones."

Everyone laughs again.

Another leader asks, "Junior, how much do you think we'd need to pull this off?"

Junior responds, "To make this really look good, we'd need about $500,000.00 American. There must also be good records for the Grand Jury."

El Catalán agrees, "Oh yes, we must always be thinking of good records for the Grand Jury."

"Está bien, who is good at copying signatures?"

Several men shout out, "El Catalán."

Junior says, "I should have known. Okay, here's a plan. Let me know what you think of it. We need an original signature of Captain Castillo. I propose we send El Catalán to Neblina, where, according to the newspapers, Captain Castillo recently went into a cave and brought out a little boy, dead unfortunately. El Catalán can send Captain Castillo, at the K-9 School in La Vista, some flowers thanking him for the kind gesture of attempting to rescue the little boy. Send the flowers with a signed return receipt requested."

Most of the men looked confused and say, "What the heck is that?"

"Take it from here, El Catalán," says Junior.

El Catalán adds, "That's when the sender would like to know for sure that the person who is supposed to receive the flowers does in fact receive them and signs his signature as proof that he received them. I'll set up a postal box in Neblina and have the return receipt sent to that address. With that I'll have a true copy of Captain Berto Castillo's signature that I can learn to copy correctly and set up a bank account with big bucks with that signature. One more thing, since secretaries often sign such packages, I'll have to designate that the signature of the recipient is the only one accepted."

Several men say, "When El Catalán talks, I don't understand much."

Another answers "It's because he speaks English, Castilian, and Catalán."

"Oh, that explains it all right."

"Right on, El Catalán," says Junior. "You should take the money with you, so you don't have to make two trips to Neblina. You can catch the bus in front of Dos Brazo's home and go directly to the airport in La Vista. From there you fly to Neblina. Get a room in a motel and send the flowers or a book, whatever. When the proof of receipt goes to your mailbox, you're in business. Take some cocaine with you and leave it in a conspicuous place in Neblina or La Vista after you set up the bank account. How much coke do we have stored around here?"

"Sorry Jefe, only about ten kilos or $300,000.00 worth if sold abroad."

Taking out his small calculator, Junior says, "That's fine, no problem Pablo. Okay, El Catalán, take $300,000.00 with you in cash and $300,000.00 in coke. Take the large sports bag. At an average price of $30,000 per kilo, that's $300,000.00. It shouldn't be too heavy for a strong guy like you. At 2.2 pounds per kilo, that's 22 pounds."

El Catalán replies, "Twenty-two pounds? That's nothing. I carry more than that all the time as we're moving 30 one kilo bags of Mama Coca for inventory and shipments."

Everyone laughs at El Catalán's use of the slang term for cocaine, e.g., Mama Coca.

Junior asks, "El Catalán, how does that price of $30,000 sound to you? We generally sell Mama Coca for less than that."

"Jefe, that's because we generally sell locally. It depends on where it is sold. In South America it is at its lowest price. In far-away foreign countries it sells for much more. That's why we figure the ten kilos are worth $300,000."

"I knew that."

Everyone laughs.

Junior continues his instructions, "Have the coke discovered someplace just after you set up the account in the bank. You should try to find the newest teller in the bank to set up the account. Most of the people there probably know Captain Castillo. Or you could rent a car and go to the drive-up window with dark glasses on and a sports cap. No teller will reject $300,000.00 because they've not absolutely certain of the identity of the person making the deposit. And one more thing that will be necessary at the bank I'm sure. You'll need some photo I.D."

El Catalán says, "We're fortunate to have the printing capability here at the shack. Thanks for thinking of that Jefe. That's important. I think I'll get two, one on a driver's license and the other as the country's I.D. card. And as for the money, make sure there are no counterfeits in the $300,000.00." Now everyone laughs.

#

Back in La Vista, the Castillo family has no idea of the huge problem that has been concocted by the Cartel de la Selva Tropical. Berto has met with Chief Medina to discuss the possibility that the Cartel will want revenge at this time, but they don't know what it will be.

In a subsequent meeting at the Police Department between the Chief and Captain Berto Castillo, the Chief says, "We need a mole in the Cartel. We can't always depend on Dos Brazos for intelligence information."

"They'd suspect any new face in their midst. They've got to be extremely wary after that ambush at the K-9 School and then the shootout in the field with the Bazooka."

"You're right Berto. We'll just have to keep our ears to the ground and try to learn in advance what they're planning to do. I'll send out a memo to the other chiefs in the nation that we suspect something is brewing and would appreciate any intelligence they might pick up relating to an act of revenge."

"That's a good idea Chief. And I'll have to keep super-alert concerning everything round about me. If I suspect that Franz is growling at something, I need to move quickly."

"I agree Berto, and we need to keep communication open with Dos Brazos. You never know, he's been such a help in the past."

"He sure has Chief. All it would take is a tip from him that something is going down."

The two men leave the Chief's office. As they start to walk to the parking lot where Berto's car is parked, the Chief's secretary, Blanca Hernández, joins them. She loves to walk by Franz and rub his back.

The Chief says, "Okay, Berto, thanks for dropping by. We had a good talk, and I feel like we are much better prepared."

"Me too Chief. I'll see you later."

Before the Chief walks away, Blanca says to Berto, "Wait a minute Berto. You remember what I said I would do when you did something meritorious?"

"I sure do, and now is as good time as ever."

She then asks the Chief, "Chief Medina, would you consider meritorious what Berto did by going into that cave a long way in the pitch black and bringing out the body of that poor little boy? Chief Camargo told me that the boy's parents were so grateful to have his body out of that cave for a proper burial."

"Yes, Blanca, there's no doubt. What Berto did on that occasion was very meritorious, and Franz too."

Berto walks over to where Blanca is standing and bends down as he waits for his kiss. Blanca holds his face in her hands and gives Berto a long kiss on the mouth. He swoons as he departs from her.

Next she kneels down, and puts her arms around Franz who by now knows Blanca very well. He is always glad to accept hugs and kisses from her. A smart dog like Franz knows she is a beautiful woman.

A few minutes later the Chief waves goodbye as Berto drives out of the parking lot with Franz in the rear area of the car. As the dog sees the Chief, he barks once at him.

The Chief laughs and says, "Big deal, I get a bark from a dog. Berto gets a kiss from a beautiful woman."

"Why Chief, you've never said that about me before."

"Well, I've wanted to on many occasions."

"Chief that seems rather meritorious for you to say after all our years together."

"I agree wholeheartedly."

Blanca walks up to the Chief and gives him a big, long kiss on the month. When they part, she notices that Chief Medina has tears in his eyes.

She says, "Chief, why the tears?"

"I've loved you for so many years. It has been rather hard. But this kiss you just gave me, makes up for all those years. Thank you Blanca."

"Chief, I didn't know you felt that way. You haven't said anything about it to me."

"As a Chief of Police who is married, I thought I should remain silent."

"Well I can guarantee you that it won't be years before you receive your next kiss. Every time you do something meritorious, you'll get a kiss from me just like Berto does."

"I'll accept that offer without any more discussion. It's a done deal."

They walk back to the office laughing and chatting all the way.

#

As Berto drives home that afternoon and parks his K-9 car, his two boys run out of the house and go to the rear of the police car. As soon as Berto comes to the rear door, the boys crowd around. Berto makes some hand signals to indicate that he needs more room to open the rear doors of the car.

Once that extra room is obtained, he opens the two doors and says, "Franz, there."

As the dog jumps down, the two boys start immediately playing and running with him. Franz is faster than they are. They can never catch him no matter how hard they try and no matter how many ambushes they set for him.

Sometimes, they pretend that the game is over and collapse on the grass. Franz is wary of them, but eventually he joins them lying on the grass with them. For a few seconds, they remain still and quiet looking at each other.

When Bobbie says, "Now," they jump on him and do everything within their power to hold his legs so that he can't get away. But his superior strength always wins out, and eventually he breaks loose from them and runs some 50 feet or so away.

Being exhausted by now, the boys return to the house. Franz follows them in, recognizing the actions of capitulation on the boys' part.

"Wash up boys, time for dinner," says Susana. Berto joins the boys as they wash their hands. Susana washes the hands of little Elizabeth.

Returning to the dinner table, Berto says grace giving thanks for all his family has, for being together, and for the meal that has been prepared for them. He gives special thanks for little Elizabeth, middle sized Miguel, and big Bobby. "Amen."

Bobbie asks, "Dad, are you really as thankful for Miguel and me as you are for little Elizabeth"

Berto responds, "Bobbie, if I tell you exactly how I feel about you, I'll have to mention your mother which will be really hard for me. Please accept that I am as thankful for you and Miguel as I am for Elizabeth. I loved your mother just like I love Susana. You three children all come from these wonderful women whom I love. Okay, understand now?"

"I think so Dad. I understand better when you mention Mom and Susana at the same time, because I love both these women the same as you do Dad."

Miguel pops in, "Hey don't forget me. I love Susana and Mom just the same too."

Susana has tears in her eyes by this time.

She says, "I love all of you."

Berto says, "Let's eat."

The family digs into a wonderful meal. Susana is a great cook just like Pilar was.

Chapter 3

The next Monday morning, Captain Berto Castillo is at his desk in the Police K-9 School. The reconstruction work to repair the damage caused by the hand grenades has been completed. Everyone is more than satisfied with the reconstruction work.

Susana comes into Berto's office with a bunch of flowers and says, "Look Berto, from the florist. Should I read the note?"

"You're always the curious one, aren't you? Okay, go ahead."

"But first since the delivery man is waiting, you need to sign for it. That way they'll know that you personally received it and it didn't get lost or lifted somewhere along the route."

Berto signs the delivery slip, gives it to Susana who walks out of Berto's office and gives the delivery man the signed receipt. He thanks her for this extra work.

Back in his office, Berto says, "The flowers are from a group of parents who appreciate what I did in attempting to find the little boy in the cave. Isn't that nice of them?"

"Yes it is Berto. They realize that all rescue attempts can't be successful."

Four days later, El Catalán drives up to the outside teller's window of the Bank of Neblina. He is driving a rental car, wearing dark glasses, and a baseball cap.

"May I help you sir?" asks the teller.

"Yes, please. I would like to set up a checking account. I'm sorry I'm so dirty from playing baseball with the kids. I hope you don't mind if I don't come in."

"No sir, that's no problem. I'll put the appropriate forms for a new account in the sliding drawer and send them to you. Just fill out the information requested and return the forms to me with the money you want to deposit."

"I hope you won't mind if I hold up the other cars."

"That's no problem either. I'll just turn on the red light and the other cars will go to the other lines. Take all the time you need."

El Catalán fills out the forms using the card returned to him when the flowers were sent to Berto with the signature of Roberto Castillo on it as a guide. He carefully copies the signature on the bank forms.

When he is finished, he puts the forms back in the sliding drawer between himself and the teller along with the $300,000.00 in cash. The teller pushes the button that brings the sliding drawer to her. She is visibly shocked as she sees the amount of money that El Catalán wants to deposit. She says that she will need two pieces of photo I.D. El Catalán puts his Roberto Castillo's driver's license and I.D. form in the drawer for the teller.

She says, "Thank you for these materials, Please wait a minute, I need to call the Assistant Manager for such a large deposit."

She leaves the area and returns a minute later with the Assistant Manager, an attractive woman in her 40s, who says, "Captain Castillo, I see you have been helping the boys with their baseball game. I didn't know you got over this way very often."

"Well the boys needed a coach so here I am, even though the trip over the mountain is rather strenuous."

"That's so nice of you. This is a rather large deposit. I'll have to check these bills to make sure they're all valid."

"Fine, take your time. I'm in no hurry. I won't be driving back to La Vista until tomorrow morning."

The Assistant Manager runs the bills through a machine that counts them and checks them as to whether or not they are counterfeit. The bills all check out, and the total is $300,000.00.

She puts the deposit slip in an envelope which she places in the sliding drawer and sends it back to Berto saying, "Here's your deposit slip Captain, $300,000.00 exactly, with not one bad bill. That wouldn't be too good if a police captain had some counterfeit bills."

El Catalán wants to stress the date for later purposes.

He asks, "Where do you print the date on the deposit slip?"

The Assistant Manager says, "There it is up in the right-hand corner along with the name of our branch, Neblina Branch Office, and our names, Anita Chávez and Mariana Mendoza. So you see, you have the date recorded, the name of the Branch Office, and our two names. Your teller is Anita Chávez, and I am Mariana Mendoza."

El Catalán says, "The only thing lacking are your phone numbers."

They all laugh. "We are both married Captain as you are."

"You can't blame a guy for trying, can you? Especially with women as beautiful as you two are."

"Well thank you very much."

After checking the deposit slip for accuracy, El Catalán returns it to its envelope. He then thanks the ladies for their help and buckles his seat belt.

"Stick 'em up." The words feared by every bank teller are heard as a man with a kerchief over his face walks into the bank with a pistol in his hand. He throws a bag to each teller and says, "Fill 'em up."

The tellers are scared and do as directed.

El Catalán knows that if he is to continue the masquerade as Captain Roberto Castillo, he must attempt to stop the robbery. He drives his car away from the bank but stops and parks in the parking lot for the mall which is adjacent to the bank. Checking the magazine on his pistol to be sure it is loaded; he puts it back in the handle of his semi-automatic pistol. Then he pulls back on the slide and inserts one shell into the chamber. He does not put the safety in the "on" position.

Walking back toward the bank, he reholsters his pistol and enters the bank as if he were any other little league baseball coach and customer coming on business.

As he walks in, the man with the pistol and a kerchief over his mouth says to him, "Stop right there and don't move. You can handle your business when I leave if there's any cash left to handle any business."

El Catalán feigns fear and moves back to the counter where the other customers have been herded.

As he does this, the robber moves his attention to other areas of the bank. El Catalán draws his pistol and shoots the robber in both thighs, **BOOM, BOOM**.

He falls from great pain dropping his pistol as he does. El Catalán quickly grabs the pistol and says, "Mariana, call the police immediately with an ambulance as well."

She does as directed.

El Catalán doesn't want to be distracted due to this robbery and shooting. He knows he needs to keep his attention on other things, and he knows he can't be present in the bank when the local police officers arrive or the press.

He must now carry out the other half of the plan that will discredit Captain Roberto Castillo. Checking the robber's pistol to be sure it is loaded, El Catalán hands it to Mariana and says, "Shoot him in the chest if he moves. The police will be here soon. I've got other business to take care of. Thanks ladies."

To reinforce that he is Captain Castillo, he kisses both Anita and Mariana on the cheek.

Mariana says, "I knew that somehow he would do that based on his reputation. Good job captain?"

"Are you talking about stopping the robbery or giving a kiss to two beautiful women?"

"Both."

The people in the bank laugh with the pressure of the robbery gone.

El Catalán reholsters his pistol and leaves the bank. Getting into his car and driving away, he passes two police cars racing to the bank. They don't pay him any special attention.

With his disguise as Captain Castillo accepted in Neblina, El Catalán knows he must hide out the rest of the day. He takes in a movie and has dinner in a dark night club.

#

That night on the streets of Neblina, street savvy and drug wise, El Catalán roams the streets looking for some undercover narcotics officers to continue to carry out his plan. Soon he comes across two officers who are dressed in fancy suits. They approach El Catalán and ask him if he is looking for something.

He says he is, but he doesn't think that these two men could provide him what he needs.

The men balk at that statement and say they could provide whatever he wants.

He says he wants $300,000.00 worth of pure cocaine, not cut with anything, especially levamisole.

They respond that they know the dangers of levamisole and stay clear of it. If they ever expect to have any resales, they say their coke must be pure.

El Catalán states that he has already purchased $300,000 worth of high-grade coke, but he can't go back to La Vista without the full $600,000 worth of good coke. He is tired of staying in the Neblina Motel and will only stay there two more nights. He arranges to meet the two men tomorrow night at the same time, 9:00 p.m., at this same location. If they have a good grade of coke in the proper amount, the purchase will be made.

"How much do you think is the proper amount?"

"You know as well as I do that the price is dependent on the quality of the coke."

El Catalán takes out his 9 mm pistol which spooks the two men somewhat. "Just to let you know I'm serious." As he puts the pistol back into his holster, he drops an envelope on the ground giving the men the impression that he is unaware of this drop. Then he walks away into the dark of the night.

The two men talk. One says, "That's an awful lot of coke. Could he be an undercover officer from the Country of Yuñeco or something like that?"

"He didn't talk like the usual coke buyer, but these guys are getting more and more sophisticated all the time. I was surprised he told us where he's staying. That's not normal."

"It could be a false address. Let's take a look at that envelope he dropped." The under-cover officer bends over, picks up the envelope, and sees that it is already opened.

"Let's check the name and address here. It says, 'Berto Castillo, La Vista Police Department.' The Envelope is empty."

"You see, he could be doing under-cover work for the National Police. I've heard of Captain Castillo. He's in charge of the K-9 School and is highly respected. There's something fishy here. Why would he want to buy coke unless he's turned dirty? And why would he want to buy coke here in Neblina unless he has turned dirty and doesn't want anyone in La Vista to know it?"

"Tomorrow night, we might make the biggest bust of our careers, $300,000.00. We've really got to be on our toes. I think we need to tell the Chief."

"No, those Chiefs communicate together too well. We'll make the bust first and then turn him in."

#

What the under-cover officers don't know is that El Catalán never intended to follow through on the purchase. He has left enough information in the town to account for the possible purchase.

He goes to the airport early the next morning and takes a plane to La Vista. In his large sports bag, he carries the coke he brought with him from camp. Hailing a taxi in front of the air terminal, he directs the cab driver to go to the rear parking lot of the police department and then drive to the front of the department and wait for him. El Catalán pays the taxi driver liberally and asks him to wait in front of the department for which he will receive a strong tip.

Walking through the parking lot, El Catalán finds the section where the officers have reserved parking spaces. The space for Captain Castillo is empty. El Catalán walks to the front of the department and asks the taxi driver if he knows where the Police K-9 School is. He says he does. El Catalán says that is the next destination.

The trip is short and as they drive by the front of the school, El Catalán sees Berto's car. Since he doesn't dare let the taxi driver know what he is up to, he asks the driver to drive through the road that goes to the back of the campus, near the track.

When they arrive there, they see numerous handlers with their K-9 dogs running around the track. El Catalán asks the driver to wait for him in the parking space he has selected so they can have a good view of the track and the wonderful dogs in training.

El Catalán leaves the taxi with the sports bag in hand. He thinks to himself, *I've ten bricks at one kilo each here. At $30,000.00 per kilo, that's the $300,000.00 we agreed upon. I hope I don't flub this assignment.*

His immediate hope is that the K-9 Car belonging to Berto will not be locked. All he can do is test the doors.

When he gets to the front of the campus, El Catalán tries the doors on Berto's K-9 car. They are all unlocked. He opens the rear passenger door on the street side hoping that no one inside the building sees him. He quickly lays the sports bag on the floor of the car, closes the door, and returns to the taxi in the rear of the campus.

"Okay, let's return to the air terminal, please."

As they drive back through the road between the campus buildings, they see another police K-9 car pull up and park behind Berto's car. El Catalán asks the taxi driver to park on the other side of the road for a few minutes.

Sergeant Pedro Morales steps out of the car and walks to the rear. Opening the two doors, he attaches his own dog to its leash and has the dog jump to the street. Then the Sergeant goes into the building with his dog on its leash and returns in a few seconds with Franz on another leash.

The Sergeant always puts Franz in the rear seat on the passenger side which requires him to open the door from the street. As the two dogs pass the rear door of Berto's K-9 car, they become very agitated, and start scratching at the pavement by the rear passenger door.

Sgt. Morales checks the rear door and opens it. Seeing the sports bag, and with probable cause to open it due to two highly trained drug dogs' registering a hit on this very location, Sgt. Morales opens the sports bag and sees that it has several bricks of cocaine in it. Leaving the bag exactly where he found it, he then goes to his own K-9 car, puts his dog in the rear, and puts Franz in the rear seat. Both dogs lie down to sleep.

Sgt. Morales takes his radio and calls, "Dispatch, this is K-9-2, patch me through to Chief Medina on his telephone please. This is a confidential call."

"K-9-2. confidential telephone call, 10-4"

"Yes, Pedro, what's up?" asks Chief Medina."

"Chief, I was just taking my dog and Franz out for their usual afternoon run, and both dogs registered a drug hit when they passed Berto's car. With probable cause due to the dogs' hit, I opened the sports bag in the rear of the car and saw cocaine. What do you want me to do?"

"Hang on. I'll be right there. Sit in your own car and keep Berto's car in sight."

The Chief runs to his car and blasts out for the K-9 School. Arriving there with his light bar clearing the way but with no siren blaring, the Chief turns off the light bar as he finds a parking spot behind Sgt. Morales.

The Chief quickly joins the Sergeant by Berto's car, opens the rear door, and sees the sports bag left there by El Catalán. He opens the sports bag to see the cocaine. Taking the bag in his left hand, the Chief closes the door quietly and tells Sergeant Morales to go on with his usual routine of running the two dogs. He tells the Sergeant to say nothing to anyone, but to meet in the Chief's office this afternoon around 4:30 p.m. for a discussion on what will be their next step. The two officers get into their cars and drive away from the front of the K-9 School.

#

El Catalán couldn't be happier. He has observed the two officers. The Chief of Police has found the cocaine in Captain Castillo's car. The plan is moving forward, better than El Catalán could have imagined in his wildest dream.

He asks the taxi driver to take him to the air terminal. Once there, El Catalán pays the cabbie with a good tip and walks to the bus stop. After a few minutes wait, he takes the bus that a few hours later will deposit him at the front of Dos Brazos' home.

#

After a bumpy bus ride, El Catalán steps down from the bus and walks the short distance to the home of Dos Brazos. Once there, he follows the format of others before him. He takes a shower in the barn, changes clothes, and puts his pistol on his belt so it is ready for quick action if needed. He next pays Dos Brazos and throws a tip to his sons. El Catalán then rents a burro to ride and another to carry the provisions that he has purchased at Dos Brazos' mini store.

He then heads into the great Rainforest. The pathway is worn down fairly well by now, so El Catalán is able to let the burro take the lead on the pathway without hardly any direction at all. The first two nights he has no shack to sleep in for protection and is therefore concerned especially about the giant and small dangerous snakes. He uses his usual technique of thorny bushes to protect him and the burros. The third night is better, since the shack is available after he checks it out for snakes.

The next day he makes it into camp where he is greeted by Junior and the others in the Cartel. They can see by the expression on El Catalan's face that he has been successful.

Junior says, "Tonight after dinner around the campfire, we'll let El Catalán tell us the story of his successful journey. I'm as anxious as anyone to get the word."

#

Previous to this, La Vista Police Chief Luis Medina and Sergeant Pedro Morales met in the Chief's office.

"Well, Pedro, you've really done it this time."

"I'm sorry Chief. Those two dogs were going crazy scratching at the door of the Captain's car. They've been trained to do that, and I've been trained to recognize the signs of a hit on drugs such as cocaine."

"I know Pedro, I was just kidding. The problem is what do we do now?"

"Chief, you've told us the same thing for many years. When faced with a difficult decision, ask yourself what you would do under normal circumstances."

"Okay, Sergeant, what would we do under normal circumstances?"

"Well, first we have a hit by two highly trained dogs on a sports bag containing cocaine. This sports bag was inside the car of a police Captain. Normally, we would talk with the D.A. and he would probably recommend that the drugs and the witnesses be taken before the Grand Jury."

"Very good Pedro. I can see why you made Sergeant so fast. You'll do the same with Lieutenant if you keep this up. Okay, I'll set up a meeting with the D.A. Would you like to go along?"

"Yes I would Chief. I'd like to follow this through, but keep in mind that I don't think Captain Berto Castillo is guilty of any drug offense. He's been set up. You noticed that the door was unlocked. If Berto had put that amount of coke in his car, he certainly would have locked all the doors. Anyone could have put that bag there. But for now, everything is done by the book."

"Okay, hang on. I'll phone the D.A. now."

The Chief clicks on the intercom to his secretary and says, "Blanquita, please try to get me the District Attorney, Felipe Ramos."

"Yes, Chief. I'll get right back to you. He may be in court."

"You always say that Blanca."

"It's almost always true Chief."

"Well, do your best, okay?"

"Yes, Chief."

Sergeant Morales asks a question knowing that there will be a few minutes' wait on the call to the District

Attorney, "How did you tag the drugs when you put them in the Property and Evidence Section?"

"I really had to think hard on that one. I labeled the sports bag, 'Cocaine Evidence, Ten Bricks, Obtained by Sgt. Pedro Morales with the date and the net weight of the drugs, which was 10 kilos, worth $300,000 at the average of $30,000 per kilo if sold out of the continent.'"

"Well thanks for that one. I'll have to remember that technique for future reference."

Blanca comes on the phone, "Chief, I can't believe it. The District Attorney is available and on the line."

"Thanks Blanca. Felipe, is that you?"

"Yes, Chief, what can I do for you?"

"We've got a sticky one here. Sgt. Pedro Morales, a K-9 Officer, was taking his dog and Berto's dog, Franz, out for their afternoon run. As they walked past Berto's K-9 car, both dogs registered a narcotics hit. Now these are highly trained dogs. They never miss. Anyway, with these two dogs acting as they were, Sgt. Morales knew he had reasonable cause to check out the car. All doors were unlocked. Inside the rear passenger seat, on the floor, he found a sports bag. Inside the bag were ten bricks of cocaine. As you know, each brick weighs one kilo.

"I met with the sergeant immediately, took the bag, and placed it in our Property and Evidence Section where it is at this time. Nothing has been said to Berto, and he has said nothing to us. To be honest, we believe he is being set up on this bust, but we want to handle it by the book. What do you suggest as the next step?"

"There's only one option, and that is the Grand Jury. I'll set it up for next week, on Wednesday at 2:00 p.m. That's their usual time to meet. Pull together all your evidence, pro and con by then, okay?"

"Yes."

"Don't tell Berto that there is a Grand Jury meeting on him. If there is probably cause, we'll have Berto before the Grand Jury the following Wednesday and hear his explanation. Is that it for now?"

"Yes, Felipe. I'm sure I'll be getting back to you in a few days."

They both ring off.

The Chief then says to Sgt. Morales, "Wait a minute, Sergeant, I've another idea."

Switching on his intercom, the Chief says, "Blanquita, get me Chief Tony Camargo in Neblina please."

"Yes, Chief."

A minute later Blanca calls the Chief on his intercom and tells him that Chief Camargo is ready.

"Hello, Tony, this is Luis in La Vista. I've got a problem."

"What is it Chief? Maybe I can help."

"This is of the highest priority. To be discussed only with me. Okay?"

"Of course Chief."

"Two of our finest narcotic dogs gave a hit on the K-9 Car of Captain Berto Castillo."

"You can't be serious. This has got to be a setup if I've ever seen one. Why, Berto was here recently as you know going into a deep, dark cave trying to rescue a little boy. He found the boy at the bottom of a 30-foot hole, got him out of the hole, talked with him, gave him some water and food, and carried him out of the cave. Then when he got the boy out, the doctor declared him dead. Berto collapsed emotionally. No, he didn't steal any contraband."

"Yes, Tony, we feel the same way. Maybe you can help prove his innocence. When we first got the word about Berto, there was some talk about his staying at a motel in Neblina and a bank account there. Can you put your investigator on it and try to find out what's going on over there?"

"Of course Chief. We'll put some additional manpower on it as well. We owe Berto, that's for sure. I'll get back to you. Oh yes, is your Grand Jury in on this one?"

"They will be as of next Wednesday at 2:00 p.m."

"Okay, Chief. We'll do the best we can. Goodbye."

"Goodbye Tony, and thanks."

After he hangs up the phone, the Chief says, "Okay, Sergeant, we're doing everything we can. If you think of anything else we should be doing, let me know. Remember, we need evidence on both sides of this problem."

Chapter 4

There are 14 members of the Grand Jury present today. Normally there would be 16, but two had other commitments they couldn't break. Twelve members in support is the required number to bring in an indictment according to the laws of Yuñeco. District Attorney Felipe Ramos is present with his investigator, Sgt. Cristóbal Valdez.

The court reporter is present with her stenographic machine. Chief Luis Medina and Sgt. Pedro Morales are present along with Chief Tony Camargo from Neblina. A few other people are present in the waiting room and will join the Grand Jury as they are called.

The D.A. says, "This session of the Grand Jury is open at this time. We have a rather serious matter to review. I'll let Sgt. Pedro Morales, a Police K-9 Officer from the La Vista Police Department, give us some background since he was present as this case developed. Sgt Morales, please."

After being sworn in, the Sergeant says, "As a police K-9 Officer, I have a highly trained German Shepherd dog that lives with my family. This dog is trained to sense drugs of all kinds, explosives, and so on. The testimony of the dog's handler is admissible in court since the dog is so highly trained.

"One day last week, I went to the Police K-9 School to get the dog of the superintendent of the school, Captain Roberto Castillo, often called just Berto. Captain Castillo has had some rather difficult rescues and needs some help with running his dog daily. Since I run my dog around the track at the school daily, Captain Castillo asked me to take his dog, Franz, as well.

"After I picked up his dog, I was walking the two dogs back to my car when both dogs stopped. They made a signal signifying that drugs were in a car that we were passing in front of the K-9 School. When these dogs signal a hit, the courts accept that as probable cause to open a car and check for contraband. Therefore, I opened the door of the car and saw a sports bag. I opened the bag and saw ten bricks of cocaine. This is typical packaging of cocaine where each brick weighs one kilo. I called the Chief because the car was a police K-9 Car belonging to Captain Berto Castillo."

Many of the Grand Jury members gasp at the identification of the car and the name of its driver.

The Sergeant continues, "The Chief came immediately, took the sports bag, and entered it into the department's Property and Evidence Section which is normal procedure. Thank you."

Sgt. Morales sits down.

The D.A. continues, "We have had our own investigator checking the banks in La Vista and Neblina to see if Captain Berto Castillo has come into large sums of money lately. Let me have Investigator Cristóbal Valdez take it from here. Sergeant."

Sergeant Valdez is sworn in and then addresses the Grand Jury, "I found a bank in Neblina where Captain Berto Castillo had an account with a rather large sum of money, $300,000.00 to be exact."

The members of the Grand Jury express surprise at such a large amount of money.

Sergeant Valdez continues, "I wanted to be sure that this account was opened by Captain Berto Castillo. In other words, are the signatures on the account the exact signatures of Captain Castillo? With rubber gloves on, I placed the deposit slip and the application form for the bank account in two plastic containers. Fortunately, I went to a special school for such training and have the proper certificate to enable me to testify in a court session as to the validity of signatures of anyone.

"Therefore, I can testify under oath that I checked the signatures on the deposit slip and the application form for the account with known signatures of Captain Castillo on record at the police department. The signatures used to open the account and make the $300,000.00 deposit were in fact done by Captain Roberto Castillo."

Everyone expresses shock and disappointment since Captain Castillo is a much-respected member of the local police department.

The D.A. says, "Thank you Mr. Investigator. Chief Medina, you have known Captain Berto Castillo as long as anyone. Would you have anything to say at this time?"

After being sworn in Chief Medina says, "Yes, thank you. As many people in this room know, Captain Berto Castillo is a much loved and much trusted member of the La Vista Police Department. He is the superintendent of the Police K-9 School. Ours is the only Police K-9 School in the country, so all the canine training for the various police departments takes place at our school.

"Recently the South American Association of Chiefs of Police held a conference here at the new hotel in La Vista. Berto was in charge of security for that conference of about 850 police chiefs and their families. Several loads of hand grenades and sticks of dynamite were found by the 19 dogs that were there with their handlers. Berto did not endear himself to the Cartel de la Selva Tropical at that time. He even had to use a Bazooka to finish off the Cartel leaders as well as a local narc who was Berto's father-in-law. Berto didn't hesitate to kill all the leaders with the Bazooka. I was standing with him when he did this. I am concerned that the Cartel has a contract out on Berto or a plan to destroy him in the eyes of the community. He has stopped their activities on more than one occasion. Thank you."

The D.A. continues, "If there is nothing else, I think it is time to vote on whether or not there should be an indictment of Captain Roberto Castillo. The charges will be possession of a controlled substance, possession of funds with the intent to buy a controlled substance, performance of the above while under color of authority, brandishment of a semi-automatic pistol in the presence of persons thought to be non-police officers, use of a police department vehicle to transport a controlled substance without authorization, and others to be determined."

Chief Tony Camargo speaks up, "Wait a minute Mr. D.A. I would like to say a word or two before you vote."

"Of course, Chief Camargo of Neblina. What would you like to say?"

Chief Camargo is sworn in and says, "Since the bank account in question in the amount of $300,000.00 was in a bank in my jurisdiction, I did a little investigating as well. We have heard an expert witness testify that the signatures on the bank deposit card and the application to open the bank account are in fact those of Captain Roberto Castillo. I would like to remind everyone that the art of reading signatures is not as accurate as the science of reading fingerprints.

"I have seen the original deposit card and the original application form to open the bank account. Fortunately, they have been kept in plastic protectors. With the permission of the D.A. I would like to have the two women from the bank who attended to Captain Castillo or whoever it was who was pretending to be Captain Castillo, share some facts with you now. The teller in the Bank of Neblina is Anita Chávez and the Assistant Manager is Mariana Mendoza."

The D.A. says, "Just a minute, Chief. These women were not scheduled to testify today. How do we know they are in fact the persons you say they are? Now Neblina may be a little lost-in-the-woods, hick town where procedures aren't very important, but in the capital city of this country, we observe procedures."

The Grand Jury Foreman stands up and says, "Mr. Ramos, we have given you complete freedom as to the procedures of this Grand Jury, but I think the time has come to call a halt to that practice. This Grand Jury exists to find the truth, not to just follow procedures. We would like to hear the testimony of these two bank employees who have made that horrible trip over the mountains from Neblina to La Vista. It is the least we can do. We'll determine the truthfulness of their testimony. Please invite the two women to join us."

"Of course Mr. Foreman," responds the D.A. "I'm sorry if I haven't let the Jury determine some of its own procedures."

After the bailiff escorts the two women into the Grand Jury room, the district attorney says, "Miss Chávez, would you please go first. The Clerk will swear you in."

After being sworn in, Anita Chávez relates, "A man with a hat, dark glasses, and coveralls came to my drive-up window and asked to open an account in the name of Roberto Castillo. I gave him the proper forms which he filled out and returned to me. I asked for the help of the Assistant Manager, Mariana Mendoza, since the amount of money was so large."

Mariana Mendoza enters her testimony after the clerk swears her in.

She adds, "When I was asked to help with the deposit, I was a little skeptical about the identity of the man. He was certainly trying to hide his identity, in my opinion. I checked the bills. They all checked out as valid with no counterfeits."

The D.A. says, "Chief, I don't understand. These women are testifying as to the identity of the depositor. His signature was accurate."

"Yes, Mr. D. A. that is true. But there is one more thing that has not been attested to. These women can testify that the only people who touched the deposit slip and the application form were Anita Chávez, Mariana Mendoza, and the depositor."

"Yes, we understand. But what's the problem?"

"The problem, Mr. D.A., is that our expert on fingerprints cannot find any fingerprints of Captain Berto Castillo on these deposit slips. The only fingerprints are those of Anita Chávez, Mariana Mendoza, and a man by the name of Juan David García Martínez, a long-time member of the Cartel de la Selva Tropical, who is known in the Cartel as El Catalán."

The members of the Grand Jury all clap. Others in the room do not, namely: the D.A., the stenographer, Chief Medina, and Sergeant Morales. The latter two are shocked, knowing that they should have checked the fingerprints on the two forms. They almost let their friend and close associate get indicted due to their lack of diligence.

The two officers look at each other. During all the clapping, the Chief leans over to his Sergeant and says, "We blew that one, Sergeant."

"We sure did. I'm glad that Chief from a little lost-in-the-woods, hick town was smart enough to have the fingerprints checked."

The D.A. says, "There being no more business, the meeting is adjourned. However, I would like to apologize to Chief Tony Camargo. It looks like it took a Chief from a "hick town" to teach me what I needed to know. A trusted man's reputation has been saved. As usual, all business conducted here is 100% confidential. Berto Castillo must never learn of this session today. And ladies from the Bank of Neblina, thank you very much for coming here today. Your expenses will be covered. You've helped save the reputation of an outstanding police officer."

The Bank's Assistant Manager, Mariana Mendoza, says, "No thanks Mr. D.A. I wouldn't have missed this for the world. I will pay my own expenses with pleasure."

Everyone laughs.

The Bank's teller adds, "That goes for me too."

Everyone laughs again.

As the crowd is breaking up, with many people shaking the hand of Chief Tony Camargo from Neblina, the D.A. says to Chief Medina, "I'd like to meet with you and Sgt. Morales in my office now please."

Chief Medina and Sgt. Morales follow the D.A. into his office. He waits for them to enter and then closes the door.

"Have a chair please."

The two officers take a chair while the D.A. takes his usual chair behind his desk.

He says, "I'm trying to control my temper, guys, I really am. I have never been so embarrassed in front of a Grand Jury as I was today. When you bring a case to me and the Grand Jury, I must assume you have done all the critical research necessary so that an indictment can be reached. That's why I'm here. To indict the criminals and convince their jury that they should be convicted for a crime. In this case, with the evidence presented by that hick town Police Chief, Tony Camargo, who used to be one of a drug Cartel's top hitmen, it was more than obvious that another drug Cartel was trying to set up Captain Berto Castillo for a fall, for a conviction on serious drug charges. His life and career would have been ruined. Fortunately, he'll never learn about all this mess.

"If you guys ever bring me another case like this, it'll be the last case you bring to this office. Goodbye."

The D.A. stands up as a sign for the other two to stand up and leave which they do.

Outside in the hallway, Sgt. Pedro Morales says, "This fiasco was my fault Chief. My dogs found the original hit in Berto's car. I should have researched it more before taking it to you."

"Maybe so Pedro, but I should have researched it more myself. There's enough blame for both of us. We'll just forget about it, and make sure it never happens again. Not a word to anyone, including our wives, got it?"

"Yes Chief, I've got it. What happens with all the drugs and money deposited in the bank now?"

"Since all the evidence is drug related, it must be sent to the National Police. And we need to make sure that it gets there. I'm putting you in charge of that transfer. Then the National Police will pay us one percent of all the contraband."

"Chief, when did they change the finder's fee from one tenth of one percent to a full one percent of the value of the contraband both the drugs and the confiscated cash?"

"The National Police Commission did that last year and made it effective on January 1 of this year. It's a good deal for us and an incentive for officers and departments all over the country.

#

Several days later, after the City Council has had its regular meeting that was written about in the local newspaper, the leaders of the Cartel de la Selva Tropical are seated around the campfire one evening.

Junior asks, "El Catalán, what's the latest in our efforts to discredit Captain Berto Castillo? That effort cost us a bit more than $600,000.00, half in cash, and half in cocaine."

"I'm sorry Chief. There's been no information in the newspaper or on the radio as far as I can find out, and there's also been a city council meeting with no reference to this project."

"What do you think happened?"

"I personally saw the police chief pick up the sports bag of cocaine. That police Captain Berto Castillo is well liked in his department. I think the chief just put the cocaine away in the evidence locker to be kept there for 75 years. End of story."

"You're probably right. Those coppers stick close together protecting each other. It's just like we do in the Cartel. One for all and all for one. That's their motto and ours as well. We really can't complain about their having such a motto. Well that's money down the drain but maybe well spent. We've learned a lot about these coppers. Anything goes to protect each other.

"Okay guys, that's enough for Captain Berto Castillo. The only way to get him out of our hair is to get him out of our heads, forget about him. What's next on the agenda?"

El Catalán responds, "Well, we learned another thing from our recent operation, and that is that our supply of cocaine is running very low. Remember?"

"Yes, El Catalán. Thanks for reminding us. If we're going to stay in the drug business, we need to replenish our supplies. What are the plans for doing this?"

Another leader of the Cartel speaks up. His nickname is El Caracol and he says, "Jefe, remember the Army Base in La Vista? It has a huge drug locker where they keep all the drugs they've confiscated, coca paste not yet processed into coke, cocaine, heroin, and marijuana. Now heroin is too dangerous to move. We've learned that lesson before. Next in line is the cocaine. It is worth the most money after heroin and the easiest to transport in one kilo bags. We're not in the business of processing coca paste, nor are we in the business of selling marijuana, it's too bulky."

"Right, El Caracol, good ideas. We keep doing the research, but we forget about it as we become involved in other projects. What say men, do we pull together a plan to hit the drug locker at the army base? Remember, they have the greatest fire power in response. Those Bazookas and .50 calibers are powerful. They can rip our cars to pieces. I think the only plan that would work would be one with very few men. An assault on an Army Base would be a massacre and we'd be the ones massacred. And if we got away, they've got those helicopters with the same weapons that could chase us any place forever. I don't know. That Army Base seems rather dangerous. But they have the greatest supply of coke, that's for sure. Is there anyone here who can fly a helicopter?"

El Catalán raises his hand and is recognized. "Now Chief, I'm not saying I can fly a copter, but I can learn. I could fly in there, set it down, have it filled with coke, and fly out of there so fast they'd never be able to catch me."

The Jefe responds, "El Catalán, I love you. You are willing to try anything for the welfare of this unit. That's what makes us successful. Are you serious about this?"

"Of course Chief. We could even fly two copters in. Imagine how much coke we could get in one run and then fly straight back to this base. We could hit the place at about 4:00 a.m. when it's dark. Then most of our flight back here would be in the dark. About the time we got to the Rainforest, it would be getting light. We know the Rainforest so well that we could compensate for any errors in direction and quickly get on the right path to this base."

"You men see, see these big words that El Catalán uses, 'compensate for any errors.' That's why El Catalán is so valuable to us. He's got an education."

El Catalán jumps in, "Guys, don't get down on me now just because I graduated from the eighth grade. I want you to know that I am a dedicated member of this Cartel, and a terrorist as far as the government is concerned."

"Don't get touchy El Catalán. We know you're one of us. We're proud to have you with us. We all benefit because of your sharp mind and quick wit. At least you're not half-quick which would make you a half-wit."

Everyone laughs including El Catalán. He walks up to Junior, and they share a strong and long embrace as everyone claps.

After everyone stops laughing and settles down again, Junior says, "El Catalán, I like the idea of using two helicopters if we can afford to buy two. If we only buy one copter, we can have an extra pilot standing by. Who would you like to go with you to share the education and training to become a helicopter pilot?"

"I would like El Caracol. We think exactly alike. What one is about to do, so is the other. That sixth sense could be helpful as we're flying out of the Army Base with a load of coke."

"You're right there. Now we need someone here at the base to coordinate with you and have the necessary troops standing by. Any suggestions?"

"Junior, I would prefer that you make that appointment. You know the group leaders better that I do. You may even want to select two and have them work together."

Junior responds, "Good idea, and I know just the two for the job. They've had lots of organizing experience as unit leaders, Manuel and Alonzo. What say guys?"

Manuel speaks up first, "Junior, you know that I always was quick to support whatever your father wanted. I'll do the same for you. If we're going to succeed following the death of the Anaconda, your father, we have to work together like never before. You can count on me for this or any other task, large or small."

The entire group claps for Manuel and his positive attitude.

Alonzo says, "Junior, I'm with you just like I was with your father. I agree with everything that Manuel said. We'll do anything you want us to do."

Junior takes his handkerchief and wipes his eyes. This commitment is more than he expected so soon after the death of his father.

He says, "Guys, you know you don't see tears in my eyes very often. The death of my father brought them to me and your commitment to help me make this a successful organization has done the same thing. You can count on me to treat you like brothers with all the respect that you deserve. There'll be no sniping behind anyone's back. If you have something to say, bring it up at the evening campfire. That way we'll understand each other and work together like no other Cartel has ever done before."

The men and women of the Cartel leadership clap again and stand around Junior patting him on the back and hugging him. He is still overcome with emotion. In just a few days after the leadership responsibilities of the Cartel were left on his back, his management team, men and women, have expressed complete support for him.

His wife comes from the kitchen. She has heard the conversation of the past ten minutes or so. She is as proud as can be of her husband. As she walks through the group, the leaders stand aside. Walking up to her husband, she gives him a big hug and a long kiss.

Everyone claps and whistles. She is gorgeous, with dark hair and the epitome of the dark eyed Latin beauty. Her name is Betty. She holds in her hand a little girl walking at her side, María Alejandra.

All the men in the Cartel admire Betty and would protect her in a minute if someone got fresh with her or threatened her life. She works alongside the other women in the Cartel, fixing meals, washing clothes, searching the Rainforest for bananas, oranges, pineapples, mangoes, lemons, grapefruit, breadfruit, nuts, chocolate, guavas, mangos, and berries. In fact, because she has a beautiful singing voice, she often leads out with the other women joining in on a variety of songs as they move through the forest. Such music keeps some wild animals away from them.

Before the group meeting breaks up, Junior talks with El Catalán and El Caracol. He brings out the large chest that has the excess money of the Cartel in it.

"How much money will you need muchachos?"

El Catalán responds, "The training for the four-week course is about $1,000 each. Yes, I've been checking. Housing and meals at a boarding house in La Vista should be about $1,500 each for the full month. Fortunately, the training takes place at the La Vista International Airport. We can take a bus from the boarding house to the airport daily. The bus fare is very cheap. Now, Junior, do you want us to buy two helicopters or steal them?"

"How much would one cost, used but in good condition?"

"From the research I've done, we're talking between $700,000.00 and $2,500,000.00. Our main problem is that we need a copter heavy and strong enough to carry a load of cocaine."

"Right," adds Junior. "We don't just need to get there, but we need to be able to bring out a heavy load of coke. Plus I imagine we should have an extra man on each copter who handles a .50 caliber machine gun to protect the crew while they're blasting out of there and trying to protect themselves as they head for home."

Junior adds, "Well, we've got more money than coke, so let's buy one. Do we have anyone in our Cartel who can act as the technician for such a copter?"

"Yes we do," says El Catalán. "Mateo was a copter mechanic in the army for three years. He should be able to fix anything in the range that we can buy."

El Caracol adds, "Mateo will do a great job. He's my cousin, you know, and a dedicated member of this Cartel."

"Great," responds Junior, "El Catalán and El Caracol, you should leave tomorrow morning. Leave your burros at Dos Brazos' house. When you get to La Vista and find some housing, buy some nice clothes and get a haircut. You need to look presentable to enter such a school."

"A haircut, Jefe, you can't be serious."

"El Catalán, I thought you said you would do anything for me." Everyone laughs.

"But a haircut, Jefe, are you certain?"

"Yes, and keep your face shaved clean."

"Oh, you really know how to hurt a guy don't you? Now I know why the other guys weren't volunteering for this opportunity."

Everyone is still laughing.

"Okay, Jefe, for you, but for no one else."

"I know El Catalán, and I appreciate your sacrifice. Now, let's get some sleep. You guys should be up early tomorrow morning. Betty, can you prepare some food for these guys tomorrow morning?"

"Yes, Junior. I'd be glad to do that, especially since they are making the supreme sacrifice in having their hair and beards cut." She laughs.

El Catalán quickly says, "Wait a minute. Nothing was said about cutting our beards."

Again the group laughs.

Junior says, "What do you think 'keep your face shaved clean' means?"

"Oh no."

Junior says, "Betty, to be sure, could you start their haircuts and beard cuts tonight with a pair of scissors?"

El Catalán groans, "Oh no, Junior, not right now."

"I'd like to see how handsome you're going to look with your hair cut."

"Okay, we might as well get it started."

"El Catalán, sit down on this chair," commands Betty to El Catalán as she puts a towel around his neck covering his shirt.

Taking a sharp scissors in one hand and a comb in the other, Betty starts to cut El Catalán's hair. Everyone stands around making wisecracks and jokes.

She tries to do a good job even though the others are laughing and want her to do a poor job. Then she starts cutting on his beard. After she cuts as close as she can with the scissors, she gets a safety razor and some hot water, soap, a can of shaving cream, and some shaving lotion. After washing his face and neck, she applies the shaving cream. Then with the safety razor, she finishes the shaving job, not cutting him anyplace. When finished, she takes a rag and soaks it in warm water which she uses to wash the shaving cream off his face. She then pats shaving lotion on his face and tries to comb his hair as well as she can.

Now the wisecracks turn to whistles of admiration. Betty brings El Catalán her mirror as Junior accompanies her and says, "Wow, what a good-looking dude. Betty, you did a great job. He really is a handsome character."

"Thanks Junior. I tried my best."

"You sure did. What do you think, El Catalán?"

"I was prepared to hate it, but Betty did a really good job. My face feels great." He rubs his face back and forth. "Yes, it really feels great. Betty, I'd give you a kiss if it weren't for the fact that Junior would never ..."

Junior says, "You deserve a kiss, El Catalán, because of your great attitude in getting a haircut. It really is part of the disguise. You would make a lot of people suspicious if you kept your hair and beard like you had it before. You'll be sure and keep it this way, right?"

"Right, Jefe."

"Okay, then get your kiss from Betty."

El Catalán is a bit hesitant as he approaches Betty for a kiss. No one has tried this before. She stands still, however. When El Catalán gets nearer, she walks over to him and plants a strong kiss on his lips. Everyone claps and laughs, including Junior. Betty steps back smiling as only she can smile. El Catalán feels pretty proud having gotten a kiss from this Latin beauty which is a gift all the men in the Cartel would pay big bucks to receive.

With that last bit of fun, Junior walks over to El Catalán and says, "El Catalán, thanks for playing along with that idea for a kiss. These are the things that keep the men loose and happy. They need to be this way if we expect them to jump into action at a moment's notice."

"Junior, I was pleased to make that sacrifice for the unit."

Junior laughs, "Some sacrifice, a kiss from the most beautiful girl in the group."

"I would only do such a thing on direct orders from you, Junior."

"I think we'd better get to bed. It's getting harder and harder to believe you."

They both laugh and head for their quarters.

#

The next morning, El Catalán and El Caracol are loading up their third burro with provisions for the trip. Betty brings them a nice lunch to help on the trek. She asks El Catalán and El Caracol to come near her. As she says, "Buena suerte," she kisses each one of them on the cheek.

El Caracol says, "Wow, I didn't think I'd be this lucky when I accepted the call to go on this assignment."

"You see, good gifts come when you volunteer to go the extra mile," adds Betty.

While both men are laughing, they mount their burros, say goodbye to Betty and Junior who has just joined them.

Junior says, "Now you guys, one last word before you leave. I've thought a lot about this possible heist from the army base. It could be a complete tragedy. I'd lose both of you. We can get all the coke we want from other sources. But either way, we need you and the copter for many reasons. So enjoy your training."

"Gracias Jefe," they both respond as they wave to those who are looking out the doorways of their tents.

El Catalán leads the way on his favorite burro who knows the pathway better than any member of the group. Both men check their pistols to be sure they are ready for any eventuality, such as a poisonous snake or a charging jaguar.

They sing as their burros take them through the jungle. Time goes fast and noon approaches quickly. They stop by a small stream with grass growing nearby. Tying their burros to a line which they string between two trees, all three animals can easily get a drink and eat fresh blades of grass. If they feel like it, they can also lie down on the wet grass.

El Catalán notices that the sky is growing darker. Covering their provisions with the tarp they brought with them, they stand in the cool rain along with the burros. The pace of the storm intensifies as rain is coming down very fast now.

El Catalán says to his companion, "Be alert, these wild beasts love to charge in this rain which cuts down on our vision and hearing a great deal. Get your pistol out, I sense some trouble coming very soon."

El Caracol says, "There it is, El Catalán, and coming fast."

Both men turn, take aim at a charging jaguar, and let go with five shots each from their 9mm pistols, **BOOM, BOOM, BOOM, BOOM, BOOM, BOOM, BOOM,**

BOOM, **BOOM**, **BOOM**. The dead jaguar slides across the wet grass stopping almost at their feet.

El Catalán says, "Hurry, insert another magazine. We may need all 18 shots in a minute or two."

Both men reload their pistols and continue to stay very alert. The burros have been in this kind of a situation before and move behind the men. They sense that the men will do everything in their power to save their lives as well as their own.

El Catalán says, "There come two cougars. You take the one on the right. I'll take the one on the left. Stand by for others."

Both men go to their special stance to maintain accuracy, with their right knee and right foot on the ground and holding their pistol firmly in their right hand resting it in their left hand as their left elbow rests on their left knee. They go to this position in about one fourth of the time it takes to describe it due to much practice. **BOOM, BOOM, BOOM, BOOM, BOOM, BOOM, BOOM, BOOM**. Two dead cougars slide across the wet grass. The men look around carefully and quietly. The rain stops its noise on the large leaves of the plants.

Both men quickly remove the used magazine from their pistols and slam another fresh magazine of 17 cartridges into the handles of their pistols. They now have 18 cartridges in their semi-automatic pistols. Next they take the two used magazines from their belts and load them with fresh bullets.

When finished, they continue to eat their lunch as the burros munch on the grass and drink from the rapidly swelling creek. Men and beasts enjoy the cool temperatures. They know it won't last long, but while it lasts, they enjoy it.

After the short rest with its attendant excitement, the small contingent is on the path again.

#

Some four hours of pleasant riding with cooler than normal temperatures later, the men see the shack. But wait, there are three burros tied up in front of the shack.

El Catalán doesn't know what to do. He has always worried about snakes in this shack but never worried about other human beings. He signals for El Caracol to stop. They move their burros behind some thick bushes where they and the burros can't be seen from the shack.

"Well, El Caracol, this is a first for me. I have never seen other humans in this shack before. I wonder who it could be."

El Caracol responds, "It could be soldiers, miners, bandits, members of another Cartel, etc. Either way, it looks like every option spells trouble."

"Very good, I think your assessment is right on. What options do we have now for spending the night?"

"We could sleep on our burros someplace along the trail, but that puts the burros at risk. We'd be dead without them. We could sleep in the trees, but that might turn out to be a real crushing experience."

El Catalán laughs, "Yes, I know what you mean."

"We could keep going on the trail but that still has some real danger related to it. And we could approach the shack and see if we could attempt to spend the night there."

El Catalán adds, "Since we don't know who is in the shack, we could wait by that stream over there hoping that some man might be coming out for water. When that happens, we could capture him and question him."

"At least that way, we'd know more than we do now."

The men decide on the latter option. Tying the burros to a tree up-stream, they wait on both sides of the stream for the hoped-for arrival of some man from the cabin. And sure enough, after a long 35 minutes, an army sergeant in full jungle uniform comes walking out of the cabin with three canteens hanging over his shoulder, obviously to fill them at the creek.

El Catalán doesn't know exactly what to do. He motions to his companion to hold still, do nothing. They wait as the army sergeant fills his canteens and returns to the shack. After the sergeant has disappeared, El Catalán says to his partner, "I don't think we should take on the army. They could be very well armed. What do you think, El Caracol?"

"You're right. They've probably got lots of ammo and grenades. We wouldn't have a chance against them. I guess we'll just have to move on."

"I don't look forward to moving through this jungle at night. We have one lantern. Would that be of any help?"

"Well, we can find out. Are you game?" El Caracol asks.

El Catalán replies with a bit of shakiness in his voice, "I sure am, and let's get going before these guys come out to look around. I wish I knew in which direction they are traveling. Several paths cross at this shack.

"Wait a minute, look at those burros. They're not army burros. The fact that there are three burros suggests that there must be two men inside, with one burro being used, like we are, for packing provisions and other things."

And at that exact second, two men dressed as soldiers come out the front door with submachine guns in their hands. Before El Catalán and El Caracol can even discuss the matter, the men start shooting their Uzis in the direction of El Catalán and El Caracol who quickly duck behind a large boulder.

"Wow, we're got a problem here. You try to take the guy on the right, and I'll go for the guy on the left."

They both lift their heads above the boulder and take aim. But before they can do anything, **BOOM**, a shot rings out.

"Oh, I've been hit in the shoulder" says El Caracol as he falls to the ground.

El Catalán takes careful aim and starts shooting his semi-automatic 9 mm pistol in rapid succession. One man standing by the shack goes down. El Catalán switches magazines rapidly and continues shooting. After 18 more shots, he switches magazines again. But before he can use his new load, he sees the second man fall to the ground with a groan.

El Catalán watches as the two men lie quietly without any moves.

El Caracol says, "I'm not too bad, just the right shoulder. Go ahead, check 'em both out. If they're alive, finish 'em off."

El Catalán walks slowly over to the entrance of the shack. He checks the pulses of both men. They are dead.

Returning to his friend, he asks him how he's doing.

"If you can cut my shirt and check out my shoulder, we'll both know a lot more."

Taking out his hunting knife, El Catalán cuts several slices up the shirt of his friend. He rips them some more and folds them back out of the way. The bullet hit El Caracol square in the shoulder, obviously shattering some bones. He needs to get to a doctor quick. But in this part of the jungle, you don't do anything quick.

El Catalán checks El Caracol's shoulder in the back and front. The bullet was stopped by the bones. He'll have to cut out the bullet and clean the wound.

"My friend, I'd better cut that bullet out and then disinfect the wound. That way you could last until we get to La Vista."

"Okay my friend, cut away. But first get me some booze."

El Catalán checks the backpack on the third burro of the dead men. Sure enough, there are several pints of whiskey. He opens the top of one and gives the bottle to El Caracol.

After he takes a few swigs, he says, "Hey that's pretty good for store-bought whiskey. Start cutting and don't stop till you're done."

El Catalán starts a small fire using some dry wood stacked under the lean-to. It takes a few minutes, but that delay helps El Caracol consume more "anesthesia." When the fire is hot, El Catalán takes his knife and puts the first couple inches of the sharp blade into the flame.

When the blade is hot and the surface is clean, El Catalán pours some cold water over the blade. It sizzles as the water touches the hot blade, but finally cools down.

El Catalán puts his left arm around his friend's neck to hold him tight. After pouring some whisky on the shoulder, he then takes the blade and cuts into the flesh of his friend's shoulder. El Caracol groans and then faints.

El Catalán knows he has to take advantage of these few seconds while his friend has lost consciousness to get the bullet that is lodged in his shoulder. Moving the tip of the blade back and forth, he finds the bullet. Putting the end of the blade under the bullet, El Catalán forces the bullet outward and flips it to the ground. He then takes the bottle of whiskey and pours the antiseptic into the wound.

His friend awakes at the pain caused by the cutting and whiskey on the wound.

"Hey, when are you going to stop?"

El Catalán says, "I'm done. The bullet is out, and I cleaned the wound with some of that precious whiskey. I need to get a clean cloth to cover the wound."

"You're done, really?"

"Yes, my friend. You were a good patient."

"Well, you were a better surgeon."

"It should hold until we can get you to a real doctor. He'll clean out the bones hit by the bullet."

El Catalán goes to their pack animal and retrieves a first aid kit. Taking a roll of gauze and adhesive tape, he returns to his friend. Next he pours whiskey over his hands.

"Hey, why are you wasting that whiskey? We need it. I need it for the pain in my arm."

"I need it more to clean my hands before I put this bandage on your shoulder. Cleanliness is next to,,,"

"Yea, I know, cleanliness is next to drunkenness."

"You're crazy."

Finished with the bandaging, El Catalán adds, "Are you all right if I check what's on that burro and inside the shack?"

"Sure, go ahead. Just leave me the bottle of whiskey."

El Catalán walks over to the burros and checks what's on the one burro used for transport of gear. He is pleased to see some canned food, extra magazines for their 9mm pistols, and two more pints of whiskey which El Caracol will be pleased to see and which may help him get out of this jungle without falling off his burro from too much pain.

He returns to his friend and says, "We should stay here tonight in the shack. I'll bury these two characters. There's some canned food and extra magazines for the pistols in the burro's backpack." He decides he won't say anything yet about the two bottles of whiskey.

El Caracol stumbles into the shack weak from the "operation" on his shoulder. He checks it out for snakes while El Catalán takes his small shovel and digs one large grave into which he places the two bodies. Later, with El Caracol at his side, he says a short prayer about man coming into this world with nothing and leaving it the same way. He asks the Lord to bless these two men and forgive them their trespasses. It is obvious that El Catalán has studied the New Testament of the Christian Bible.

#

The night's rest was fitful for El Catalán but peaceful for El Caracol, obviously due to the last drops of the bottle of whiskey. As they pack up to leave the shack, El Caracol asks if there is any more whiskey in the pack of the burro.

This is the question that El Catalán was hesitant to receive. He has to answer the truth. He tries to fudge a bit by saying, "I think there is one more bottle. Let me check. But it would have to last you a long time, two days."

"No problem, just enough to get the edge off the pain. I don't want to waste it getting drunk. It's too precious. It's a long ride to a doctor's office. I don't imagine that Dos Brazos has what I really need, some morphine injections. That would do the trick."

El Catalán helps his friend get on his burro. El Catalán then gets on his own burro all the time holding the rope to the string of four burros. El Caracol leads out with El Catalán following while holding onto the rope that controls the string of burros. They are the two pack burros and the two burros used by the men who were just buried.

El Catalán thinks, *These extra burros should be good trading material with Dos Brazos.*

Fortunately, the trip goes smoothly from this point on. Morning and afternoon showers of 20 or so minutes each keep the contingent cool and make for some excitement. Each evening, they are able to find an opening that provides the ability to see some 50 meters in each direction. They have to keep a fire burning and one must stand watch at all times. While some cougars are in the area, they don't like the fire or an occasional shot from a pistol.

#

Eventually they can see the home of Dos Brazos in the distance. His children see them, and start yelling so that everyone is aware of the approaching group. When they arrive, Dos Brazos is out to greet them along with his many children.

The first question El Caracol has is: "Do you have any morphine. I've been shot in the shoulder and this butcher of El Catalán did a job on me."

"Well that's the thanks I get."

"I was just kidding my dear, old friend. Without your help, I would probably be dead."

Dos Brazos says, "Yes, I have some morphine, and there is a doctor just two houses down. Would you like me to send one of my children to get him? Dr. Mendonza is a good doctor"

"Please do, Dos Brazos. I'd be eternally grateful."

Dos Brazos sends one of his older boys to see to the important task of finding the doctor.

"Come on in and have a seat. We have a table with strong lighting. We know it's a little ancient, but it's kept very clean and we call it our operating table. Here, let me show you some of the devices we have made so the doctor can adjust parts of the table to suit the operating needs."

Dos Brazos is so proud of his table that he takes some time showing off the various parts that accomplish what is needed in a modern operating table.

And just then, there is a knock at the door which is opened by Dos Brazos.

"Doctor Mendonza, how nice of you to come so quickly. We have a man here who's been shot in the shoulder, but his friend took out the bullet and tried to keep the wound clean with whiskey."

"Well, that's better than nothing," says the good doctor. But we can do better here, can't we Dos Brazos?"

"We sure can. I'll get out the necessary articles. You see guys, I'm the doctor's assistant."

Speaking to El Caracol, Doctor Mendonza says, "How many tetanus shots have you had?"

"Tetanus shots, what's that?"

The doctor laughs, "That's what I figured."

El Catalán and El Caracol take a seat and watch as the two men prepare to perform an operation on El Caracol. First they go to the sink and wash their hands and wrists frantically. Dos Brazos' oldest daughter, Susana, age 17, or as she always says, "17 going on 18," shows up and scrubs herself as well. Then she dries her hands with a clean towel, after which she gives similar towels to the two men. When their hands are dry, she sprinkles some powder on their hands and helps each one put on antiseptic vinyl gloves.

Both Cartel men can't help but stare at Susana. How beautiful she is. Her long black hair shows the Indian background she gets from her father, Dos Brazos. Her high cheekbones she gets from her mother. She stands tall and straight with complete devotion to what she is doing.

El Catalán whispers to El Caracol, "She would have my vote in any beauty contest."

"Mine too," adds El Caracol.

Susana approaches the two men taking El Caracol by the hand, which he enjoys, and helps him lie down on the "operating table." She then places a clean pillow under his head which helps him relax a bit.

"Would you like a morphine shot?"

"Boy, would I."

She then gives him a mild morphine shot which puts him immediately to sleep.

Dr. Mendonza asks, "Susana, please give the patient a shot of the anti-tetanus serum before we begin."

"Yes, Doctor," she says as she goes to a small cabinet and withdraws the necessary item. Removing the protective end from the syringe, she squirts out a bit of liquid and air. Taking an alcohol pad, she cleans a spot on his shoulder. Then she jabs the needle into his shoulder and deftly administers the anti-tetanus serum.

"Okay, now for some alcohol," says Susana.

She removes the antiseptic protection on the top of a bottle of alcohol and places the bottle on the counter.

Next she removes the bandage from the shoulder of El Caracol and takes the bottle of alcohol and cleans the wound. The doctor comes forward and examines the wound.

He says, "El Catalán, you did a good job taking the bullet out, but you missed a few items. There are several bone chips here that must have been giving him lots of pain. Once we get those out, his pain will be reduced significantly."

The doctor goes to work with Susana handing him the tools as he needs them, and Dos Brazos keeping the doctor's forehead and his eye lids dry. The doctor demonstrates real professionalism as he takes out the bone chips cleanly with El Caracol lying quietly. Finally, Doctor Mendonza puts down his operating tools and looks carefully into the wounded area to be sure he has removed all the bone chips.

"Uh oh," he says, "Here's one little bone sliver trying to hide out and cause trouble much later."

Susana hands him a sterilized pair of tweezers. He grabs the small bone sliver and removes it from the shoulder wound.

Then he says with an air of satisfaction, "That's it. We got 'em all, I think. Thanks Susana and Dos Brazos. No surgeon ever had a better trained team around him during an operation."

Dr. Mendonza adds, "Hey El Catalán, can you help bring El Caracol over to this faucet? I want to wash his shoulder with warm water with some pressure. I know it's a bit different than in a hospital, but we have to make do here."

The men do as requested. El Caracol is still under the influence of the morphine, but the men are able to hold his shoulder under the warm water that is kept at a pretty strong spray.

Dr. Mendonza says, "Here Susana, take some of this antibacterial soap. Suds it up really good all around his shoulder." Then the doctor puts a household strainer under the shoulder that is being cleaned.

She does as requested after he squirts the soap into her antiseptic gloves. It is obvious that they are doing whatever they can in these primitive conditions to observe antiseptic conditions in their little hospital room.

"Now Susana, wash the soap off as well as you can."

She diligently washes his shoulder from every possible angle. Dos Brazos' wife brings some more antiseptic towels. Susana takes one and dries her own hands. She then takes another and dries El Caracol's shoulder very gently patting only. He is beginning to regain consciousness after the morphine shot.

As Susana leads El Caracol back to the hospital bed, he thanks her for taking care of him. She says she is pleased to do it. She helps him lie down on the bed after which she places a clean sheet over him. She then folds another clean sheet over his neck and chest leaving just his shoulder exposed.

The doctor brings the strainer to the table and says, "Susana and El Caracol, look. What do you see in the bottom of the strainer?"

They both strain their eyes and finally zero in on a very small sliver of bone in the bottom of the strainer.

The doctor says, "I'm very sorry El Caracol. Here's one I missed. Without an X-Ray machine, we have to invent our own technology. I have learned that warm water with some pressure will bring out bone slivers that I can't even see. It's primitive, but it works."

"That's great doc. It'll save a lot of pain later, won't it?"

"It sure will."

Speaking to the group the doctor says, "He needs rest now and later some mild food. Susana, will you put a fresh bandage on this wound after you apply some broad-spectrum antibiotic cream?"

"Of course Doctor. Father, would you hold his arm steady so I can get a good bandage around his shoulder?"

Dos Brazos complains, "Look at this daughter of mine, giving me orders all over the place."

Susana says, "Hush, this is tricky work and must be done right and can't be disturbed with someone talking."

Doctor Mendonza says, "She's right Dos Brazos."

"Okay, okay, I guess my daughter is now giving me orders."

The doctor supervises the bandaging of the left shoulder.

"Perfect," he says. "this girl has got what it takes to be a surgery room nurse."

"Thank you Doctor."

Before Dr. Mendonza leaves the room, he gives an antibiotic shot to El Caracol.

As Dos Brazos, El Catalán, and the doctor relax in the other room talking about this and that, finally the question is asked, "Who shot El Caracol?"

"A dead man," responds El Catalán. That's the end of the subject.

"Doctor, how long do you think my friend will have to have bed rest before he can take the bus to La Vista?"

"After probably two days more. In other words, on the third day. Don't rush it."

Susana comes into the room and says, "Mom and the other girls made a large pot of chicken soup and hot rolls. This should be good for our patient as well as the entire group."

Everyone agrees and quickly goes to wash up. When they return, there is a lineup of people taking a plate for rolls and a bowl for soup. They then stack two rolls around the soup with the final item being a glass of lemonade. Everyone takes a place around a large dining room table and starts to enjoy a sumptuous meal. Dos Brazos doesn't even look at the diners, he just starts to say grace. Hearing it, everyone else stops talking and eating. He is grateful for the medical help provided to his friend, El Caracol.

After dinner, Susana says, "Doctor Mendonza, is it too early to serve the patient some soup?"

"No I don't think so. Try it."

Susana ladles out a bowl of chicken soup and along with a roll and some lemonade heads into the "operating room." She knocks quietly and then enters. "El Caracol, may I come in? I'm the nurse who helped in the operation."

El Caracol looks to his right to see a pretty young lady dressed in a nurse's uniform wanting to help him. He thinks, *There's no way I'm going to miss this opportunity.*

"Come on in, pull up a chair, and let me see what you've got to eat. I understand patients need to be fed really mild food after an operation. What do you have there?"

"Chicken soup, a roll, and lemonade."

"Oh boy, let's get at it."

Susana starts to feed him. He could probably feed himself, but it's more fun being fed by this beautiful young woman. El Caracol continues to eat and drink with Susana's help until all the food and drink are gone.

"So you're the nurse who helped me, is that right?"

"Yes, that's right."

"I understand that Dos Brazos is your father, is that right?"

"Yes, that's right."

"How do you explain your being so beautiful with an ugly father like yours?"

"Hey, don't talk about my father that way. When you get to know him, you'll realize how beautiful he is. Did you know that he served as the doctor's assistant during the operation today?"

"No I didn't. You're right, I didn't realize how beautiful he is."

"He has assembled this little operating room right here on the edge of the Rainforest. We're able to do some rather sophisticated operations for people coming out of the Rainforest having been injured by wild animals, falls from burros, etc. We usually recommend they go to the hospital when they get to La Vista, but all reports are positive as to the work done here, You watch, I bet Dr. Mendonza will recommend the same thing for you.

"Now you should get some more rest, sleep right through till breakfast. You've had a good meal, and should sleep well. If the pain returns to your arm, let me know and I'll give you one more mild morphine shot, but that'll be the last one. From here on out, it's over the counter pills. We don't want to get you hooked on morphine. It's a strong drug and very addictive, but very helpful for the kind of pain you had when you arrived here. I'll close the drapes so you can have it dark here."

"You wouldn't want to stay with me, would you?"

"Why are you men all alike? You want the girls near you."

"Take one look in the mirror, and you'll see why I want you near me."

"Oh you're silly. Goodnight and sleep well."

Chapter 5

Three days later, El Catalán and El Caracol wait at the bus stop for the bus that stops in front of the home of Dos Brazos. The men left some money with Dr. Mendonza for his professional services, with Susana for the same reason, and with Dos Brazos to refurbish the medical supplies for his "hospital room" and for the room and board for several days. Susana is sad to see them leave, but knows that El Caracol must get to a hospital ASAP. She kisses both men on the cheeks for which they are grateful.

El Catalán is pleased with the "hospital" that Dos Brazos has assembled. He is especially grateful for the help given to his friend, El Caracol. He calls Dos Brazos over before he boards the bus.

"Dos Brazos, those three extra burros we brought in the other day. They're yours to use, rent, sell, whatever. We appreciate very much your little hospital in the jungle."

"Hey, thanks very much. I can trade them for lots of supplies for the family. Goodbye."

Boarding the bus, the two Cartel men wave at the kids and the family and then settle back for the ride to La Vista. El Caracol does not have a temperature for which everyone is grateful. The pain in his shoulder is decreasing with each passing day.

They soon are asleep on the bus along with most of the other passengers. A few hours later, the bus stops at the La Vista International Airport. The two men disembark and take a taxi to the La Vista Hospital.

Arriving at the admission counter in the hospital, El Caracol explains his problem. A clerk walks them both back to the emergency room. After another explanation, one of the doctors in the E.R. quickly asks a nurse to take all the vital signs of El Caracol. The doctor knows that the possibility of severe infection is possible after hearing the explanation given to him by El Caracol.

Another nurse puts on antiseptic gloves and removes the bandage from the shoulder of El Caracol. The doctor approaches and hears the report on vital signs from the first nurse. He is pleased. He then dons antiseptic gloves himself and checks the wound. He is even more pleased. He takes a powerful magnifying glass searching for bone splinters. He finds none. He asks the nurse to arrange for X-Rays of his shoulder and blood tests.

The nurse puts El Caracol into a wheelchair and pushes him to the X-Ray laboratory. He is a bit embarrassed to be pushed by a pretty nurse through the halls of the hospital. Then the nurse pushes him to the lab for blood tests. She shows the technician the order from the doctor as to which specific tests he wants performed on El Caracol.

After the blood tests are finished, the nurse wheels El Caracol to a room near the E.R. area. She helps him take off his clothes and put on a hospital gown. The results from the blood test will take several hours.

El Caracol immediately goes to sleep. However, the doctor comes into the room and says, "Sr. Caracol, I am amazed at the results of the tests taken so far. The X-Ray shows no bone slivers of any size. Your temperature, blood pressure, blood glucose, oxygen, pulse are all in good shape for a man your age. The only tests we are waiting on are the more sophisticated blood tests. They take a bit longer. So you can just rest here for the remainder of the day.

I would suspect, based on what we've seen so far, that your other tests will have the same great results and you should be able to leave the hospital this evening. I don't know who attended you in the Rainforest, but they certainly know their business about operating room procedures, antiseptic conditions in the operating room and the various tools needed in the E.R. area."

El Caracol adds, "And they have the best-looking nurse you've ever seen."

The men laugh.

"Goodbye doctor, and thanks. Can we pay the bill upon leaving this evening.?"

"Sure, just stop at the business office near the elevators on the main floor."

#

Four days later, the two men from the Rainforest have rented a room in a boarding house near the airport, purchased some clothes on the advice of the clerk in the men's store, enrolled in a four-weeks' class to start in one and one-half weeks on the basics of flying a helicopter. They feel that they are doing well, especially when they take into consideration the bullet that caught El Caracol in his shoulder.

Waiting for formal instruction to begin, each day El Catalán and El Caracol spend some time at the airport watching the helicopters with the student pilots. They also spend some time in the aviation library checking on loads that can be carried by the various copters. They realize that this is purely a business venture, and the proceeds must surpass the expenses by a great deal.

By the time the class starts, El Caracol feels he should be in good physical condition and be able to use both his hands and arms as he learns about flying a copter. They wonder what kind of copter they will learn to fly, how much a similar one would cost, where they can purchase such a copter, etc.

#

Finally the big day has arrived. Their first instruction to learn how to fly a helicopter is about to begin. But naturally, it begins in a traditional classroom. Both men agree that it is rather complicated, but it is the only task before them. They learn about three different types of copters, small, medium, and large. The price goes up as the size goes up. In the classroom, they learn about copters produced by various nations, used copters, lift load, altitudes. They have to remember that they live and work sometimes at high altitudes. Therefore, they must suggest to Junior a model that can operate at high altitudes.

As the weeks progress, both men become more familiar with the helicopters. Just a few days before graduation, they write a letter to Junior. Such letters are sent to the house of Dos Brazos, and the next passerby going into the Amazon Rainforest to the Cartel hideout takes the letters to the Cartel leader, Junior.

Their letter reads,

"Jefe Junior,

"We finish r training course this Friday. We have learnt a lot. Recomendashuns are follows: By one used 4 seatur copter, price for model is $1,000,000.00. Front seats pilot and co-pi; Remove co-pi seat and 2 back seats, replace with load that is now over 200 kilos of u-know-what. 4 fuel set up gas stashun at Dos Brazos place, with regulur gas and aviashun gas. Be quiet partner with majur gasoline produsir, investment $250,000.00 2 build landing pad 4 copters and addishunal pad 4 cars with sales pumps. There is great need 4 such a stashun near the Rainforest 4 the 2 companies that fly turistas ovur the Rainforest and 4 people in the area needing gas 4 their cars and tracturs. Even the State Patrol and the Army need gas stashun in that area, ha, ha. We would by all r gas there. Aviashun gas, or avegas as it is kalled, is more spensive that regulur gas. Avegas is sumtimes kalled AVGAS. Note: Jet planes kan not use eithur 1 of these 2 gases.

"Another suggestshun: Have 2 burros pull wagon with 2 50-gallon kans of aviashun gas into r camp to have on hand for emurgencies.

"If you agre, we could meet with Jefes from gas company. You wouldn't recognize us now, with our good-looking haircuts, and no face hair, plus super sports clothing and business suits. Jefes from gas company would think we were top brass from anothure firm, quiet partners.

"Anyway, these are some thoughts for u to think about. Oh yes, in case u haven't heard, El Caracol got shot in the shouldur in a battle with 2 dead men at the shack. Doctor at Dos Brazos fixed him up with help from Susana, daughter of Dos Brazos, and the old man himself helping around the operatin table. I took El Caracol immediate to the hospital when we finally got to La Vista. The doctor at the hospital after many tests said the doctor at Dos Brazos place did a good job, very antaseptic, as in very clean, which was necessary for him. If u ever want to see a butaful girl, age 17, stop by Dos Brazos place. His daughter is the most butaful girl I have ever sen. She sure could not have got it from her Dad.

"We will see you in a week or so.

"El Catalán and El Caracol (the wounded snail.) P.S. We both red this story 2 check the spelling. We aggreed on all words excep 1, namely, tracturs. El Caracol says tracturs, I say tracters. El Caracol one the koin tos so we used his word. Otherwise, we feel all uthur words are speled correctly. Goodby."

Putting the letter in an envelope, El Catalán addresses it, buys a stamp at the motel manager's place, and posts the envelope. It should arrive at Dos Brazos' place in two days, but no one could guess when it might get to the headquarters of the Cartel de la Selva Tropical.

#

In his newly rebuilt office at the Police K-9 School, Captain Berto Castillo answers the phone, "Berto here."

"Berto, this is Colonel Mario Núñez at the Army Base. I have an invitation for you. Tomorrow the private helicopter training company on the other side of the airport is having its graduation. The day should come when your department will need to buy a helicopter. Most of the companies selling copters will be there with at least one of their models. This doesn't happen very often when so many copters are in the same place at the same time here in La Vista. How would you like to go with me and see the graduation as well as stroll throughout the display area of the copters?"

"Hey that does sound good. I think Chief Medina should be there as well. He's the one who would have to make any recommendation to the Police Commission."

"You're right. I'll give him a call. The graduation is at 1000 hours. I'll come by and pick you up at 0930 hours. If the Chief wants to go, we can drive by his office as well. What say?"

"Sounds good to me. I'll be standing by. Goodbye."

Berto walks into his secretary's and wife's office, where Susana is hard at work.

"Hi Honey. I just heard from Mario Núñez at the Army Base. He's invited me to a display tomorrow of helicopters at the airport. He'll invite the Chief as well."

"That sounds like fun, Berto. I'd like to see that as well, but we need someone to man the office, or is that to woman the office?"

"Whatever, you're needed here, sorry."

She asks, "Will you be able to join me for lunch in the staff lunchroom today?"

"Sure Honey. Give me a yell when you're ready to leave."

"Okay, Captain Castillo, will do." She salutes from her desk.

He laughs.

#

The following day, at 0930 hours, Berto walks through Susana's office, gives her a kiss, and says "goodbye Dear."

"Have fun. I imagine you'll have lunch together someplace."

"I imagine."

Berto walks to the front of the school and looks down the street. An official Yuñeco Army car, driven by a military chauffeur, is approaching. The car pulls up to the curb and stops. Colonel Núñez opens the door from the inside and says, "Hi Berto. Come on it."

"Okay, let's go. Hi Chief Medina. I'm glad you could go too."

Colonel Núñez says, "Driver, to the air station on the other side of the commercial airport where they're having a show of helicopters today."

"Yes sir," responds the driver. The trip to the airport is short. The drive to the other side of the airfield is slower since the chauffeur must be aware of planes landing from time to time. But eventually they arrive at the location for the graduation ceremonies and the display of many helicopters.

"Look Chief, have you ever seen so many copters at the same time?"

"Never Berto. I'd like to really look them over after the graduation ceremonies."

The car stops with the three men leaving and taking a seat inside one of the large hangars for the graduation ceremonies. There is a program on each chair.

The Chief says, "Let's see who's graduating today."

The men read all the names.

Chief Medina says, "Oh no, not Juan David García Martínez."

Berto inquires, "Chief, what's the problem with him. I've never heard that name before."

"Oh it's just a case before the Grand Jury that I heard about long ago. No problem."

"Good, do you know any others of the graduates?"

Colonel Mario Núñez speaks up, "Our unit has a graduate among the group, Sgt. Luisa Marcón. She's a great sergeant. I hate to lose her as a leader, but she will be a great asset working with us as a copter pilot. She knows our tactics perfectly."

The Chief responds, "It'll take a month to get a copter and her assigned, don't you think?"

"You're right, Chief. No use worrying about it now. It might work out perfectly as I think about it. Look, there's the brass going up to the stage and microphone."

After the usual preliminary speeches by various leaders, the important part arrives, the reading of the list of names of the graduates. Chief Medina is very focused on the man who was involved in the Grand Jury case against Berto. Fortunately, Berto to this day knows nothing about it.

The Chief wants to see if El Catalán has a companion in the group of graduates since every pilot needs a co-pilot. When the name of Juan David García Martínez is read, it is followed by a man named Federico Hernando Rodríguez, II. As the other names are read, the Chief notes the two men, same kind of haircuts, suits, shoes, etc. The Chief concludes these two men have been trained together to help the Cartel. He figures he must tell Colonel Mario Núñez since copters and drugs in and around the Rainforest are in the jurisdiction of the Yuñeco Army.

After the ceremonies are concluded, the Chief tells Berto to check out the copters while he talks with Colonel Núñez. Taking him aside, he brings Mario up to date on the attempt at discrediting Berto in the Grand Jury and that the main Cartel man who was trying to do this was El Catalán. He shows and circles his real name on the program. The Chief requests complete confidentiality on this issue, but says he feels the Colonel has a need to know. The Colonel thanks him for sharing that info. They then join Berto as they check out the copters. When Berto moves ahead, the Chief tells Mario to keep an eye on El Catalán to see what kind of copter he is interested in buying.

The men stroll through the copters, some parked in the hangars, and others parked outside. Various ones have "Sold" written on them with the name of the buyer and the price.

They come to a four-seat copter. The description taped on its side says, "Used: Price is $1,000,000.00. Front seat for co-pilot and rear seats can be removed. Additional carrying load is now greatly increased. Sold to Juan David García Martínez. Three other versions of this model will be available in two weeks at same price."

Mario says, "Well Chief, I guess we know what model of helicopter the Cartel de la Selva Tropical will be flying."

Chief Medina wishes that the Colonel had not made that comment. He'll have to wait and see how Berto responds.

Berto asks, "Mario, how will you know that?"

"Berto, we have learned that this Juan David García Martínez is a representative of the Cartel de la Selva Tropical."

"That's good news Mario. Congratulations on learning that. I suppose my unit couldn't give you any help."

"I don't think so, Berto. We'll probably have to go after them with our copters that are much faster and can carry a heavier load. Plus we have increased armament, rockets, .50 cal machine guns, etc."

The Chief jumps into this conversation at this point. "Mario, I think Berto was referring to his K-9 Dogs. If his department can offer any help, give him a call."

"Okay, guys, shall do. Are you ready to go? Have you seen all you wanted to see?"

The Chief responds, "I've seen much more than I expected to see."

"And you Berto?"

"I didn't have any particular aspirations as far as what I might see so I'm ready to go. How about you Mario?"

"I'm sort of like the Chief. I've seen and learned much more than I expected, so this has been a very profitable day."

"Good, let's go then," echoes Berto.

#

Colonel Mario Núñez meets with his supervisor, General Miguel Escobar.

"Yes, that's right General. The Cartel de la Selva Tropical bought a helicopter. With the seats for the copilot and the two passengers removed, there is lots of room for a great amount of freight as in cocaine."

"Freight huh? How much weight could the copter carry in cocaine?"

"Well, that's easy. With three seats removed, the coke could equal the weight of three adults, say 165 pounds or 75 kilos each. That's 225 kilos or about 500 pounds."

"And what do you figure would be the value of such an amount of cocaine?"

Colonel Núñez responds, "It depends on a variety of things such as location of the sale, how trusted the dealer is for quality of the coke, and the purity of the coke. It could sell anywhere from $12,000-$32,000 per kilo. The price we use for calculations is $30,000 when sold abroad."

Taking out his little calculator, the Colonel pushes in the numbers for the average price of $30,000 per kilo times 225 kilos and gets the answer of $6,750,000 which he shares with General Escobar.

The only response he gets is "Wow."

"Yes, General, 'Wow.' Their base is in our boundaries. Would you like us to take out the base?"

General Escobar respondes, "No Coronel. If that is a typical Cartel base, it will include lots of women and children. We need to destroy the copter just after it leaves the base loaded with cocaine. That will require some heavy intelligence. And remember, we can't destroy it while it's still in the base. Who do we have from the intelligence community who could help us?"

"Well there's always Dos Brazos. But if he were ever suspected, his entire family would be wiped out. No we don't even get near him about this issue. We need to find a member of a foreign Indian Tribe, and that's not the Llumista Indians. Remember, it's the Llumista Tribe that's working with the Cartel."

"Okay, Colonel, this is simple. Just give me the names of the Indian tribes who hate the Llumista Indians."

"The problem is General, those that hate the Llumista Indians also fear them. We'd have to convince them that we would destroy the Copter Crew and the Llumista warriors. If word got back to the Llumista Tribe that a certain other tribe helped the Yuñeco Army destroy their new copter with its load of cocaine, that would be the end of the other tribe."

"What tribe has the guts to take on the Llumista Tribe?"

"In our experience, only the Yuñeco Indians."

"Uh oh, that's a problem."

"What kind of a problem, General?"

"The Yuñeco Indians are the favorite Indian Tribe of the President of the Republic, President Restrepo. He feels it is his personal responsibility to protect them."

"Would it be wise to approach the President about talking with the leadership of the Yuñeco Tribe requesting some help?"

The General shows a little more enthusiasm. "If the President knew the purpose of the need for the information, he might feel differently about the request."

The General picks up his intercom phone and asks his secretary to join him. When she does, he says, "Please contact the President's secretary. Now what's her name? Oh yes, it's Ana Martínez. Colonel Núñez and I would like to meet with the President ASAP. Thanks."

The officers continue talking while the secretary makes the call. She returns to the General's office in just a few minutes.

"Excuse me General. The President can meet with you tomorrow morning at 1000 hours. He said you officers might be out of bed by that time."

They laugh. Knowing his sense of humor, they are not offended at all.

"Okay, Colonel Núñez, I'll pick you up tomorrow morning by 0945 hours. Is that okay? Will you be out of bed by then?"

They all three laugh.

The Colonel responds, "I'll make a superhuman effort to be out of bed by then and ready to go."

He salutes his commanding officer and starts to leave the office with Captain Berto Castillo of the local police department at his side.

General Escobar states, "Captain Castillo, I just took it for granted that you'd like to go along on this venture since you're the one who brought it to us. It could be somewhat dangerous. We'll have body armor for you."

"Good General. Yes, I'd like to go. I'll have to check with my Chief first though. Thanks for the invite." The two officers leave the General's office.

#

That evening as soon as he returns home, Captain Berto Castillo takes his famous German Shepherd dog, Franz, out for a run. The usual neighbors are running their dogs as well. They greet the Colonel, knowing that his profession could take him from them at any time after a shootout with Cartel or bank robbers. They also know that he carries his 9 mm pistol with him at all times and one word from him and his faithful dog, Franz, would jump and rip the arm off a possible assailant. They usually give Berto and Franz a wide berth. In fact, everyone knows that Franz meets no dog that is his match during their morning or evening runs. The interesting part to the owners, is they believe their dogs know it too since their dogs also give Franz a wide berth.

#

After a shower and seated at the dinner table with his family, Berto advises the family of his meeting with the President tomorrow morning. The boys are excited. Little Elizabeth doesn't understand but is excited since the others are as well.

Susana expresses some concern for the life of her husband. He tries to tell her that all will be well and that the meeting is a planning meeting only.

#

At 1000 hours the next morning, the Army car drives up in front of the Government House. Its passengers disembark in a good mood. They are: General Miguel Escobar, Colonel Mario Núñez both of the Yuñeco Army, and Captain Berto Castillo, Superintendent of the La Vista Police K-9 School.

After identifying themselves to the guard at the entrance, they enter and walk down the hall to the President's office. Entering the secretary's office first, General Escobar says, "Hi Ana, how are you these days?"

"Just fine General Escobar. We haven't seen you for a while. I guess things in your world have been overly quiet."

"Yes, Ana, that's true, but that may all change any minute now."

"Well go right in and see what you can do to get things hopping."

"Thank you very much. We'll see you as we leave."

"I hope so General."

The three men walk into the President's office. First he looks at a sheet prepared by his secretary listing the names, ranks, and responsibilities of each officer in the group."

Recognizing rank first, he steps from behind his desk and says, "Miguel, I haven't seen you for a while. Are you all right?"

"Yes, General, tip top."

The President laughs at the General's choice of words. Continuing to recognize the Army first, he says, "Mario, what have you dreamed up now? Has your life gotten so slow that you need to go into the Amazon Rainforest again?"

"I'll let the General fill you in on that Sir."

"And Berto. Are you at the bottom of all this trouble?"

Berto responds, "Well, you might say that, and you might not."

They all laugh.

"Sit down men. General, from the top please."

"Yes sir, Mr. President. Captain Castillo has learned that two men from the Cartel de la Selva Tropical have recently learned to fly a helicopter. In fact, they've bought a helicopter which will seat a pilot and at least 225 kilos of cocaine, or 225 bricks at one kilo each.

"We believe that soon they will fly the copter to their camp in the rainforest, load it with coke and then fly to a spot where they can transfer the drugs to trucks, boats, or airplanes for distribution worldwide."

The President says, "Then this agrees with our recent intelligence from our high-flying spy plane."

General Escobar asks, "May I inquire about that?"

"Of course Miguel. I thought you would have been advised of that by now. We need to fill that hole. Our spy plane photographed a helicopter in a clearing at the cartel camp on a pass. Later it appeared that camouflage had been placed in the exact spot. The pilot was just fortunate to make the first pass before the camouflage was put in place."

The officers appeared stunned by this news, but not surprised.

The General then looks toward Berto, "While I already know the answer to this question, Captain Castillo, how much would 225 bricks of cocaine be worth on the street?"

Taking out his little calculator, Berto says as he pushes in the numbers, "You have to remember that cocaine sells for a wide variety of prices, depending on many factors. But as an example, let's use an average price of $30,000 per kilo. Remember that one kilo is approximately 2.2 pounds. Multiply that $30,000 per brick times 225 and you've got $6,750,000."

The President is astounded, "Berto did you say, 'six million seven hundred fifty thousand dollars?'"

"Yes, Mr. President, I did."

"Well, gentlemen, I can see why you're here. General, what's your plan?"

"We'd like to get some Yuñeco Indians to keep watch for us and notify us when the helicopter is getting loaded with cocaine, and then when the copter takes off."

"Uh oh, you want to put my Yuñeco Indians at risk, do you?"

"No we don't Mr. President. That's the last thing we'd want to do, as our past actions have demonstrated."

"Yes, that's true isn't it? I'm sorry. I forgot the many good things your units have done for my Indians. But what about this time?"

"We think the Yuñeco Indians could keep watch on the Cartel from a great distance. There are a number of hills with tall trees on them surrounding the Cartel's camp grounds. There is another option, Mr. President."

"Well, tell me please."

"Since the Cartel's home base is located within the boundaries of Yuñeco, a high-flying spy plane could fly over the Cartel's base daily with all its cameras running. The film from the day could be developed quickly, and we could analyze what is taking place at the Cartel campground. Once we know the copter is in the air, we would send jets to take it out of the air."

Colonel Núñez interrupts, "General and Mr. President, please pardon my interruption. It is very unusual for a fast jet to take out a helicopter that can bounce all over the place unless the jet is using heat seeking missiles, and even then the missile can lose its lock or tracking. But heat seeking missiles can also be used from the ground with a shoulder launcher against a slower copter just a short distance away."

The President says, "Do I detect another trip into the Rainforest by Intelligence Unit One for the purpose of taking out a copter loaded with cocaine with Colonel Núñez in charge?"

Everyone laughs.

General Escobar says, "Mr. President, I think you're right. Mario, tell us what you have in mind."

"Well gentlemen, my Unit has more experience in the Amazon Rainforest that any other group in Yuñeco. We know what equipment to take to keep antidotes fresh that are used against a wide range of snakes. We are familiar with the Llumista Indians and their tricks and curare tipped darts or arrows. We also know the correct antidote to take against curare. We are familiar with the heat, the downpours of rain, the paths used by the Llumista Indians, how to move a group through the rainforest which protects the troops in the best possible way, and so on."

"General, what do you think?"

"Mr. President, he's right. Nobody can challenge his data. His Unit is the best in the Rainforest, there's no doubt about that."

Berto adds, "Wait a minute gentlemen. When I informed you of the Cartel and its efforts to buy a copter to carry cocaine, I didn't want to put the lives of soldiers at risk in the Rainforest fighting Indians with curare tipped weapons."

Everyone laughs.

General Escobar adds, "Listen to him now that the cat is out of the bag."

President Restrepo says, "I've got another meeting in 15 minutes gentlemen. Let's bring closure to this discussion."

General Escobar says, "Mr. President, I think we would like your opinion. Is it worth the risk to take out 225 kilos of cocaine? Is it worth the risk sending in Intelligence Unit One to take out that copter? And last but not least, if Intelligence Unit One is going into the Rainforest again, should we add to their mission some additional targets?"

The President grabs his coat and hat, gives his bodyguards the high sign that it is time to leave, and says, "The answer to your three questions is 'yes.' Goodbye gentlemen. Mario, best of luck, and take care of yourself and your men and women."

"Thank you Mr. President," Mario says as the President leaves his office with his security force around him.

General Escobar says, "Wow, that was quick. Mario, I hope you know what you got yourself in for."

"So do I Miguel."

The General continues, "Let's head for my office and start the planning for this mission."

Off they go saying "Goodbye" to Ana as they leave her office.

She says, "That'll teach you to request something of the President." She laughs.

General Escobar says, "Oh that's right, she's been asked to listen in to all the President's conferences."

Ana adds, "Mario, you take care now. Remember, that Rainforest is dangerous."

#

Back in the office of General Escobar, the men are seated around his small conference table. The General asks his secretary to bring him the satellite map of the Amazon Rainforest.

General Escobar says, "Okay, Mario, this is your show."

Berto says, "Hey, wait a minute. There was no show until I came along. And that's what I want to do. I want to go along."

General Escobar says, "You wait a minute, civilian. This is an Army show."

Berto responds, "There's no show unless I reveal what I know about the Cartel, where their hideout is, where their shack is for rest on their treks, etc."

"Hey guys, it looks like he wants to play hardball," responds the General. "What do we do now?"

Colonel Mario Núñez says, "His boss probably wouldn't let him go even if he wanted to."

"I already checked on that. My boss, Police Chief Luis Medina, says if you guys will take me, I can go."

"Aha, there's the question," says the General. "'If you guys will take me.'"

Mario says, "But General, he's got us pinned. He knows the intel on this mission. Without him, we might as well stay home."

Berto laughs.

So does the General who says, "So what's the decision, Mario?"

"Well, I don't like being bested in arm wrestling. Wait a minute, if Berto can beat me in arm wrestling, we'll take him. If he can't, then he supplies the intel and stays home. Is that a deal Berto?"

Knowing the reputation that Mario has in all contests involving physical strength, Berto is hesitant and says, "Yea, sure, I've been in the hospital so many times this past year, they keep a permanent room reserved for me. How about a contest with the 9mm pistol? Most shots cutting black in the center of the target with 5 shots in the magazine at 50 feet."

The General looks at Mario and says, "What say Mario? This seems to be more even. I know that Berto has been laid up a number of times after chasing criminals with his dog."

"Okay, that sound fair to me. If I win, he's out but his intelligence is in. If he wins, he's in along with his intelligence. This afternoon at 1400 hours we'll meet at the shooting range, with no laser sights."

The General says, "Okay, with planning to commence tomorrow morning at 0830 hours in this office. See you at the shooting range."

The men disband.

#

At 1400 hours the men meet at the pistol range on the Army Base. With two officers squaring off, General Escobar has decided that he'd better be there to act as judge.

He explains the rules, "First, I'll flip a coin. Mario, you call the coin, 'heads or tails' while the coin is in the air. If you win the flip, you have the choice of going first or last. The one who goes first will shoot five shots and then the other one will shoot five shots. This will continue in groups of five shots until all 15 shots are expended. The range master at the end of the target range will do his usual thing of lowering the target and yelling out the number of bullets that have cut black, in other words, have cut someplace in the center of the target. Does everyone understand the rules?"

Both men agree that they understand the rules.

General Escobar says, "Okay, here goes the coin."

He flips the coin in the air as Colonel Mario Núñez calls "heads."

The coin lands on the wooden counter in front of the shooters and spins a few times, finally stopping with "tails" showing.

General Escobar says, "Berto, you win. In what order would you like to go?"

"I'd prefer to go last."

"Okay, you've got it. Mario, it's your turn."

The two men step back giving Colonel Mario Núñez sufficient room.

Putting his left elbow on the counter with his right wrist resting in his left hand, Colonel Núñez takes careful aim and then squeezes off five shots, **BOOM, BOOM, BOOM, BOOM, BOOM**.

The man at the end of the target range makes the exchange of targets and yells out, "All five bullets cut black."

Berto walks up to the counter as Mario joins the General to the rear. Taking the same position as Mario, Berto carefully squeezes off five shots, **BOOM, BOOM, BOOM, BOOM, BOOM**.

The range master exchanges the targets and yells out, "All five bullets cut black."

Mario and Berto repeat their performance and both cut black five times on their second round of five shouts.

The General says, "This is close guys. Each one has cut black ten times. These last five shots will make the difference. Mario, you're up."

Again taking his position at the counter, Mario rests his shooting arm as before and squeezes off five shots, **BOOM, BOOM, BOOM, BOOM, BOOM**.

The range master exchanges the targets, but does not yell out the usual information.

Instead he says, "I'll need some extra time. General Escobar, I'd appreciate your joining me to help determine the results of these last five shots."

"Sure Sergeant," yells out General Escobar as he runs to the end of the pistol range and steps down into the trench to help the range master analyze the results accurately. The range master hands the General a magnifying glass. He takes it and looks at the five holes in the target, saying, "Sarge, I see why you called for another judge. Two of these shots are really close, but I believe all five cut the black."

The sergeant says, "That was my conclusion after I looked very carefully at the results. Thanks General. You can return and have Berto take his last five shots. Thanks for your help."

The sergeant yells out, "All five bullets cut black."

As the General is walking back to the counter, Berto is thinking to himself, *If I win, Susana will be alone with the three children for several days, and if I get killed in that Rainforest by some snake, jaguar, or curare tipped arrow, she'll be alone to raise the kids. But my integrity demands my best performance.*

The General says, "Okay Berto, you know what the situation is. Good luck.'

Berto walks up to the counter, puts his safety in the off position and takes careful aim, **BOOM**, **BOOM**, **BOOM**, **BOOM**, **BOOM**.

The range master exchanges the targets. After a few minutes, he yells out, "All five bullets cut black."

General Escobar says, "I propose five shots at 75 feet. Do you men agree?"

Both men say "Yes," and nod their heads.

The General yells out, "Sergeant, we're going to take five shots each at 75 feet. Would you please move over to the 75 feet range?"

"Yes Sir," responds the range master as he moves to the next target range and sets up the targets.

"Mario, you still go first, okay Berto?"

"Of course, General."

Mario takes his preferred position and lets go with five shots, **BOOM, BOOM, BOOM, BOOM, BOOM**.

The range master exchanges the targets and in a few minutes yells out, "All five bullets cut black."

"Whew, that was close," says Mario.

Berto takes his preferred position and squeezes off five shots, **BOOM, BOOM, BOOM, BOOM, BOOM**.

The range master exchanges the targets and after a few minutes yells out, "Four bullets cut black."

Berto groans, "Oh no. How did that happen?"

Colonel Mario Núñez responds, "That always happens when you meet a better man."

They all three laugh and return to their cars.

As they arrive at their cars, the General says, "Don't forget, tomorrow morning at 0830 hours. Our goal is to plan an attack on the helicopter carrying 225 kilos of cocaine by the Cartel de la Selva Tropical. We'll use five men with shoulder fired heat seeking missiles. They weigh about 55 pounds apiece when assembled completely. These new missiles can lock on to a target from about any position. They don't need to be fired behind the heat produced by the engine like the older missiles did. Mario, how many troops do you want to take with you into the jungle?"

"In addition to the five soldiers with the missile launchers, the two EMTs with antidotes for snakes and curare, as well as two or three cowboys to tends the burros, I'd like to take the entire unit. We could very easily meet up with a contingent of Llumista Indians with vengeance on their minds. And we've learned that the best way to march is to go in three separate lines."

Tears come to the Colonel's eyes as he remembers those who went with him on earlier missions into the jungle and are now dead or no longer in the unit.

The General knows the history of these people and has to fight tears himself. He loved them just as Mario did and was also very close to them for many years.

General Escobar says, "Let me pass this idea by the top brass so we can get their nod of approval. I understand the need for so many troops. This is the only way to attempt to provide protection to the unit. You have too many good men and women who have been with you for many years, from the beginning to be exact. How many women will you take with you?"

"General, we have had from the beginning the motto that all women go on all missions. That's the motto that made them work harder than any women I've ever seen, climbing the rope, doing pushups, all the upper body exercises that require so much upper body strength. Very few women can do what our women can do, and that includes hand to hand combat, accuracy on the 9 mm pistol range and throwing hand grenades, shooting with the sniper rifle from a position of secrecy, marching day after day on very little food if necessary."

The General says, "Mario, you don't have to convince me. I'll get back to you as soon as I hear from the top brass. And there's no use having a planning meeting until we get the word from them. Stand by for a phone call."

Chapter 6

That evening around the Castillo dinner table, the boys are asking their father about the meeting he had with the Army officials and the President. He tells them that he almost had a chance to go into the Amazon Rainforest in search of the "bad guys."

His wife says, "Berto, that can't be true. What kind of responsibility is that for a husband? The odds that anyone going into the Rainforest and returning are slim at best."

"Dear, you didn't hear me. I said I almost had a chance to go into the Rainforest. I'm not going. Do you understand? I'm not going. Got it?"

"Yes, Dear, I've got it."

Susana pushes her chair back, walks around the table to where her husband is seated, and gives him a kiss on the lips.

"Thank you Dear," he says.

"You're welcome, Dear."

The subject is probably dropped completely and forever.

#

The next day at work, Susana answers the phone. "Yes, General Escobar, one moment please."

"Berto, General Escobar is on the phone."

"Thank you Dear. ...Hi General Escobar, what's the word?"

"Hi Berto, the top brass will only approve dropping by parachute from a helicopter four of our best team members. They will be selected from the Army's Parachute Jumping Team. Obviously, they'll get hung up in the canopy of the Rainforest, but from there they can rappel down to the forest floor with all their gear on their backs. Then it will be up to them to set up a perimeter of missile launchers and wait for the copter with the cocaine to take off. They'll have to get close enough to the take-off point to be able to take down the copter before it gets too far or too high."

"Well General, thanks for calling. I'll keep all this very confidential. It seems to me to be a good plan. Those members of the Army's Parachuting Jumping Team are the best. Does this mean that Mario won't be going?"

"That's right, Berto. He'll help in the planning with the Jumping Team, but beyond that it's up to the jumpers."

"Then you won't even need my input, right?"

"Right Berto. Thanks for standing by, but this will be an All-Army affair. But I wanted you to know what the plan is since you and your people were the ones to discover this cocaine transport in the first place."

"Thanks, General, and good luck to the Army. Goodbye."

"Goodbye Berto. Oh one more thing, Berto. Since you discovered this cocaine moving plan, any cocaine that we confiscate will be yours as far as the bounty is concerned. Do you know what I'm talking about?"

"I sure do General, you're talking about money, that's m-o-n-e-y, with a capital 'M.' But how will you know the value of the cocaine if you destroy all or most of it with missiles?"

"You've already told us it weighs 225 kilos. We've picked up radio transmissions from the Jungle speaking of moving 225 kilos of hi-grade cocaine. We can check the quality of the cocaine by testing some of it that survives the attack. I think your K-9 School is about to receive a huge amount of plata."

"I don't care whether you call it 'plata' or silver. Just be sure and send the check for the cocaine's recovery and destruction our way."

"I'll make sure personally that you get the check. I may even hand deliver it myself."

#

As Berto returns home that evening, Franz hears the front door opening and runs down the hall to greet him. Hearing the large dog running down the hallway, Berto quickly puts his brief case on the floor with his pistol belt beside it. He then sits down with his back propped against the door and prepares for the onslaught that will soon come his way.

"Hey Franz, how are you doing?"

The dog keeps running and crashes into Berto who puts his arms around the German Shepherd and hugs him several times. He then turns him on his back and starts a strong rub on his chest. Franz is making his usual noises indicating that he is enjoying this attention.

Susana, Elizabeth, Bobbie, and Miguel all stand in the hallway watching this rare event since Berto has been so busy at work lately leaving little time to play with the dog.

Berto flips over on his back and lets Franz get the best of him, growling and shoving his nose into Berto's chest as Berto yells out for mercy. But the dog gives him none.

Bobbie and Miguel want to join in the fun, so they jump on their dad and help Franz win this wrestling match. Finally, after another ten minutes of this tussle, the three members of the family tire from exhaustion. Franz is barely panting. Berto falls onto his back and says, "I give up."

Franz has learned that phrase. He barks twice to acknowledge his win in the wrestling match.

Taking his brief case with him, Berto crashes onto the sofa with one boy on each side. He picks up his little girl, Elizabeth, and holds her on his lap. She enjoys this position, feeling it is the best one with her father's arms around her. Berto kisses her twice on the cheeks.

"Someday Elizabeth, are you going to want to wrestle with Franz, the boys, and me?"

"No, Daddy, Franz is big for me."

Everyone laughs. They all agree that Franz is indeed too big for the petite, little girl.

Susana has to bring a kitchen chair over to the sofa so she can get in on the ensuing conversation. The two boys always take one side of their father and Elizabeth sits on Berto's lap. This leaves no room for the mother of the family.

#

As the family is recuperating from the wrestling with Franz, the telephone rings again. Berto, on hands and knees, crawls over to the phone and says, "Hi, Berto here."

He listens intently for several minutes and then says, "Thank you. I'll have to check with the Chief. Goodbye."

After he hangs up the phone, his wife, Susana, asks, "What was that Dear?"

"You're not going to like it, Dear. I'm sorry."

"Okay, I'm not going to like it, but what was it Dear?

"That was General Escobar. The brass in charge of the parachuting team don't want to put their men at any more risk than is necessary."

"Of course they don't. But why the phone call, Dear?"

"The Brass want me to accompany the parachutists on their entire mission."

"Yea, yea," yell the boys. They like more action for their dad. Little Elizabeth also yells in her tiny voice, "Yea, yea."

Susana says, "I knew it, I just knew it. They always need you to lead the way, don't they?"

"Well Dear, I know the area, the flora and the fauna."

"Don't give me those fancy words. What do they mean?"

"They mean the plant life and animal life."

"In other words, the poisonous plants and the dangerous animals, right?"

"Right Dear. Don't you think that it's important to have someone on the mission who knows the flora and fauna?"

"Yes, but why must it always be you?"

"Well, I might not be going anyway. I have to get the clearance from the Chief. Let me go in the bedroom where it's quieter, and I can phone the Chief."

"When you said you had to check with the 'Chief' on the phone, I thought you were referring to me."

"Sure, Honey. you may be the Chief. But in the home, I refer to you as my wife."

"Oh that's nice. Thank you."

"You're welcome, Dear. I'll go phone the Chief now."'

Berto leaves the confusion of the front room and goes into his and Susana's bedroom. Closing the door after him, he dials the Chief's number and waits a few seconds.

"Hi Chief. Berto here. We've got a problem. General Escobar phoned. If we expect to receive the finder's fee from the drug bust in the jungle by shooting down the helicopter with the 225 kilos of cocaine, a member of the department has to be present and involved."

The Chief responds, "Good, that's the way the law is written. I was wondering about that. Everything's on the up and up. You know how the regulations are."

"Yes, Susana will lose four cylinders, but it's part of my job. Since I've never parachuted before, I'll probably go down in tandem with someone else who is an experienced jumper. Then when we get hung up in the canopy, we can break loose from our chute and rappel down. That I've done before many times, so it won't be a problem."

Berto listens to the Chief's response and then says, "Thanks Chief. I felt we couldn't lose so much money in that finder's fee. Goodbye."

Berto returns to the front room to see his family seated on the overstuffed couch and chairs waiting for him to let them know his plans. Berto decides to let it out quickly and get it over with.

"I assume you all want to know what I'm going to be doing this next week. Well, here's the answer to that question. I'm going on a mission with the Army's parachute team and jump into the Amazon Rainforest. Any more than that I can't tell you. You don't need to worry about me since I'll have some experienced soldiers around me, and we'll return home as soon as possible."

Susana starts to cry. "I knew it. They just can't leave you alone."

Bobbie puts his arm around his mother and says, "Now Mom, don't feel so bad, Dad always comes home, you know that so don't worry."

Miguel joins his brother, "Mom, have faith like you're always telling us to do. We'll pray every night for Dad in our family prayer, won't we?"

Sobbing, she says, "Yes we will Dear. We'll pray every meal too."

Little Elizabeth climbs up on her mother's lap and says, "Mommy, don't feel bad. Daddy come home and take care of us."

Susana puts her arms around the sweet little girl whose faith is as strong as a mountain.

She says, "Berto, with the kind of support we have in these three wonderful children, we can't lose. You'll come home safely to us like in other missions. But let me get you the emergency syringe with the single dose of morphine in case you need it."

"Thanks Dear," responds Berto. "And I really appreciate this attitude from you and the kids."

#

The following Monday, Berto is at the headquarters of the Army's parachute division at the Air Base. He is invited to join the jumping team at its meeting in a small conference room with the commander of the mission, Lt. Coronel Francisco Padilla, and his three team members, Lieutenants Linda Delacruz, Ricardo Montoya, and Javier Moreno. After introductions are made all around, Captain Roberto Castillo takes a seat and is prepared to get down to work.

Col. Padilla says, "Captain, we are aware that you have not jumped before. But that is no problem. You can jump in tandem with me. It's smooth as silk. I'm concerned, however, if we both land in the canopy at the top of the trees together, that'll be too much weight, and we might just crash right on through the canopy and get hung up some distance underneath the trees in the dark. Therefore, as we approach the canopy, I'll cut you loose and push you away, so you'll land in the canopy at one location and I'll maneuver my chute quickly and land several feet away from you. Can you handle that?"

"Sure, just don't cut me loose too far above the canopy. If you do, I'll be a flying bomb and crash right on through the canopy and land on the ground with a broken shoulder, back, neck, nose, arms, legs, fingers, and toes. Hey that rhymes."

Everyone laughs.

The Colonel continues, "Good show, Captain, good show. We also understand that you have rappelled many times before. I think the average distance from the canopy to the ground below is about 100 feet. Those trees really grow tall, don't they?"

"They sure do. And we have to be careful at all times. The small poisonous snake, the coral snake, the large anaconda and the large boa constrictor, as well as other poisonous snakes are a constant problem. I assume we'll have Uzis."

Colonel Padilla says, "Yes, Berto, we'll have Uzis and the newest version of the stinger that can heat seek from almost any angle. We won't have much of a chance to get a copter as it takes off, so we'll have to be alert. Our plan as you can see before you, is to station ourselves in five locations around the Cartel Camp. Then when a copter takes off, we'll have to react quickly with our stingers. They should bring the copter down quickly."

The Colonel continues speaking to the group, "Now as for tomorrow. You can get up at any time you want as long as you have eaten your biggest meal and picked up your gear by 1800 hours. We will take off in one copter at 2000 hours. The copter is outfitted with the maximum armament if needed. But we'll be over the drop zone in the dark, around 2120 hours, and hope to jump quickly, together, and quietly from about 1,500 feet. Our chutes will deploy as soon as we're safely away from the copter. Then we'll be in the canopy before we know it.

"When we land, we'll plan on remaining in that position for about five minutes trying to get the lay of the location where we've landed. No talking please. There could be all kinds of guards under the trees. I'll use the owl horn to signal to you. When you hear the first hoot, start repelling down one at a time alphabetically by last name, got it? Wait about three minutes between drops. Those who go first must be prepared to protect the others who come later. As soon as all five of us are on the ground, we'll gather up in some bushes getting the lay of the land again. That's 'Point A.'

"Then we'll disburse to five different locations waiting for the cartel copter to take off. As soon as we've taken out the copter, we'll return to 'Point A.' So mark your bearings when you leave 'Point A' in the beginning. After we return to 'Point A,' we'll have about a 100-meter dash to an open field where I will radio our copter to meet us. The copter will be hovering about one-half mile away and be ready to come in and pick us up at my signal. If the copter is running out of gas waiting for our signal, another copter of the same type will take its place. They can keep up this rotation for as long as necessary. A large gas tanker truck is parked at the edge of the Rainforest but far away from the Dos Brazos home. We don't want to have him implicated in any way.

"Now, if something happens to me, Captain Castillo, who is next in rank, will take over. He'll have a radio and the frequency to contact the copter. If someone doesn't report to the gathering point, don't go back looking for that person. A few seconds going back for a dead body or even a wounded person could cost the lives of all the others.

"Now we have a woman with us, as you've certainly noticed, Lt. Linda Delacruz. Her first name is appropriate. We've been trained to make no special considerations for females in our crews. Linda knows this and volunteered for this mission. Of course we do what we can to protect each other, but we don't do anything foolish to go back for someone already shot to pieces.

"Now I know this may be hard for all of you, especially those whose mothers have taught you to respect women, girls, sisters, etc. That's a nice trait around the dinner table, but out here, it's not acceptable. Any man caught doing some macho act to save a woman will be recommended upon our return for transfer to a regular army division. The parachute division cannot afford that luxury. Berto, this may be all new to you. Do you understand the rule as I have explained it to you?"

Berto answers, "I have many women in my K-9 Corps who are expected to be ready for battle at any moment just like the men. And they are expected to be physically fit to follow their German Shepherd dogs up the side of a mountain. They're great and make a valuable contribution to our unit. I'm sure yours do the same."

"That's good Berto. We're all on the same wavelength then. I'm going to dismiss you now for some food and sleep. Tomorrow evening, we leave for the jungle. Too bad there's no camera person going with us. This action would make a great movie. See you tomorrow."

Javier says, "Colonel if I might. As you know I was an attorney before I joined the paratroopers. Captain Castillo's answer to your question is called in the legal profession, 'non-responsive.' In other words, he spoke when you asked him to, but his answer was in no way related to the question."

The Colonel says, "I'm not going to get hung up in legalese. See you later."

The group breaks up.

Linda walks over to Berto and asks, "Hey stranger, how'd you like to have a partner for dinner?"

"I sure would. I don't even know where the officers' mess is."

"Just follow me and we'll dine together if you don't mind."

"Mind? It's a pleasure to be able to dine with the prettiest girl on the base."

"Well thank you Berto. I've heard about you, but I wasn't sure till now."

"Heard about me? What do you mean?"

"I mean that any girl with you will automatically become the prettiest girl on the base and the most important girl in your life, after your wife and daughter, of course."

"Oh you know about my wife and daughter, do you?"

"Yes, Captain. I understand that your wife is really the prettiest girl on the base and your little daughter is fast becoming her competition."

Berto laughs. "I'd like to know where you get your information."

"Sorry Captain, my source of intelligence is hush hush, you know, very confidential."

"Oh you're too much. Hush hush, very confidential. What's next?"

"Next is dinner, right there in that officers' mess as the sign says."

"Okay, if you're not going to talk, at least we can eat."

#

After a good night's sleep and much rest during the day, Berto and the others are preparing their gear in the parachute shack. Berto checks over his stinger missile launcher. It has an I.D. tag attached to it with some instructions which Berto reads, "This is a 'fire and forget' missile. It is heat seeking and can take out a plane up to 11,500 feet in altitude. Don't think that you have to be able to see the aircraft in order to shoot it down. It you have an indication of its general location, shoot. The missile is fast and can out-climb any plane."

Berto thinks, *Wow, these newer versions are sure hot. I want to get at least one piece of that cartel's copter.*

Berto says to Linda, "How about a good meal before we launch?"

"Great. I'm hungry."

Then she yells out, "Hey you guys, who wants to join us for our final meal before launch?"

The others say they are not ready yet and will come along later to the officers' mess.

This doesn't upset Berto.

#

At exactly 8:00 p.m. the Army's newest model helicopter, loaded with the parachute team, takes off and quietly heads for some altitude. The pilot quickly finds the road with car lights that leads to the home of Dos Brazos which is the entrance to the Rainforest. He figures the trip will take about one hour to the Rainforest where Dos Brazos lives and then another twenty minutes or so to the camp of the Cartel de la Selva Tropical. GPS technology is being used to insure an exact location for the drop of the parachutists. They should hit the target right on the button.

All the lights are turned off on the copter, both inside and outside. While these are not normal rules for flying in the dark, the security of this mission takes precedence. There is no talking among the five parachutists during the flight. Each person is left to his or her own thoughts. They all know that this could be their last flight and their last day on earth.

As they reach the edge of the Rainforest, Berto looks out the window and sees the home of Dos Brazos. Everyone should be in bed now, but he is able to see the yard lights that surround the barn and the corrals. Suddenly after that, all is dark as the copter moves over the rainforest.

Everyone checks his watch and sees that it took the one hour as predicted to get to the edge of the jungle. The thick darkness below adds to the danger inherent in a parachute drop into the Rainforest. Every one of the five shows this concern as the copter moves along at a quick pace. They all realize that this particular helicopter is one of the quietest copters in the service. This should help them at the beginning of their mission.

After another wait in silence, the red light comes on alerting everyone to stand and prepare for the jump. Colonel Padilla comes back and hooks Berto behind him with a harness.

He tells Berto, "Don't worry about this chute. It's extra-large, made to hold two people. Remember, I'll cut you free at the last moment. By the way, we jump first."

"Okay, I'm ready," responds Berto.

The five parachutists line up at the opening preparing for the jump. They hook their lines to the wire overhead so that their chutes will be deployed automatically.

Berto looks around in the dark. He sees that Linda is right behind him. He reaches his hand back and squeezes her arm as a show of support. She returns the kindness and squeezes his shoulder.

Everyone is looking at the red light. There it goes. It is now green.

Colonel Padilla puts his arms back around Berto and steps out of the copter with Berto attached to him by the harness. Down they go into the black wilderness. Berto is especially worried because soon he will be cut loose and free fall into the canopy of the Rainforest.

The 1,500 feet go by quickly, and Col. Padilla cuts Berto loose with a push to the rear. In an instant Berto falls into the canopy which holds him tight due to its thickness.

Well, that wasn't as bad as I was expecting. Now if the rest of the mission will go just as well.

Berto holds his position and with the little starlight that exists he is able to see the others land in the canopy. After the last soldier hits the canopy, all is quiet and remains that way.

Berto remembers that they will rappel down in alphabetical order. *Now what were their last names? No wait, I don't need to worry. With my last name starting with a 'C,' I rappel down first and wait for the others who will come every three minutes, or was that five minutes?*

Assuming they have been perched in the canopy for five minutes, Berto decides it is time for him to rappel down.

He hears the sound of an owl, *Oh that's right. The hoot of the owl is the signal for the first one to rappel down.*

He attaches his nylon rope to a strong branch, works his way through the other branches and the vines of the canopy, and starts his drop. It goes well, and soon he is on the ground. He detaches his rappelling equipment, and moves to the nearest group of bushes to wait.

Soon, Lt. Linda Delacruz lands on the ground near where Berto is stationed. After she cuts herself loose, Berto whispers, "Linda."

She quickly joins him and takes hold of his hand as the two dinner partners are now partners in warfare. Every three minutes another parachutist rappels down to the jungle floor and joins the others.

Lt. Colonel Francisco Padilla is the last one to join the group. In charge of this operation, he takes a minute or two to be sure his small contingent is in good shape physically and mentally.

Once he makes the decision that all is well, he says, "Okay, troops, time to move out. We'll call this position twelve o'clock. The camp is dead ahead of us, about 300 feet. Can you see those lamps through the trees?"

Everyone answers in the affirmative.

"Okay, Berto, you stay at twelve o'clock after you get as close to the camp as you can. Keep your stinger at the ready.

"Linda, you take three o'clock; Javier, you take five o'clock; Ricardo, you take eight o'clock' and I'll take ten o'clock. Now if our intelligence is correct from the mole in the Cartel, the helicopter should take off at dawn. Now dawn is a loose word, so we need to be alert starting as soon as 0500, but, who knows when it'll start to get light in this maze of trees and bushes and that great canopy. Whatever, we'll be ready. As soon as we start shooting stinger missiles, we'll have a small army out to get us. Keep your Uzi standing by for defensive purposes.

"If you have to leave your stinger here, perish the thought, destroy it so it can never be used again. But preferably bring it back with you even if it doesn't work any longer. This will be the gathering point right here at the bushes. When we return here, we'll wait a maximum of three minutes for the others. After that, we'll head for the pickup station where our own copter should be waiting for us. Remember, it has lots of fire power. If we can get to it, I think we'll get the protection we need.

"Another important thing. I've placed you at various locations using the hand of a clock. This was done for purposes of shooting at a rising helicopter from all angles. But, it has another aspect as well, which is related to friendly fire. As soon as you shoot your stinger, grab your Uzi and head for the gathering point. Be careful in any use you make of the Uzi until you get to about 10:00 o'clock to 2:00 o'clock. When the group is within those parameters, feel free to shoot your Uzi for protection. But the important thing is to return to the gathering point.

"I hate to even mention this last item. You are now in the middle of the great Amazon Rainforest. It is loaded with wild beasts and poisonous snakes. When you finally station yourself to wait it out till morning, your body will give off some heat. There are snakes that can sense that heat. If you shoot at a snake, you'll give away the presence of the entire mission. If a snake comes your way and you feel you have to try to kill it, please use your knife or a rock. This will not be easy in the dark. We have no antidotes with us. A bite from some of these snakes would spell a certain death in a few minutes. I want to thank you now for volunteering for this mission. If it rains during the night, that should be helpful in destroying our scent cones, our scent trails, our odor and any other smells we put out. That would be a blessing. Pray for rain. Those little creeks that always follow a rain, are a blessing. Stand out in the rain. Get as wet as you can. Cool down your body, kill any odor you may be giving off. That could help protect you from those blasted snakes. Enough of that.

"Okay, all hands in the middle."

The five soldiers make a circle and place their hands in the middle on top of the others' hands. The leader quietly says, "God bless this mission. Protect us from snakes and wild animals, and bring us all home safely."

They break their grip, and everyone moves out quietly toward his assigned station. Berto moves out slowly but maintains his 12:00 o'clock position. As soon as he gets close to the Cartel camp, he stops and kneels down. He can't see the others due to the dense foliage, but he knows about where they are. He then leans back against a tree but keeps a lookout for any snakes.

The night proceeds slowly. The members of the mission listen to the sounds of the jungle at night. The birds dominate while beasts of the jungle add their roars to the symphony of sounds.

Berto looks at his watch and presses its stem. The face lights up to reveal the time. It is three forty a.m. Even though the night is dark, Berto notices that the jungle becomes even darker. He looks up into the sky through a hole in the canopy and sees a bank of clouds blot out the light from the stars. Soon Berto can feel tiny drops of water on his hands. Within a very few minutes, the jungle is alive with large drops of water from a cloudburst of torrential rain. Remembering the instructions, Berto takes a small tarp from his pocket and covers his Uzi and his stinger. Then he steps out from underneath the tree and lets the downpour soak him and his clothing completely. Cooler than he has been in a long time, he returns to stand next to the giant tree where he was before. He notices small creeks beginning to form from the heavy rainfall. He returns to the open spot and lets himself be soaked again. Fortunately, the rain keeps up.

Berto thinks, *Dear God, thank you for the lifesaving rain. May it protect us from snakes and other wild animals.*

As he says these words to himself, he sees the eyes of what he believes are two jaguars moving through the trees. They are trying to catch the scent of their dinner, but due to the rain, they sense nothing but the odor of wet leaves from the many wet bushes and soaked trees.

Berto keeps his Uzi at the ready but doesn't move an inch. He watches the powerful jungle inhabitants as they continue to move away from him. *Dear God, thank you for such immediate protection. Those two jungle cats would have ripped me to pieces, that's for sure.*

Eventually the rain stops but not before Berto has the opportunity to step out from his tree and get soaked again.

This is the best shower I've ever had; he thinks to himself.

Looking again at his watch, he realizes that the rain has lasted forty-five minutes. As the clouds move away in the skies, the light from the stars returns.

Berto and the others continue to maintain their stations as the darkness of the night begins to disappear. Berto looks over to where Linda is stationed and can see her through the darkness. When he realizes that she is looking at him, he waves to her. She waves back.

They continue to wait. It is such a beautiful morning in the jungle. Berto feels sad that soon the sound of gunshots will destroy the silence. He readies his stinger.

#

And then suddenly, in the Cartel camp a guard yells out, "Wake up everyone. We've been surrounded."

El Catalán yells to his partner, El Caracol, "Have Mateo warm up the copter. I need to get out of here with that load of cocaine and fast."

El Caracol dresses quickly and runs off to find the mechanic for the copter.

When he does, he says, "Mateo, El Catalán needs to leave immediately with the Army around us. Warm up the copter while he is getting ready. After a twenty second warm-up, he'll be there. Thanks."

"Okay, El Caracol. I'll get on it right now."

Mateo runs to the middle of the clearing where the copter is secured with camouflage. He removes the tall stakes that were holding the camouflage above the copter. After he drags the camouflage away from the copter, he starts the powerful engine.

Berto has been observing this activity in the center of the Cartel camp. He knows exactly what their plans are, get that copter out of here fast. It is hard to do, but Berto and the others wait.

The Cartel men have loaded their weapons and taken up a position of defense in their tents and shacks. Once they locate the exact positions of the Army personnel, they start firing. A few bursts from the soldiers' Uzis and the Cartel men take better shelter.

During this skirmish, El Catalán has finished dressing and attaching his pistol and other gear to his belt. He is now ready to run to the copter.

However, at the same time, the mechanic, Mateo, is still removing the various ropes that secure the copter to the ground.

Berto can feel the heat from the engine of the copter as it warms up. *These missiles are heat seeking. I can't wait any longer. There is no better time than the present to take out that copter. I don't dare even wait until that one guy is out of there. How will the Colonel feel about such an action before the copter even takes off? I don't know and I don't care. He can't bust me to private. I'm not in the Army.*

Aiming his stinger at the rear of the engine of the copter, Berto pulls the trigger that sends a deadly missile into the engine.

BOOM goes the missile as it explodes inside the engine. The soldiers in the group take this as a signal to fire their stingers also. Four more stinger missiles are sent flying toward the copter. Since the copter is now on fire, the missiles have no trouble seeking out the heat generated by the burning copter.

BOOOOM echo the four missiles that hit the target basically at the same time. Mateo perishes in the white heat of the explosions.

Now the mission has been completed, and it is essential that all five parachutists find their way back to the gathering point by the bushes where they first rappelled down.

A rifle cracks as it sends its bullet from a Cartel member in a tent into the right arm of Linda. She falls to the ground and groans. Berto witnesses this and crawls to her aid.

"Berto, you know the rules. Leave me here."

"Rules, mules, I'm not leaving you here. Let me see your right arm."

He checks her arm that is bleeding and says, "The bullet went right through your forearm. I don't think any bone was hit, what luck, but it is bleeding rather profusely. Let me bandage it."

"No Berto, go."

"Shut up, I'm busy." Berto cuts the sleeve of his shirt and wraps it around the bleeding area of Linda's arm. Then he cuts his other sleeve and makes a sling which he quickly puts around her neck and arm.

"Come on kiddo, let me help you as we crawl out of here back to the gathering point."

Positioning himself on her right, Berto puts his arm around Linda and acts as her second arm. Together they crawl back to where Berto was stationed.

Then he says, "I think we can stand up now and hurry back to the gathering point, although I prefer the position where I have my arm around you."

"Oh Berto, you never change do you?"

They start moving fast and soon arrive at the gathering point where they hide in the bushes with other soldiers.

Berto says, "Where's the Colonel?"

Javier responds, "I saw him take a blast from an Uzi. I think he's a goner."

"Where was that?"

"Right at his original station, 10:00 o'clock, right?"

Berto realizes that he is now in command, "Okay, I'll call in the copter to the pick-up station, about one-half mile from here. In the meantime, I'll go back and see if I can help the Colonel."

Javier says, "But Berto, remember our rule."

"Like I told Linda, rules, mules, they can't bust me to private in the Army, I'm not in the Army. Go."

The group takes off running as Berto works his way through the trees to where he figures the 10:00 o'clock position should be. Hearing a noise behind him, Berto quickly takes a defensive position behind a huge tree. Soon Linda comes up to him crawling as best she can.

"Why you little disobedient squirt, you. What are you doing here?"

"I thought you might need some help."

"Okay, we can discuss this later. Let's find the Colonel, and we've only a few minutes to do it, quietly."

As soon as they stop talking, they hear the groans of a wounded soldier on the ground.

They both hurry to the spot and see their Colonel lying on the ground moaning in great pain.

Berto does a quick look over. "I think he got sprayed in the legs with an Uzi. It looks like he has been hit several times. He's in real pain. Let me give him a shot of morphine."

Linda says, "A shot of morphine. Where'd that come from?"

"Oh I always take some on my missions." Berto takes the syringe from his shirt pocket, removes the needle guard, and pushes the needle through the Colonel's pants into his thigh. He then pushes the piston to empty the syringe of the pain killing fluid.

The Colonel immediately relaxes and falls asleep.

"Linda, cut one sleeve from his shirt and take care of the wounds in his right leg. I'll do the same for his left leg, but quickly."

They wrap the Colonel's legs tightly in an attempt to slow down the bleeding.

A voice rings out from one of the tents of the Cartel, "Look, it's that Police Captain Berto Castillo trying to help a wounded soldier. We should have known he would be involved in this raid."

Hearing this, Berto realizes he must hurry or be killed, "Okay Sweetheart, let's lift him and walk him out of here. You take his right side so you can use your good left arm. I'll take the other side. I think we'd better drag him for a while. Standing up around here might not be too safe."

"Okay Sweetheart," she says.

They look at each other and smile. Then off they go dragging their patient. Once they get back to the gathering point, it seems safe enough to stand and move out to the pick-up station much more quickly. They are running for their lives.

Soon they can hear the whirling blades of a helicopter. Berto says silently, *Please wait for us.*

A few feet down the pathway, they see Javier.

He yells, "Come on."

He then rushes to replace Linda who is exhausted by now. Her right arm is hurting even more.

There was never a more welcome sight to Berto than the helicopter in the clearing waiting for them. They get on board with the help of two EMTs in the copter. Berto explains quickly what he knows about Colonel Padilla's condition. He tells them that he gave him a shot of morphine.

They are quite impressed that the Police Captain would have such an item on him in these conditions. As soon as the Colonel and Linda are strapped into stretchers, the copter takes off and heads for the Army base.

Linda calls Berto to her side, "Berto, the EMT said he was going to give me a shot of morphine to help with the pain while they're patching up my arm. Before they do that, I wanted to thank you for coming back to get me."

"Hey, you don't think I'd leave such a beautiful girl alone in the jungle do you?"

He then gives her a tender kiss at the same time as the EMT gives her an injection of morphine. When Berto releases her, she is asleep. Berto then moves out of the way of the EMTs.

He takes a seat and collapses from the strenuous activity of the morning.

The flight back is productive with the EMTs working all the time doing what they know best. It takes little time to patch up Linda, but the Colonel is another story. He has four bullet wounds in his legs. Both legs are broken where the bullets ripped through his flesh. His soldiers are saddened to see their leader in such bad condition, but they know that soon he will be in the hospital.

And that is exactly where the pilot lands the copter when they arrive in La Vista. Medical teams rush out to the landing pad and take the two patients on gurneys quickly into operating rooms. Both have x-rays taken of Linda's right arm and the Colonel's legs completely.

The copter leaves the hospital landing pad and heads to the airport and the copter base there. As it is landing, Berto sees his family waiting for him, along with Franz. He waves to them. They all see him and wave back.

Little Elizabeth says, "See Mommy, Daddy come back and take care of us."

Susana starts to cry at these words of faith of a little child. But she is not the only one crying. The entire family is fighting tears except Franz whose tail is wagging a mile a minute.

When the copter's blades stop whirling, Berto jumps down from the copter and runs to his family. After hugs and kisses, Berto sees what looks like the family of Colonel Padilla.

"Pardon me Susana. I need to talk to the wife of Colonel Padilla. He's in the hospital."

Berto walks over to the other family waiting and says, "Mrs. Padilla?"

"Yes, Captain, where is my husband?"

"He was shot in the legs and we left him at the hospital. Would you like me to drive you and your two children there?"

"No thanks Captain. You have your own family to care for. How bad is he?"

"I really can't tell. Fortunately, I had a syringe of morphine with me and gave him a shot as soon as I found him. He went immediately to sleep."

"Oh thank goodness. That was nice of you to help him like that. I'll leave now for the hospital."

"Okay, I'll be over there myself later today. Lt. Linda Delacruz was also shot, much less severe, in the right arm. She's also at the hospital."

"I thought the rule was to leave wounded personnel in the field."

"That's right. That's the Army's rule. I'm in the La Vista Police Department so I figured the rule didn't apply to me."

"God bless you Captain. Thanks to you, I still have my husband." She leans forward and kisses Berto on the mouth and hugs him.

"Come on kids, to the hospital to see Daddy."

As they walk away, Susana comes up to Berto and says, "More hugs and kisses from a strange woman. Why does this always happen?"

"I guess she was appreciative because I saved her husband's life."

"That'll do it every time. Let's go home."

But before they can leave the tarmac, another woman approaches Berto.

"Captain, can you tell me anything about my daughter, Linda Delacruz? I'm her mother."

"Yes I can. We were together on this mission. She was shot in the right arm, not seriously. I wrapped her arm and gave her a sling. She was dropped off at the hospital before we landed here. The EMTs wanted to have some x-rays taken and to have the surgeons check their work before she is released. They also gave her a shot of morphine on the copter to help her with the pain."

"How did she make it back to the copter? I thought the unit had a rule that no one was to go back for a wounded comrade."

"That's true. That's the rule. But you see, I'm not in the Army. I'm a La Vista Police Captain and the Army's rules don't apply to me."

"Are you saying you went back for Linda?"

"Yes, Ma'am. As I told her she is too pretty to leave on the jungle floor."

"Yes, she is, isn't she? Thank you Captain for this extra effort on behalf of my daughter. I couldn't stand losing her." The woman leans forward and kisses Berto on the cheek.

"I'll head for the hospital now."

"Good idea. I'll be there later myself to see how Linda is doing."

Susana comes over to Berto again and says, "I have no comment to make. It'll be of no value. Now, let's go home, okay?"

"Okay Dear. You drive please so I can be with the kids."

#

After a great, warm shower and shave, Berto dresses in a fresh uniform and has lunch with his family. Afterwards, he says, "You'll have to excuse me now. I want to go to the hospital to see the two members of our team who were shot."

"Okay Dear. I'm sure they'll appreciate that. Let me give you a kiss before the others do."

"Oh Susana, you're silly."

He kisses her and returns to his bedroom to put on his pistol belt. Whenever in uniform, he must wear his pistol.

Kissing all the children goodbye, Berto gives Franz a good rubdown and then goes to his K-9 police car. Franz looks out the window of the front room. He can't understand why he isn't going with Berto in the K-9 car.

Soon Berto arrives at the hospital and parks his car. Chief Medina and Blanca drive up at the same time. The Chief rushes out of his car and hurries over to Berto's car. He gives Berto a big hug. "We heard there were two casualties and thought you might be one of them."

"No Chief, the casualties are Colonel Padilla, the team leader with four shots in the legs, and Lt. Linda Delacruz, with a glazing shot to the right arm."

Blanca arrives a bit after the Chief and puts her arms around Berto crying all the while.

"I thought you were shot, Berto. Oh thank the Lord."

"Yes, Blanca, thank the Lord. It was pretty dicey there for a while."

The Chief asks, "Did you accomplish your mission?"

"Yes Chief. Our presence was discovered by a guard who yelled out. They started warming up the copter with the cocaine. I felt the heat from the engines. Remembering that

I had a stinger which, as you know, is a heat seeking missile, I decided to not wait any longer. I blasted the copter with my stinger, and then the other four did the same. What a blast! They probably heard it at Dos Brazos' house. Then we got outta there as fast as we could."

"Well we're glad you did, but sorry that the entire group didn't make it without wounds."

Berto adds, "We'd better go into the hospital. I want to see how the others are doing."

In they go where the receptionist tells them the room numbers of the two patients.

Berto says, "I want to see how Colonel Padilla is doing. He was really shot up."

Peeking his head around the doorway to Colonel Padilla's room, Berto sees the Colonel's wife whom he met earlier at the airport. She motions him to come in with his group.

Berto walks in with Chief Medina and Blanca. He introduces the Police Chief and the chief's secretary to Mrs. Padilla and Colonel Padilla who has just finished a light lunch.

"Berto, how nice of you to come. Have a seat. I need to give you some disciplinary talk."

Everyone laughs.

"I understand it was you who brought me off the battlefield and gave me a shot of morphine to boot. Don't you know that's against the rules. We leave the wounded on the field of battle."

"Well Colonel, I never really did understand those rules. You remember that Javier said my answer was non-responsive. I'm very sorry. I didn't mean to be disobedient."

Blanca says, "Watch Chief. He'll do it again. He always squirms out of the responsibility for his words and actions that are against the rules."

Mrs. Padilla adds, "As for me, I'm glad he was non-responsive in his answer. He saved the life of my husband, and that's all that counts."

Berto says, "There you see Blanca. What's important, the rule or the life? Colonel Padilla, are you going to bust me to a private?"

"I would if I could, but I have no authority over you."

"You don't? Oh I didn't know that. So I stay a Captain, is that right?"

"That's right Berto."

Blanca adds, "You see, he says, 'I didn't know you had no authority over me.' Didn't know. Who wants to bet he didn't know? He always knows."

Everyone laughs.

Berto says, "Let's change the subject. Colonel, what do the medics say about your condition?"

"Well, I guess my running days are over. A broken bone in each leg and air conditioning in each leg to boot."

"What are they going to do for the broken bones?"

"They're setting the legs this afternoon and we'll see if they mend themselves. If they don't, it's pins and braces internally. Ugh. How is Linda doing?"

"I don't know yet Colonel. I'm going down there now and will come back with the news in just a moment. If you others would stay here with the Colonel, I'll be right back."

#

Berto leaves the Colonel's room, walks down the hall, and stops at Linda's room number.

He knocks firmly and hears, "Come in please, Berto."

Berto enters and says, "How did you know 'twas I?"

"Oh such fancy English. I knew 'twas you because I knew you would visit me as soon as you could, and no one else could have such a macho knock on a door."

Berto laughs and pulls up a chair beside Linda. There are no other visitors at this time.

"Where's your mom?"

"She phoned and said she didn't want to visit until you finished your visit."

"Well isn't that nice of her? What did she think might be going on here?"

"I guess she figured you'd want to give me a kiss and a hug."

"Okay, if that's what your mom wants, that's what you're going to get."

"Wait a minute Captain Berto, if you think you can kiss me whenever...."

Berto puts his arms around Linda and gives her a tender kiss that lasts more than a few seconds. When they part, they both have tears in their eyes.

She says, "Berto, why the tears?"

"Linda, why the tears?

They both respond at the same time saying, "I thought I had lost you."

Berto holds her hand and they enjoy an extended conversation.

Finally, Berto says, "I'd better get going. I told Colonel Padilla that I'd report right back as to your condition. You feel pretty good to me. In fact, you feel wonderful to me. You really are soft; did you know that?"

"Don't let that get around. A female paratrooper can't be soft you know."

"You'll always be soft, and there's nothing you can do about it."

Linda smiles which about knocks Berto off his chair. He has seen many beautiful women smile in his career, but none has a smile like Linda except his little Elizabeth.

"Before you leave Berto, with all kidding aside, thanks for that wonderful kiss and hug, and thanks for coming back to save my life. I think I am in love with you. Is that possible?"

"I know I love you Linda. I knew it the first moment I saw you. And thank you for that wonderful kiss. I'll be back if you promise every time I visit, I'll get a kiss like that one."

"I promise."

Berto kisses her hand and says, "Goodbye."

But before he leaves, he says, "Oh I forgot. I'm supposed to report on your condition after being shot."

"Tell them that I'm doing fine. The bullet didn't hit the bone. The worry now is infection, so I should be here at least three more days for rest and recuperation."

"Thanks for the report. I'll see you later for you know what."

Linda laughs and says, "Goodbye Bertito."

He then runs out the door and down the hall to the Colonel's room. Walking in slowly, as if he had all the time in the world, he hears the Colonel ask, "How is Linda?"

"She's great Colonel."

Everyone laughs.

"No, I meant, how is she doing after being shot?"

"She's great. The bullet didn't hit any bone. The concern now is infection, so they want to keep her here for at least three more days for rest and recuperation."

"Thanks. That sounds like a pretty good report, much better than mine. But I'm glad Linda isn't wounded seriously. I guess in a day or so, I can have someone put me in a wheelchair. Then they can take me to Linda's room for a visit."

"I would imagine so," adds Berto.

Chapter 7

The next week Berto reports to work at the Police K-9 School. He sees on his desk a strange envelope. Checking it, he is surprised to see airline tickets from La Vista to Independence Island to leave in two days with the return date to be determined later.

"Susana, what's this with these airline tickets?"

"Well, you agreed to serve as the Chief of Security for the Continental Games to be held next year in the new country of Independence Island, and you agreed to go to Independence Island for orientation and planning so that security would be at its best for the games. Hence, the airline tickets."

"It's just that I had forgotten all about it with all the other things going on. Wednesday, huh? I assume they have made room and board arrangements for me."

"Yes, check that telegram on your desk for info on that item."

"A five-star hotel. You can't get better than that. I also see you printed some pages from the Internet on the hotel. Look at that swimming pool. What an interesting shape."

"Oh yes, Berto, there are lots of interesting shapes around a swimming pool."

"Now Susana, stop being jealous of people you don't even know. To continue, I'll bet the temperature is rather warm there. I'll have to do a lot of planning in the swimming pool."

"No you won't. The rooms are air conditioned. Notice that you'll be met by the Chief of Police when you arrive at the airport. He'll be your main contact and liaison. That's Chief Arturo Méndez. He's been Chief there since the Country was organized. They're really proud of their new country. There's a good article on the Internet for an explanation of how the country was organized and how it broke off from other islands in the Caribbean. They've wanted their independence for a long time, so when they finally got it, they called their country Independence Island. That makes sense, doesn't it?"

"It sure does."

#

In the camp of the Cartel de la Selva Tropical, the people have just finished cleaning the camp site up after the raid by the parachutists. Following this, they hold a very important meeting. Junior has asked El Catalán to direct the meeting.

El Catalán says, "Until we get rid of this Police Captain Berto Castillo, we'll never be able to do anything."

El Caracol responds, "Well, I've picked up some interesting news from one of my sources in the Caribbean. You probably all know that there's a new country there, among the islands. It's called Independence Island. They're starting to plan for their Independence Day, which is next year. And guess who they have asked to be in charge of security during the three-day festivities?"

Everyone responds, "Captain Berto Castillo."

"Right on the nose. El Catalán, if we want to nail that bum, this week is the time and there's the place. He will not be surrounded by his usual group of buddies, coppers, and others. He's going there this Wednesday for some planning sessions with the leaders of the country. I'll bet we can nail him on Thursday or Friday. Or we could even plant a bomb in the plane and bring it down when it gets to a specific altitude."

"This bomb stuff," replies El Catalán, "takes too many innocent people out and we get some very bad publicity. If we just take out one police official, there's not such a big fuss."

El Caracol adds, "You're right. What do you want us to do?"

"Let's meet right after this meeting and do some planning. We don't have much time. Someone has to first get out of the Rainforest to La Vista, then fly to Independence Island."

El Caracol says amid laughter from the others, "Okay, as long as I'm one to go on this mission. That Berto killed my cousin, Mateo, when he shot that missile into the helicopter. Mateo was warming up the copter for the takeoff that never took place. Plus Berto destroyed an expensive copter and 225 kilos of cocaine. He really took a great deal of money from us when he did that. And I happen to be one that thinks he was behind the entire operation. He's not in the Army. He's a copper. All the others were in Army uniforms. Yes, we need to eliminate that Berto copper as soon as possible."

El Catalán says, "Relax El Caracol. You'll not only go on the mission, but you will also be the leader. We need a leader who is passionate about the goal of the mission."

"Hey guys, if we keep listening to El Catalán, our speech will really improve, and we'll be able to understand him when he speaks all those fancy words."

Everyone laughs, including El Catalán.

When the meeting breaks up, El Catalán remains along with several leaders including El Caracol.

El Catalán says, "El Caracol, do you have a plan?"

"Sí, Mano." (El Caracol refers to his associate as "Mano" short for the Spanish word hermano or brother.)

"Share it with us."

"Okay. My plan is to have one person go alone to Independence Island without any weapons of any type."

"And who do you recommend as this person?"

"I recommend El Caracol."

Everyone laughs.

"What a surprise," laughs El Catalán. "I can't imagine why you would recommend yourself."

"You said it Mano. 'We need a leader who is passionate about the goal of the mission.'"

Everyone laughs again.

El Catalán says, "I'm not so sure I want you to learn those fancy words."

"My plan is this: There's always lots of sport fishing off those islands. There would be many sports items and sporting goods stores on the Island. I would buy a good rifle with a scope, say a .270 which is a very dangerous rifle. I'd scout the place and find out the best spot to nail that copper. Then I'd plan my route of escape. Perhaps hit the copper just before a plane takes off for the continent. It makes no difference where I land. From there I would go to La Vista, then the bus, and then the burro to our camp. I don't believe the security will be as tight for him now as it will be during the games."

El Catalán asks his other leaders, "How many can support the plan as presented by El Caracol?"

All the hands go up.

"Good decision. El Caracol, we'll hold your coat while you go and fight."

Everyone laughs.

"I'll have to leave early tomorrow morning and try to make the trip in two days. Which is that strongest burro again?"

Several answer, "Carlos, he's the biggest and the strongest."

"Okay, is he well rested or has he been on a mission lately?"

One cowboy responds, "He's well fed and well rested. As long as he gets his food, water, and rest, he'll go and go. He's a great burro. You could just leave him at Dos Brazos place and pick him up on the return trip. He'd be rested again. Just make sure Dos Brazos understands that he's not to be used for any other purpose. Sometimes, because he is so strong, they give him extra assignments while the other burros are resting. If you emphasize this with Dos Brazos, he'll protect the burro from any other work."

"Great, thanks for that information. If we can get several good rains during the trek, we can both keep cool and make better time. When it rains, we won't seek shelter, we'll go into high gear."

"That's fine," responds the cowboy, "but remember, those jaguars like to hunt in the rain because the other animals' vision is cut way down and their sense of smell is reduced as well."

"Thanks, that's more good information. I'll take two pistols and one Uzi and leave them at Dos Brazos in the barn where Dos Brazos points out they'll be safe. I think I'll also take a pair of goggles so I can move right through the bush and rain easier."

"Sure, but remember, Carlos doesn't have any goggles, but he has two eyes which he needs for good vision. And he also represents a large amount of meat for the jaguars and the cougars, as well as some other animals."

"Hey, I'll protect him with my life. If he gets killed, I won't have a chance to survive. So if you have any other suggestions about Carlos, let me know. I want to protect him as well as I can.

"I'll meet with the other wranglers and we'll write up a list of things to know about Carlos. Each cowboy probably has a few suggestions to help him. He's not afraid of anything. He'll charge a jaguar just as fast as a jag will charge him. That's a problem. The jag would just put one bite on Carlos' neck and with more force than you can even imagine, poor Carlos would collapse. Carlos thinks he can turn around at a charging jag and give him one kick like the world has never seen before. He thinks he could kick the jag to the moon. I don't think so, I'm sorry."

Another cowboy joins in the conversation. "You need to know; however, I've seen Carlos kick a jag that was charging him. That jag was thrown about forty feet. When he regained his breath, I've never seen a jag run as fast as that one did in the opposite direction while Carlos was taking a few gulps of water from a nearby creek. He's a great companion in the jungle. And one more thing. He doesn't mind his rider shooting a pistol while on the run. The noise doesn't bother him in the least. And be sure and treat him with kindness. He reacts in kind if someone mistreats him."

"Don't worry about that. I don't mess with guys who are bigger and stronger than I am."

Everyone laughs as the group breaks up.

Junior and El Catalán remain behind with El Caracol.

El Catalán takes a few extra minutes to talk with his friend, "El Caracol, you be careful on this mission. If you can't get that copper on this mission, we'll have another opportunity I'm sure. He can't avoid us forever. What time do you expect to leave in the morning?"

"About 5:30, just as dawn is breaking. I need every minute of daylight. I'll write you a letter as soon as I arrive on the Island of Independence. If anything of importance happens, I'll write another letter. When I'm ready to come home, there's no use in writing. I can get home faster than the letter."

"Good, old friend. Be careful in the jungle. You might send us a short note when you get to the home of Dos

Brazos, so we'll know you made it through the jungle safely."

"Okay, and if I'm in a hurry to grab a bus, I'll ask one of the girls of Dos Brazos to write. Either way you'll get a letter when I arrive there."

"Good idea. We'll look forward to your notes and letters. Now get a good night's rest. You'll need it for two days on the back of Carlos. He likes to trot and can go for hours like that. He'll shake your bones up as he trots. But that's the fastest way for him to move through the jungle. And don't worry about the route. He's knows the route to the home of Dos Brazos like the back of his hoof."

El Caracol laughs, and the men leave for their respective tents.

But first, Junior commends El Catalán for the way he conducted the meeting and for the plan of action that was developed.

#

True to his word, the next morning at 5:30 a.m., El Caracol, on the back of Carlos, heads out of camp. As he looks toward the tents of Junior and El Catalán, he sees them both standing with lanterns shaking back and forth. He waves to them. They wave back. And suddenly he disappears into the jungle, and no one from the camp can see him.

And true to El Catalán's word, Carlos hits his stride, a strong, and bumpy ride through the jungle as if he were a trotting horse. However, El Caracol is pleased with the pace and committed to hanging in there as long as Carlos can keep it up.

Remembering the cautions about wild animals, El Caracol draws one of his pistols and pulls the slide back to insert a cartridge into the chamber. He leaves the safety in the off position so he will be immediately ready to shoot if the need arises.

And the need arises sooner than he ever expected. He hears faintly the sound of an animal running. Although he can't see any other animal, he can hear one. He turns around on his saddle and sees a jaguar about 50 feet behind them and closing the distance between them fast.

Knowing that the jag will be upon them soon, El Caracol starts shooting his 9 mm semi-automatic pistol, **BOOM**, **BOOM**, **BOOM**, **BOOM**, **BOOM**. After five shots the jag falls dead and slides on the wet grass.

All through this episode, Carlo kept up his trotting pace and didn't show any reaction due to the attack of the jag and the noise of the pistol.

El Caracol thinks, *I can't relax for even a few seconds. If that jag had caught up to us, he would have made mincemeat of both of us.*

For the remainder of the morning, everything goes well for the duo. Carlos slows down every 15 minutes and walks for about five minutes. Then, without any prodding, he starts trotting again and the pace picks up for another 15 minutes.

Finally at high noon, El Caracol sees a nice meadow with a creek of fresh water.

"Whoa, Carlos, time to eat and rest."

Carlos gradually pulls over to a stop. El Caracol jumps off him and leads him to a tree by the creek where he tethers him so he can drink the clear, cold water and eat fresh grass. El Caracol takes some food from the backpack, sits down, and enjoys the rest and food.

He knows he doesn't dare lie down. He would soon be asleep and for how long?

But he remembers to take the time to reload the five cartridges in his pistol. He always wants a full load of cartridges in the pistol's magazine.

After 30 minutes' rest and relaxation, El Caracol leans over the creek and takes a big drink of the water. Then he splashes water all over his face, head, and shirt. He takes his hat, turns it upside down, and fills it with water from the creek. He then holds his hat in front of Carlos who drinks slowly from the hat.

With everyone satisfied, El Caracol says, "Time to move on Carlos."

He then puts one foot in the stirrup and climbs aboard the faithful burro.

"Let's go Carlos, get up, get up."

Soon they are moving along at the usual trotting speed. El Caracol gets out his pistol and prepares for any attack from a beast of the jungle.

The afternoon goes well. Both enjoy the mid-afternoon driving rain which lasts about 20 minutes and cools and refreshes them. El Caracol is saddened when they pass the usual shack. But if he is to arrive in La Vista after two days' ride, he can't stop at the shack as the Cartel members usually do.

Finally as it is just about pitch dark, another meadow looms a few yards ahead.

"Whoa Carlos. Time to stop for the day."

Carlos slows down gradually and stops in the meadow near the usual creek that flows through it. El Caracol's biggest concern now is the safety of the burro. He drives a stake in the ground in the middle of the meadow away from any trees but right next to the creek. Then he tethers Carlos to the stake. Next he looks for some tall bushes with lots of sharp thorns. With his knife, he cuts the bushes at their roots and pulls them over to Carlos where he encircles him with the bushes.

This should at least keep the wild animals away from you for long enough to awaken me.

He takes some more thorny bushes and makes another circle but smaller this time for himself to use as protection.

eak up on their prey as the noise from the storm masks ly sounds from the wild animals.

El Caracol continually looks all around him trying to ot some movement of a wild animal. Suddenly, Carlos icks and lifts his front hooves making all sorts of wild oises. El Caracol was fortunate enough to be able to stay n the burro's back. He looks all around. All he sees are the ees on all sides and a fallen log across the trail in front of em.

Wait a minute, he thinks to himself. *That's not a fallen g, that's an anaconda snake about 20 feet long waiting or some unsuspecting meal to come along the trail.*

El Caracol dismounts and goes to the backpack on Carlos where he finds his Uzi submachine gun. Taking it rom its holster, he walks in front of Carlos and visually ollows along the giant snake at a safe distance until he inds its head, for certain.

Remembering the cautions from his comrades, he decides to empty his weapon into the brain or head of the horrible animal. Taking aim, he pulls the trigger which releases an onslaught of 9 mm bullets most of which hit their target. The giant snake shakes and vibrates to its final seconds of life.

El Caracol thinks, *Just as well. You kill your meals by squeezing them to death.*

He reloads the Uzi, replaces it in the backpack on Carlos, and mounts Carlos again. He then leads the burro far around the "fallen log" and returns him to the pathway. Off they go again at the same trot which seems natural by now to El Caracol.

Lunch, though meager, tastes good. Carlos enjoys the wet grass and the cool water from a creek. Both enjoy the rainstorm of the afternoon. Cool again, they continue the trotting.

After Carlos has had enough water from the cree[k], cuts some tall grass and throws it inside the circle o[f] for Carlos.

Soon they are both asleep among the night soun[ds of the] jungle. Two cougars on the prowl catch the scent o[f] and El Caracol. They approach the circle of thorn[s] trying to find a passageway through the bushes. E[very] often they try to move through the bushes but ge[t] with one or more sharp thorns. This brings a loud cry from the wounded animal. El Caracol is awake these sounds. He takes his pistol and watches for moments as the cougars continue to search for an en[trance] to where the burro is tethered.

After a while, the cougars try to enter where El C[aracol] is lying. He figures this is close enough, so he shoo[ts] shots into the air, "**BOOM, BOOM**."

The cougars jump as if they had been hit. Then the[y are] off running never to be seen again.

The rest of the night goes peacefully. Even befor[e the] first rays of the sun make their way through the tree[s and] bushes, El Caracol is up having his breakfast. Carl[os is] doing the same. Then El Caracol pushes a couple bu[shes] away from his encirclement and does the same for Ca[rlos]. A good drink of cool water for both man and beast is final task before the trip of the day.

The morning air is fresh and cool which puts an extr[a bit] of energy in both travelers. El Caracol mounts the bu[rro] and off they go. The animal quickly hits his stride, trotting which he can keep up for a long time. However Caracol pays the price of the trotting, as he bounces al[ong] on the saddle.

Lunch is a repeat of the previous day, and the afternc[on] is cooled by another downpour with its accompanyi[ng] wind. El Caracol remembers that he was told that so[me] wild beasts take advantage of this kind of weather a[nd]

As the sun starts its attempt to rest for the night, El Caracol sees the lights from the windows of the house of Dos Brazos. The nearer they get, the brighter the house lights and the darker the night sky become.

The children of Mr. and Mrs. Dos Brazos hear the sound of the trotting burro. They come running and greet El Caracol and Carlos.

El Caracol asks the boys to put Carlos in the corral after removing his load. He also tells them that Carlos has made the trip from the Cartel's camp in two days, and is very tired. He warns the boys that Carlos is not to be used for any purpose while waiting for the return of El Caracol.

"When is the next bus for La Vista?"

"One left here one hour ago. The last bus will leave here in two hours."

Dos Brazos arrives on the scene, "Hey El Caracol. That'll give you time for a good shower and a good dinner."

The two men shake hands and Dos Brazos walks with El Caracol to the barn where the shower is located. It is now a warm shower for 50 centavos, which the men of the jungle gladly pay.

"As soon as you are finished with your shower, come into the house. The meal is waiting. You'll enjoy it: deer steaks, baked potatoes, other vegetables and fruits, and cake for dessert."

#

No shower ever felt better to the human body thinks El Caracol. *This hot water makes quite a difference. Maybe I can get rid of all the bumps from that trotting burro.*

After his shower, El Caracol dries and dresses in his "city dress."

He then walks to the house and knocks on the back door.

"Come on in El Caracol. We're glad to have you. Do you need any medical services after coming through the jungle?"

"No thanks. I'm fine. We made it in two days."

Everyone says, "Two days. How is that possible?"

"It's only possible on a burro like Carlos, who is the biggest and strongest burro we have."

Dos Brazos says, "That's quite a record. I don't think it will ever be broken."

El Caracol responds, "Mrs. Dos Brazos, this meal is wonderful. I didn't realize how hungry I was."

"Well we're glad to have you and to have you enjoy the meal. The kids say you're leaving on the last bus of the day."

"Yes, that's correct. I should be back in a couple days and if you don't mind will square up with you financially at that time. And one special request, Carlos has gone all out for two days. He is exhausted and needs all the rest he can get. Please don't let anyone use him for any purpose. I will sure appreciate it. Also please make sure he has hay and fresh water all the time. That was a real task for him. I'm sure proud of him. We had trouble with one jaguar, two cougars, and one anaconda snake. Carlos didn't show any fear and was right on target all the time."

The kids are all impressed with the wild animals that were encountered by El Caracol and Carlos.

After finishing his meal, El Caracol says, "I think I'll shave and then go to the bus stop."

"Shave? You? What's happening to all the men of the jungle?"

"We have decided that whenever we go into the cities, we need to have a shave. The girls are more impressed that way."

Everyone laughs. Dos Brazos says, "Okay, finally a reason that makes sense."

Again, everyone laughs.

#

After several hours on the bus, El Caracol disembarks at the Yuñeco International Airport. He takes his bag and walks into the air terminal. There are only a few people in the various lines for tickets on the airplanes at this late hour.

El Caracol checks the large computer board to see what kind of service will get him to Independence Island. He doesn't expect a non-stop flight from La Vista to Independence Island, but in that regard he is surprised. There is a Sudamérica Air flight leaving tomorrow morning at 1030 hours flying non-stop to Independence Island.

He thinks, *What luck.*

After purchasing his ticket for tomorrow, El Caracol walks to the motel up the street from the airport. Booking his room, he takes the plastic key, opens the door, goes inside and locks the door behind him. He then drops his bag, takes off his clothes, hangs them up in the closet, and crashes into the bed pulling one blanket over him in this air-conditioned room.

#

He doesn't move until the phone rings at 6:30 a.m.

Slowly taking the phone, he says, "Hello."

"Good morning. This is your wake-up call."

"Thank you Miss."

El Caracol hits the shower, dries and dresses, goes to the motel restaurant for breakfast and then returns to his room to pick up his bag. He knows that he must arrive early at the airport for the security checks, luggage checks, etc.

#

Once at the airport terminal, he starts the process. He goes through passport control for a quick stamp on his passport. Next a luggage check. All is well. He then walks to the waiting area for his flight. Almost before he knows it, his flight is called. He walks down the ramp, enters the plane, and finds his reserved seat.

Soon the flight attendant is giving all the instructions for flying over water, wearing life jackets, etc. as the plane taxies out to the runway. El Caracol hears the motors rev up for a last-minute check. Then down the runway they go at an ever-increasing speed. Soon the plane leans back and heads for 32,000 feet which takes a while at maximum power of the engines. El Caracol never did like flying and this is no different.

Sleeping on the flight makes it easier for people like El Caracol. And the slow glide to the final destination is not so nerve wracking. The approach over the ocean seems strange to El Caracol, but soon the plane is over land and touching down on the runway at Independence Island. The reverse thrusters heighten the pressure on El Caracol and a few others, but that doesn't last long, just enough to really slow the plane down. It then turns and taxies up to its assigned gate. Then it stops and the engines are turned off.

Safe at last, thinks El Caracol who exits the plane in turn with the others.

With his one small bag, he takes the next taxi in line and tells the taxi driver, "I want to do some big game hunting with a .270 rifle and scope. Can you take me to a sporting goods store where I can buy such things?"

"Sure enough man, after that where?"

"If you'll come in with me and help if needed, then I have to go to a hotel near the police department."

"Sure enough man, let's go."

The taxi spins its front wheels as it heads for the sporting goods store. The driver stops in front of the store about the way he left the taxi line at the airport.

El Caracol thinks, *I may be in more danger on the ground with this driver than flying at 32,000 feet.*

They both exit the taxi and go into the sporting goods store heading straight for the rack of high-powered rifles.

"May I help you man?"

"Sure, I'm going big game hunting and would like a .270 with a good scope. What kind of game do you have on the island?"

"Hey man, we have good hunting for deer and wild pigs. Be careful they're dangerous. The deer aren't too large, but they taste very good as steaks and roasts, man.

"Here's a nice .270 with a scope already attached. This is the most popular deer rifle in the States man. It is extremely accurate. I'd recommend taking a few practice shots before you go hunting so you'll know the rifle. I can give you this rifle, man, with scope, one box of 25 cartridges, and a cleaning kit for $1,000.00 man.

"By the way, man, the Hotel near the police department has privileges to use the police rifle range. You can rent a taxi or a car to take you there. It's just up the mountain road far enough so the noise doesn't bother the guests of the hotel, man. You show your hotel key to access the rifle range, man. They have targets placed every hundred yards up to 600 yards, man. I check the sights on all my rifles there. It's a privilege they give me to use the range, man."

El Caracol asks the taxi driver, "What do you think? How is the rifle and the price, man?" (El Caracol is quick to pick up the local language custom.)

"There is no question. This is the best deer rifle in any country and especially with that scope. You won't miss your target, that's for sure. However, I think the price is a little high."

The clerk quickly jumps into the conversation since he doesn't want to lose this sale, "I can see you are a tourist. We always like to treat our tourists very well so they will return. For you, I can let the rifle, scope, and cartridges go for $900.00. You won't find such a price at any store on the island."

The taxi driver says, "I agree, that is a very good price for a superior rifle."

"Sold," says El Caracol.

"And to show you how we treat our tourists, I'll add a nice nylon case for the rifle at no extra price. Now if you want a leather case, that'll cost another hundred dollars, man."

"No, the nylon case will be just fine and protect the rifle very well.

"Now I need a good pair of binoculars."

The clerk says, "Right over here you will find several pairs of the best on the market, man"

El Caracol wastes no time in selecting and paying for a good pair of binoculars. After paying for them, he opens his bag and puts the binoculars away where they won't get broken."

#

As they leave the store, El Caracol thanks the taxi driver for his help in getting a good price for the rifle. He then asks, "Do you know where that hotel is he was talking about?"

"I sure do. My sister works there in the reservation department."

"Let's go there, man."

The taxi driver smiles as he drives for the hotel.

In a few minutes, they pull up in front of a large, five-star hotel named El Hotel de Independencia. El Caracol says in his best Spanish, "Qué fantástico."

"You're right there, that's for sure. If you would like, I could go in with you and we could talk with my sister to help in getting you a nice room for a good price."

"That's a good idea. I would appreciate that very much."

The taxi driver pulls his taxi over to the reserved space for taxis. Taking the bag and gun case, the taxi driver says, "Let's go man. Hey by the way, my name is Pablo. How about you?"

"I'm El Caracol." He didn't really like giving his name but if he is to receive some help from Pablo's sister in getting a good deal on a room, he'll have to use the name on his credit card and other I.D.

Pablo leads the way into the plush hotel. Seeing his sister, he says, "There she is, at the main counter. Her name is Virginia. Let's see what we can get."

"Hi Sis. This is a friend of mine, El Caracol. He's visiting our new country and chose of all the hotels yours. You should be honored. What can you do for him as far as a nice room with a stupendous view?"

"Let me check on what's available right now." She starts operating her computer and finds the list she is looking for, "Rooms available by price."

"Are you alone Mr. Caracol?"

"Yes I am."

"Okay man. Here's the room I was looking for. It just became vacant. It's on the corner of the building at the tenth floor, room 1050. You have window views on two sides, one of the ocean and the other of the islands as well. And I am authorized to provide a special price for VIPs, and as a friend of Pablo's, you certainly qualify as a VIP. The special price is $80.00 per night."

El Caracol says, "That's a good deal. I'll take it."

After filling out the various paperwork, El Caracol thanks Virginia and asks, "Could you get me the room number of a person for a $20.00 tip?"

"As a VIP friend of Pablo's, there's no need for a tip, but thank you anyway. Who's the person?"

"He's a friend of mine. We are both here to help plan the security for the upcoming International Games."

"Well that is important. And his name?"

"His name is Captain Roberto or Berto for short, Castillo. A police captain from Yuñeco."

"Now I see, both of you are from Yuñeco. I heard about the great job you did for security at the police chiefs' convention in La Vista. I hope you can do the same great job here. Let me see, my computer tells me that this Berto Castillo checked in yesterday and is in room 815.

"Thank you very much Virginia. Are you married?"

"I was, but my husband died doing some deep-sea diving work for a recovery company."

"I'm sorry. May I ask, any children?"

"No."

"I don't mean to insult you, but you could remedy a situation where a hotel guest was alone."

"Yes, that's right man."

"Could you personally remedy that situation? You are a beautiful woman, and I would enjoy getting to know you better."

"What specifically do you have in mind?"

"Hotel rooms get very lonely. I would enjoy just talking with you looking out that window that shows the various islands all lit up at night."

"Is that all you had in mind?"

"Yes, it is. I promise that as Pablo's sister, I would treat you with the greatest respect and you would enjoy the night. We could have a nice dinner in the room enjoying the beautiful ocean view."

"Well there is some risk involved since I really don't know you very well. May I discuss this first with Pablo?"

"Of course you may. I'll walk around the floor a bit while you are talking with Pablo."

As El Caracol walks off, Virginia motions for her brother to join her at the counter.

He walks over and asks, "What's up Sis?"

"I have a problem. El Caracol has asked me to spend tonight with him. Just a nice dinner in his room. What do you think Pablo? Is there too much risk involved?"

"I don't think so Sis. He's tipped me graciously and lined me up for another trip with a $100.00 tip. You would obviously get a generous tip as well without any complications. I think you could trust him without worrying one bit. When do you get off work?

"In 40 minutes."

"Nothing could be better. Take a chance Sis. You'll be all right. If you have a problem with him, just call me and I'll be there in a flash."

"Okay Pablo thanks. I know you wouldn't let me get into any difficult situation."

She motions for El Caracol to talk with her and says, "I'm off in 40 minutes. Could we eat dinner first since I had no lunch?"

"Whatever you want Virginia. I'll be waiting for you in room 1050. We can order dinner immediately, whatever you want."

"I'll see you there in a few minutes. Chao."

El Caracol then walks over to the corner of the room where taxi driver, Pablo, is waiting.

"Pablo, do you have a card with your cell phone number in case I need a taxi?"

Opening his wallet, Pablo hands El Caracol his business card which he reads carefully to be sure he understands everything completely.

"Pablo, you've been a big help to me when you didn't need to. Here's a token of my gratitude, $50.00. If I need another taxi, I'll give you a call. In fact, I know I'll need a taxi when I leave here. Could you be available at a site designated by me for a rapid trip to the airport, for a $100.00 tip?"

"For a $100.00 tip, I could be anyplace at any time waiting for you, and I would not leave until I had you in the back seat."

"Okay man, now for another question, how is your memory?"

"I have the worst memory of anyone on the island. I never remember names, faces, trips taken, luggage, etc. The better the tip, for some reason, the worse my memory."

El Caracol laughs and says, "That's good. I'll be contacting you for sure concerning my trip to the airport.

Does it make any difference if the trip is in the middle of the night?"

"None whatsoever, man. I sleep anytime, anyplace."

"Okay, I'll be going to my room now and contact you later. Thanks for all your help and your sister's help as well. Chao."

#

El Caracol takes a quick shower and puts on a light robe to help with this hot weather. Hearing a knock at the door, he walks over to it and opens it.

"Hi Virginia, come on in."

Pablo's sister, Virginia, walks in and then grabs the menu off the TV table.

El Caracol laughs, "You must be hungry."

"I said I had no lunch, remember?"

"Well you just pick out whatever you want, and I'll do the same. Then I'll phone room service."

Virginia takes some time looking over the entire menu carefully. When she grabs a pad of paper and a pen from the desk, El Caracol concludes she is ready to order. She writes down several items and gives El Caracol the list.

Reading it over, he says, "You are hungry. You shouldn't go so long without eating. It's not good for you."

"I was so busy with reservations that I couldn't find time to take a lunch break."

"Excuse me a moment, and I'll check over the menu."

"Of course. Take your time," responds Virginia as she walks over to the window to admire the view.

El Caracol finally picks up the phone and calls room service. He gives the order which is not too complicated since they both order prime rib with all the trimmings.

El Caracol laughs, "Guess what I ordered?"

"No really? You didn't get prime rib like I did?"

"I sure did. That's a good sign. We both think along the same lines."

Virginia laughs, "I see you have already showered. I'll do the same. Here's something for you to read while I'm in the shower. This is the map of the hotel grounds with the schedule of Colonel Berto Castillo starting tomorrow. It also shows the exact location on the map where he'll be at specific times. You'll probably get one of these when you report for duty tomorrow, don't you imagine?"

"I'm sure I will, but this gives me a little heads-up time, thanks to you. That'll get you a $20.00 tip for anticipating my needs."

Virginia says, "El Caracol, this is a new experience for me, staying with a man in his room. You don't have to give me a tip for such things. I'm here with you because I want to be, not because you will give me some tips."

"I know that, but please give me the pleasure of leaving some money with you when I want to. I'll be gone soon and will not have another opportunity to leave some money with you."

"Okay, if that's the way you want it. But please don't talk about being gone soon just as we are beginning to know each other and have a good time. I think I will miss you when you are gone, and that makes me sad, and I don't like to be sad."

El Caracol approaches her, puts his arms around her, and hugs her gently. "Don't be sad, Virginia, there's nothing to be sad about. We're here together in this magnificent room with an incredible view. Go ahead and take your shower and when you're done, we'll enjoy prime rib together."

She kisses El Caracol on the cheek and runs off to the shower. Soon El Caracol can hear the water from the shower and the singing voice of Virginia.

Wow, she has a beautiful voice.

Soon the water in the shower is shut off and the singing continues. After a couple more minutes, Virginia steps out of the bathroom like some European Queen in a beautiful pink robe that has a sleeping gown underneath it.

El Caracol whistles. "Hey there, you look beautiful."

And just on cue, there is a knock on the door. Virginia returns to the bathroom and closes the door. As an employee of the hotel she is not supposed to be in rooms with guests.

El Caracol goes to the door of the room, opens it, and shows in the steward with his tray of two hot dinners, prime ribs with all the trimmings. After he lays the tray down on the small table in the room, El Caracol thanks him and gives him a generous tip.

After the steward leaves, El Caracol goes to the bathroom and knocks on the door.

He asks, "Anyone live in this house?"

Opening the door, Virginia emerges more beautiful than before since she has had more time to fix her hair and makeup.

They both sit down at the small table and start to enjoy a marvelous meal with all the trimmings.

#

After dinner, El Caracol escorts Virginia to the couch and says, "Help me figure this map out, would you please?"

"Of course. This is the standard map that the hotel uses with the same method for marking locations of various people during the day. For example, let's take your friend, Captain Berto Castillo. He's listed as person 'A.' There are three others listed alphabetically. That means he will have three others with him as guards who will be armed with high powered weapons. It doesn't say here who they are, but you are probably one of them.

"Now for example, the hotel manager is listed as person '1' with his staff that will be needed during the walk-through tomorrow listed as persons '2 through 5.' And on and on it goes.

"Now for timing. According to this plan, person 'A' will be in the basketball and badminton courts at 10:30 a.m. tomorrow morning."

El Caracol asks, "Where will he be before that tomorrow morning?"

"At 9:00 a.m., he'll be in the grand ballroom. See, right here on the map. Then he crosses the foot bridge and goes to the athletic part of the hotel property, starting at the basketball and badminton courts."

"What's this about a foot bridge?"

Virginia responds, "Maybe you haven't noticed it yet, but there's a foot bridge going over the main highway that brings people from the airport to the hotel building. The foot bridge takes pedestrians to the recreation complex that belongs to the hotel.

"According to this schedule, Captain Castillo will check out this overpass from 10:15 a.m. until 10:25 a.m. Then as previously announced, he'll arrive at the basketball and badminton courts at 10:30 a.m. This Captain Castillo of yours is certain punctual, isn't he?"

"Oh yes, you can count on him to observe this schedule."

As he says this to Virginia, El Caracol relaxes on the couch holding Virginia's hand and thinking of what he has just learned.

He thinks hard, *Where would be the best place to make a hit on Captain Castillo? I think the foot bridge is tailor made for me. As Berto is inspecting the bridge for perhaps dynamite, with my .270 caliber and scope, I could nail that bum who has become a thorn in our side. But where should I make the hit from?*

He hesitates a bit, *How about the top of the building? Let me see, if I make the hit at 10:20 a.m., I can rush to take the elevator down, pick up my bag at the concierge, and then go outside to catch Pablo in the cab. The drive to the airport is about 15 minutes. That would put me at the airport around 10:40 a.m. So I'll need a plane to anywhere in South America leaving at 10:50 a.m. I'll need to make the reservations tonight.*

"Virginia, can a guest view this marvelous scene from the top of the hotel?"

"Oh yes. The top of the hotel is open from 8:00 a.m. until 11:00 a.m. After that, it gets too hot and windy."

El Caracol responds, "That makes a lot of sense. When do you have to go to work in the morning?"

"I have the day shift starting at 8:00 a.m."

"You'll want breakfast in the room, won't you?"

"That would be nice to order breakfast in the room. How about a scrumptious meal at 7:00 a.m.?"

"Okay, I'll order it now. What would you like for this scrumptious meal?" he says as he takes paper and pen in hand.

"Scrambled eggs with fried potatoes, lots of toast of white bread, and hot cinnamon rolls with raisins and nuts and jam and butter. Hot chocolate for four people. "

"Well, that certainly is a scrumptious meal. I can hardly wait."

El Caracol picks up the phone, dials room service, and orders the breakfast as suggested by Virginia.

Then he leans back again on the couch holding Virginia's hand. Soon he falls asleep still holding Virginia's hand.

Two hours later, Virginia says to El Caracol, "Hey sleepy head. Time to get up."

Surprised, he responds, "I've got to make reservations for a plane tomorrow morning."

"Oh no El Caracol. Can't you stay over a few days more?"

"You have no idea how much I'd love to stay over now that I've met you. But previous commitments don't permit that. I'll be coming back and since I know where you work, I can contact you easily. And now, me for the phone."

El Caracol walks over to the phone in the room and dials a general phone number for airplane flights.

"Hi this is El Caracol, I need a flight tomorrow morning at 10:50 a.m. to South America."

"Wow, that's rather vague," is the response from the reservation clerk.

"Don't worry about it. Ten fifty a.m. on the dot. What do you have?"

"Let me check my computer list by time of departure. Here's a flight at exactly 10:50 a.m. for Colquequile. Will that be okay?"

"That'll be perfect, thank you." After he gives the reservation clerk his credit card number and address where his credit card bills are mailed, the clerk figures his identity is verified and puts through the reservation.

"Can you put down that I will be arriving at the last minute, and they shouldn't give my seat to anyone else. Also put down if I miss the plane, charge the ticket to the credit card number. In other words, I want that seat reserved for me, got it?"

"Got it Señor Caracol."

"Goodbye Señorita."

"Goodbye Señor Caracol."

As he rings off, he calls his favorite taxi driver.

"Pablo, El Caracol here. I'll need you in front of the hotel at exactly 10:20 a.m. tomorrow morning. If I'm a few minutes late, you'll wait right?"

"Right, El Caracol. Where do you want me to be waiting?"

"Almost exactly in front of the hotel, but across the street. There's always that line of taxis that would cause you problems. But if you wait across the street as if you were waiting for a passenger from a plane, the traffic cop wouldn't cause any problems, right?"

"Right. I had that same situation before. We taxi drivers are told to wait across the street so the whole thing is a bit organized."

"Okay, I'll see you there at about 10:20 to 10: 25 a.m."

"It's a deal."

They both ring off.

What else do I need to do?

After some consideration, he decides he has done all the planning necessary for tomorrow's important hit.

#

Early the next morning as they are preparing for the day's activities, there is a knock at the door. Virginia disappears into the bathroom. El Caracol opens the door and sees three policemen coming into the room.

"Pardon the interruption. We're checking all the rooms that have recent arrivals."

El Caracol says, "We're getting ready to leave after we have breakfast. My girl works here and prefers not to reveal her identity."

"Of course, we're not here to disturb peoples' vacations. We're just being alert during the practice security check we're having today."

"Oh yes, I heard about it. Good luck guys. This kind of alertness will do the job, that's for sure."

"Thanks for your understanding Sr. Caracol. I notice you have what looks like a high-powered rifle in the corner."

"Would you like to see it? I'm rather proud of it."

"Of course."

El Caracol unzips the zipper that holds the case around the rifle. Then he pulls out his beautiful .270 with scope. The first thing he does is pull the bolt handle back and leave the bolt open to assure the officers that there is no bullet in the chamber."

He holds the rifle out for anyone who wants to handle it.

The sergeant takes the rifle and looks it over carefully. He then closes the bolt so he can look out the window and see how well the scope works.

"Wow, what great magnification."

"Yes, as you know with scopes, it's lower that's important in case the animal is close. So this is a three by nine-forty. At three it'll give me a good field of view for close shots, and at nine it'll give me a good size target for one that is far away. This is probably the most popular scope on the market."

"What do you hunt on the island?"

"Well, I'm starting today. I guess the original game animals were brought to the island many years ago by the Spanish. They say I can get good shots at fallow deer or wild boar. I'll be careful with those latter beasts. They can rip you to shreds if they're not killed quickly."

"How about the fallow deer. What size can you expect?"

"The big bucks can weigh up to 150 pounds. They grow a nice set of antlers each year. Like other deer, they're skittish, jump quickly, and move out fast."

"Hey guys, we need to get out on our own island and try for some of those fallow deer. One hundred and fifty pounds can put a lot of meat in the freezer. Well, we'd better be running now. Good luck in your hunting. Goodbye."

As the police start to close the door, the room steward comes into the room with breakfast, steaming hot.

El Caracol pays and tips the steward who thanks him and slowly begins to leave the room, although he is curious as to who is in the bathroom. He has seen some beautiful women if he hesitates a few seconds before he leaves the room. However, that technique doesn't work this morning. Virginia doesn't come out of the bathroom until the steward closes the door behind him and Caracol knocks on the bathroom door. Then out she comes with her hair combed and looking like a million dollars.

After breakfast and brushing of teeth, the two pack their small bags and are ready to leave. El Caracol says he will be leaving for the airport in a while and will spend his waiting time in the hotel room.

Virginia has tears in her eyes.

"Don't cry beautiful," says El Caracol. "If something happens to me, you'll be safe and sound here on the island. A good man will come along, and you'll get married and have six kids of your own."

"Caracol, I don't understand what you're saying, but I know one thing, I don't like it. You're talking like I won't see you again."

"Virginia, we never know when our number is up. So we have to tell those that we love that we love them and not regret it later that we kept silent. So Virginia Dear, remember that I do love you."

"I will Caracol. Now let me kiss you and run. I'm going to start crying really bad here in a minute."

El Caracol kisses her for a long time, after which she grabs her bag and leaves the room with tears streaming down her face.

Sitting down on the couch, El Caracol turns on the television. In a few minutes, a bell rings on the television signifying exactly 8:00 a.m. Then a movie comes on.

El Caracol thinks, *Good. This will probably last a couple hours which should put me right on schedule.*

El Caracol takes out his rifle and cleaning liquids. First removing the bolt, he looks down the barrel with the room lamp at the opening for the bolt. He can see the shiny metal with its lands and groves twisting their way up the barrel. Since he has sufficient time, he decides to thoroughly clean the rifle and lightly oil it where needed.

After taking his time to clean the rifle, El Caracol relaxes and dozes while partially watching the movie.

Later, he glances up at the clock on the wall. It is now 10:01 o'clock. He loads his .270 with four cartridges of 130 grain bullets. He knows this will give him a flat trajectory which is essential in the job before him. What he aims at, he will hit. He returns the cleaning kit to his bag.

Another glance at the wall tells him he has five minutes left if he wishes to get to the roof of the hotel by 10:15 a.m. Taking his binoculars from his small bag and hanging them around his neck, he quickly leaves the room with bag and rifle in hand. When the empty elevator arrives, he punches the button with the small sign above it that reads 'Roof Top.'

#

In the meantime, Captain Berto Castillo has started his tour of the facilities to provide for the security at the hotel during the week of the Continental Games. He is now in the kitchen and just about done. A glance at his wristwatch tells him it is time to check out the foot bridge.

At the same time, El Caracol reaches the roof top by means of the elevator. He has decided to not leave his small bag with the concierge. He has kept it. As he leaves the elevator, he places his bag by the corner of the wall where the elevator starts. A few people are observing the sights on the other side of the roof.

El Caracol then walks slowly to the edge of the building with its four-foot-high parapet that is actually an extension of the concrete walls of the hotel. The walls are 12 inches thick, and provide safety to anyone on the roof.

Looking over the edge of the parapet, El Caracol sees the security planning group begin to assemble on the foot bridge. Only one man is in uniform. El Caracol quickly takes his binoculars and checks out the group. He sees that the uniformed officer is a police officer. From the gold bars on his shoulders, it is apparent that he is holds at least the rank of lieutenant or above.

That's got to be Captain Berto Castillo, I know it. It's now or never for a quick shot from this great .270 caliber.

Quickly removing his rifle from its case and inserting a cartridge into the chamber, El Caracol lays the rifle across the parapet. With the wall to steady his aim, he looks through the scope and sees a greatly magnified view of Captain Berto Castillo.

Aha, two bars. He is a captain.

He aims for his chest.

Then he thinks, *He probably has on a bullet proof vest. So a chest shot wouldn't do much. I'll try a head shot, but the chances of missing are greatly increased.*

Moving his cross hairs on the scope, he places them directly between Captain Castillo's eyes.

Just before El Caracol squeezes off his first shot, one of Berto's comrades hands him a map of the City of Independencia. However, the pass isn't too accurate as the map falls to the ground and Berto bends over to pick it up. This happens just as El Caracol squeezes the trigger of his .270 rifle.

BOOM goes the sound of the powerful .270 rifle with the bullet bouncing off the concrete of the foot bridge behind where Berto was standing.

Berto yells out, "Everyone down in the corners."

They all follow Berto's directions as he draws his semi-automatic pistol.

Meanwhile on the roof, El Caracol ducking down himself, understands exactly what has happened and why he missed with his first shot. He quickly pulls back on the bolt and injects another cartridge into the chamber.

He slowly peeks his head over the wall to see everyone with his coat or jacket off. Even Berto has removed his jacket with its golden bars on each shoulder. El Caracol looks through his rifles scope for the captain. He can't believe the captain is a chicken and is hiding someplace.

Wait, there he is. He can't hide that military tie and military shirt. Caracol takes another aim.

But Berto from his location can see the morning sun providentially bouncing off the lens of the .270 scope.

Berto thinks as quickly as he can, *My bullets that miss the target and go over the building will just land in the bay on the other side of the hotel and not cause any damage or hurt anyone.*

After pulling back on the slide and releasing it, the pistol is now ready to shoot with 17 cartridges available without any more pulling or pushing of any parts except the trigger.

Berto takes careful aim at the partial figure on the top of the building and fires his entire load: **BOOM, BOOM, BOOM, BOOM, BOOM, BOOM, BOOM, BOOM, BOOM, BOOM, BOOM, BOOM, BOOM, BOOM, BOOM, BOOM, BOOM**.

Pushing the button that drops the empty magazine from the bottom of the pistol, Berto takes another fresh magazine from his belt, rams it into the handle of the pistol, picks up his empty magazine from the concrete passageway, and starts running toward the hotel. Once inside the hotel, he grabs an elevator for the roof top. Arriving there in what seems like a long time, he emerges with his pistol at the ready.

He sees a group of people assembled by the wall where they can see the concrete foot bridge.

"Move back, please," Berto yells as he approaches the crowd.

As they move back, Berto can see the gunman. He has all the usual trappings of a Cartel hitman as Berto has come to know them.

El Caracol shows signs of being hit with four bullets before he fell to the ground.

Berto leans over and feels his pulse. It is very weak. Taking his portable phone, he calls the management of the hotel, "We need an ambulance from the hospital with two EMTs and a stretcher on top of the hotel. Please send up some hotel attendants or police officers to help with crowd control up here. No cameras please or newspaper persons."

In a few minutes, hotel employees begin to appear followed by regular police officers from the community. Berto assigns them to particular locations as he asks the crowd that was already there to take the elevators to whatever floor they want.

Several minutes later, two EMTs appear with a stretcher and two other police officers. By this time, the roof top is free of tourists and others who were on top of the building when the action commenced.

Berto gives the police officers the explanation of what took place.

The manager of the hotel says, "Berto, this is proof that we need a strong security presence during our conference. I assume you'll be drawing up some plans as to our needs, drug sniffing dogs, police officers in general, and so on. And based on this incident, we need to really lock this upper door and turn off the elevator to the roof top. The only ones on the roof top should be four police officers in three shifts. And we need three sergeants, it seems to me, checking who the officers on duty really are and so on. They should constantly keep in touch with you."

"Hey, you sound like a police captain or at least a lieutenant the way you're barking out orders."

"I'm sorry Berto. I was usurping your position and responsibility, wasn't I? Thanks for reminding me. I'll manage the hotel, and you manage the security detachment and details."

Just then an employee of the hotel comes banging on the elevator. She is crying and demands to be admitted.

Berto says, "I'll handle it," as he walks over to the elevator to greet Virginia.

"Captain, please have a heart here. I had dinner with El Caracol last evening. Let me see him before you remove him, please."

Berto feels he can learn something from this woman, so he escorts her to the body lying in the shade of the parapet. She leans down and kisses El Caracol.

She then looks up at Berto and asks, "What happened here?"

"He's a Cartel hitman and tried to kill me with his rifle when I was on the footbridge. I had to shoot back and emptied my pistol at him. It looks like I hit him four times."

Returning to El Caracol, Virginia says, "Hey, Caracol, you're breaking your promise. You said we'd be together next year, remember? What happened? Don't leave me just as I've found you."

She bursts into tears. El Caracol takes her hand and with his other hand rubs her hair.

"I'll be all right Virginia. You watch. The bullet hasn't been made yet that can kill El Caracol."

The EMTs say, "We need to get him to the hospital fast. Please don't hinder our passage."

El Caracol says, "I'll see you later Sweetheart," and then his head falls to the right. The EMTs put him down and check his vital signs. Then they pull the blanket over his face.

"We're sorry Miss. He's dead. Thank you for getting here in time before he died."

Virginia really sobs now. Berto puts his arm around her and tries to console her.

"He said your name was Virginia."

"Yes he did. He was El Caracol. He worked for a business from the Amazon Rainforest. I never really knew what he did. Please excuse me, I need to get back to work. If you want to talk with me, just give me a call at the reservation desk and ask for Virginia. Then we can arrange a meeting if you need one."

"Yes, Miss, we can do that. Thanks for your help, and please accept our profoundest condolences."

Virginia returns to the elevator and goes down to the hotel lobby where she works. But first she goes to the ladies room to wash her face and comb her hair. She is very sad.

Back on top of the roof, Berto says, "Come on guys, we've got an inspection tour to finish. We're about 30 minutes behind schedule."

In her office, Virginia phones the airlines that Caracol made the reservations with last night. She advises them that El Caracol has just died from gunshot wounds, therefore he will not be taking the flight he made a reservation for.

Next she phones the office of Captain Berto Castillo in La Vista. Susana answers the phone and identifies herself.

"Susana, this is Virginia María Escobedo, the reservation clerk at the Hotel de Independencia, on the Island where Berto is working. Berto had to shoot and kill a man known as El Caracol. Do you know of this man?"

Susana responds that she knows of this man.

"Would you please get word to his family and friends that he tried to shoot Captain Berto Castillo, but the police Captain emptied his pistol at El Caracol and killed him. The Independence Police have just taken him away to the morgue. If his family and or friends want to claim the body, please let me know if they want my help. I work in the Hotel de Independencia, at the reservations desk. I could help act as an intermediary between his family and the police. I had dinner last night with El Caracol. He was nice and we liked each other. I think if left alone, we could have developed a serious relationship." Then she breaks into sobs and tears.

Susana says, "Virginia, I understand completely. I am married to Captain Berto Castillo. If I can be of any help,

I'll be available. I'll contact someone right now who lives on the edge of the Amazon Rainforest who can get the word to his family and friends. Goodbye Virginia."

"Goodbye Susana."

Chapter 8

A few weeks after the episode on the Island of Independence, Berto is home enjoying his family again. Susana is concerned that the Cartel will try something like they tried last time.

Franz senses someone at the door. The family has learned to recognize his reactions to various sounds. Elizabeth slides off her father's lap and lets him go to the front door. He opens it to reveal four men with bandanas tied around their faces to mask their identities.

"Back inside quick," shouts one of the men.

Berto does as ordered.

As the four masked men follow Berto to the front room, Franz is upset when he sees the pistols and the masks. He waits for a command from Berto, but it does not come.

The leader of the group says, "Everyone, sit down on the sofa …now."

The family sits on the sofa and awaits the next order.

Berto calls Franz to sit on the floor in front of him with his back facing him.

"Okay, guys, now what? What are you doing in our house? We're a peaceful family who wouldn't hurt a fly."

The leader says, "You're Berto Castillo, aren't you? You're a captain in the police force, aren't you?"

"Yes I am, so what?" Berto notices that one man pulls up a chair near Franz and keeps his pistol and attention trained on the police dog.

"So plenty. You've given us a lot of trouble, not just here in La Vista but also in Neblina, and on the Island of Independence. We've had a trial, and you've been convicted."

"Convicted? Convicted of what?"

"Convicted of being an enemy of the state."

"Of what state?"

"Of the State of the Cartel de la Selva Tropical. And the penalty has been affixed and will be carried out now."

"Wait a minute guys. What penalty? Give me a chance to at least say a word in our behalf."

"You already spoke with a Bazooka, remember? Two missiles and you wiped out a large part of our leadership. And you recently killed El Caracol on the Island of Independence. Those are the crimes, murder, and the penalty is death for your family and your dog. But we'll leave you alive to suffer the loss of your family."

"No, wait, since I committed the crime, I should receive the penalty, not my wife or children, or even the dog."

"Yea, that's the way you'd like it, isn't it? No luck today, Captain. Now shut up or we'll gag you."

As the men prepare to kill Berto's family, his mind is racing like never before. *What to do? How to stop this assassination of my family? Where is my pistol? Oh yes, I left it in the hallway. How many could Franz take out while I tried to take out another?*

Realizing that he has almost no time, Berto springs into action, yelling at the same time, "Franz, sic'em, sic'em."

As the dog also moves into action, Berto hears the sound of gunshots and then all goes black.

#

Three hours later while lying on the floor, Berto hears a knocking sound as if it were miles away. Gradually it gets louder, until he hears the sound of the kitchen door being smashed in. Everything is like a dream. Next he hears a voice that he recognizes, but he can't identify it for sure.

The voice says, "Dispatch, this is Lt. Neto Ramírez of the K-9 School. I'm at the home of Captain Berto Castillo. His entire family has been killed. Franz was shot in the leg and the stomach. He hid under a bed and is still alive. The Captain seems to still be alive. Send one ambulance and four vehicles from the mortuary services division and one ambulance from the local veterinary hospital. Over and out."

Berto next feels a cold, wet rag on his forehead. He tries to open his eyes, which he can do, but he can't see anything. His head hurts and someone tries to stop the bleeding.

"Berto, Berto, this is Neto. What happened?"

"What happened? I can't remember. Give me some time to get things together. I can't even see."

"That's no surprise. You've got an egg on top of your head. You've been hit very hard. I'm trying to stop the bleeding now."

"Neto, what about my family?"

"Berto, they're all dead, Susana, Miguel, Bobbie, and Elizabeth. Franz was shot in the leg and the stomach and hid under a bed."

"Oh no, no Neto. Are you sure?"

"Yes, Berto. I'm so sorry."

Sirens are heard in the distance. The first car to pull up belongs to Police Chief Luis Medina accompanied by his secretary, Blanca Hernández. They are followed by several police cars, mortuary service vehicles, and a police ambulance. The final vehicle is the ambulance from the Veterinary Hospital.

Berto hears people coming in and out of his house, but his senses are so damaged that he is unable to discern who they are and what they are doing.

Soon two EMTs come over to Berto along with Blanca who says, "Berto, oh Berto, what a tragedy. The EMTs will take you to the hospital now. I'll go with them in the back of the ambulance. I'll be right beside you all the while holding your hand."

"Thank you Blanca," whispers Berto.

It helps him to have a familiar voice and person next to him during this stage when he isn't even sure where he is or what has happened. But he does recognize Blanca's voice.

Then another familiar voice speaks to him, "Berto, this is Chief Medina. I've asked Blanca to stay with you as long as she can. I'll meet you at the hospital and try to explain to you what has happened. I've put Sergeant Pedro Morales in charge of the investigation of this crime. He'll be at the hospital later to take your statement."

Berto again whispers, "Thank you Chief. Are all my children and Susana really dead, Chief?"

"Yes, Berto."

"And Franz?"

"He's been wounded in the leg and the stomach. It looks like he then hid under the bed in your room. He lost a lot of blood dragging himself there. How does your head feel?"

"It hurts like crazy."

"Hey, one of you EMTs. Berto's in a lot of pain. Can you help him?"

"Chief, we'd like him to hang on a bit longer, so the emergency room doctors can get accurate vital signs and be able to discern the condition of his head. Then, I'm sure, they'll give him some help with the pain. It won't be long. We're leaving now."

The EMTs place Berto on a stretcher and lift him with Blanca at his side holding his hand. He squeezes her hand with tears flowing from his blinded eyes.

The impact of what has happened to his family is beginning to sink in. The EMTs take him to the ambulance and place him in the rear, strapping him in for security. Blanca steps into the ambulance, sits down beside Berto, and continues to hold his hand.

Berto asks, "Blanca, what's all that noise? It sounds like a bunch of people talking."

"That's what it is, Berto. Your neighbors are all standing outside your house and are saddened to see you taken into the ambulance."

One EMT slams the rear door of the ambulance shut and runs to the passenger side in the front of the ambulance. With its light bar flashing and siren screaming, the ambulance takes off for the hospital at a high speed.

Within a few minutes, the ambulance pulls into the emergency entrance to the hospital followed by Chief Medina's car. Two army vehicles are parked close by.

As Berto is taken into the emergency room and put on a moving gurney, he sees other faces he recognizes, General Escobar and Colonel Núñez. Somehow they got the word and moved quickly.

They remain outside as Berto is placed in a cubicle in the ER with all kinds of equipment. The Chief with the two soldiers joins a tearful Blanca in the waiting room.

The doctor in charge, Dr. Francisco Gutiérrez, slowly asks Berto four questions, "What's your name? Where do you live? What is your telephone number? On a scale of one to ten with ten being very severe, how is your pain level now?"

Berto listens to the questions and thinks hard on the answers. However, he can't remember three of the questions. I'm sorry Doctor, I can't remember the first questions. On the pain level question, I'd say I'm about an eight or nine."

Dr. Gutiérrez says to the EMTs, "Since the bleeding is stopped from his head, I want a CT Scan STAT."

The EMTs wheel Berto out of the ER down a hallway and into the room holding the CT machine. The tests are done quickly with and without contrast. The results are sent electronically to the radiologist who interprets the images and attaches his comments. In a few minutes after Berto returns to the ER, Dr. Gutiérrez is able to read the results of the CT Scans.

He says to his fellow surgeons and assistants as they crowd around a large video screen, "Well, there's one thing for sure. This isn't the first time Captain Castillo has been hit on the head with great force. Talk about Traumatic Brain Injury. His head can't take any more of these hits. One more, and his brain will swell such that he will die quickly. Now for the present, the next 48 hours will tell the story. At this point in time, it doesn't look like we'll have to cut out any of his skull to release pressure on his brain. However, future CT Scans will confirm those suspicions.

"As for medications to help relieve the pain, Captain Castillo is one tough character, so we'll use a minimum of medication for pain relief. I'd like to have him ready for a CT Scan at any time with a minimum of medications in him. The nurses will keep him here in the ER until I release him. The EMTs can return to their normal duties, and thank you everyone. You all did an outstanding job with this patient. He is still alive, thanks to you."

The nurses push the gurney to a private room in the ER area while the others return to their normal duties appreciative of the kind words from the doctor.

Dr. Gutiérrez goes to the waiting room and sits down to talk with the people waiting to hear about Captain Castillo.

After Chief Medina introduces everyone to the doctor, Dr. Gutiérrez says, "I'm sure you all know this, but that Captain Castillo is one tough customer. A CT Scan tells us that this is not his first Traumatic Brain Injury."

Chief Medina adds, "Yes, Doctor, that's true. He was hit on the head during his duty down by the Blue River and who knows how many other times."

The Doctor continues, "Right now we're going to do some watching and waiting. We've giving him some pain killers and will be taking him in for additional CT Scans as needed. He'll be here for a while under the best conditions. If there is swelling in his brain, we'll cut a portion of his skull away to relieve the pressure on his brain."

Blanca starts to cry.

The Doctor says, "Oh, I'm sorry, I thought his wife was killed in this horrible episode."

The Chief says, "She was Doctor. This is my secretary, Blanca Hernández. We're a pretty close-knit group at the police department. Blanca and Berto have worked together for many years."

The Doctor leaves the waiting room while the Chief asks the others to stay.

The Chief says, "There's one thing that needs to be taken care of. Berto's entire family was killed. I'll contact his brother and sister, Pablo and María. They'll want to take charge of the funeral arrangements. The killers, in my opinion, were the Cartel de la Selva Tropical. But we'll take care of them later."

#

Several days later, the same group meets in the waiting room of the hospital.

Blanca says, "Chief, that was a nice eulogy you gave at the funeral services for Berto's family."

"It was the most difficult eulogy I've ever given, a wife and three children with one being a very young and beautiful little daughter."

Blanca says, "Look, here comes Dr. Gutiérrez."

Mario observes, "He doesn't look very happy."

The Doctor enters the waiting room, checks to be sure the room is empty of other people not associated with Berto, and takes a chair.

Dr. Gutiérrez says, "I have good news for you today. The latest CT Scan tells us that what swelling there was is beginning to recede. His vision has returned, and he is eating better. His memory is slowly returning with some new techniques we are trying. He says the culprits who killed his family were from the Cartel de la Selva Tropical."

General Escobar says, "I shall ask the brass for permission to send Unit One into the Rainforest to wipe out the Cartel de la Selva Tropical, leaving the women and children alive. We'll have to bring them out and set them up in an agrarian society."

Colonel Mario Núñez adds, "General, all I need is 48 hours to put together the excursion to do the job. My people are used to traveling in the Rainforest."

Chief Medina says, "Wait a minute here. This offense was committed against all the police jurisdictions of Yuñeco. I think we should be permitted to do this job. This is not a job for the Army except we might need your helicopters to get us in and out."

General Escobar asks, "You have a plan, Chief?"

Chief Medina answers, "I sure do, but let me meet with some other chiefs first and see what they think of it. Then if they agree, I'll share it with you, okay?"

The General responds, "Okay by me. Mario, what do you think?"

"That's fine with me too."

#

Several days later, after Berto's condition has improved greatly as well as that of Franz, Chief Medina has called a meeting of all the Chiefs in the Country of Yuñeco. The Chiefs booked rooms at the La Vista Blue River Hotel. The Hotel management, upon learning the reason for the meeting and what happened to Captain Castillo, offered the rooms and meals at a significant reduction from the usual price. The meeting is being held in one of the many conference rooms of the hotel.

After light refreshments are served, Chief Medina says, "Okay guys and gals, let's get started. First, thanks for coming to this meeting on such short notice. I don't know how many of you are aware of the reason for this meeting.

"Not long ago, four masked men of the Cartel de la Selva Tropical burst into the home of Captain Berto Castillo, Superintendent of the Police K-9 School. They were angry with him for the great job he had done in providing security at this very hotel for the annual police chiefs' conference and for his taking out one of their top men, El Caracol, on the Island of Independence.

"They shot and killed his wife and three children. When they shot his famous dog, Franz, the dog ran and hid under a bed.

"Then they hit Berto on the head very hard. He has been in the hospital ever since trying to regain his vision, his memory, his strength, etc.

"The Army wanted to go into the Amazon Rainforest to kill the men of the Cartel. I told their officials that there might be a chance that the Police Chiefs of Yuñeco might just want to perform this raid ourselves. What's your opinion gentlemen and ladies?"

Chief Tony Camargo from Neblina says, "Hey, when I needed an officer with a trailing dog to help find a little boy lost in a cave, Berto and Franz were on my front step in less than 24 hours. For one, I want to settle the score with the Cartel de la Selva Tropical personally."

Another Chief asks, "Luis, I've heard some horrible stories about the Army's traveling in the Amazon Rainforest, snakes, wild beasts, Llumista Indians with curare tipped arrows. Is your plan any different?"

"Yes, it is. The Army has agreed to supply helicopters for those of us who want to fly in, parachute down at night, and land in the jungle canopy. From there we would rappel down to the jungle floor. The next morning we would attack with Bazookas and Uzis the men in the Cartel camp, blow any helicopters they may have and the same with all the cocaine and other drugs we can find. Then we head back to a staging point where the Army helicopters would pick us up. We'd be outta there in less than 24 hours. Now, I know that some of you have never parachuted before. But the experts say that there is no use practicing for such a jump. We'd have just as much chance for a safe jump into the jungle on that jump as we would practicing a first jump elsewhere."

One Chief asks, "If one of us got killed, would our department's life insurance be valid? Remember, this would not be an official mission of our own department."

Chief Medina responds, "I checked that one with the insurance carrier. Their rep told me that if your local police commission approves the trip for the Chief as a valid attempt to eliminate the Cartel and that fact is written into the minutes, the insurance will be valid."

Another Chief asks, "Now I know we all are familiar with the Uzi, but how many know how to use a Bazooka?"

"Good question, how many can use a Bazooka?"

Most of the Chiefs in the room raise their hand.

"Good. We're in great shape as far as that is concerned."

Another Chief says, "Where would we leave from?"

Chief Medina responds, "Since the Army Base is here in La Vista, the copters would leave from here. Also, my department has several Bazookas with missiles, so that also works out well. I'd think that we would leave around 11:30 p.m. in a couple weeks, giving each Chief time to check with his or her police commission."

The discussion continues for another 30 minutes until Neblina Chief Tony Camargo says, "I think we've beaten this subject to death. Let's have a vote."

The others agree that the issue should be voted on.

Chief Medina says, "Okay, all in favor of the mission to eliminate the leadership of the Cartel de la Selva Tropical as described, leaving two weeks from tonight at 11:30 p.m. please raise your hands."

Every Chief in the room raises his/her hand.

"Okay Guys and Gals, thanks for your support. Now I realize that some of you may not be able to get the support you need from your local police commission. Don't worry about it. All who can get the support will meet here. Let your commission know that the family that was assassinated by the Cartel was the family of the Captain who had the 19 German Shepherd dogs at the conference and protected all of us and our families.

"Let's meet here in this conference room at 10:00 p.m. two weeks from tonight. I'll have a bus to take us to the airport, the Army side where we'll have a few minutes for orientation from the parachute team on using parachutes and rappelling gear. By the way, is there anyone here who plans on going who is already experienced in parachutes and/or rappelling gear?"

Five hands go into the air.

"That's great. What a help that will be. I assume you had experience in the Army."

The four men and one woman confirm that their experience came during their service in the Army.

The Chief continues, "This support will be such a shot in the arm for Berto. He'll want to go, but the doctors aren't about to let him do that. One more bump on his head, and he's dead, boom, just like that. The CT Scans revealed the other solid hits he's taken over the years. His head is worse than one of those North American football quarterbacks who are getting pounded every week during their football season.

"Okay Guys and Gals, time to go home. Thanks for coming such great distances for such a short meeting. I hope you agree that it was worth the trip."

As the Chiefs stand to leave, most of them thank Chief Medina for setting up the meeting and tell him not to worry about the distance. In their opinion, such a meeting was long overdue.

"The Cartel de la Selva Tropical needs to be wiped out," is the consensus of all the Chiefs at the meeting.

#

The following Monday morning, Chief Medina and his secretary, Blanca Hernández, visit Berto in the hospital. They find him in the physical therapy room with all the rehabilitation equipment.

Blanca says, "Hey Berto, how are you doing?"

"Right now, I'm hot and ready for a shower."

Chief Medina says, "Not physically, Berto, how are you progressing?"

"The doctor says I'm making great progress, but I can't have another bump on the head."

"Yes, he told us that too. One more head bump, and you're six feet under."

"Thanks Chief, I'll look forward to that."

While this may be a joke to the two men, it is a reason for tears from Blanca. She tries to hide the fact that she is crying, but the men notice it easily. The Chief puts his arm around her and hands her a box of tissue. She takes a few pieces and wipes her eyes.

The Chief says, "Berto and Blanca, I've got some very unusual news for you, especially you Berto. Are you ready for it?"

Berto responds, "Of course Chief."

The Chief asks, "Do you know where next year's Continental Games are being held?"

Blanca jumps in quickly, "I know."

Berto says, "I don't know. I can't even remember my name after that hit I got."

Blanca says, "The Games start on the tenth of May and end on the fifteenth. There, I got it right, I bet."

The Chief continues, "Okay smarty pants, that's when it will be held. But where will it be held?"

Hearing no response to his question, the Chief continues, "Okay, I'll answer my own question. Next year's Continental Games will be held on one of the islands in the Caribbean. The Island is used to having various types of competition, but this will be the first time they've tried track and field."

Berto says, "That's interesting, but why are you bringing it up now? It seems I've heard about this competition before, but I can't remember when or where."

"Here's the news: Many of us Police Chiefs throughout the continent received a telegram from the Planning Committee asking for help with security at the Games. They only sent the telegrams to departments that have Police K-9 Teams. They especially want dogs that are trained in trailing for explosives or sniffing luggage for explosives."

Berto waits a few seconds before he responds, "Wow, I assume they'll pay all the expenses."

"That's right Berto."

Blanca asks, "What about the doctors? Will they approve such a trip and such duty for Berto? Will he be safe flying at over 30,000 feet and standing on his feet all day long?"

The Chief responds, "We'll have a meeting with the doctors and the physical therapists. They'll make the final decision, of course, based on whether or not Berto even wants to go. You wouldn't be able to see the Games. They especially said they need K-9 Teams on the bus routes and at the airport to check all the luggage and packages being carried by tourists, fans, etc."

"Yes, I'd like to go. The change would be good for me, I think, but the docs will make the final decision. Chief, thanks for bringing that news. Blanca, you're crying again, why now?"

"Berto, I'm worried about you and that not so hard head of yours. Chief, here's an idea: Berto could wear one of those very expensive motorcycle helmets. They look great and people would just think he was a motorcycle officer on special assignment. If he were hit on the head or fell down for some reason, I think one of those helmets would protect him."

The Chief adds, "I think you have a good idea Blanca. It'll also be a good chance for Berto to get used to such a helmet. I know some departments where all officers wear such helmets, whether they're in a squad car or on a motorcycle. If an officer is involved in a car crash, such a helmet has proven to be of great value as he gets bounced around in the car. I know the Police Commission would be interested in using Berto to field test such a helmet.

"Blanca, tomorrow we need to go through the police catalogs on motorcycle gear and find a very high-quality helmet for Berto that we could show off at the next meeting of the Police Commission. Berto, what size hat do you wear?"

Without thinking for even a second, Berto says, "I wear an extra-large hat, size 7 5/8."

Blanca says, "Did you hear that Chief? Without thinking, Berto remembered his exact hat size. His memory is gradually coming back. Yeaaaaaaaa."

Berto joins in, "Blanca and Chief, I really appreciate your concern in this regard. I know those motorcycle helmets are of the highest quality. When an officer gets in a struggle with a thief or such, the helmet is a great advantage. Also, I'd like to see our logo on the side in bright colors. This would really impress the girls, I'm sure."

Blanca says, "Chief, did you hear that? Already, the first thing he's really interested in are the girls. He'll probably meet a flock of them on the buses and will be having dates during all his free time."

"I have to keep close to the local citizens. A lot of good information can be obtained that way. That's my only reason for wanting to check out the gals."

"Yea, sure Berto. If you think we're going to buy that story, you're crazy. In fact, you may be crazy anyway. I think you faked that hit on the head so you could have some mattress time and be ready for some special assignment like this Continental Games bit."

Berto breaks into tears which surprises the Chief and Blanca a great deal. They both remember the brain specialist telling them that unusual behavior could be expected from Berto or anyone else for that matter who has experienced such a strong hit on the head. The doctor's instructions to them were to not pay a lot of attention to the tears, just change the subject but don't let Berto think it's no big deal, because it is.

Blanca moves over to Berto and says, "Have you been a good boy today Berto?"

"Ask my physical therapist."

She does and he responds, "Yes, Blanca, Berto's been a good boy. He's the hardest worker in the class."

Berto says, "I know where you're going with that question Blanca. If I've been a good boy, I get a kiss, right, I remember you said that."

"Listen Chief. Berto says he remembers my promise. That's also a good sign. I'll give him his positive reward kiss right now."

By this time, all the men in the therapy room are watching Blanca. She is one of the most beautiful women they have ever seen, and her discussion about a kiss as a reward has certainly drawn their attention.

Blanca leans over and kisses Berto on the lips, lightly but for a long time.

All the men in the room whistle and hoot. Blanca pretends to be embarrassed, but she isn't. Berto is the hero of the day for receiving a kiss from such a beautiful woman.

Several of the men yell out, "I've been a good boy too."

Blanca laughs, "If you were as good looking as Berto, I might consider it."

Everyone really laughs including the Chief and Berto.

Blanca asks, "Chief, you never did tell us where the Games will be held next year?"

"That's right. They'll be held in the Caribbean Sea on Independence Island. They have recently finished construction of a new airport with a very long runway. In addition, their track and field at the University of Independence Island has just been refurbished. As a new country, they've never participated in the Olympics before. They'd like to hold this event as a tune-up for their own athletes to see if they're ready for world competition. They're really anxious to host this event but are concerned about security."

Berto says, "And that's where Franz and I come in, right?"

"Right," is heard by Chief Medina and Blanca.

The Chief adds, "Berto, based on your experience here at the Hotel, they want you to head up the security for the Games, coordinating naturally with the local police."

"Good, I can do that. I'd rather be in charge any day."

Everyone listening in the rehab room laughs at that remark.

Blanca says to Chief Medina, "Chief, there's someone in the hall that wants to speak with both of us."

"Okay, let's go."

The Chief and his secretary excuse themselves and go into the hall.

The Chief says, "Blanca, I don't see anyone out here. What are you pulling on me?"

"Nothing Chief, but you were just talking about an invitation to the Continental Games on the Island of Independence. Berto already received such as invitation, went there to check out the place, met many people, and received plans so he could start preparing for the security of the games. That's where he took out that hitman, El Caracol. Now there's this same invitation but much later than the first. What's going on here?"

"Blanca, I'm sorry, I should have told you. Berto has completely forgotten about his invitation and prior visit to the islands, his planning with the security team there, and his shooting El Caracol from the foot bridge to the top of the hotel, which was quite a shot with a pistol I want to tell you."

"Forgot about all that?"

"Yes, Blanca, so we have to go along with the situation and pretend this is the first invitation we received. Can you do it?"

"Of course I can do it, but it'll seem a bit awkward."

Chapter 9

As they leave the hospital, the Chief and Blanca talk about the progress that Berto is making with his memory.

Blanca says, "I think we need to talk with the psychologist about the kinds of questions we can ask Berto. I'm sure he's reached the state where he can be challenged a bit to help his memory relearn the many things he's forgotten."

"Good idea, Blanca. Let's go back in the hospital now and find the psychologist."

They return to the hospital checking the name plates on the doors as they walk down the hall of the first floor. Eventually they find what they are looking for, "Dr. Pablo Costa, Psychologist in Residence."

The Chief says, "I know Dr. Costa. He's a member of the same service club I belong to."

"Good, that may help," responds Blanca.

Opening the door, they see the Doctor's secretary, with a name plate on her desk that reads, "Verónica Castellanos."

The Chief says, "Miss Castellanos, is Doctor Costa available? Please tell him the Chief of Police would like to speak with him for a few minutes."

"Of course, Chief. Just a moment please," she says as she leaves her desk and walks into the Doctor's inner office.

She says, "Dr. Costa, the Chief of Police would like to speak with you for a few minutes."

"Uh oh, he's finally caught up with me, huh?"

His secretary laughs.

"Please show Luis in. I'd be glad to talk with him."

The secretary leaves the doctor's office and transmits the message to Chief Medina and Blanca. They are escorted into the office and asked to sit down.

"Hi Luis. What's up? It isn't the day for our weekly meeting, is it?"

"No, Pablo. I just have a need for your help with a problem. By the way, this is my secretary, Blanca Hernández."

The doctor shakes hands with Blanca as they both exchange greetings.

"Okay, what's your problem?"

"You remember reading about Captain Berto Castillo, the Superintendent of the Police K-9 School? He's suffered several severe hits to the head in the course of his duties over the past few years. A recent one has really put him in another world. Now we know what traumatic brain injury means."

"Yes, Luis. I've already met with him, administered a variety of tests, and come to some conclusions."

The Chief says, "We would like to know what can be done if anything to help his memory improve."

We recommend that the patient be provided with a laptop computer to help in this endeavor. Can you get him a laptop?"

Blanca responds, "He will definitely have one at his office. I'll personally get it and bring it to him."

"Good," replies Dr. Costa.

The Chief says, "We'll be going now. That was short and sweet. Thanks for that suggestion Doc. It'll be a big help."

"I'm glad you stopped by. We'll work hard with Berto. By the way, does he have a place where he can go after his time at the hospital is ended? I know his immediate family was killed by the Cartel?"

Blanca immediately enters the conversation, "He can stay at my house where I can take care of him."

The Chief says, "But Blanca, you're needed at the office."

"I think I'm needed more at home with Berto. You can get a good assistant from the secretarial pool. Well, come to think of it, his injury and loss of his family were job related. Hence any expense to get him back on the job comes under workers' compensation. And it doesn't hurt that I'm also a registered nurse."

"Let me think about it Blanca. At first glance, it does sound pretty good. I know the workers' comp liaison would prefer to have Berto in a private home rather than here at the hospital. It would be much less expensive."

Blanca adds, "And Chief, it sounds like the job they have in store for Berto at the International Games is more executive than a permanent assignment at the airport or a bus route. Returning to more personal matters, what would people think if Berto remained an extended period of time at my home?"

Dr. Costa says, "Oh posh, people don't pay any attention to such things anymore, especially with someone like Captain Castillo who has been wounded."

The Chief adds, "That's right. The people I know would appreciate your helping Berto when he needs it. He's as respected as you are."

Blanca adds, "Okay, we'll check with Berto the next time we see him to find out how he feels about it."

#

The following week, Chief Medina and Blanca Hernández meet with the team of doctors who are supervising the medical attention given to Captain Berto Castillo.

After everyone has had the opportunity to speak, the doctor in charge says, "Let me summarize. I believe I'm hearing that since Berto will be sent to live at the home of Miss Blanca Hernández, who is a registered nurse and the Chief's secretary, he will get extended attention and care. In this case, I think we can release him next Monday.

"As for the job overseeing the security of the Continental Games on Independence Island, if Miss Hernández will accompany him as his secretary to take a good part of the load off him, the dog, Franz, can go along but under no conditions is Berto to run alongside Franz again. The dog will have to be restricted to airport control and inspection of luggage. Obviously the same is true for train stations or bus stations. And the idea of a motorcycle helmet is an excellent idea. Be sure and proceed with that idea as soon as possible."

Chief Medina says, "We have already purchased a helmet for Berto. He'll start wearing it as of today."

"May we see it?" asks the doctor.

"Of course. It's right here. I'll pass it around. Check it out for protection of the various parts of the head, not just for its beauty."

The Chief removes a beautiful blue and white helmet from a sack and passes it to his left.

The doctor in charge says, "Let's take five minutes while we pass this helmet around. If you have any concerns, make a note that you can give to me."

Chief Medina says, "This helmet passes all the various tests for a person who participates in motorcycle races. However, after one fall, the helmet must be discarded even though it costs $900.00. The same general rule will apply for Berto. After one hit on the helmet, it will be discarded because it can be weakened without our knowing it."

Everyone agrees that is a good idea regardless of the cost.

One of the doctors asks, "Can I put it on?"

The Chief responds, "Of course, although it is rather large at 7 5/8."

Various doctors try on the helmet. They all ask another doctor to hit them on the head. Each one is pleased with the results of the hit.

Chief Medina says, "Yes, that helmet can withstand a very hard hit on the head."

After the break, a poll is taken of the doctors and their views on the helmet. Everyone agrees that it is a good choice and likes the idea of discarding the helmet after a serious hit on the head.

The meeting is adjourned with the decision that Chief Medina and Blanca can accompany the doctor who will give Berto the good news.

#

In Berto's room, Blanca stands against a wall as the doctor and Chief Medina give Berto the news. As she observes Berto's reaction when he is told that he can stay at Blanca's home, she begins to cry.

Berto says, "Blanca come over here."

She hesitantly walks over to the hospital bed with tears in her eyes.

Berto asks her to sit on the chair beside the bed which she does. He then turns in the bed and puts his arms around Blanca as best he can. He hugs her tightly. She cries even more now.

Berto says, "Blanca, what a nice thing to do for me. Taking care of me starting next week. You'll get awfully tired of me under foot."

"No Berto. You need some help if you're going to recuperate from this horrible injury. I'm happy to be the one to provide that help."

"Aren't you afraid of what people will say?"

"Not in the least. Your recuperation is much more important that what people might say."

"Okay, if that's the way you feel about it. I'll certainly enjoy having you care for me. What does that entail, Doctor?"

"You can walk, but you must have Blanca at your side. You could get dizzy very fast and fall. No more showers for a while. It's the bathtub for you. Again, that standing on a slippery surface is rather dangerous. Blanca'll have to bathe you in the tub. Also, she'll have to help you dress. No more standing up to dress. You'll have to sit on the edge of the bed while she helps you dress. No more shaving while standing. If you have an electric razor, use it sitting down in front of a mirror."

"I have an electric razor."

"Good. Now here at the hospital, all the beds have sides which can be pulled up so the patient can't fall out of the bed."

Blanca adds, "I don't have such a bed, I'm sorry."

Chief Medina says, "The purchase of such a bed from the hospital supply store will be perfectly proper as an expense of the injury."

The doctor asks, "How large is your bedroom, Blanca?"

"It's very large, in an old-fashioned home. I only have my single bed in the master bedroom."

"Good, put the new bed in that same bedroom. I'd rather have Berto sleeping in a room where you're close by. That way in case of a problem, you can hear him and react quickly."

Berto says, "Now I know what it means to have a live-in patient."

Everyone laughs.

"Feed him in bed for a while, and then gradually help him go to the dining room table. After a while, he should be able to walk alone to the table.

"Now Berto, I need to go, but let me stress one thing to you. You can't have any more falls or be hit on the head ever again. Don't put yourself in a position where you might be hit on the head. Use your dog, Franz, more. Call in backup. Every investigation of a mysterious nature might result in your getting hit on the head. Wear your helmet all the time at first in Blanca's home during the day. Whenever you have to walk, wear your helmet. Whenever you have to drive in a car, wear your helmet. You'll need to be brought to the hospital from time to time for us to check you. Wear your helmet, even when you are walking down the hall to the examination room. Have you got that?"

"I'm sure if I forget, Nurse Hernández will be right there reminding me."

"Chief," asks the doctor, "if you don't mind my asking, what are the financial considerations with Blanca helping Berto all the time?"

"Since this is a work-related injury, all expenses will be covered by workers compensation. That includes Berto's salary as well as Blanca's. In either case, we'd have to hire a full-time nurse. I'll get a new secretary from the secretary's pool. This time I'll get a good-looking secretary."

Everyone laughs since Blanca is known to be the most beautiful secretary in the police department.

The Chief walks over to Blanca, hugs her, and says, "Can you forgive me for that comment, beautiful?"

"Yes, Chief, this one time I can forgive you."

The Chief kisses her on the cheek and says with tears in his eyes, "I'll miss you like crazy."

"Me too you, Chief," she says with tears in her eyes.

The doctor says, "I'd better leave here, or I'll start crying." Off he goes out the door.

#

The following Monday, an ambulance from the hospital brings Berto to the home of Blanca. Two EMTs carry him in a stretcher into the house to be greeted by Blanca who says, "Right in this master bedroom guys. Just plunk him down in that hospital bed. Pull up the sides when you're done so he won't escape."

Everyone laughs.

"Escape, will you? I'm not a prisoner. I'm a patient," adds Berto.

"Of course, a patient." The EMTs lift Berto gently from the stretcher to the hospital bed. He sits up with two pillows behind him.

As the EMTs leave, Blanca thanks them following which she returns to the master bedroom.

Berto asks, "Where's Franz?"

"He's in his bed in the guest room. I don't dare let him in here. He'd be all over you which is the last thing you need."

"How is he doing?"

"About like you. He needs rest and recuperation. Don't worry about him. He knows me and takes directions better than you do."

"You'll watch over him, right?"

"Yes Berto."

As she walks over to Berto, he lowers the protective siding. With Blanca standing beside him, Berto grabs her and pulls her onto the bed where he gives her a big kiss on the mouth.

"Whoa cowboy," responds Blanca as she slips out of the bed and lifts the railing back to its protective position. "Boy, are you a fast worker?"

"That wasn't a fast worker. That was just a sign of affection and appreciation for what you are doing for me."

"If you keep that up, you'll be right back in the hospital. I'm your nurse."

"Oh, I'm sorry. I must have misunderstood."

"What a joke. I've heard about you from the other secretaries. How much you love the hugs and kisses. Well, Buddy, those days are over forever."

"Forever? You can't be serious. How can I survive without an occasional kiss from you?"

"Well, maybe an occasional kiss if you're a good boy, just like the rules in the hospital."

"Okay, show me now what you mean."

"Don't you ever stop operating?"

"Blanca, I've never told anyone this before, and I'm completely serious. As you know, I lost my beloved wife. If I don't get some occasional affection from you, I'll waste away thinking no one cares for me anymore."

Berto begins to cry again, but this is not just an occasional tear. He starts sobbing and has to grab a tissue from the box near his bed.

Blanca puts her hands on his head. "Berto, I understand completely. What you have been through almost no one would ever comprehend. I'll try hard to meet your needs, I promise, if you won't take advantage of me."

"I won't, I promise. Just let me hold you from time to time. I don't need to kiss you every moment, but I do need to hold you from time to time. You feel so good and perk me up when you're close to me."

"Okay, I think we understand each other. Put the side down on the bed and let me hug you."

Berto quickly unhooks and drops the siding of the bed. Blanca moves close to him and holds him tightly to her. Berto was correct in his evaluation of such a move. He perks up and smiles. When she withdraws from him, she can see the smile on his face. She gives him a quick kiss and says, "Was that something like you were talking about?"

"Yes, Blanca, that was exactly what I was talking about."

"That was special for a little boy who needs his mother, and you qualify."

"I sure do, and I feel much better now. Thank you Blanca."

Blanca pulls up the side rail and shows Berto the electric control for the foot and head tilt.

"You should really love it here. I'll get some magazines for you. Any preference as to books?"

"Get me one of those electronic screens where I can order any book I want."

"Okay. As for now, it's time to eat lunch. What would you like?"

"I feel like I've already been fed my lunch."

"Oh Berto."

"You can't imagine how good you felt to me. With that positive reinforcement, you could get me to do anything."

"Positive reinforcement?"

"I really have to admit that being held close to you is certainly a pleasant reward."

"Oh you're silly, but I have to admit that you're learning some important things. So you think I'm a pleasant reward, or a stimulus which increases the frequency of a particular behavior?

"You sure are."

Blanca laughs. "We studied all about that in nursing school, particularly in dealing with children. Now don't get touchy, I didn't say you were a child."

"I don't mind being a child with you around Mom."

Blanca responds, "I'm beginning to understand, and it makes sense to me. You see I'm learning too. Now for lunch, I'll make a couple sandwiches, with some fruit, cookies, and milk. Okay?"

Berto answers, "That'll be great. Shall I come out there to eat?"

"Not yet. You heard the doctor's instructions."

Chapter 10

Night falls and time for preparing for bed arrives in the home of Blanca Hernández. When she walks into her bedroom and sees Berto in his hospital bed reading she says, "Time for a bath, little one."

"Okay, are you going to have any trouble with this? You've never been married, you know."

"Yes, Berto, I've never been married, but I was a nurse for many years bathing all sorts of people. No it won't bother me. Will it bother you?"

"Not in the least."

"Okay, let's go. This will be a nightly episode."

Berto undresses with the help of Blanca and walks slowly into the bathroom. She tells him that she will leave for a few minutes for him to take care of his personal needs.

A few minutes later, Berto calls out, "Okay, Mom, come and get me."

She previously filled the tub with warm water and helps Berto step into the tub and sit down.

"How's the temperature of the water?"

"Great. Do it like this every night and we're in business."

"Yea, and what business?"

"I'll have to think on that answer for a while, Nurse Hernández."

Blanca takes a washcloth and soap and washes Berto's body from face to toes.

"This feels so good. I haven't had a bath for many years. I always used to take showers."

"Me too Berto. Okay, here's a washcloth for you to wash your private parts."

Berto takes the warm washcloth and does as directed.

"Time to stand up and get out. Now slowly, let me help you."

Blanca helps Berto step dripping wet out of the tub onto the safety of the carpeted floor. As he holds onto the grab bar, she dries him as well as she can. He takes a small towel and finishes the drying job.

Blanca hands him his pajamas and helps him put them on. She can see that he is starting to get weak, so she sets him down on the chair in the bathroom to rest a few minutes.

When he feels stronger, Blanca helps him into bed after which she pulls up the side rail.

"Mommy, do I get a kiss good night?"

"Of course son."

Blanca kisses Berto on the mouth for several seconds.

"Thank you Mommy. Now I can sleep well."

As Blanca looks into Berto's eyes before saying "goodnight," she notices something that no nurse wants to see in the eyes of a patient who has suffered a traumatic brain injury, eye pupils of different sizes.

She says nothing but, "Goodnight Berto. I'll be coming back in a few minutes myself after I let Franz out."

"Thank you for taking care of Franz."

"I'll leave the lights on until I return, okay?"

"Sure, that'll be fine."

Closing the door, she moves quickly to her phone and calls the ER at the local hospital.

"Dr. Francisco Gutiérrez please."

She breathes a sigh of relief when she is informed that Dr. Gutiérrez is on duty."

"Doctor, this is Blanca Hernández. Berto Castillo, as you know, is staying at my house during his recuperation. I just put him down to bed and noticed that his pupils are of different sizes."

"Thanks for noticing that Blanca. That is a key sign as you know. I'll send an ambulance over to your house without siren and flashing lights. They'll bring Berto back here to the ER for some exams."

"Thank you doctor. You have my address?"

"Yes, we have all the addresses in every ambulance where TBI patients are staying. Goodbye."

"Goodbye Doctor."

Blanca lets Franz out for a few minutes and then returns to her bedroom. As soon as she does, Franz rushes over to Berto's bed and tries to get the side rail down. Blanca follows the dog and lowers the rail. As soon as she does, Franz puts his front paws on the bed and starts licking Berto's arms. The dog is obviously very agitated.

All this activity brings more anxiety to Blanca. She is very glad that she phoned the doctor since she has read of some dogs' being sensitive to impending seizures of their masters.

Berto says, "Blanca, what's going on here? Why is Franz so agitated?"

Blanca has a problem now, to tell what she suspects or not. She decides to tell the whole story.

"Berto, when I looked into your eyes before leaving the bedroom a few minutes ago, I noticed your pupils were of different sizes. This is one of the signs of impending problems for a person who has suffered a traumatic brain injury. I phoned Dr. Gutiérrez at the ER. He's sending an ambulance right over to take you back to the ER. Then when I returned to your room, I too was disturbed by

Franz's behavior. Some dogs are known to sense an impending problem, such as a seizure for their master."

As she is talking, Blanca notices that Berto is beginning to have a seizure. He is beginning to shake and stare straight ahead. Even though Blanca talks to him, he does not respond. Although she is a trained nurse, it is hard for Blanca to hold back tears.

She hears a knock at the door. She rushes to open it and admits two EMTs with a stretcher.

"In here guys. I believe he is having a seizure right now."

The EMTs move quickly into Blanca's bedroom and see Berto. He is still shaking and staring straight ahead.

"What is your name?" asks the senior EMT.

Berto does not respond.

The other EMT takes a flashlight and shines it across both of Berto's eyes. His pupils do not move. They continue to maintain their irregular size.

The EMTs take his vital signs.

The Senior EMT says, "Let's get him outta here fast."

They put Berto on the stretcher and move quickly out of the house to the back of the ambulance, placing Berto inside and strapping him tightly. Blanca tells them she will follow along in her car.

Returning to her house and kneeling down by Franz, she rubs his head and back and says, "Franz, good dog. I need to go to the hospital now. I won't leave you alone too long. There's food and water in your special tray. You be a good boy, and I'll be back soon."

She hugs the dog, leaves the room, and closes the door to the room. Passing by the small table at the foot of the stairs, she picks up her purse and cell phone.

As soon as she leaves her house, she gets into her car and heads for the hospital.

When she gets to the hospital, she heads for the waiting room. Knowing that the doctors in the ER will have no information at this time, she takes her cell phone and calls Police Chief Luis Medina.

"Chief, this is Blanca. I'm at the ER with Berto. He started to show some signs that typically lead to a seizure, so I called the doctor here at the ER. The doctor sent an ambulance, and Berto is here now for tests, etc. ... Yes, he was having a seizure when the EMTs arrived at my house. That is not too uncommon, to have a seizure several weeks and even months after a traumatic brain injury. After he is done in the ER, they'll send him to room 506 which is a specialized room for people in conditions such as his. There's a room next door for a night doctor to sleep in and be quickly available if needed. There is also lots of specialized equipment in room 506 for traumatic brain injured patients. In addition, it's out of the way and not too noticeable if a Cartel sends a hitman to find him and kill him."

The Chief responds, "Blanca, thanks for the call. I'll be right there and that idea about a room on the fifth floor for Berto is a good one. I'll make sure there's a guard at the door to that room day and night."

"Thanks Chief. I'll see you in a few minutes. Goodbye."

Chapter 11

At the headquarters of the Cartel deep in the Amazon Jungle, Junior is leading a meeting of the various Cartel sub-leaders. He says, "The latest report from La Vista is that Captain Berto Castillo is still alive in the hospital there. The newspaper said he had a seizure and was close to death. Maybe it's time we helped him on his journey."

Everyone laughs.

"But the problem is the same we had in the beginning of this venture, how to do it?"

El Catalán says, "In a hospital such things are easy. First we get a white uniform like everyone wears. So the disguise is easy. Then the hitman in white sneaks into Berto's room. With a syringe loaded with some poison he gives Castillo a shot in the tube coming from the IV bag into his arm."

Junior says, "What the heck's an IV bag?"

"That's the bag of liquid hanging above almost every patient to make sure he doesn't get dehydrated. That means to be sure the patient doesn't die from thirst. The hitman sneaks into the room, and puts the needle of the syringe into the tube leading from the bag of IV into the patient's blood stream. The poison gets to the patient's heart quickly, and he dies. It takes the docs at the hospital a long time to figure out what happened. The only problem is to figure out how to get into Captain Castillo's room. One good way is to climb up the fire escape and enter through a window. And then leave by the same window."

Junior says, "Hey, that sounds like a great plan. First, I think we need to send one person to the hospital to check the layout, the schedule of the nurses, and so on. It's too bad we can't send a woman as a nurse. A woman would have a much better chance to get into that room. If everything looks easy, then that person should do the hit immediately."

Junior's wife, Betty, speaks up, "Hey, how about sending me? I've sat here for a long time just listening to you guys plan a large number of activities without ever saying a word. Well I'm finally speaking up. You said a woman could do this better than a man. Well, here I am, ready to go. Just help me get the syringe with the poison and the white dress belonging to a nurse."

Junior replies, "No way Sweetheart. You're staying with me."

"Okay, you go with me, and I'll be staying with you."

Everyone laughs.

Several say, "She got you there Jefe."

Junior thinks about the proposition for a while.

He then asks one of his closest compatriots, "El Catalán, what do you think of this idea?"

"Well Jefe, I would never say this under any other conditions, but I think it's time for you to take such an assignment in the field. Staying here all the time makes a man rusty. Such a mission would sharpen your senses and especially with Betty. The two of you would really enjoy working together on such an important mission."

"I was afraid you would say something like that."

Again, everyone laughs.

"Betty, are you sure you want to do this? We might not make it back, one of us or both of us."

"Yes, Junior, I know that. But I need a little respect around here besides being something to look at. Maybe if I did this with you, the guys would look at me differently."

Several speak out, "I don't ever want to look at you differently."

Everyone laughs again.

Junior says, "Take it easy guys, you're getting close to some trouble with me. Betty is mine, and your job is to always protect her. Oh heck, I know you will do that at the risk of your own lives. Forgive me, huh?"

Everyone nods his head up and down.

"Okay, let's get serious now. Give me some time to think about this and talk with a few of you. If I lost Betty, you'd have the hardest Jefe in the world to get along with."

El Catalán says, "We know that Junior. If we lost Betty, it'd be very hard on all of us. We all love her as you know."

"Yes, I know."

"But to really be a part of this Cartel, each one should take a share of the dangerous missions. If you two took this mission and succeeded, you'd really be proud of yourselves and understand much better what the rest of us go through when we go on a mission."

"As usual, El Catalán has convinced me. He always does. Okay, here it is. If I get killed on this mission, El Catalán takes over the leadership of the Cartel with no arguments from anyone, got it?"

All heads go up and down.

"If I don't make it back and Betty does, she's free to choose her man, got it?"

All heads go up and down again.

"I'd like four men to go with us on the burros to Dos Brazos' place and bring the burros back here. El Catalán will select the four persons, men, or women, and the four will select the food and weapons that we will take. I think we have lots of our own syringes since we occasionally sell heroin. Prepare four for Betty, using liquid rat poison in the largest syringes that we have. Prepare some decent civilian clothes for Betty and me to change into after a shower at Dos Brazos' place. You see, I remember you've told me that Dos Brazos has a great shower now. That way, we'll really look proper for the trip on the bus to the hospital."

One Cartel member yells out, "Hey Junior, you'll have to have Betty cut your hair and shave you like she did for the last two that went on a mission."

Now everyone is looking carefully at Junior to see his reaction.

He says, "You're right. What's good for you guys is good for me too. It may save my life looking like a regular guy. What say Betty, right after lunch?"

"Of course Junior, I've been waiting to cut your hair and shave you for a long time now. But first you need to take a shower and soap down your hair and beard."

"Okay, I knew there would be a catch to it."

El Catalán says, "Pardon me Junior, if I may say a word. You guys check out what you have just witnessed. Did you notice the manner that Junior accepted the need for a haircut and a shave? That's real leadership. He's one of us and will do whatever it takes to accomplish the mission. Three cheers for Junior."

Everyone yells, "Hip, hip, hooray. Hip, hip, hooray. Hip, hip, hooray." Then they all clap while Betty gives Junior a big hug to show her pride in his leadership as well.

#

The following morning, Junior, Betty, and four other members of the Cartel are ready to leave the camp. The six riders are atop burros. Two other burros are with the group carrying food supplies for the three-day trip.

Junior gives last minute instructions, "Okay, let the head burro lead the group. He knows the path better than we do. Keep alert for hanging snakes that appear to be branches or vines. Also, these burros are tasty meat for a charging cougar or jaguar. Fire first and ask questions later.

"Of the group, Betty and I will keep an eye open to the front, number four will look to the right, number three to the left, number two to the right rear, and number one to the left rear. This should give us good vision as we try to anticipate any attack. Any animal at some distance that stays there leave alone. If a beast starts an attack, alert the group and start firing. We all have Uzis with thirty-two 9 mm shells each and semi-automatic 9 mm pistols with seventeen shells each.

"We'll stop at the cabin for the night. And don't forget, the Llumista Indians still use darts and arrows dipped in curare. We have no antidote against curare. If you're hit by a poisonous dart or arrow, there's nothing we can do for you unless you want a bullet in the head. Keep an eye out for those Indians as well. Good luck to us all."

#

As the morning sun peers through the trees, the group proceeds amid cheers from many members of the cartel. Each rider knows the danger of the Rainforest so there isn't much social chatter as all are intense on their lookout duty. This is the first trip that Betty has taken through the Rainforest in a long time. The last time was when she was a little girl. She is excited and happy to be going along finally.

#

After several hours of a pleasant and uneventful ride, Junior reins up his burro and says to the group, "Let's break out some lunch but keep moving as we eat. I think we'll be safer that way."

One wrangler moves to the side of a pack burro and opens the side pockets to find the lunch. He takes enough for everyone and distributes the food as he moves back and forth through the group.

Some three hours later, black clouds appear as the afternoon wears on. Soon the tiny group is inundated in a cool rain that refreshes everyone, even the burros.

Junior yells out trying to be heard over the sound of the storm, "Remember, some of these wild beasts like these storms because they can sneak up on people in the mist of the rains and noise of the storm. Keep alert."

Thirty minutes pass by, and the sky becomes blue and the heat intensifies. But all members of the group appreciate moving along in wet clothing that keeps them cooler. All members are also appreciative that no wild beasts took advantage of the storm to attack them.

Another two hours pass and Junior yells out, "There's the cabin." The riders direct their animals toward the cabin.

Everyone knows this means a chance for a rest and a night's sleep under a roof. In addition, there is a lean-to where the burros may rest and eat the grass that is there.

The wranglers lead the burros to their resting place and unload their packs and saddles from them. Betty directs the men as they take into the cabin those items needed for dinner. The main item is a large pot filled with stew that was prepared in camp.

The men check the inside of the cabin to be sure there are no snakes or other problems present.

Betty asks one of the men to start a fire so she can prepare a hot meal. The cabin has a fireplace with a device that can hold a large pot over the fire. Betty hangs the pot on the device and swings it over the fire. Since the stew was not cold, it heats up quickly. Bread is brought forth with a preserve made from wild berries.

Everyone enjoys the meal and the chat as they feel much safer in the cabin. They alternate taking turns outside as guard of the cabin, the group, and the burros.

Blankets are laid out all over the floor and each one picks his place to sleep. As they take their places including guard duty, the sound of wild animals can be heard from various locations in the jungle. Each one lies quietly listening to the sounds. Some are made by animals fighting. They all check to be sure their Uzis and pistols are within a few inches from their sleeping place. Soon they are all asleep. Two hours later, two men change guard duty. This occurs every two hours from 10:00 p.m. till 6:00 a.m.

Junior holds Betty's hand during most of the night. He wants to be sure she is nearby and safe.

The next morning, some hot coffee is prepared, and rolls, bananas, and oranges are available for those who want them. They are used to a light so called "continental breakfast." Everyone comments on how good the breakfast tastes.

As soon as breakfast is over, the group makes ready to leave without wasting any time. The burros are fed and watered. Saddles are strapped on the burros as well as the supplies on the pack animals. In a few minutes more, the group is off and moving again.

Junior says to Betty, "Betty, there's one thing I didn't mention in our planning sessions. When we go into the city, we try to talk like the city folk or else they'll think we're a bunch of hicks. Can you do that?"

"Sure Junior. I am aware that at the Cartel camp we talk one way and another way when we are among educated people. It'll be fun trying out my new language."

"Thanks Betty, that'll help. It'll be like talking to El Catalán."

They both laugh.

#

This pattern of travel is followed for two more days with little change in sequence. The food grows scarcer with each passing meal, but finally Junior yells out, "Here come the kids of Dos Brazos."

Several children of various ages come running to greet the strangers. They lead the group to the corrals behind the home of Dos Brazos. After the saddles and packs are removed from the burros, the tired but faithful animals are led into the corrals where they quickly spot the hay and water.

Dos Brazos joins the group. He hasn't seen Junior for a long time.

"Hey Junior. Welcome to my home, you, and your entire group. I see you have lost a lot of your hair."

"Thank you Dos Brazos for your greeting. Yes, Betty cut my hair while everyone was laughing at me. By the way, I understand you have a shower now."

"Yes, you are all welcome to use it. It is in the barn. I'll have one of the kids show you. Who'll go first?"

"The one woman in our group, Betty."

"Oh good, Betty is in your group. I haven't seen her in a long time. Where is she?"

"She's tending the burros. She'll be right here any minute now."

At this moment, Betty rounds the corner from the corrals and sees Dos Brazos who quickly walks over to her, gives her a big hug and a kiss on the cheek.

"Betty, it's been a long time since you're been here."

"That's right, Dos Brazos. You've sure got a pack of kids."

"They are a blessing from the Lord. And Betty, Junior says you are the first to use our shower."

"Thank you Junior," Betty replies as she takes the bag containing her city clothes from Junior. Then she takes the hand of a teen-age girl who leads her to the barn and the shower.

"What's your name?" asks Betty.

"I'm Vera."

"Glad to meet you Vera. Thanks for helping me. How old are you?"

"Although I'm short for my age, I'm 16 years old. I don't get to see pretty women very often except my older sister."

"Oh yes, I've heard of her. She's beautiful, correct?"

"She sure is. It's fun to watch the men make a big fuss over her. I bet they do the same thing over you since you are so pretty. As for the shower, for 50 cents we have hot water now."

Betty replies, "That's great. I'll really like that."

"It'll be cold at first until you adjust it."

Vera watches as Betty takes out her fresh clothing from her bag that she will wear into the City of La Vista.

Betty quickly disrobes and hangs her jungle clothing on a hook that Vera points out near the shower. Then taking the handle, Betty turns on the water as she steps into the shower.

"Oh, this is cold." Then she adjusts the water so that it is nice and warm. She takes a plastic bottle of shampoo and washes her hair. Then with a bar of soap she washes her complete body. After she washes the shampoo from her hair and the soap from her body, she hears a voice. It's Vera again.

"Betty, I'm sorry. I didn't show you where the towels are."

As Betty turns off the water, she opens the shower door but stays in the shower dripping water. Vera hands her a large, dry towel.

"Thank you. I'd better get dry before I get out of the shower and start shivering."

"Oh nobody shivers in this part of the Rainforest. It's always so warm."

"We'll see," Betty says as she quickly dries herself. After stepping out of the shower, she finds her clean clothes and puts them on while saying, "You're right Vera. I'm not shivering any longer."

Vera laughs. "You see, I told you. May I call you Betty?"

"Of course, everyone does. Thank you for staying and watching over me when I took a shower. What can I do for you?"

"Well, if you don't mind. You are so pretty. Can I kiss you and get a kiss from you?"

"You mean two kisses?"

"Yes, if you don't mind?"

"That would be nice. Stand up here on the bench. I'll help you."

Betty helps Vera stand up straight and tall on the bench while maintaining her balance.

"You are so pretty yourself Vera. It'll be a pleasure to kiss you. Are you ready?"

"Oh yes, I am, and thank you."

Betty takes Vera's head in her hands and gives her a big kiss on her cheek after which she hugs her. Vera then gives Betty a kiss on the cheek.

Vera replies, "Oh that was so nice Betty. I love you. That was such a nice kiss. I'll always remember it, always. Goodbye. Oh and one more thing, when you were ready to get into the shower, you were so pretty."

"You're a pretty young lady yourself. Someday you'll be a pretty woman and not a young lady. Maybe we can be friends till then. Would you like that?"

"I sure would. Can I write you a letter from time to time?"

"Oh you can write at your age, can you? That's wonderful. I'll look forward to your letters. I live in the jungle you know. Just give your letters to someone coming into the Rainforest to the Cartel de la Selva Tropical."

"Will you write back to me?"

"I sure will, you'll see."

Betty gives Vera another kiss on the cheek and helps her down from the bench.

"Goodbye Betty. Remember, I'll always love you."

"I'll always love you too Vera."

Vera runs off with a smile of happiness on her face.

#

After a night's rest by the guests in a variety of tents, the wife and older daughters of Dos Brazos fix a tasty meal for the visitors and feed them on the picnic table in the back yard. Then the visitors lay their plans for the next few days.

Junior asks, "Dos Brazos, would it be all right if my four men stayed in your back yard for a couple days and nights? Betty and I have some business that will keep us in La Vista for a few days. It would make no sense for the four men to return to our camp and then come back here. We can pay you for all expenses and whatever else you charge."

"Of course they can stay. You're right that it would make no sense for them to return to your camp and then turn right around again and come back here. I'll not charge them anything if they can meet my one condition."

"What's the condition?"

"I've got eight new horses that need to be broken. Your men appear to be cowboys. If they could take the time and bumps to break the horses, there would be no charge for their staying here."

Junior looks at his men. Each one is moving his head up and down.

One says, "Junior and Dos Brazos, that would be great. We haven't had the opportunity to show a horse who's boss in a long time. It would really help the waiting time go fast and be a lot of fun. But we would want to at least pay Dos Brazos and his wife for the food we would eat and some extra for the shower and towels that we would use."

Dos Brazos wife adds, "I think you men have some clothes that need washing as well. I'd be glad to do that as part of the bargain."

Everyone laughs.

Junior adds, "Well it looks like a deal. Thanks for the opportunity. These men are cowboys, as you guessed Dos

Brazos, and good ones too. Your kids will really enjoy watching them break the horses. Perhaps your older boys can ask some questions about how to break a horse. They could learn a lot."

Chapter 12

The next morning, at exactly 9:00 a.m., the bus stops in front of the home of Dos Brazos. All the family and cowboys are outside ready to wave goodbye to Junior and Betty.

One wrangler puts his arms around Junior and says, "Jefe, you know this could be a dangerous assignment. We may never see you again. Remember what your men think of you and how much we have appreciated your leadership."

"Gracias Rafael. I'll be all right, but if I'm not and Betty returns alone, take care of her, please."

"Yes, Jefe, I promise, with my life I'll protect her."

"Gracias Rafael. Chao."

Vera runs over to Betty and hugs her. Betty gives Vera a kiss on the cheek and hugs her.

"You'll come back, right Betty?"

"Yes, Darling. I'll see you in a few days. Goodbye."

Taking Betty's hand and their one suitcase, Junior leads Betty onto the bus. After paying the fee, they take a seat in the middle of the bus. As the bus departs, Betty and Junior wave at their friends and associates standing at the bus stop who are all waving back at them.

The bus stops from time to time as it makes its way to La Vista. Gradually Junior and Betty doze in their seat even though the ride is not too comfortable. This helps pass the time quickly.

Eventually they hear the driver yell, "La Vista International Airport, next stop."

Junior says, "Come on Betty, we get off here."

Taking the suitcase from the overhead rack, Junior leads Betty by the hand as they depart the bus saying goodbye to the other passengers.

Once on the sidewalk in front of the airport, Betty says, "Junior, why did we get off so soon?"

"The guys tell me they always get off here at the airport. It makes people think we're taking a flight to some foreign country. After a short walk in the terminal, we take a taxi from here to a hotel generally. That makes other people think we have just come in on a flight from a foreign country. We'll want the hotel that is closest to the hospital. There is generally a large hotel near a hospital for the families from out of town who want to visit patients."

Junior leads Betty on a short walk through the terminal and then back outside to the row of taxis. They get into the one at the head of the row.

The driver asks, "Where to please?"

"What's the name of that hotel near the hospital. I forget."

"Oh that's the Hotel Montoya."

"That's right. That's where we want to go please."

The driver leaves the airport area by a maze of roads, but finally gets onto the highway that leads to the hospital. Soon they stop in front of the Hotel Montoya. After Junior pays the driver, he and Betty walk into the lobby of the hotel and head for the counter to check in.

#

Ten minutes later, the bell boy opens the door to room 404, leaves the bag on the special rack for suitcases, opens the drapes, and waits for a tip. Junior tips the boy liberally and closes the door after he leaves.

Betty goes to the window and looks out over the City.

"Oh look, Junior, one block away, the hospital, see."

Junior walks to the window and is pleased to see the hospital so close.

Junior says, "Sweetheart, I'm not sure about this mission. This may be our last time together."

"You're worried, aren't you Junior? It's like El Catalán said, 'Since you don't go on missions very often, you've gotten rusty.'"

"Maybe that's it."

#

After breakfast the next morning, Junior says, "I'm going to walk over to the hospital, check things out, and buy you a nurse's uniform with white shoes and white stockings. What sizes do you wear?"

Betty responds, "Size eight in the dress with size seven in the shoes and stockings."

Junior adds, "It's better that we are not seen together right now."

"I guess you're right, but I hate to see you go. You won't try anything risky, will you?"

"No, of course not, Betty. You just stay here, relax, watch some television, and I'll be back before lunch. Now give me a kiss goodbye."

"I don't like the way you said that."

Junior kisses Betty for the longest time. Afterwards, he turns and leaves the room.

The walk to the hospital is pleasant enough, with birds singing everywhere as they jump across the freshly watered lawns looking for something to eat. As he arrives at the hospital, Junior walks in and goes past the receptionist's desk as if he belonged there.

First, he thinks, *I need to find out which room Captain Berto Castillo is in.*

He decides the best way to do that is to start walking along the entire bottom floor, take the stairs to the next floor up, and walk its entire length, and continue that pattern until he comes across a room with a police guard.

He notes an abundance of police officers in the building. He stops at the end of the first-floor hallway and looks out the window. He sees a large number of police cars in the parking lot.

Uh oh, they suspect a hit on the good captain. This won't be as easy as we thought. I need to check out the fire escapes once I learn what room he's in.

Junior continues his walking pattern. When he takes the stairways to the fifth floor, he opens the door to the hallway and immediately sees several policemen in front of room 506. He walks past the room and concludes that Berto is in this particular room.

Next he goes to the floor below and finds that room 406 is empty. He goes inside and checks the window. It is large with only a single pane. Much to his disappointment, the window is locked tight with a handle that clamps down firmly on the frame of the window.

He thinks, *If all the windows are like this, we've got a problem to solve. Wait, this won't be so hard. Betty enters as a nurse, opens the window for me standing outside waiting for her, and in I go.*

Returning to the first floor, he finds the room where they sell nurses' uniforms. Walking inside like he owned the place; he tells the clerk that his wife asked him to pick up another white uniform for her. He tells the clerk that they live in a rural area where such uniforms are not available. Giving the clerk the size that he wants, he looks over the other materials for sale as the clerk selects a uniform.

The clerk says, "The uniforms come in various materials: 100 percent cotton which is cool but requires ironing, a mix of cotton and polyester which keeps a press better but is warmer to wear, and so on."

Junior likes the idea of the cooler uniform and requests that one. He then asks about white shoes to go with the uniform and white stockings. He gives her the sizes. The clerk says that those are very common sizes for the younger nurses. She then goes to the storeroom and returns with the appropriate shoes and stockings.

Junior looks everything over and is pleased with the quality of the material and craftsmanship. "I'll take them, thank you."

After paying for the clothing, Junior leaves the hospital. As he walks across the hospital grounds, he checks out the fire escapes and is pleased. Each room has an entrance to the fire escape by means of the window. In addition, there is one ladder on each side of the hospital and one at the front and back of the hospital, for a total of four in all.

This place was built to exit patients quickly in case of a fire, Junior thinks to himself.

Back in the hotel at the entrance to room 404, he takes his plastic key and opens the door. He finds an anxious Betty who comes running to him.

"I thought the police must have taken you."

"Oh Betty, relax. This will be a piece of cake."

They spend the rest of the day relaxing, watching television, and sleeping. After having dinner in the hotel restaurant, they pack their few things in their one bag. Betty then dresses in her nurse's uniform. It fits perfectly with her beauty contest shape. She places her other clothing in the bag that Junior carries.

After it gets dark, Betty takes out two syringes loaded with rat poison. The needles are protected so that no one would be accidentally pricked. A serious injury or death could result from such an accident. She places the syringes in a small zipper case that looks very professional.

Junior puts his arms around her and says, "If something happens and we get separated, you take a taxi to the airport and then the bus to the home of Dos Brazos and his family. They'll take care of you until I arrive, or our cowboys will escort you back to our camp."

"Junior, you really have some fears about this project, don't you?"

"Well, it helps to keep sharp by being a bit concerned about a mission. Everything will go just fine. Here's what we'll do. I'll climb the fire escape and wait outside the window of room 506, remember that number, 506. A few minutes after I arrive outside the window, you'll take the elevator to the fifth floor, get out, and walk with determination to room 506. There'll be at least one or two police officers outside room 506. Just tell them that you need to take the vital signs of the patient and will be just a few minutes.

"Enter the room and inject the poison into the tube that feeds into the patient's arm. The poison will go straight into his blood stream and he will be dead in a very few minutes. After you have injected the poison, put the shield back on the needle and place the equipment back into your small case. Then come to the window and open it using all your strength. I'll help you out the window, and we'll go down the fire escape. Hey that's a good name for it, an escape. Then we'll head for the airport by taxi, and get the late evening bus to Dos Brazos' home. Got it?"

"Yes, Junior, I've got it. I hope I don't flub it up. I've never killed anyone before, you know."

"Just remember all the pain this police officer has caused the Cartel. That should give you enough motivation."

"I hope so. How much time do you think the police officers will allow me to stay in the hospital room before they get concerned?"

"I'd guess about two to three minutes, so you need to move fast."

"Okay, Junior, I'm ready. Let's go."

He kisses her long and hard after which he picks up their only bag. She takes her small case, and they leave the room hand in hand.

Junior stops long enough at the receptionist's counter to pay their bill for the room and meals.

The walk across the large grassy area is pleasant. They are not used to such mild temperatures at this time of the evening. When they arrive at the side of the hospital building where the fire escape starts, Junior hides their bag behind some bushes. Fortunately, no one else is walking in their area.

Junior says, "As soon as I wave from the fifth-floor level, you go into the hospital and head for room 506." He kisses her again and starts to climb the ladder.

Betty quickly moves back from the building so that her white uniform does not call attention to Junior's activity.

When he waves to her from the fifth-floor level, she starts to walk toward the entrance of the hospital. Her heart is pounding like never before. She has never been given such an assignment by the Cartel before. She wonders, *Can I do it? Will I be caught by the police?*

After walking up the concrete steps of the entrance to the hospital, Betty walks in with determination and goes directly to the elevators. Fortunately, the door is open as one elevator is waiting for its next passengers. She steps in and pushes the button for floor 5. She knows her time is short now.

As she exits the elevator, she maintains her professional demeanor as best she can and walks to room 506. Just then a police sergeant is coming down the hall from the opposite direction.

Betty thinks, *Should I just keep walking right on by the room?*

But fortune is with her. Just as she approaches the policeman at the door, the sergeant calls out to him.

He turns to talk with the sergeant as Betty says, "I need to take the patient's vital signs."

The officer waves her into the room and that is where she goes. *What luck. If this will just continue.*

She sees Junior at the Window and waves quickly at him. She decides she will unlock the window before she does anything else. While doing that, she notices that Junior is carrying his pistol in his hand. She then turns on one of the small lamps near the bed.

She removes one of the syringes from the small case she is carrying. Walking around to the other side of the bed where the IV bag is hanging as she was instructed, she pulls up a chair by the bed near Berto's arm and sits down. Then she removes the protective shield from the needle. She looks carefully at Berto's arm and sees the tube that is attached to his arm. She then prepares to insert the deadly needle into the IV tube.

However, she looks at Berto who is sleeping. Suddenly she is overwhelmed with the thought of what she is about to do, kill with rat poison a highly respected man and police officer. She cannot do it. Placing the syringe on the tray next to the bed, she collapses onto the bed crying.

Berto wakes from a deep sleep. He doesn't know who is lying against his bed crying.

Is it Pilar or Susana crying over the deaths of our children?

He puts his hand on Betty's head and strokes her hair gently.

Junior is going wild as he watches this scene from the window. He pulls the window open from the bottom and slips into the room. At the exact same moment, a police officer enters the room from the hallway and draws his pistol. The officer and Junior shoot at each other at the same time, **BOOOM**, with both falling dead to the floor.

Berto is still in a bit of a trance.

He asks, "What's your name?"

"Betty."

Continuing with his hand on Betty's head, Berto pulls her close to him and kisses her gently on her forehead.

He then says, "You need to leave quickly. God bless you."

She asks, "May I write to you?"

"Of course, at the Police K-9 School."

Betty grabs her syringe materials, puts them into her small bag, moves a chair to the window, and leaves the room through the window. Instead of going straight down a ladder, she moves quietly along the ramp until she comes to the rear of the hospital where it is darker. Now she goes down the ladder quickly.

She wants to shed the nurse's uniform. Walking carefully between the hospital building and the bushes that surround it, she moves along the wall until she comes to the place where Junior left their bag of clothes. She quickly changes clothes placing the nurse's uniform with white shoes and stockings in the bag along with the small bag containing the syringes. She straightens her usual clothing to be sure all is right.

Walking away from the area at the side of the hospital with the bag in her hand, she hails a cab telling the driver to go to the airport. As soon as they drive away from the rear of the hospital, several police cars with flashing lights and blaring sirens come rushing to the hospital.

When the cab arrives at the airport, Betty pays the cabbie and walks into the terminal to give the driver the impression that she is taking a flight. While there, she goes to the cosmetics and ladies wear counter. She must hurry so she doesn't spend a lot of time selecting a small black bag that contains all the necessary cosmetic items a woman would want while traveling. She thinks to herself; *A woman needs certain cosmetics no matter where she lives.*

She then buys a beautiful nightgown, lightweight for sleeping in the jungle. In addition, she buys a small, pink suitcase to carry all the items. After paying for them, she places everything in the suitcase. Next she walks calmly through the terminal and exits at the opposite end from where she entered. There it is. The bus stop.

What's that loud noise? she asks herself. Looking down the street at the front of the airport terminal, she sees a large trash truck approaching with a man standing at the rear who occasionally steps down from the truck and pushes a cart onto the back of the truck where it is lifted and dumped into the rear of the truck. Occasionally, he pushes a lever that starts a hydraulic press that crushes all the trash together so that the maximum load of trash can be taken on each trip to the city trash yard.

As the truck approaches a trash cart near the bus stop, Betty takes her large bag and pink suitcase and waits for the truck to stop. When it does, the man in the rear steps down and heads for the sidewalk to get the trash cart. With his attention diverted, Betty pretends to be walking across the street behind the trash truck. However, as she gets to the middle of the street, she throws her large bag into the back of the trash truck keeping her recent purchase of a pink suitcase. Then she walks to the front of the truck and returns to the bus stop. When the trash truck leaves the area, Betty watches as the attendant pushes the lever that crushes all the trash together, pushing from the rear. She smiles and hopes that she has no evidence on her to tie her into the attempted murder at the hospital.

She sits quietly at the bus stop thinking about her experience in the hospital. She realizes that her hesitancy to kill Berto cost Junior his life. *How will I report this to the Cartel leadership?*

Her mind then moves to the tenderness with which Berto treated her. He stroked her hair so softly. He seemed to understand exactly what she was going through. Then he warned her to leave. He cared for her.

She says to herself; *I'm beginning to understand why so many people love this police K-9 Superintendent, Captain Berto Castillo. He cares about others no matter who they are. I'm going to write to him.*

She engages others on the bench at the bus stop in conversation. She wants to appear like one of them. She remembers that she had changed her accent a bit since she came to the big city. She didn't want to sound like a "hick" as Junior told her.

She is sitting near several other country folk and engages them in conversation as she tries to return to her "hick" dialect. She gets better with each passing sentence. As she does, the county folk warm up to her and enjoy talking with her since she is so pretty.

Soon a police car stops in front of the air terminal as other police cars move down and stop at other locations. One officer steps out and asks all the people at the bus stop to produce some identification and explain where they're going.

When the officer gets to Betty, she experiences the usual reaction from men to her beauty. She says she has been in La Vista visiting her sister. She is now going back to her home "near the Amazon Jungle."

The officer says, "How can a woman as pretty as you live near the Amazon Jungle?"

"That's where my husband works so that's where we live, heat and all."

"What kind of work does your husband do?"

"Two kinds, he seeks special berries that grow only in the jungle that have medicinal uses, and he seeks hard wood trees for later harvesting leaving the forest in good condition as he goes. He's a conservationist as well as a woodsman."

The officer continues the conversation, "What do you have in that pink suitcase?"

Betty doesn't say a word. She just passes the suitcase to the officer. He opens the bag and examines its contents. Then he lifts the beautiful nightgown and holds it as high as he can.

"Oh, lady's stuff, right?"

Everyone at the bus stop laughs as he returns the bag to Betty who says, "Right."

The officer is impressed with the contents of the suitcase and doesn't even ask Betty for her identification, a thing that is not unknown to her. As the officer leaves, she says a silent prayer thanking the Lord for protecting her to this point.

Someone at the bus stop says, "Did you see how that pretty woman changed her way of speaking when she spoke to the policeman. And did you see how that policeman melted when he was talking with her. Ma'am, does that happen often?"

Since the question was asked sincerely, Betty decides to answer accordingly.

"Yes, that happens often. I need to speak several dialects so the police will not bother me. (Changing back to her Jungle accent.) Isn't it funny the way men react when talking to a girl? They just fall all over themselves."

"You mean when talking to a pretty girl."

Everyone at the bus stop laughs at this comment and the way Betty is able to move back and forth with her way of speaking.

She says to them, "Thank you for being so nice and understanding. I usually never explain such things to people, but you all seemed so kind and helpful. Thanks again."

One of the men walks up in front of Betty, takes her hand, and pretending to melt to the sidewalk says, "You're welcome Miss. Thank you."

Everyone laughs again.

As they do so, the bus rounds the corner and stops in front of the group. Everyone steps back and lets Betty get into the bus first.

"Now, com'on you guys, let's don't carry this too far."

Again the group laughs, and all the people at the bus stop board the bus. The driver is glad to see such a friendly group of people board his bus. It is not always this way.

Betty selects a seat at the side of the bus, leans back, and quickly goes to sleep.

#

On the fifth floor of the hospital, there is nothing but chaos and commotion. Berto knows he must remain silent or he'll be involved in a murder investigation as a witness.

The two bodies remain on the floor while the police officers from ballistics check over the two guns and the two dead men, one a police office and the other, they don't know what.

A doctor comes into the room and says rather loudly, "You officers must be quieter than this. I have a man here who is a patient and could die at any moment. It is Captain Berto Castillo, Superintendent of the K-9 School. He's been hit on the head so many times that his brain may swell to the point that we'll have to cut his skull open. Even then we may not save him. Please help us help the Captain."

The officers hush down and move outside the room to conduct much of their business in the hall. The doctor asks a nurse to stand by Captain Berto Castillo's bed and make sure he is protected from these loud noises or anything that might be harmful to him.

The nurse takes the responsibility seriously. Whenever a police investigator starts to question Berto, the nurse stops him immediately and says in Spanish, "No se puede."

Berto pretends he is still out from pain pills and keeps his eyes closed as he listens to the ongoing conversation. He decides he will continue his silence until he has time to talk with Chief Medina or the doctor in private.

After another ten minutes, the two bodies are removed and the doctor returns saying, "That's it people, everyone out, and that's an order."

The detectives are not at all happy taking orders from the doctor. Usually they are in charge of a crime scene investigation.

Soon Chief Medina and his secretary, Blanca, enter the room. The nurse is hesitant to order the Chief of Police out of the room.

"You may stay if you'll promise to remain only about ten minutes. Anything longer than that will require permission from the Doctor."

She leaves the room. Berto opens his eyes and sees the Chief and Blanca whom he has missed. He takes her by the hand as she pulls up a chair for herself.

The Chief says, "Okay, Berto, what's happened here?"

Berto relates as best he can what he knows, "I woke up with this beautiful woman dressed in a nurse's uniform about ready to inject something into the IV tube. But she couldn't do it. She broke down crying and laid her head on the bed. I though it must be one of my previous wives, Pilar or Susana. Just then a man came in the window with a pistol and had a shootout with the officer who was guarding the door. Both were killed.

"Chief, I didn't share any of this information with the investigating team. I feigned sleep and just listened. I wanted to speak with you first. I should mention that the woman at the side of the bed who was about to use the needle on me was one of the most beautiful women I've ever seen, present company excepted."

Blanca says, "Listen to that will you Chief? A woman was about to inject some horrible substance into Berto's blood stream and all he was thinking about is how pretty she was."

"Now Blanca, don't criticize a man lying on what could have been his death bed, and what still might be his death bed."

Blanca starts crying. Berto strokes her arm, saying, "Cálmate Blanca, cálmate."

He then addresses Chief Medina, "Chief what should I do with this story I just told you? If I ever had to go on a witness stand and reveal this information, I could be accused of withholding evidence. If I share the story with a detective in the next half hour, I could say I have been out of it due to the pain killing drugs. I don't know what to do."

Chief Medina says, "Berto, you just identified what to do. You have no choice. You must speak with a detective ASAP. What do you think?"

"You're right Chief. Will you call one of the detectives into the room please?"

"Of course. Come on Blanca, we'd better be going."

The Chief and Blanca leave. Berto knows that in a few minutes a detective will enter the room and he must give a straight story about what happened. It must agree with any testimony he might have to give in a legal setting at a later date.

The door opens and in come two detectives. One is carrying a tape recorder.

"Hi Berto, do you remember us, Detectives Ortega and Murrillo?"

"Sure guys. Thanks for coming in to talk with me."

Detective Ortega says, "Our pleasure. The Chief said you were beginning to come out of the effect of the pain medicine they have been giving you. I hope things are clearing up for you now. Here, let's get this recorder on."

His partner, Detective Murrillo, turns on the tape recorder and places it on the tray which he pushes up close to Berto.

Berto says, "Okay, here's my best attempt. But I must say for the record, I can't vouch too much for the accuracy of what I'm about to say. The drugs they give me to sleep are powerful and sometimes in the middle of the night I wake up. It's like being in a fog.

"For example, when I first realized that something was happening in this room a few hours ago, I thought one of my former wives, Pilar or Susana, was sitting by the bed with her head on the blankets crying over the deaths of our children.

"I stroked her hair. I don't know when I realized that it was some other woman. I could see that she had a syringe in her hand, and it occurred to me that perhaps she was there to kill me, but didn't have the commitment or strength to do it. She was crying, I thought, because of her failure to carry out her assignment, or it occurred to me that she couldn't do it because she had never killed another human being before and just couldn't do it. I don't know the exact reason for the tears and sobbing, only she would know.

"Then I heard the door open. At the exact same time, I heard the window open. Two pistols were fired at the same time and two men fell to the floor, one of whom was the police officer sent here to guard me. I remember feeling so bad about his being shot.

"At that time, the woman took her bag with the syringe and pushed a chair over to the window. She then left the room with the aid of the chair through the window."

Detective Ortega asks, "Did you speak with the woman? Did she speak with you?"

"I'll have to claim ignorance on that one. My memory is so vague even now and my head hurts like crazy. I do not recall any conversation between me and the woman. If there had been, I don't know what it would have been about. Talking with a woman who was about to kill me with a syringe is a horrible thought. I just can't remember any talking."

"We understand Berto. We talked with the doctor before we came in here. He supported everything you've said as to how you felt and the effect of the pain killing drugs on your head and your mind, even to the hallucination where you thought your previous wives were crying at your side. We're sorry we had to bother you. Please accept out condolences on the death of Susana and your children."

Detective Murrillo turns off the tape recorder. The two men stand up, say goodbye, and leave the hospital room.

Berto thinks to himself, *Well it looks like the good doctor supported my statement as to effect of the drugs. I hated to use the standard 'I do not recall.' I would have sounded like some criminal character trying to avoid prosecution. I hope I never have to appear in court concerning any of this.*

Berto hears a knock at the door followed by his doctor coming into the room.

Berto thinks quickly, *My conversation with the doc better square with what I told the detectives or I'm dead in the water. He could very well be asked to testify as well.*

"Hi Berto. Boy when you have excitement, you really go all out, don't you?"

"Well, I don't like to see the death of a police officer who was sent to protect me."

"You're right, I'm sorry. How are you feeling now? Is anything clearing up for you as to what happened?"

"Not really doc. I had what you call a hallucination I guess as I was awakened this morning by all the noise and activity. I thought my two previous wives were at the side of the bed crying over the deaths of our children. It took me a long time to realize that wasn't the case. I even put my hand on the woman's head, whoever she was. I saw a syringe in her hand. I have to assume she was sent to kill me but couldn't follow through with the horrible deed. It just wasn't in her to kill another human being. Or at least that's my interpretation of what was going on."

The doctor adds, "Well, if you ever have to give any testimony in court on what happened this morning, I'd be there first telling the court that your testimony wouldn't be worth beans. You know how when you've had anesthesia or something like that you are told to not sign any legal papers for 24 hours. It's the same concept. That hallucination is proof of what I'm saying. No judge that I know of would even permit your testimony. You were just too full of drugs that can cause hallucinations when preceded by all the hits to the head that you've had."

#

A bright morning welcomes the inter-county bus as it stops in front of the house of Dos Brazos. Three children of Dos Brazos wait behind the bus bench to see if they know any of the passengers who disembark from the bus at this time.

There she is. The kids will be happy to see Betty.

Vera is the first to reach the passengers as they disperse to their various homes.

"Vera, over here," in a loud voice yells Betty.

"Betty," says Vera as she runs to Betty for a big hug and a kiss. Vera is happy to see her special friend again.

"Betty, are you going to stay with us for a while?"

"I'll have to talk first with your dad to see if there is room to put me up for a few nights."

"Oh Betty, I have a double bed. You could sleep with me. I would love that."

"Well let's see first what your father says."

Hand in hand the beautiful woman and the teen-age girl walk to the home of Dos Brazos who comes out the front door to greet them.

He says to Betty, "Don't you steal the heart of my little girl. Promise me."

Betty laughs and says, "I promise Dos Brazos."

Betty explains an abbreviated version of her mission that failed in La Vista with the death of Junior.

"I wonder if you could put me up for a while. I'm not up to a trip into the rainforest right now."

Dos Brazos replies, "Betty, we would love to have you here for a few days and nights. We're a little crowded right now. You'd have to bunk with someone. Your cowboys are still here, you know, working hard at breaking horses."

"That's right, I remember."

Vera immediately enters the conversation, "Oh Dad, I have a double bed. There's lots of room for Betty to join me."

"I figured you'd say that you little squirt. You two will probably talk most of the night. Remember, you both need your sleep, so don't spend too much time gabbing away."

"Okay Dad. I promise."

Betty adds, "Okay Dad, I promise."

They all laugh as Vera hugs Betty.

Dos Brazos says, "Betty, since your men haven't finished breaking all my horses yet, I hope you can stay until they do."

Vera rather rudely jumps into the conversation, "Yes, Dad, she can stay as long as the men need to break in the horses."

Dos Brazos replies, "Vera, I don't believe I was talking to you. I was asking Betty a question. It was for her to answer, not you squirt."

"Oh Betty and Dad, I'm so sorry for being rude. Please forgive me. It's just that I want Betty to stay with us for as long as possible."

Dos Brazos and Betty laugh.

Betty says, "She is a little squirt, isn't she Dos Brazos?"

Vera turns red from embarrassment.

Betty puts her arm around Vera's head saying, "I'll stay longer on one condition."

Dos Brazos responds, "Which is?"

"That I can sleep with Vera."

Vera looks quickly at her father waiting for his important response.

"Done, with much pleasure. We're always glad to have you stay with us. It only happens once every five years or so."

Vera hugs Betty saying, "Oh Betty, I'm so happy that you are staying. Thanks for wanting to stay with us and with me especially."

Dos Brazos gives Betty a hug and says, "I'd better check on your cowboys. I think these horses have been a little more trouble than they expected." And off he walks leaving the two girls together.

Vera says, "Betty, here's a surprise. The showers in the house have warm water too now. We have a large propane tank in back hidden by the bushes. We even have a gas stove and each of the three bathrooms has a small water heater that heats the water as you take a shower. It doesn't have a large tank to store hot water. It just heats what you need and saves money that way."

"How big is your shower?" asks Betty

"Big enough for you and me at the same time," responds Vera.

"Yea, a warm shower for us both. How neat."

#

Back at the hospital Berto continues to improve. The two detectives Ortega and Murrillo visit him from time to time.

Detective Ortega says, "Hi Berto. We need your help."

"How is that?"

"With the death of a policeman, there will soon be a Coroner's Jury. You could be the chief witness."

"You've got it all wrong Detective. According to the doctor and to use his words, my testimony 'wouldn't be worth beans.'"

"How is that Berto?"

"The doctor said I was so deeply injected with pain killing drugs and a head problem, he doesn't know of a judge who would accept my testimony. I was having so many hallucinations during that period of time, even that very night of the officer's being killed, that the doctor would demand to testify before I do and tell the judge why my testimony would not be acceptable. I'm sorry guys, I've never been in a situation like this before."

"Well, this is bad news, but we understand Berto. We know you'd rather be in there doing your job as you have on hundreds of times before, but hallucinations we can't deal with. We'll just have to count you out and explain the reason for it. Of course, we'll have to talk with the doctor so the judge will understand the official medical language."

Berto adds, "That's a good idea Detective Ortega. Even I don't understand the official medical language. I just lie here and go through whatever tests they shove at me, and I can tell you it's really a drag. I'd much rather be with you guys on the firing line."

"Okay Berto, we'll be leaving and try to see the doctor today. Good luck to you. I know you're going through a lot of pain except for the many pain killing drugs."

"They're going to start weaning me off the drugs starting tomorrow, gradually. I hope I can handle the pain without the drugs. I think I've become an addict, having been on these drugs for such a long time."

Detective Murrillo says, "What kind of withdrawal pains did the doctor say you'd have?"

"That's why it's going to take so long to get off the drugs. It'll be a slow and long process. However, that way he says the withdrawal pains will be much less and with my own determination, I should be able to make it without too much trouble. I just need to keep busy, eat a healthy diet, read a lot, watch some good television, and so on."

Detective Ortega says, "Do you mind if we come by and visit you in a few weeks? We'd like to see how you're doing at that time."

"That'd be great guys. I'd love to have you come by and keep me up on all the latest gossip in the department. I'm lucky to have an assistant administrator at the K-9 School who really knows the ropes. He'll have to break in a new secretary. Oh no, here come the tears. The previous secretary was my wife, and she was killed with my children by the Cartel. I've got to stop referring to them. Maybe you'd better leave now. I hate to cry in the presence of my fellow officers. Please excuse me."

"Nothing to excuse Berto. We'll see you later."

As the two officers leave the hospital room, they can hear Berto break into sobs as he lets himself go with his tears.

Detective Ortega says, "Let's hope we never have to experience what Berto is going through right now, the pain following the murder of your wife and children."

Chapter 13

At the Dos Brazos home, Vera and Betty are watching the cowboys as they break in the horses. Betty has told the cowboys of the death of their leader, Junior. They all expected that possibility and had a premonition of it. They discuss it over the evening campfire.

They had asked some Llumista Indians to relay the message from Betty to the members of the Cartel deep in the rainforest. Word came back that the Cartel members had received the message and were looking forward to Betty's return with the cowboys when their commitment to break in Dos Brazos' horses is completed.

After dinner, everyone retires for the night.

#

The next morning early, Dos Brazos knocks on the door. When Vera answers, he says, "Time to get up girls. Betty and her cowboys will be leaving in 45 minutes for their home. She'll need time to eat."

"Okay Dad."

Vera fights tears, "I didn't think you would be leaving so soon."

"Neither did I," says Betty as she jumps out of bed and dresses in her jungle dress that has been washed and placed on the dresser in Vera's bedroom.

"Wasn't that nice of your Mom? Look at these clean clothes. They're clean enough to die in."

"Oh Betty, don't say that. You're going home safely."

"Okay, if you insist, I'll do it."

They dress fast and are downstairs for a large breakfast of hotcakes, bacon and eggs with fresh milk. Afterwards, Betty thanks Sra. Dos Brazos for her kindnesses and runs back up to the bedroom to brush her teeth. After this, she lays out on the bed all the items she bought in the airport store as gifts to Vera who remained in the kitchen to help wash the dishes

Betty then rushes back downstairs and goes outside to see the cowboys putting the final loading touches on the burros.

Dos Brazos says to the cowboys, "Guys, thanks a lot for breaking those horses. My boys will keep them in good shape now. I'll rent them out regularly, so they'll mean a lot of cash to our household. And with so many kids, especially girls, there are lots of expenses in the family."

Everyone laughs.

Vera comes over to Betty and hugs her tightly.

Betty says, "You write, and I'll write, okay?"

"Okay," answers Vera.

Rafael, the cowboy who promised Junior he would watch over Betty, comes over and stands by in case Betty needs any help mounting the burro.

Rafael yells out, "Let's go cowboys."

The contingent sets out with Rafael in the lead followed by Betty and the other cowboys. Next come the burros carrying provisions and lastly is a cowboy who stands guard. They all wave to the family of Dos Brazos.

Soon they are in the jungle and civilization is left behind.

Rafael yells out, "Cowboys, check your pistols and other armament."

All the cowboys including Betty check their pistols, Uzis, etc. All weapons seem to be in good condition and ready for action if needed. Betty hopes they won't be needed.

And at that exact moment a small curare tipped arrow flies through the air and hits Betty in the neck.

"Oh that hurts. Guys, I've been hit with an arrow."

She tries to step off her burro but falls to the ground in the process.

Rafael hurries to Betty's side. He turns her over on her stomach and can see exactly where the small arrow penetrated her neck.

"Betty, this will hurt. But I've got to get this arrow out as soon as possible."

"Give me a piece of leather to bite on and go ahead. I know it must be done now."

Rafael takes a piece of leather that he carries as a good luck piece and puts it into Betty's mouth.

Rafael asks one of the cowboys to hold Betty's head so that she doesn't move. He then takes his hunting knife and cuts into her neck so he can remove the arrowhead. Suddenly the arrow shaft itself, as planned by the Indians, comes loose from the arrowhead. Rafael doesn't fret over this problem. He quickly disposes of the arrow shaft and with his neckerchief, takes hold of the arrowhead and with tremendous pressure from his fingers pulls the arrowhead from Betty's neck.

She faints from the pain. Rafael squeezes around the wound to get it to bleed as much as possible. He then wraps his neckerchief around her neck and says, "Men, we need to get Betty back to Dos Brazos' place as soon as possible. We'll return in a trot. Which is the strongest burro?

One cowboy steps forward and says, "Mine, Carlos, is the largest and the strongest."

Rafael adds one more question. "Who is the lightest cowboy in the group."

Another cowboy, Manoel, steps forward. "I am. I weigh 68 kilos."

Rafael continues, "Okay, Manoel, get on the strongest burro, Carlos. We'll hand Betty up to you and with me in the lead we'll return to the home of Dos Brazos and try to get some professional help for Betty. Let's go men."

The group turns around in order and with Rafael in the lead, off they go at a measured trot. The bouncing is horrible, but the burros can last longer at this speed than at any other. After a time that seems like an eternity, the group rides into the corral area of Dos Brazos where he is working with his animals.

"Well Rafael, what brings you back here so suddenly?'

"Betty has been shot in the neck with a curare tipped arrow. I cut it out but did a rather horrible job of doing it I'm sure."

By this time, all the Dos Brazos older children have come to the corral area.

Dos Brazos says, "You boys of mine, take Betty up to Vera's bed. I'll take a burro and try to get the doctor down the street."

The boys do as directed while Dos Brazos rides off on his mission.

His wife leads the boys as they carry Betty up to Vera's room. As soon as Vera realizes what has happened, she goes to pieces. Her mother chastises her and tells her to get some clean bandages. She gains control of herself and does as told by her mother.

Dos Brazos returns and says, "The doctor is in La Vista today. Maybe we can get some help from the Army."

Upstairs Betty is delirious, saying, "Berto Castillo, Berto, where are you?"

Dos Brazos wife reports this to Dos Brazos.

He takes the new family phone and calls the army base, Colonel Mario Núñez.

"Mario, this is Dos Brazos. A good friend of ours and the woman who stopped the killing of Captain Berto Castillo at the hospital recently has been hit by a curare arrow. She is here at my home now, but the local doctor is gone to La Vista today. Is there any chance you can send a doctor here in a copter to save this woman's life?"

"I'll try, Dos Brazos. I'll phone back in no more than 20 minutes. Goodbye."

#

The Colonel runs the chain of command and finally gets approval to help this woman who "saved the life of a good friend, Berto Castillo."

Within a few minutes, a medivac copter leaves the Army base with a doctor aboard carrying antidote for the poison curare. If they can only get there in time. In addition, one of the soldiers who has been to Dos Brazos place several times is aboard the copter as a guide.

Even though Captain Berto Castillo is also aboard, they are not sure of his ability to locate the Dos Brazos home. Fortunately, the highway is straight and goes almost directly to the home of Dos Brazos. The copter pilot locates the highway and puts the copter at maximum speed.

In 50 minutes the soldier says, "There it is, the house of Dos Brazos." The pilot lands the copter near the home in a freshly cut field of wheat. Berto is helped out of the copter gently after the doctor is rushed to the upper room in the house.

As Berto works his way up the stairs, he enters the bedroom of Vera where Betty lies on her bed.

Berto has only met Betty once but he recognizes her. Bending to his knees, he whispers into Betty's ear, "Betty, this is Captain Berto Castillo. Thank you for saving my life in the hospital."

"I'm sorry Berto for what I was going to do. It was my assignment, but I just couldn't do it. I had never taken the life of a human being before and couldn't do it on that occasion. I hope you can forgive me."

"Of course Betty. I forgive you easily. Now, what kind of a situation have you gotten yourself into?"

"It seems some Indian shot me with a curare tipped arrowhead that separated from its shaft. Rafael took the arrowhead out and tried to get me to a doctor in time, but I'm afraid it's too late. The poison has already worked its dirty deed. I don't have much time left. Is Vera here?"

Berto turns around and says, "Is Vera here."

The children are standing around the wall. Vera steps forward and goes over to Betty.

"Kneel down Vera."

Vera kneels down as Berto moves aside a bit. Betty takes Vera's hand and says, "You won't forget our time together, will you Vera?"

Vera can't stop crying but sobs out the words, "Yes Betty. I shall never forget our beautiful time together and the beautiful things you left me."

"That's good. I'll love you forever."

"But Betty, please don't leave us."

"I have to. My time has come Sweetheart."

Vera can't talk anymore, so she stands up and leaves the room.

Berto asks the doctor what's the word.

The Doctor says, "Berto, we're just too late. Rafael tried his best to extract the arrowhead and did a good job. But the poison causes a complete paralysis in her ability to breathe. It is not a pleasant way to die."

Berto moves back on his knees as he takes Betty by the hand.

She says, "Hey Copper. We didn't have much time together but it sure was special. I didn't have it in me to inject that poison into your system."

"Of course you didn't Betty, you're too good a woman to do such a thing. I wish we could have had more time together. But we'll have time together when I join you in Paradise."

"I'll be waiting for you. We have been studying the *Bible* and about Paradise. I hope the Lord knows I'm a penitent sinner. Uh oh, I think I'm going now. Please kiss me."

With growing tears running down his cheeks, Berto leans over and gives Betty a very tender kiss. As he is doing so, he feels her body go limp. She is dead.

Berto leans on her body and says, "Betty, don't leave me."

Vera returns and tells all the children to leave the room. When they do, she returns again and kneels beside Berto saying, "Do you mind Berto if I join you? I loved her so much."

"Of course," Berto sobs out as he puts one arm around Vera. Side by side, they hold each other and lie beside Betty's body, crying and sobbing like two little children.

The doctor and the pilot come into the room where the doctor says, "Berto, we need to get this copter back to its base and I need to get back to some serious operations."

Berto responds, "Go ahead without me guys, and thanks a million for coming so fast in an effort to save this wonderful woman. I'll stay and help with the funeral and then go home by bus."

The doctor says, "Don't do that Berto. Just phone your school and have someone drive a car to pick you up."

"Good idea, Doctor. Thanks, I'll do that. Thank the brass for letting you make this trip, especially General Escobar."

"We will Berto. Goodbye. Drop in and see us when you get back to the base. We'd like to hear how the funeral went."

"Will do. Goodbye and have a safe journey."

The two officers leave the room which is quiet except for the sobs of Vera as she holds Betty's hand.

Next, Dos Brazos comes in and signals for Berto to join him outside the room.

"Let's go outside where we can talk," Dos Brazos says.

Berto responds, "Fine."

As they walk, they pass the cowboys sitting around the picnic table.

Berto says, "Guys, come with us please."

Rafael and his fellow cowboys join the pair as they walk. Dos Brazos leads the group a short distance to a place that has obviously become the family graveyard under some wide trees.

Berto says, "What a restful place for a family graveyard. I assume that's what this is."

Dos Brazos responds as the cowboys join him and Berto, "Yes, guys, this is the graveyard for our family and friends. With your permission, we'd like to bury Betty here."

All the cowboys nod their heads in the affirmative. Some say, "Sounds good to me. Junior would like this beautiful place for Betty."

Dos Brazos says, "What do you say Berto, could you try to get in touch with the graveyard services and see if Junior has been buried yet? Maybe if he hasn't been buried yet, someone could get a car and drive him here today with his body in a casket."

All the cowboys agree with that possibility.

Berto is actually not in favor of this idea. He doesn't like the idea of Junior and Betty being buried next to each other, but he is trapped.

Berto says, "Dos Brazos, may I use your phone?"

"Of course, Berto. Go right ahead."

Berto enters the house and goes straight to the phone. He asks information for the number of the Army Base in La Vista. He is patched directly through with no waiting. The operator must think this is an emergency call.

"This is Captain Berto Castillo of the La Vista Police Department. I'd like to talk with someone from mortuary services."

"Yes captain. Stand by."

"Hello."

"Hello, is this mortuary services?"

"Yes."

"Good. I have a unique request. This is Captain Berto Castillo of the La Vista Police Department. Have you buried yet the body of Junior of the Cartel?"

Berto listens a while and then says, "Today? This is luck. I am at the home of the best friend the Army ever had, Dos Brazos by the Amazon Rainforest. Junior's wife just died from a poisonous arrow from an Indian. We are getting ready to bury her in a beautiful graveyard maintained by Dos Brazos.

"Oh you've heard of Dos Brazos. Could you send the body of Junior to the home of Dos Brazos in a casket so we can bury him beside his wife?

"I understand the brass. Please try to secure permission from General Miguel Escobar. Tell him of this call from me, Captain Berto Castillo. I'll phone back in 30 minutes. Thanks for your help. Goodbye."

Berto returns to the picnic table where the cowboys and Dos Brazos are assembled. He brings them up to date on his call to the military base.

The men spend the next few minutes sitting around the table telling stories of Betty and Junior.

Just then Vera comes running out of the house, "Berto, there's someone on the phone that wants to talk with you. His name is General Miguel Escobar."

"Okay, I'll take it." He rushes into the house for the phone.

"Hello, General Escobar, Captain Castillo here. I'm sure you heard about the shootout in my hospital room between a member of the Cartel named Junior and a police officer that ended with the deaths of both. The original plan was for Junior's wife, Betty, to insert some poison into the IV that was going into my body, but fortunately for me she couldn't kill another human being. In her return to the Amazon Rainforest she was killed by a poisonous arrow from an Indian.

"We wish to thank you for sending a copter with a doctor, but it was too late. We are about to bury Betty in the family graveyard of Dos Brazos whom you certainly know. We would appreciate your sending a vehicle with the body of Junior so the two can be buried side by side. That's our request and I appreciate your listening to it."

Berto waits to listen to the response of General Escobar who says, "I've been very close to this action in the Amazon Rainforest. And I know of your personal fight with Cartel members that has resulted in a number of serious hits to the head. And by the way, you should still be in your hospital room as I understand it. But you see your duty and do it first worrying about your own condition later. You'd better get back to the hospital as soon as possible. I guess the only way I can accomplish that is to send a hearse with the body of Junior. It'll go with siren blaring and red lights flashing. After it arrives and one hour later, the hearse will return with you in the front seat, I hope."

"Thank you General. You have been more than kind. We'll stand by for the hearse and have the funeral as soon as it gets here. Then I'll return in it to the hospital, I promise. Thanks again and goodbye."

"Goodbye Captain. You get back in bed fast, and that's an order."

"Yes, Sir."

Berto rings off and walks a little slower, per the instructions from the General, to the back yard where his companions are waiting.

"The General gave the green light. A hearse will leave the base immediately at high speed. We've got a short time to dig two graves, side by side."

Dos Brazos says, "Okay, you boys and you cowboys, let's get to it. There are several very good shovels in the barn. Where would you like the graves Berto?"

"I think that's for Rafael and the cowboys to decide."

"Right. Rafael, talk with your compatriots and let us know in two minutes."

The cowboys walk off by themselves and talk of the decision to be made.

Rafael says, "Guys, you realize that we are close to that police captain who has been a thorn in our sides for a long time now. This mission had one goal and that was to kill him. How are we going to explain to the new boss that we worked with him here and didn't eliminate him?"

One of the cowboys responds, "Don't you think there's been enough killing on this trip? We've lost both Junior and Betty to killing. Our new boss is an educated man. I think he will agree with us. Stop the killing."

The other cowboys agree.

Rafael says, "Okay guys, that's it. It may cost us our lives, but I agree. At the burial of Junior and Betty, there'll be no more killings. You saw the captain's response when Dos Brazos asked him where the burial site should be. He said that's for us to decide. I think we've made a mistake about this police captain. It's time to call a halt to killing him."

The others agree.

They return to the graveyard and look over several possible sites, under trees, in the sun, etc.

Finally they return to Dos Brazos and ask him to go with them. By now the boys have returned from the barn with several shovels. Other family members are also present.

They all walk over to a small incline with a tree on top. Rafael takes two shovels and with his booted foot pushes one into the ground, and about four- and one-half feet from the first shovel pushes the second shovel into the ground.

Dos Brazos says, "Those are too close to each other for two graves."

Rafael responds, "We know that, but they are perfect for one large grave for two caskets side by side."

This brings tears to the eyes of the children, the wife of Dos Brazos, and Vera.

Dos Brazos says, "Measure the one casket we have in the garage now for Betty and double the width. You boys can do that. As soon as you have the measurements, we'll draw a line in the dirt and start digging from there."

Dos Brazos' sons run off with the challenge given to them. Soon they return with some measurements written on a piece of paper.

The oldest boy says, "We did some calculations keeping in mind that the two caskets will be next to each other and we wanted the measurements to be simple with some extra room. Conclusion: For each casket we should have 36 inches wide and 96 inches long. Or in other words, we need one hole 72 inches by 96 inches for the two caskets. This way there will be no problems."

Another son brings forward a measuring tape. With his Dad's help, they measure the four corners of a rectangle 72 inches by 96 inches. Dos Brazos takes a stick and draws in the dirt the rectangle per the measurements given. When finished, it looks perfect.

The cowboys grab a shovel and start digging at the four corners, so they are not too close to each other. Every ten minutes or so, Dos Brazos and his three oldest sons trade places with the cowboys. No one will let Berto work.

In fact, Dos Brazos says, "Berto, you've done your part. You should go into the house and rest a while. You've had a difficult morning."

Berto responds, "Normally I'd argue with that conclusion, but under the circumstances, I think I'd better rest. Call me if you need me for anything."

Off he walks into the house and then into the front room where the women are seated, many of them still fighting tears. Even though they didn't see Betty very often, they all loved her for her beauty and kindness.

Berto sees an empty seat by Vera which he takes. He puts his arm around her and hugs her. She lays her head on his shoulder and goes to sleep in about five minutes. She too is exhausted. Berto lays his head on Vera's head. He then goes to sleep. The others laugh very quietly since they don't want to awaken Berto or Vera.

In one hour and 45 minutes, Dos Brazos comes into the house and sees the two still asleep. However, with his walking on the wooden floor, they wake up.

Dos Brazos says, "The double grave is finished."

Everyone wants to see it, so they all stand up and stretch a bit. Berto removes his arm from around Vera. He rubs it since it is sore after being held in the same position for so long.

Vera says, "Let's go outside and see how the progress is coming along."

"Okay Vera. Lead the way."

They walk outside and up the small incline to the location where the double grave has been dug.

Berto looks at it and says, "Perfect in all measurements. Do you have two long ropes to lower the caskets to the bottom of the grave?"

One of Dos Brazos sons shows Berto two long ropes of high quality that have been oiled and rubbed many times.

He says, "We use these only for funerals."

Berto says, "Listen. Do you hear that siren? It's stopped now. We're on schedule."

At this time, an Army hearse drives into the back yard. The soldiers push the casket over to the side.

The officer in charge says, "Will some of you guys bring out the other casket and place it in the back of the hearse next to this casket?"

"Sure," the boys reply.

Off they go up to Vera's bedroom where Betty has been placed in a casket. It is rather primitive, obviously made with hand tools, but with the same love that any casket could ever be made. The casket does not have any professionally made handles, just pieces of rope sticking out at four places for the men to carry the casket.

The boys grab hold of the casket at the four different locations and lift it down the stairs. They then carry the casket to the hearse where they gently place one end of it into the rear of the hearse. The two soldiers help them push the casket back into the hearse all the way so that it lies exactly beside the casket of Junior.

The hearse is then driven the short distance to the grave site.

Everyone gathers around the grave site. It is apparent that the family has done this before. Dos Brazos acts the role of the presiding minister and starts the ceremony. He asks his daughters to sing a song. This they do with feeling and love. It is apparent that they have learned the various parts, soprano, second soprano, and alto. When they finish, there is not a dry eye in the place, including the two soldiers who brought the hearse.

Dos Brazos then delivers the eulogy since he knew both persons the best. He makes no pretense at correct language. He just speaks from his heart. Some of his stories are funny which draws a subdued laughter. Other stories tell of Betty's willingness to help his daughters and of the things she left with the girls. He mentions that all who knew Betty loved her.

Berto says to himself, *That's for sure, and I'm one of them.*

The stories about Junior tell more of his leadership qualities and how his men would follow him anywhere, even into the jaws of a python or the grip of an anaconda. The cowboys in the crowd nod their heads up and down as they know personally the truth of the statements.

When he finishes, he says a loud "Amen," followed by the same spirited "Amen" from everyone in the crowd.

Dos Brazos continues to lead as he directs the cowboys to take the two ropes and place them under the casket of Junior. Once the ropes are adjusted, the cowboys move the casket to a position over the grave.

Dos Brazos gives the sign for the men to lower the casket slowly so he can direct them to place the casket on one side of the grave. The casket slides down the oiled ropes smoothly. It fits perfectly. The boys who supplied the measurements are proud of their contribution.

Next the cowboys repeat the process with the ropes and Betty's casket. This is a little more difficult since this casket has to fit in exactly next to the casket of Junior. Again the cowboys let the casket slide gently and slowly. With Dos Brazos directing, the casket falls into place at the side of Junior's casket. The cowboys pull up the ropes and give them to the eldest son of Dos Brazos.

Dos Brazos asks each one present to take a shovel full of dirt and throw it onto the caskets. This is hard for almost everyone to do. Berto has the hardest time throwing dirt on top of Betty's casket. He thinks, *Who would have ever thought that this woman who knelt by my hospital bed with a deadly syringe in her hand is now lying in that casket where I just threw a shovel full of dirt?*

When everyone is finished taking part in this ritual, Dos Brazos says to his sons, "Boys, please cover in the hole. Tamp it down occasionally so that after it rains it won't sink in depth. When the boys are finished, girls I'd like you to plan a simple flower garden for this spot."

The eldest son of Dos Brazos asks, "Dad, can I make the headstone of wood? I knew both of them and how they spelled their names. I don't know their birth dates, but I do know their dates of death. Maybe I could leave room for their birth dates for later when I find out."

"Thank you son. Yes, that would be nice. Use that cedar you got the last time you visited La Vista. It will withstand the elements and the bugs better than most other wood."

Berto says, "Okay soldiers, I know you have to get back. I'm ready when you are."

"Yes Sir" comes the reply from both the soldiers.

Berto does the rounds of shaking hands with the boys and hugging the wife and girls. Vera sneaks a quick kiss which makes Berto smile.

Once this is done, Berto thanks Dos Brazos for all his help. He then gets into the rear seat of the hearse.

As they drive away, the entire family waves at Berto who returns their waves. He sees that the boys are working hard at filling in the grave.

Once the hearse arrives on the smooth highway, Berto quickly falls asleep and remains so for the rest of the trip to La Vista.

Chapter 14

As soon as the hearse arrives back in La Vista, the Army driver heads for the hospital saying, "These were our orders, Captain. They want to give you a complete checkup, especially since you've been running all around the country."

Stopping in front of the hospital, the driver turns off the motor to the hearse, takes the keys from the ignition, and accompanies Berto up the steps.

"Hey, you guys don't even trust me to report into the hospital."

"Berto that's not it. You're still a bit shaky on your feet. I'm here to help."

"Oh I don't need any help climbing stairs."

At the very moment he says this, Berto stumbles on the edge of the next step. The Army driver is quick to respond and catches Berto before he falls onto the concrete steps.

"Oops, I spoke too soon, didn't I?"

"Yes sir, you did."

"Thanks for being here."

"You're welcome sir."

When they get into the hospital and stand at the check-in counter, the receiving nurse says, "Well, look who's here. Good evening Captain Castillo. We're putting you right in the emergency examination room for starters according to instructions from your doctor."

She pushes a button. Very soon an intern comes down the hall to help.

He asks the Army driver, "Does he need any help as he walks?"

Berto says, "That depends on who you're talking to."

"Okay, Sergeant, does he need any help as he walks?"

"Yes."

"Thank you for that complete and accurate answer."

Berto puts his arm on the sergeant's shoulder and says, "Thanks for all your help. I'm just sorry we couldn't save Betty. I'll never be able to live that down." Tears form in Berto's eyes.

"Many people tried to save her, Captain. You can't do any more than that. I'd better run now. Good luck in your recuperation from all that banging on your head."

The intern walks with Berto to the emergency examination room. A nurse is waiting for him.

She hands Berto a hospital nightgown. "Here it is Captain. As you remember, it ties in the back. I can help you with that if you wish."

"I wish."

"Okay, I'll be back in a few minutes and finish tying you up and then we can put you on the examination table where the doctor would like to check you over after your having been gone so long."

"Thank you Nurse (he looks at her name tag) Alicia."

She leaves the room as he starts to undress. There is a locker where he puts his clothing, everything except his socks. After he puts on the hospital gown, there is a knock at the door.

"Come in, Nurse Alicia."

She walks in with a big smile on her face, "You remembered my name."

"How could I ever forget the name of such a beautiful nurse?"

"There it is, only a few minutes. I've been warned about you Don Juan."

"My name is Roberto or Berto for short."

"Berto may be your name, but your personality makes you Don Juan."

They both laugh. She gives him a hug and says, "I thought I'd do that before you did."

Now they really laugh.

Berto says, "Okay, you win. What's next?"

"Over to the examination bed. But first turn around and let me tie you up."

Berto turns around. She begins to tie him up starting at the top. As she gradually works her way down, she gives him a smack on the right buttock."

"Ouch, that hurt," yells Berto.

Nurse Alicia says, "It felt good to me."

They both laugh again as she finishes tying up all the strings. She gives him another hug from the back and says, "You sure are a lot of fun. I'm glad I'm single."

"You are? Well this is getting better all the time. I suppose you have memorized your phone number by now?"

"I sure have. It's 856-8907. Here, I wrote it on this piece of paper. Shall I put it in your locker?"

"I hope so."

The emergency room doctor knocks politely and enters the examination room.

"So this is the famous police Captain Berto Castillo who runs all over the country with a good chance of experiencing a severe seizure which could plant him six feet under."

"Now Doctor, I take better care of myself than that."

"I'm Doctor González, your neurosurgeon. Get up on the bed please. I'll raise the head part for your comfort. Nurse Alicia, please get a warm blanket and put it over the Captain. He seems to be shivering."

"Of course Doctor."

As Berto gets into the bed, Nurse Alicia places a warm blanket over him.

He pulls it up to his chin saying, "Now this feels good."

First the doctor looks into Berto's eyes with his specialized equipment.

"Berto, I'm sure you've been told this before. Your pupils are definitely not of the same size. How many serious concussions have you experienced in your professional life?"

"I couldn't even guess, lots, that's for sure. My career has been rather violent. The guys I play with are rough and tough. For some reason, they all have another person in the background waiting to hit me on the head with something very hard."

"Nurse Alicia, take Berto down the hall for a CT Scan. I'll meet both of you here later to review the results from the radiologist."

"Yes, Doctor."

Nurse Alicia starts to push Berto's bed on wheels out the room and down the hall. As she pushes, she puts one hand on his shoulder which is covered by the blanket. It is a physical sign of support from her to him. He brings his hand back and places it on top of her hand. She feels him relax as he does this."

She says, "Berto, I'm praying for you. May God bless you."

"Thank you Alicia."

At the CT Scan room, she turns Berto over to the technician and waits in the hall.

#

Later, Berto, Alicia, and Doctor González are back in the special emergency room where the doctor is preparing to report on the results of the CT Scan.

"Before I review the results of the CT Scan, I need to tell you that there is a more sophisticated, and more expensive, test call the MRI, or Magnetic Resonance Imaging Test. We may need to have one of those taken next. The CT scan tells us of immediate damage following a Traumatic Brain Injury, especially bone damage. The MRI will tell us of damage to vessels, arteries, and so on. Now with these injuries, the secondary damage is relevant. By that, I mean you might not notice the damage for weeks or months. Berto, how are you doing in the headache field?"

"Horribly. I have a constant headache that's getting worse not better. None of the meds I can get help in the least."

Doctor González hesitantly adds, "I hate to say it, but I need you to take that other test, the MRI. Only then will we know the situation inside your head. Have you ever had an MRI before?"

"Yes, Doctor. Immediately after my last injury to the head."

"While you're taking this MRI, I'll call up on the computer the results of that previous test and any CT Scans you might have had previously. Sometimes the worst results from TBI come well after the original blow to the head. It's been sufficient time now that we will be able to see any serious changes that might be occurring inside your head. Nurse Alicia, please take Berto to the MRI room. I'll phone down and make the appointment."

"Yes, Doctor." She starts to push the bed through the doorway and down the hall. With tears in her eyes, she puts her hand on his shoulder as before. He reacts as before with his hand on hers. She can feel him relax as he did the first time.

"Berto, you remember how the MRI goes, don't you?"

"Oh yes, I'll never forget that noisy machine. It was scary the first time, to be put inside that giant tube. I thought I'd have claustrophobia. I was lucky that the technician gave me some headphones with music playing which helped keep my attention away from the problem at hand."

"You've got it. Just keep your mind on something else that's beautiful."

She continues her walk to the MRI room. Once there she knocks on the door.

A technician responds and says, "Hi Nurse Alicia. Dr. González just phoned. Come right in. We have sufficient time until my next appointment."

Berto says, "Oh Goodie."

Alicia and the technician laugh.

Alicia says, "I'll leave you now Berto and will be outside the room waiting for you. Okay?"

"Okay as long as you don't leave me."

"I won't, I promise." She leaves the room.

The technician explains the process to Berto and gets things underway.

Their first attempt at a start is not successful. However, once Berto takes off his shoes with their metal ringlets that set off the giant magnets of the MRI Machine, all goes well. That is, all goes well as long as Berto can hang on tightly to the edge of the railing and concentrate on the music coming over the internal radio system.

When told that the exam is over, Berto says, "Whoopee, aren't I lucky."

The technician opens the door and in walks Nurse Alicia. By this time Berto is out of the "Tube of Fear" and back on his rolling bed with a blanket over him.

She asks the technician if she can move Berto back to his hospital room. Given the green light, Nurse Alicia pushes the bed out the doorway and starts down the hall.

When they reach the doorway to Berto's hospital room, a nurse tells them that Dr. González is in a team meeting concerning Berto.

"The doctor will soon receive the radiologist's report on the recent MRI. He will be with you ASAP."

Nurse Alicia pushes Berto into his room.

#

Later Dr. González walks into the room and says to the nurse, "Pull up a chair and sit-down Alicia. You need to know what's going on here since you are Berto's special nurse."

Alicia pulls up a chair and listens intently.

Dr. González says, "Well Berto, I'm glad you're tough because you'll have to be to take what I'm going to tell you."

The doctor notices with that news Berto grabs Nurse Alicia's hand.

The doctor continues, "We've done about every test there is for cases like yours. In most injuries or sicknesses, the patient starts out in a bad condition, takes medicines, gets lots of rest, and gradually returns to regular health and strength. However, in these traumatic brain injury cases, that is not necessarily the pattern. In cases of TBI, the patient can seem to be improving but after a while it's impossible to ascertain how long this can be. As I was saying, after a while, the patient becomes sicker due to developing problems in the brain. And that is what we have in your case."

Berto says, "Okay, so what is the developing problem in my case?"

"Our TBI team has just met on this. And once again after seeing your CT Scan and your MRI results, it is apparent that your brain is injured, is swelling, is bleeding in one specific location, and we will have to cut your skull open to relieve the pressure. We have been very successful with this operation. Once part of the skull is removed and the pressure is off the brain, we can find where the bleeding is taking place and stop it, and you'll start to improve. We'll have to keep you in the hospital for quite a while during recovery."

"What will you put in to replace the part of the skull you have to remove?"

"That depends," answers Dr. González. "If the injured part is clean and can be removed without any problems, we can sometimes use the original part of the skull as a replacement. If there is lots of trauma to the injured part of the skull, we'll have to remove it and discard it, replacing it with one of several substances we have for this case. In addition, you need to be very careful to not hit the open part of the brain since the protective skull will have been removed."

Berto responds, "That makes sense."

"We'll monitor you very carefully to make sure no bleeding starts up. Generally, we stop the bleeding quickly, and that's that. Now there will be some therapy after this operation. Your memory will be less sharp. Some of your body movements will not be the same. You shouldn't walk any place without help. That's what Nurse Alicia is for, and I can see that she has already developed a special care for you."

Berto and Alicia laugh.

"Now Nurse Alicia has a five-day a week shift, eight hours per day. Therefore, she can't be with you all the time. You understand that don't you?"

Nurse Alicia interrupts, "Doctor if I want an extended shift, I can get it. We are always short on nurses and the personnel office is pleased to accommodate requests for extended hours. I'm not sure I could leave Berto in the hands of another nurse very often."

Berto adds, "Alicia, your health is important too, remember. You need your rest, a good diet, etc. I'll track your shifts to be sure you're not overworking."

They all laugh.

Berto asks, "When will this operation take place?"

"In two weeks, about 7:00 a.m. in Operation Room Number Four. They will start to prep you about 5:30 a.m. in a room reserved for that near the operation room. You might ask Alicia to make a few contacts for you so that your close friends and family know of the operation. Oh, I'm sorry for my reference to your family."

"I have a brother and a sister, Pablo and María."

"Good. Alicia can contact them for you."

"I'll have lots of help that morning so don't worry about anything. The anesthesiologist will be in to see you early in the morning in the prep room. Ask him any questions you might have. He'll give you some pre-op meds that will help you to relax. Once in the operation room, he'll put you to sleep and it will seem like no time at all until the operation is over. You'll wake up in the Post Anesthesia Care Unit. I'll be in to see you in that location."

Chapter 15

Meanwhile in the camp of the Cartel de la Selva Tropical the word has reached the members that Berto has to undergo a serious brain operation due to their act of violence. Whether or not he will live is beyond the ability of the doctors to know.

Unfortunately, the same is true for Berto's trusted dog, Franz. His wounds are more serious that anyone imagined. The staff members at the Veterinary Hospital have worked all out to save the life of Berto's famous German Shepherd dog.

The leadership of the Cartel has changed from Anaconda to Junior and now to Rafael who is a different sort of person than his predecessors. Everyone knows that Junior wanted El Catalán to take the leadership position if necessary. However, El Catalán recommended Rafael for that position.

At the very moment that the neurosurgeon, Dr. González, is involved in examining Berto, Rafael is demonstrating his style of leadership by looking to the future.

He says, "The Cartel has been on the same track for a long time now without making any real progress. I had the chance to get to know that Captain Berto Castillo when we were breaking horses at the home of Dos Brazos. He's a great guy and a good leader. I think we could deal with him."

"Deal with him? What do you mean Rafael?" asks a senior cartel member.

"I mean this continued dealing in illicit drugs may be getting us some cash but nothing else. I think there is much more to living that just accumulating cash. For example, the land in the immediate vicinity of our camp is rich in a treasure we know almost nothing of. Are you aware that most of the plants in our area can be used to make medicines of great value? We could cultivate and harvest the growing of these plants. I checked on this while in the capital. Why even the cocaine, marijuana, and occasional heroin that we sell can be used profitably to make important medicines. And if we were involved in this industry, we wouldn't have to always be on the lookout for the federales and the coppers."

"Okay, Rafael, that may sound pretty good, but what's your proposal?"

"My proposal is for me and one other to go to the capital city, meet with the President and a couple officers from the Army. And remember, this is not a one-way deal. We would benefit from this agreement. For our commitment to stop dealing in illicit drugs, we would need help in setting up a new industry of drugs that are helpful to the world. We would eventually need a railroad built into the rainforest, from La Vista to our camp. The products could be flown all over the world easily from the railhead. I tell you I'm really exciting about this idea. How would you like your children to grow up in peace? I know I would. And I would propose that the beginning of this agreement be the day at noon that Captain Berto Castillo undergoes his brain operation. We could dedicate the peace agreement to the life and commitment of Captain Berto Castillo. Just ask some of the cowboys what they think of Berto."

"Good idea," speaks up one. "Tell us guys about this Berto person whose family of a wife and three children we killed and almost killed him with a lightning hit on the head."

One of the cowboys responds, "While we were waiting at Dos Brazos, Berto made sure we were taken care of, rooms, beds, showers like I've never had before, and meals cooked by one of the prettiest gals I've ever seen. And this Berto, he didn't show any anger toward us even after the great loss he suffered and the hit on the head that may still take his life."

Rafael continues, "I personally know that he has had a struggle with forgiving us for killing his family and almost killing him. He is still struggling with it, but he is a Christian man and feels that if he is to obtain forgiveness for his own sins, he must forgive others who sin again him."

One member of the Cartel speaks up, "I know that scripture. It's included in the Lord's prayer and in the verses right after the Lord's prayer. It's true for all us guys."

One says, "Hey look, we've got a preacher among us." Many of the group laugh.

A couple others say, "Don't knock it. We've been having some meetings with those who are interesting in learning more about Christianity. You could benefit by joining with us, every Monday evening after dinner."

A few more laugh.

Rafael says, "Hey, I'm glad to hear that. If we're going to keep up with the rapid advance of this world, we need to have study groups on lots of subjects. Congratulations Guys, I'm proud of you."

This time everyone claps.

"Okay, I want a vote. I don't wish to threaten anyone, but if I am to continue leading this crew, I need to know how you feel about the things I've been talking about here these past few minutes. Let's have a show of hands of those who can support me in this attempt to establish an industry of using the plants around us to build a pharmaceutical, pardon the fancy word guys, a pharmaceutical company to help develop different medicines that will bring good things to people everywhere. We will expect these companies to build a railroad to our camp. Look how easy it would be for our wives to travel from here to La Vista. Okay, all in favor, raise your hands."

Rafael takes the count.

"I feel that about seventy-five percent of the group support the idea. Okay, usually we have a much higher percentage supporting a proposal than that. Then let me put it to you a little differently. Some may say this isn't fair, but we are at the crossroads men. I feel it in my bones."

He takes his boot and makes a straight mark in the dirt about thirty feet long.

"You men who didn't support the idea please step across this line." About twenty-five percent of the men step across the line.

"Thanks for your honesty men. When I took over the leadership of this clan, we agreed that honesty would be the keyword, and no one would be looked down upon for his opinion. I respect you all for stepping across the line.

"Now one more thing before you vote again. I cannot lead where you cannot follow. I'm going to ask you to vote again. If at least seventy-five percent of those remaining don't support this idea, I shall leave the camp with my family, head for La Vista, and live among the city folk. You can then select another leader."

Lots of groans and complaints are heard. Most of the men want Rafael to continue as their leader. They feel that the future looks brighter under his leadership.

"Okay, now we'll have a second vote of only those who voted against the proposal on the first go-around. Of those mentioned, how many can now support the proposal as it has been explained to you?"

Almost all the hands go into the air. Rafael asks another man to count the total number of men who crossed the line and the total number of men with their hands in the air.

In a few minutes, the man reports that twenty-four men crossed the line and twenty-two voted in favor of the proposition. There is lots of clapping and yelling.

Rafael says, "Okay, time to move into action. I would appreciate you cowboys getting two burros ready for a trip tomorrow morning to the home of Dos Brazos. Paco, you'll be going with me. We'll get to see Dos Brazos' beautiful daughters, Vera and Susana, before all the others, what luck."

Paco lets out a yell, "Yahoo."

Everyone laughs.

"Also pack us a third burro with provisions and bullets for our pistols and Uzis if we run into trouble. Maybe in the future, we can sit back comfortably in a train and enjoy a quick trip to La Vista, "

As the meeting breaks up. Many of the men stand around discussing the proposal and the future possibilities it could mean for the Cartel.

#

The next morning, Rafael and Paco are ready and raring to go. The burros are also ready and the strongest and biggest, Carlos, who was ridden back to camp after the deaths of El Caracol and Betty, is loaded with provisions and ammunition.

Rafael checks to be sure Carlos is not overloaded. Once convinced that his cowboys know how to properly pack a burro with a heavy load, he yells outs, "Yahoo," as he throws his cowboy hat into the air.

After he retrieves his hat, Rafael mounts his burro and says, "Let's get going burro." The trip begins in great spirits.

Everyone laughs and claps as Paco joins Rafael with Carlos the burro bringing up the rear.

The heat of the day is upon them quickly. However, they are used to it and pay it no attention as they enjoy an uneventful ride through dangerous territory.

As lunch time approaches, Paco slows down a bit. An inviting meadow lies ahead. He and Rafael decide the burros need a rest and lunch too.

Rafael pulls over by a streamlet and dismounts. Paco does the same and the two men lift most of the load off Carlos. The animals enjoy the cool water of the streamlet and the fresh green grass growing in the meadow. Paco takes from Carlos' pack the lunches prepared for Rafael and himself.

After a refreshing lunch, both men enjoy walking around to stretch their legs but keep their Uzis at the ready with a couple extra magazines also available just in case.

The heat of the day brings with it the storm of the day. Black clouds form quickly with an accompanying wind. The downpour starts fiercely with only a few seconds' introduction. The temperature drops immediately as men and beasts enjoy the cool rain.

Ten minutes later, the storm stops as quickly as it started.

Rafael says, "Okay let's load up again. Everyone should be cooler now."

After loading up, the men mount their burros and off they go again with Carlos the mighty burro bringing up the rear.

Fortunately, the trip goes smoothly, with the first night spent in the shack and another night in the open. Although they hear the sounds of the animals of the jungle, none challenges them for which they are grateful. It is this kind of protection that makes the men of the jungle rather religious by nature. Not that they are of a particular faith, just Christian men, who pray by themselves regularly due to the dangers they face daily.

Soon they see the cabin and corrals of Dos Brazos. His children see the visitors at the same time and take off running to greet the two men. The children are excited to see these men of the jungle, strong men, rugged men, who face danger at every turn when they make the trip from the Cartel hangout to the home of Dos Brazos. The children, by habit, first check to see if any one of the men is wounded or hurt in any way. As soon as they determine that the two men are not injured, they do not need to hold in their enthusiasm at seeing them.

Everyone knows Rafael the new leader of the Cartel. Two of the smaller kids run beside the burros and ask the men to lift them up for the final ride to their destination. The men lean over and pick up the light-weight children and put them over their saddles. The kids think they are famous cowboys of the jungle and the pampas to the south.

When they arrive at the corrals, the boys jump down while the men get off their saddles slowly. They are tired and sore from the three-day ride. One of Dos Brazos' boys unlocks the gate to the corral and after the three burros are unloaded, he opens the gate. The kids always enjoy watching the burros run to the water trough and then to the haystack. Finally, they get the rest, food, and water they need and deserve after such a long ride in the heat and humidity of the rainforest.

Dos Brazos comes out of his house to greet the men. A big Latin embrace is shared by Rafael and Dos Brazos and then by Dos Brazos and Paco. Even though these latter two have never met, they share many things in common living near and in the rainforest. It is this camaraderie that permits them to share a big embrace inherent in their culture.

"What's the mission this time amigo?" asks Dos Brazos of Rafael.

Rafael first introduces his companion, Paco, to Dos Brazos. Next he briefly explains the mission of attempting to secure the support of the Government to build a railroad from La Vista to somewhere near the home of Dos Brazos. Later they hope to see the railroad extended to the Cartel camp deep in the rainforest. He explains that the purpose of the railroad is to move the pharmaceutical plants of the rainforest that Rafael and his people will obtain as their part of the deal.

Rafael asks, "Dos Brazos, before we proceed any further with this proposal, we need to have your support. Will a railroad close to your home be a problem for you and your family? Will it bring a bunch of ruffians near your home and put your daughters especially at risk? What do you think?"

Dos Brazos, a man of experience in many ways responds, "I think I better take some time to discuss this with my wife and children. When are you leaving for La Vista? There are no more buses this evening. The first one is at 8:00 a.m. tomorrow morning. You're welcome to stay in my barn. There are some nice beds there and a wonderful shower. I'm not kidding guys. It is now a wonderful shower. I had a plumber install a hot water heater like we have in the house. If you're willing to pay fifty cents per shower, it'll pay for the propane that is used to heat the water for the shower. If you like cold water showers, be my guest at no cost."

Both men are quick to pull out from their pockets a fifty-cent piece.

Rafael says, "There's no argument there."

All three laugh.

Dos Brazos says, "Okay, I'll let you know how the family feels about this proposal before you hit the hay tonight, about 9:00 p.m. And don't forget, dinner is served in one hour as made by my wife and older girls."

As Dos Brazos leaves, Vera comes running into the barn. "Hey guys, anyone know anything about the condition of Captain Berto Castillo and his K-9 dog, Franz?"

Rafael explains to Vera the situation on Berto and the brain operation coming up in several days. He also says that Franz is not doing well.

Vera says, "If I could only get my hands, or better yet, my guns on those guys that hit Berto hard on the head and shot Franz, I'd nail them to our barn door."

Vera obviously doesn't suspect that Rafael and Paco were among the group that assaulted Berto and Franz and killed Berto's family.

As Vera is talking, the two men look at each other not a bit proud of what they did. The Monday night meetings on religion at their camp have helped them to understand the severity of that act and the difficult task of obtaining forgiveness for that act. They are sincerely sorry for the violence against Berto's family and look for a way to demonstrate that sorrow.

This move to work with the government in securing pharmaceutical drugs from the great Amazon Rainforest and discontinue trading in illicit drugs is part of the demonstration of their sorrow for what they did to Berto and his family. And they must tell Berto of their participation in the horrible deed and seek his forgiveness for this act that took his family from him. They don't know if Berto is the kind of a person who can forgive them for killing his family.

The men now realize that they have hurt others with their killing of Berto and his family. Here is a beautiful, young girl expressing great anger at the ones who committed the act. She has obviously been hurt as well by the deed.

Rafael thinks, *I will try out something on this girl to see how she feels about forgiveness.*

"Vera, how do you feel about this gang that killed Berto's family and wounded Berto and Franz seriously? Now this is not a joke, this is a serious question. What if a couple men from this gang came to you and asked your sincere forgiveness for what they had done? Let's say they seriously are sorry for this act, and they want your forgiveness. Could you forgive them?"

Vera says, "Oh, what a hard question. However, I know the answer without even thinking. You see, I go to the local Sunday School near here every Sunday morning and have for many years. I have studied this situation with Pastor Mora. Here then is my answer and I'm serious.

"I know from studying the Bible and the discussions with Pastor Mora that if I ever expect the Lord to forgive me of my sins, I must forgive those who sin against me. Now this horrible act against Berto and his family is a sin of the worst kind. Yes, I could forgive these men because I want and hope the Lord will forgive me of my sins. There's your answer in a nutshell."

She continues, "However, these men have another problem, and that is obtaining forgiveness from the Lord for their sin of murder. That's a different question. The sin of murder is a very serious one. In fact, it is one of the Ten Commandments. I don't know the answer to that one. Each case I'm sure is different. But Berto and his family were such wonderful people, from what I've been told. I think it would be almost if not impossible to obtain forgiveness for murdering Berto's wife and sweet children. Oh I'd better run. It's my turn tonight to set the table. See you at dinner."

And in a flash, out the barn door she runs for the mansion house.

Paco says, "Well, Rafael, there's your answer from a Christian young lady who has studied the subject. I hope Berto has studied it as well. If not, he might just shoot us on the spot."

"How do you feel about that idea, Paco?"

"Sometimes I'd rather be dead that burdened like one of our burros with this load, being responsible for the deaths of so many wonderful people, including little children. Boy I really shivered the other day when in our discussion someone read the verse about it is better to be cast into the sea with a millstone around our neck than offend one of these little children."

Rafael continues the discussion, "You too huh? I felt that one as well. I don't want a millstone hung around my neck and be thrown into the sea. Those millstones are heavy. It would take a few men just to put it around your neck."

Just then Vera appears at the barn door, "Hey guys, time to eat." And off she runs. The two men follow at a slower pace.

The discussion at the dinner table is about the trip the men had in the jungle, what they saw, what they didn't see, how dangerous it was, and did they see any Indians trailing them?

The kids are sorry to hear that there weren't any Indians trailing them so there could be a fight. Dos Brazos has to calm the kids down from their talk of warlike activities. He apologizes to the two men for the kids' concentrating on Indians and battles.

After dinner is finished, Dos Brazos tells the family to stay in their seats as he wants to discuss something important with all the family that the two men brought for their consideration.

Rafael and Paco thank the women for the super meal cooked only as country folk can prepare a meal of chicken and vegetables with hot rolls, wild honey, and apple pie for dessert.

The two men leave so that Dos Brazos can discuss the important matter with his family.

Rafael says, "Let's take a short walk around the neighborhood."

That decided, off they go. As they pass the house with the sign of the Physician and Surgeon, Paco says, "If that doctor had been at home when Betty was hit with an arrow tipped with curare, she may be alive today. Let's walk over to the small hill where she and Junior were buried."

As they reach the small hill, they see the bench installed near where the gravesite is located.

Rafael says, "I don't know Paco. That curare is deadly, especially a shot in the neck. Even if the doctor had been at home, I don't think Betty could have survived. You know, as we talk of pharmaceuticals, let's talk of a small kit that anyone could carry. If a person is hit with an arrow or dart dipped in curare, one injection from the contents of the kit, and the person lives. Now there's a real contribution."

Paco replies, "We'll need the chemists to do the research to know how to do that. That's why we must speak with the President."

After the men return to the home of Dos Brazos, they head for the barn. Dos Brazos is there waiting for them. They sit down on the old furniture that has been placed in the barn for those who pass the night with the family.

Rafael asks, "Dos Brazos, did you have time to talk with your family about our proposal?"

"Yes, they were all very interested in the subject. Everyone supports the idea of having a train come here from La Vista to pick up the plants that can be made into good drugs. Also they like the idea of passengers riding on the train. They feel this would be easier for the women who need to go to the big city every so often to buy special materials and for the men who need to go there to get special tools and supplies."

Rafael says, "That's good to hear. Where would you suggest the train should stop when it comes here? In other words, how close do you want the train to come by your house? Now remember, those trains are noisy and make a lot of smoke."

"We talked about that too. Everyone agrees that someday the train would probably go on to the base in the jungle. Therefore, the best place is on the upstream side of the bridge before it comes over the river. If the soil there is strong enough for the bridge to hold cars and trucks, it should be strong enough for a bridge to hold a train. So for now, the best place is on the upstream side of the bridge."

"That sounds good. The advanced planning should impress the officials we are going to meet with. What do you think Paco?"

"They did a good job of planning. I hope the people in La Vista can support the idea as well. Now let's hit the hay, I'm tired. It's been a long day."

Dos Brazos says, "Goodnight men, have a good night's sleep. I'll see you at breakfast, 7:00 a.m. You'll have plenty of time to catch the bus for the big city."

"Goodnight Dos Brazos."

#

The next morning, the women serve another outstanding meal. After breakfast, the children assemble by the bus stop to say goodbye to the two men as they leave for the city.

Vera's last words are, "Find out for me, please, how Captain Berto Castillo is doing."

"Okay little one," says Rafael.

When the bus pulls up to the stop, several other people have joined Rafael and Paco at the bus stop.

The kids all yell, "Goodbye."

Everyone on the bus replies, "Goodbye."

The bus starts its bumpy voyage to La Vista from the bus stop in front of the home of Dos Brazos and picks up country folk as it travels through the various counties. It seems that everyone knows everyone else on the bus, so the trip is a friendly one with some singing and social chatter.

The first stop in La Vista is at the International Airport. Several passengers get off at this stop. Rafael and Paco continue on to the stop in front of the Army Base. Everyone bids them, "Goodbye," as Rafael and Paco step down from the bus.

They proceed to walk to the main gate of the Army Base where they are stopped by two guards with rifles at the ready.

"And where do you think you're going?"

"We'd like to speak with Colonel Mario Núñez."

"Oh you would? Well let's find out if Colonel Núñez wants to speak with you. What are your names and where are you from?"

"We are Rafael and Paco from the Cartel de la Selva Tropical."

As soon as the guards hear these last few words, they take the safeties off their rifles and aim their weapons at the two men from the jungle.

Rafael says, "Please, we don't want any trouble. All we want to do is speak with Colonel Núñez or if he is busy we would like to speak with General Miguel Escobar."

The guard says, "Let's start with the Colonel." He dials the extension for Intelligence Unit One.

The secretary, Olivia Duarte, answers, "Intelligence Unit One. How may I help you?"

"Olivia, we've got two hillbillies from the jungle who want to speak with Colonel Núñez. Their names are Rafael and Paco."

"Oh yes, send them in please. I'm sure the Colonel will want to speak with them since they are representatives of the Cartel de la Selva Tropical."

"Okay, if that's what you want, I'll send them in." He hangs up the phone and walks out to the gate.

"Okay men, do you have any identification?"

The two men look at each other. "Identification?" asks Rafael. "He's Paco, and I'm Rafael."

The two guards look at each other. Fortunately, at this time Olivia comes walking over to the main gate from her building. The guards explain the problem, that the two men have no official identification.

Olivia says, "That's no surprise. No one else in the jungle has I.D. either. I'll vouch for them."

"Okay, Olivia, they're yours."

"Come on Rafael and Paco. Let's go see Colonel Núñez."

Off the trio goes chatting all the way.

As they walk into the headquarters building of Intelligence Unit One, Colonel Núñez comes out from his office to greet them. Olivia introduces them and returns to her office.

In the main office, Colonel Núñez says, "Okay, guys, you must be aware that I don't make it a habit to meet with men from the Cartel de la Selva Tropical. It was your men who killed the family of Captain Berto Castillo and hit him so hard on the head that he has to have a special operation from which he may never recover. Why are you here?"

Rafael takes the lead, "We have come to realize that what we did to the family of Captain Berto was wrong. We are sorry and have decided to stop dealing in illicit drugs. We would like to make a deal with the government asking them to build a railroad from La Vista to the jungle's edge for now and eventually to our camp in the jungle. We of the Cartel will put down our weapons and start a program of collecting the plants that can make special medicines that save lives. We know a lot about these plants. In addition, we know a lot about living in the jungle so we can work there safely without any harm from the wild animals and beasts that live there."

"Are you guys serious?" asks the Colonel.

"Of course. We didn't make this trip on that bumpy bus and three days on burros in the jungle just to see La Vista. We want to talk with the President and your superior officer, General Miguel Escobar. We feel they have the authority to make such an agreement with our Cartel."

Colonel Núñez says, "Well, I can't guarantee that I can set up such a meeting, but I'll certainly try. Please take a seat out there in the conference room while I go talk with General Escobar in his office. I should be back in a few minutes."

"Thanks." The two men take chairs in the conference room while the Colonel leaves the building.

#

Twenty minutes later, Colonel Núñez returns to the building with General Escobar at his side. The Colonel makes the introductions.

General Escobar says, "Rafael and Paco, that's it, right?"

"Right," responds Rafael.

General Escobar says, "The proposal that Mario explained to me was so farfetched that I had to come here personally. Are you aware that Captain Berto Castillo is a good friend to everyone in this unit? His family was loved by everyone here. And you killed them all. The doctors aren't sure that Captain Castillo will survive the operation that is scheduled for him in just a few days. And his wonderful trailing dog, Franz, a beautiful German Shepherd who was so smart and so well trained. You shot him twice. What makes you think we would make any kind of a deal with men who would do that to these people?"

Paco says, "Rafael, I'd like to say a word."

"Sure Paco, go right ahead," responds Rafael.

"You see sirs, it's like this. First, you need to know that Rafael has been elected as the leader of our Cartel, officially. Now, we have started a little study group every Monday night on the Bible. We have a member of our

Cartel who is pretty smart when it comes to the Bible. We have been studying the Lord's Prayer. It says there and in the few verses right after those famous verses that we will be forgiven by the Lord only as we forgive others. We hope Captain Castillo knows those verses as well. We figure we need forgiveness from Captain Castillo. Now we know that is a hard thing, since we killed his entire family and as you said he may die any day now.

"We are trying to make up for all the bad that we have done. If the Cartel could start collecting plants that are only found in our region of the Amazon Rainforest, we figure that some scientists could make some lifesaving drugs from them. In other words, saving lives is the only thing we figure we can do to show to Captain Castillo that we really regret taking the lives of his family. Now most men could never forgive us for what we did. They'd probably shoot us on the spot as soon as they see us. But we have heard some marvelous things about this Captain Berto, as he is called. We figure if anyone could ever forgive us for the horrible thing we did, it would be Captain Berto."

The General asks, "And what is it that you are asking in return as a Drug Cartel that has been very active in transporting drugs for many years?"

Rafael adds, "We would need a way to transport the good plants from the jungle to La Vista where they could be processed. In other words, we would need a train from La Vista to the edge of the jungle, near where Dos Brazos lives. Do you know Dos Brazos and where he lives?"

Both the military officers respond in the affirmative.

The General says, "Come with me to the board where we have a map of Yuñeco. This train idea may not be as difficult as you think. I believe, although you haven't mentioned it yet, that the large pharmaceutical companies would want to get in on this proposal. And I can tell you, we'd need their financial backing, that's for sure.

"Now look here at this map, do you see this red colored line with small lines crossing it every so often?"

Both men respond that they see the red line.

The General continues, "That line represents train lines at the present time in Yuñeco. As you can see, one line leaves La Vista and goes toward the Amazon Jungle but turns about 40 miles before it gets there and goes in another direction. In other words, the train line would only have to be extended about 40 miles and not the 200 miles that La Vista is from the home of Dos Brazos."

Rafael and Paco become more enthused after hearing this information.

Rafael says, "Now here is another part of our proposal. We would like to sign such an agreement with the government and the train companies on the day that Berto has his brain operation, at 12:00 noon and call it 'National Day of Forgiveness,' to be recognized each year. Maybe with so many people thinking of Berto on that day, the Lord might look kindly on Berto and save his life."

General Escobar looks at Colonel Núñez. Both hardened soldiers begin to have tears in their eyes as they are impressed with the thinking of these two jungle inhabitants.

General Escobar says, "I'll have to talk with the President first. And he may want to talk with you. As you can imagine, he has not been a very happy man with your activities over the years. You would really need some forgiveness from him as well as Berto. Where will you be staying?"

Rafael says, "We came here immediately when we got off the bus, so we haven't checked into any motel yet."

"Please inform Colonel Núñez of the name of the motel where you are staying when you get one. And don't worry, we won't raid the place. I'll have to give you a paper of permission to be in the City legally, so you won't get arrested."

Rafael says, "Thanks, I hadn't thought of that."

The General goes to Olivia's office and asks for a piece of official stationery and an envelope. He then sits down at a table in the conference room and pens the letter he was speaking of. Afterwards, he gives it to Rafael.

"And you'd like to see the signing day known in the future as 'National Day of Forgiveness,' is that right?"

Rafael responds, "If possible."

Colonel Núñez says, "Speaking of Captain Castillo, if you're going to ask his forgiveness, I think we should be moving. General, with your permission, I'd like to drive these two men to the hospital and oversee their meeting with Captain Castillo."

"Of course Mario. Please do that. When you get back, give me a call. I'd like to know how Berto handles this."

The Colonel salutes his superior officer and leads the two men out of the building into the parking lot where they get into his car and drive to the hospital.

The trip to the hospital is short. Colonel Núñez parks his car in the hospital parking lot and leads the men up the steps to the receptionist's desk.

"Hi, I'm Colonel Núñez from the Army First Intelligence Unit. These men are my guests, and we would like to talk with Captain Berto Castillo for a few minutes, please."

Picking up her phone, the receptionist says, "Nurse Alicia, Colonel Núñez is here with two associates and would like to speak with Captain Berto...Okay, thanks, I'll send them right down."

Speaking to the three men, the receptionist says, "Nurse Alicia is with Captain Berto Castillo. Take the elevator across the hall to the fifth floor. Nurse Alicia will meet you waiting in the hall of the fifth floor. She'll take you in to see Captain Berto. Be sure and tell the police officer on duty at the door who you are and why you're here."

"Thank you," responds Colonel Núñez.

As the men cross the hall for the elevator, Rafael says, "I hope we don't have any trouble with the police officer at the door."

"So do I," adds Colonel Núñez. "You don't have any weapons on you, do you?"

Both Rafael and Paco say, "No."

Once inside the elevator, Rafael pushes the button for the fifth floor. Up they whiz to the floor indicated. After the elevator door opens, the three men step out, look in both directions, and see a nurse waving at them from the doorway of a room down the hallway. Off they walk toward her.

"Hi, I'm nurse Alicia. And you are?"

Colonel Núñez responds, "I'm Colonel Núñez, commander of the Army's First Intelligence Unit. These two men are Rafael and Paco from the Amazon Jungle where they work. They have stayed with Dos Brazos and have come to talk with Captain Berto. This morning they talked with General Miguel Escobar."

When the police officer hears the names of the top brass, he relaxes and asks if anyone is carrying a weapon. Colonel Núñez says he is and is required to do so when in uniform. The other two men say they are not carrying any weapons.

The guard says, "Okay, you all may go in to see Berto."

Nurse Alicia leads the way and says, "Colonel, would you please make the introductions."

"Of course Nurse Alicia." Seeing Berto in his hospital bed, Colonel Núñez says, "Captain Berto, we've met before. I don't know if you remember."

"I don't remember a lot of things." Since Berto laughs after that comment, the others join him in the laughter.

"I'm just kidding, Colonel. Yes, I remember you, Colonel Mario Núñez. I've visited you and your beautiful secretary, Olivia, in your headquarters building."

The Colonel responds, "I knew you wouldn't forget Olivia. She is beautiful."

Berto continues, "But I don't recognize these two men. I have to judge from the way they are dressed that they are from the Amazon Jungle."

"Yes, Berto, they are, and they have met this morning with me and General Miguel Escobar. Then they wanted to meet with you and make a proposal. Are you physically up to handling some information that might upset you? We don't want to impair your health with your operation so close."

"No I'm fine. They keep me drugged just enough so I can handle anything. I never thought I could handle the upcoming operation or even talk about it, but I've been able to do that. Now, let's don't waste any more time. Come on guys, give me the word. What's going on?"

Colonel Núñez says, "These two men are Rafael and Paco, the top representatives of the Cartel de la Selva Tropical."

Nurse Alicia is not pleased that Colonel Núñez sprung this introduction on Berto this way. She watches Berto's reaction carefully and checks the technology that is hooked to Berto to see that his blood pressure and other vital signs maintain acceptable numbers.

Berto says, "Well Mario, you really dropped that one on me quickly, didn't you? Where's my pistol?" Then Berto laughs again. Rafael and Paco relax.

Rafael takes over the conversation at this point introducing himself as the new chief of the Cartel and that he wants to make some important changes in the Cartel's operations. He then explains their proposal to extend the railway to the house of Dos Brazos and cultivate and harvest native medicinal plants of the jungle. Then they would ship them by train to La Vista.

Rafael also says that he and Paco are there to seek Berto's forgiveness for killing his entire family and wounding his dog, Franz. As a sign of continued friendship between the Cartel and the Government, Rafael says they would like to sign the agreement with the government at exactly 12:00 noon on the day of Berto's operation. He hopes that by doing this in this manner that many people will be praying for Berto. Also, and he says he talked with General Escobar about this idea; he wants the date of Berto's operation to be known as 'The National Day of Forgiveness" or at least "The National Day of Remembrance."

Berto responds, "Remembrance? I'll remember. That's for sure. You mean forgiveness, don't you? Call it what it is: For killing my entire family."

Then Berto starts to cry with big tears running down his face. Nurse Alicia moves closer to him and puts her arm around his head.

Paco says, "Berto, we know there is nothing we can do to bring back your family. We also know that we will have to carry eternally the burden of our acts of murder. We know that what we ask of you is a very difficult thing to do, forgive the men who killed your entire family. We got this idea in our weekly Bible study group."

Berto says, "Well what do you know?" as Nurse Alicia wipe the tears from his eyes. "Cartel members studying the Bible."

Rafael says, "Yes, Berto. Under my leadership, this will be a new Cartel with great changes. The men support my proposals. They are tired of killing and being killed. They want their children to grow up in peace. We will work in the jungle sun hard to show our commitment to this proposition."

Nurse Alicia keeps a close eye on Berto. She also checks his vital statistics as registered by the equipment around his bed. All signs look good.

Berto says, "Do I have some time to think this over? This is a mighty big decision. I loved my family, you know. I had two teen-age boys and one little, new, beautiful girl. You are asking a lot from me. I'd actually prefer to draw my trusty 9 mm pistol and send both of you to Hell right now." Again the tears start rolling down Berto's face.

Colonel Núñez senses that Berto is about to lose it due to the anger he has kept in for a long time now.

He says, "Berto, we'd better be going now. Thanks for seeing us and listening to their proposal. Could you give us your answer in 24 hours, or by 1600 hours tomorrow?"

"Yes, I can do that. But don't come here for the answer. Just phone Nurse Alicia. If you come here and my answer is negative, bullets may be flying and I'm, or at least I was, an expert shot."

"Yes, I remember. Okay Berto, I'll personally phone at 1600 hours tomorrow on the dot. Goodbye."

Rafael and Paco say, "Goodbye," as well. So does Nurse Alicia.

The three men leave the room. Nurse Alicia sits down on the bed beside Berto. He puts his arms around her and asks, "What do I do, Alicia? Is their request even a reasonable one? Forgive them for killing my wife and children and almost killing Franz? And the docs say that Franz may still pass on."

Nurse Alicia asks, "Are you willing to listen to me for a while?"

"Of course, that's why I asked, Silly." He kisses her on the cheek.

"Okay, here's my readout of this thing: I believe Rafael when he says he wants to bring new leadership to the Cartel, that most of the family leaders are tired of seeing their children killed by the soldiers of the Army. They are also tired of killing. They even have a Bible study group. There's so much more in that statement than we could ever imagine.

"You have a marvelous opportunity to show thousands, even millions of people, what religion is all about. If you can do this thing, it'll be talked about for years after your death. The annual 'National Day of Forgiveness' will be celebrated, and people will ask why. Once again, the beautiful message of maximum forgiveness will be told. The Cartel de la Selva Tropical will be changed to a business for people who have been raised and lived their lives in that hot, humid, and dangerous environment. It's up to you Berto. I'll stop talking now."

"Thanks Alicia, I appreciate your thoughts on this subject. You really are a Christian, aren't you?"

"Yes I am, Berto. A Christian doesn't just talk his religion, he acts his religion. When you see Pilar and Susana again in Paradise, they'd be so proud of you. You should read about these things in the first part of the New Testament."

"I think I will, and right now. Please get me the Bible that's on the counter over there."

Nurse Alicia takes the Bible to Berto and opens it to the first book in the New Testament, Matthew.

She says, "See these first four books, Matthew, Mark, Luke, and John. They tell of the work that Jesus did among the people and talk of His Prayer, or the Lord's Prayer, and many other important things."

"Good, there is no better time for me to read these first four books than right now, before I have to make the decision of my life. I'll read all night if I have to."

Nurse Alicia takes a chair and picks up some handwork she has been doing as she keeps a constant watch over Berto. Berto leans back in his hospital bed and starts to read the New Testament. He is looking for guidance in this very important decision that he must make.

#

Berto reads most of the night. He finishes the first four books of the New Testament. At 3:30 a.m. he finally falls asleep and is still asleep as Nurse Alicia brings him his breakfast. She peeks into his room but sees he is still asleep. She decides to let him sleep as long as he wants this morning since every time she checked him last night he was wide awake reading.

Nurse Alicia sits in the room quietly as she keeps extensive notes of what has happened. She tries to remember everything that was said by Colonel Núñez and the others. Just as she finishes, Berto moves in his bed and stretches.

"Good morning, Alicia." Looking at the clock, he says, "Hey, you let me sleep until 9:40 a.m. You've never done that before."

"That's right, but you never spent most of the night reading before either."

"I'm hungry."

"Of course you're hungry. So am I. I'll check to see if the kitchen staff kept our breakfasts in the oven as I asked. You can wash up while I'm gone. Wait, no you can't. I need to be here when you leave that bed. You wash up first while I wait right here. When you're done and back safely in bed, I'll go get breakfast for both of us."

"Sounds good Alicia. I'll just be a minute," he says as he leaves his bed and goes to the private bathroom."

A few minutes later, he returns to his bed and tells Alicia she can leave now.

Off she goes to the kitchen.

A few minutes later, she returns with two trays that are covered in most places. She puts one tray on the movable table by Berto's bed. Berto moves the tray over to his bed and removes the covering revealing a delicious, steaming hot breakfast of bacon and two eggs, toast, orange juice, and milk.

"Oh boy, does this ever look good."

Berto begins to eat his breakfast which he enjoys a great deal. Alicia returns to the chair and enjoys hers as well.

"Alicia, this is a very good breakfast. Thanks for protecting it for me in the oven."

"You're welcome Sir."

When they are finished eating, she takes both trays and places them on the floor in the hall.

Berto says, "Now back to the bathroom to brush my teeth." He starts to get out of bed but is very dizzy. Alicia grabs his arm and helps him stand up. She walks with him to the bathroom and holds him tightly as he brushes his teeth. When he is finished, Alicia walks with him back to the bed.

"Can I go back to sleep for a while, Alicia. With my tummy full and a night with little sleep, I'd like to rest some more."

"Go right ahead. I'll be watching over you every minute."

She helps him into the bed and puts the blankets over him. He lies back, and gets warm very fast. As soon as he does, he is asleep. Alicia smiles and kisses him on the forehead. She takes a magazine that she bought before taking the elevator this morning. There is an article on Berto and Franz. Surprised, she opens the magazine to the proper page. After reading a few paragraphs, she too falls asleep. Her night wasn't very restful either.

Both sleep for several hours. Berto wakes up first shouting, "Hey what kind of looking after is this? You're sound asleep."

The shouting awakens Nurse Alicia.

She opens her eyes and says, "Who could be sound asleep with your raving and ranting like this. I've been awake all the time, just with my eyes closed."

"Yea, sure, your eyes closed. Come here close, let me see those eyes. I can tell whether eyes have been sleeping or not."

Nurse Alicia steps out of her chair and walks over close to Berto to show him her eyes. However, this entire action is a ruse. Berto wants a kiss. As Alicia gets really close to him, he grabs her head with both his hands and holding her tightly kisses her hard and long on the mouth.

"I should have known you were preparing a trick. If you want a kiss, all you have to do is ask."

"It's more fun stealing one," says Berto as he laughs.

Alicia says, "I'll get even with you, just watch and be alert. I'm as smart as you any day. I'll steal a kiss some time when you don't expect it."

Berto repeats her previous words, "If you want a kiss, all you have to do is ask."

"Yes, but it's more fun stealing one."

"Copycat, copycat. And you said you were as smart as me any day. Now you're just copying what I said. That doesn't take much brain power."

When Alicia hears the word "brain," she breaks into tears. The operation is tomorrow morning. They have been trying to pretend it was further off, but can't do it any longer.

Alicia puts her arms around Berto and holds him tight. "I can't lose you Berto, I can't."

She sobs and sobs deeply.

Berto holds her tightly.

"I know it's easy for me to talk, but Alicia you won't lose me, you'll see. Please don't cry, it hurts me when you do."

"Okay, I'll stop. And by the way Dear, it's almost 1600 hours. Remember, Colonel Mario Núñez is going to phone at 4:00 p.m. on the dot. Do you have your answer ready that you want me to give to him?"

"Yes I do."

"Well, when are you going to share your answer with me so I can tell the Colonel when he calls?"

"I'll tell you my answer at 3:58 p.m. I want to hold it until the last minute in case I want to change it."

"Okay Dear, I understand. But don't forget. In fact, I'd appreciate your writing the answer on a piece of paper so there won't be any error in transmitting the response. Many mistakes have been made when transferring important information verbally. This is too important to make an error in communication."

Berto replies, "Hey, you are smart. Please give me a pen and some paper and some time to write the answer."

Alicia does as requested and returns to her chair, picks up her magazine, and resumes her reading while Berto writes. When he is finished, he asks for an envelope which Alicia gets for him.

She then moves her chair back next to his bed and holds his hand. They both realize that time is short for their being together prior to the operation. A doctor could come in at any moment throwing the place in increased anxiety and fear since this operation is extremely serious and delicate.

Holding hands, they don't talk,

And sure enough, a few minutes later, the anesthetist knocks lightly on the door giving Alicia time to stand and move the chair back. She then goes to the door and welcomes the doctor.

"Good afternoon Berto. How are you feeling this afternoon?"

"Anxious to get this operation over with."

"That's understandable. Let me see your chart. How have your vital signs been?"

He takes a clipboard from the end of the bed and reads over it carefully.

"It looks like you have gradually been getting better as you prepare for this operation. That's the way we like our patients."

Nurse Alicia says, "He has been eating well also, Doctor."

"That's another good sign. All of this wouldn't have anything to do with the assigned nurse being here almost 24 hours a day would it?"

Berto says, "It sure would."

Alicia says, "I have no comment to make."

The two men laugh.

Pulling a chair up to the bedside, the doctor says, "Okay Berto, now to be serious. Do you have any questions before this operation?"

"Yes, how long will it take?"

"That's a good question for the neurosurgeon. Ask him when he comes in to see you later today."

"Okay, I will. You guys always avoid the hard questions."

Alicia says, "Now Berto, there's some professional ethics operating here. The surgeon wouldn't want another doctor giving out information different from what he'll tell you."

"Okay, that makes sense. You see doctor, a simple answer will do the job."

"Sure, especially when it comes from a beautiful nurse."

They all laugh.

Taking a small pamphlet from his pocket, the doctor says, "This small pamphlet will answer most of your questions. Other patients have said it really helped calm them down before the operation. It was written by a real pro."

Berto says, "Oh, who wrote it?"

"I did."

Everyone laughs again as the doctor hands the pamphlet to Berto.

"I'll be going along now. You'll see me again before the operation if you have any questions. I leave you in the capable hands of your nurse."

The doctor starts to leave the room.

Alicia accompanies the doctor to the door with tears in her eyes, saying, "Please doctor, don't let me lose Berto."

She then kisses the doctor on the cheek, "I couldn't stand it if we lost him."

"We'll all do our best Alicia." He then kisses her on the cheek and leaves the room.

As the doctor starts to close the door, the head nurse approaches him and enters Berto's room.

"Good afternoon. How are you two doing? I suspect with the time for the operation approaching, Nurse Alicia, you are getting more nervous. I'm here to relieve you of duty and send you home to get some sleep and meals. I'm very aware of the schedule you have been keeping. I'll give both of you five minutes to say your goodbyes and then Alicia, it's home for you."

"Oh no, please."

"Now you know the rules. One word from me and that's it. I'll be back in five minutes. We have to start getting this patient ready for his operation as you know."

She leaves the room.

Alicia runs over to Berto crying all the way.

Berto says, "Now Honey, it's the same way in the police department. When an officer gets too close to a person involved in a case, we're relieved of duty. Now calm down, stop crying, and wipe the tears from your face so I can kiss you a few times. I need those kisses to get me through this operation."

Alicia does as directed and let's Berto kiss her all over her beautiful face. Alicia kneels by the bed and holding Berto's hand says a silent prayer. When she is finished, she sits on the side of the bed and tells Berto that she can take care of him in her home after the operation.

There is another knock at the door and in comes the head nurse.

"Time to go Alicia. Get some rest and come back no sooner than 8:00 a.m. tomorrow morning. I've put you on a day of vacation, so you'll be free tomorrow to go and be where you want to be."

"Thank you Head Nurse. I was wondering what the best way would be to handle that."

Then looking at Berto, Alicia blows him a kiss and walks out the door. She heads for the parking lot, looks around for her car, and finding it gets inside, starts the motor and drives out of the lot heading for home.

Back in Berto's room, the nurse from the operating room comes inside and gives Berto the first preparation pill prior to the operation. He will need to take a series of pills so that his blood is not too thin or too thick. The nurse tells him that one of the main problems in this operation on his head is related to the removal of his skull cap. Will there be veins attached to the underside of his skull which will start bleeding profusely when the skull cap is removed?

At this time, the neurosurgeon enters the room and walks over to Berto saying, "Do you remember me? I'm the surgeon who is in charge of this operation."

"Of course Dr. González, I remember you. As a police officer, you may be the guy I have to track down if this operation fails."

"Well I see you haven't completely lost your memory or your sense of humor. I'm here to explain a few things to you. Unfortunately, we learned through the periodic CT Scans and MRIs that your brain is swelling causing abnormal pressure against your brain. For that reason, we have to cut away a portion of your skull, or a craniotomy. In addition, we have seen blood clots that need to be removed so the removal of a portion of your skull will be helpful to us in that we'd have to do it anyway even if there were no swelling."

"Oh boy, good luck again."

"Well, I have been waiting until the last possible minute hoping that the swelling would stop, but it hasn't. I can't wait any longer, so we operate tomorrow morning. But before we do, you have some guests outside that want to explain something of great interest to you. May we admit these guests?"

"Of course."

Dr. González opens the door and admits the following: Police Chief Luis Medina pushing a baby carriage; Blanca, the Chief's secretary; Rafael and Paco of the Cartel de la Selva Tropical; and Colonel Mario Núñez.

First the Chief pushes the baby carriage over to Berto who looks inside and sees his trusted dog of many years and many actions.

"Franz, Franz, how are you?"

The dog recognizes Berto and licks his hand when Berto rubs his chest. Berto starts to cry. It has been a long time since his K-9 companion licked his hand.

"Oh Franz, I've missed you so much. Don't ever leave me like that again."

The dog issues a faint bark.

Colonel Núñez says, "Look Berto, it's exactly 4:00 p.m., time for your decision on the proposal made yesterday to you by Rafael and Paco."

Berto takes the piece of paper he prepared and says that he has written his response so there will be no confusion as to what he is saying.

He reads, "TO: RAFAEL AND PACO, What you ask of me is greater than anything I have ever been asked to do. Normally, I would shoot both of you and be done with it. But Nurse Alicia has explained to me some of the eternal implications of your request. Therefore, I forgive both of you, Rafael and Paco, and others in the Cartel who killed my family. I also consent to your using my name if you will include the name of my trusted German Shepherd dog, Franz, on any bronze statuette in memory of this National Day of Forgiveness. Let it be heard annually throughout the country and help to bring peace to the Country of Yuñeco that we love. I hereby request the National Railroad to extend the railway the additional 40 miles or so that are needed to link the jungle to the capital. I also request that the pharmaceutical companies work with the Railroad. May the work of the former Cartel members in bringing native vegetation from the jungle to the Capital City for processing be a major success. May this effort bring an end to many diseases and pain suffered by people all over the world. This way the Cartel de la Selva Tropical will go down in history as the benefactor of a large number of human beings, children and adults, who will bless the Cartel forever for its willingness to change its way of life and pursue another that will bring life to many persons. Signed: "Captain Berto Castillo and K-9 Dog Franz, La Vista Police Department"

Everyone with tears in his eyes claps at this humane decision on the part of Berto.

Dr. González says, "I understand that in 24 hours, exactly at 4:00 p.m. tomorrow, a cannon will sound from the platform in front of the City Building. This too will be part of the annual celebration as a 'National Day of Forgiveness.'"

Rafael and Paco are so overcome with the forgiving attitude of Captain Berto that with tears in their eyes they asked to be excused from the room.

Captain Berto says, "Don't worry guys. I left my pistol at home. Feel free to stay."

All the others laugh at Berto's continuing humorous attitude.

Rafael and Paco thank everyone for their kindness and say they would like to visit the City lawn so they can be there the next day when the cannon is shot.

Berto says, "That's just fine guys. Take some cotton for your ears. That cannon is loud."

The two Cartel representatives leave the room.

Dr. González says, "You people, and that includes Franz, are invited to return to the recovery room tomorrow at 3:50 p.m. so you can celebrate the day and hour at 4:00 p.m. with Berto."

Almost everyone claps and leaves the room.

Berto says, "That sure is nice what everyone is willing to do to bring peace to this country."

The surgeon stays with Berto for last minute instructions.

#

On the afternoon of the next day, the entire city seems to be aware of the operation that Berto is undergoing. The local morning newspaper carries in large print the announcement of the operation and the ceremony at 4:00 p.m. to announce the agreement with the Government, the Railroad, and the Pharmaceutical Companies. In addition the cannon on the front lawn of the City Building will blast out at 4:00 p.m. announcing the first annual "National Day of Forgiveness" in honor of Captain Berto Castillo and his K-9 Dog Franz.

Many churches in the City are open all day long as people come in to pray for Berto's survival from this complicated medical operation. Many stores in the center of the city have prepared large signs telling of the events of the day. The mayor stops by the city offices to learn how things are going with Berto. But there is no information yet. A portable blackboard has been placed at the entrance to the City Building to keep people updated as to the operation as soon as such information is made available.

Many people fast during the day as they dedicate this a day of prayer. As 3:30 p.m. comes, a large group of people begins to assemble on the lawn in front of the City Building with Rafael and Paco among them.

The officials who will oversee the ceremony from the lawn are also starting to gather, namely: General Miguel

Escobar and Colonel Mario Núñez of the Army; the President of the National Railroad; and the two Presidents of the major pharmaceutical companies in the nation. Also present on the stand are Sr. and Sra. Dos Brazos.

Another group of people assembles on the lawn in front of the hospital.

At 3:50 p.m. per their arrangement with the hospital staff, the people invited to see Berto in the recovery room are dressed in white sterile hospital gowns. They wash their hands vigorously. Afterwards, they put on white gloves and hospital masks over their mouth and nose.

The select few are: Pablo Castillo and Maria Castillo Rodríguez, Berto's brother and sister; Police Chief Luis Medina and his secretary, Blanca; Nurse Alicia, and Vera, young daughter of the family of Dos Brazos.

The Chief leads the group into the recovery room pushing a baby carriage with the K-9 dog Franz who has been washed thoroughly, disinfected, and covered in white. The German Shepherd is trying to recover from his recent operation following two gunshots to his body.

At a few minutes to four o'clock, the operation room nurse and the neurosurgeon, Dr. González, push the hospital bed with Berto through the doorway and park it in the recovery room. Surprisingly, Berto is coming out of the anesthesia fast. The surgery staff realized that Berto is strong and used a minimum of anesthesia.

Berto recognizes everyone and says, "Hi guys and gals. Thanks for coming to see me."

Chief Medina wheels Franz over to the hospital bed. When Franz sees Berto, he puts his paws on the side of the baby carriage and lifts himself up and over the side onto the hospital bed. He then lies down beside Berto who recognizes what Franz is doing. After lying down, Franz puts his head on Berto's lap and finally relaxes as Berto rubs his head.

The nurses look at the Doctor. It is a shock to them to see a dog in the recovery room so soon after a patient has had a serious operation. This has never been done before. But the doctor waves everyone off realizing the importance to the patient and the dog of this act.

The guests in the recovery room keep glancing at the clock on the wall. Four o'clock is fast approaching. They keep their eyes on the windows where the sound of the cannon will be heard the loudest.

Meanwhile back on the podium in front of the City Building, the Mayor is leading the ceremony as planned. Many of the citizens of the community are there. After the mayor reads the statement that Berto presented the day before, everyone waits anxiously for 4:00 p.m. They don't hear the city's cannon very often.

Thirty seconds before the appointed hour, four men in uniform from the National Guard step forward and check the giant cannon. All is ready.

Exactly at 4:00 p.m., **BOOOOM** sounds the cannon with its echo bouncing throughout the city. People everywhere in the City hear the sound that starts the annual celebration of the National Day of Forgiveness. People are shaking hands and hugging strangers throughout the large gatherings in front of the City Building, in front of the hospital, in stores, in businesses, and on the sidewalks of the city.

Back in the hospital room, those invited to share the event with Berto turn their attention from the windows back to Berto and Franz. But neither one is moving. Berto's head has fallen on the head of his faithful dog. Dr. González checks the vital signs of Berto and Franz.

The Doctor then says, "They are both dead."

Everyone in the room bursts into tears and sobs. Nurse Alicia, Vera, and Blanca surround the bed and kneel with their hands on Berto and Franz. They cry as loud as they have ever cried before. Berto's brother and sister along with Chief Medina are in tears.

A reporter from the radio station barely opens the door and glances into the room to get the official word. One look is all it takes. He sees the dead Berto and Franz surrounded by everyone in the room crying as loud as they can.

He rushes to the phone and calls his station. Soon, throughout the city and the country goes the word that Captain Berto Castillo and his faithful K-9 dog, Franz, have died from wounds suffered from an attack on the family of the police captain by members of the Cartel de la Selva Tropical.

Rafael and Paco feel the severity and responsibility of their having killed Berto and Franz. They appreciate the challenge given to them by Berto, to be active in the new program but they are now afraid. They move quickly into the City Building and go into the men's room on the second floor. They are afraid to leave the building. With the word getting out concerning Berto's death, will the people rise up against them?

The Nation's President goes on the radio saying, "These deaths cannot be in vain. Berto wanted this to be a National Day of Forgiveness. He was able to forgive the Cartel for having killed his family. In the same way, we must all be able to forgive those who have hurt us. Only in this way, can the sacrifice of Captain Berto Castillo and his faithful K-9 dog, Franz, mean anything."

The President declares that this date and starting time of 4:00 p.m. will henceforth be a "National Day of Forgiveness" in memory of Police Captain Berto Castillo and his faithful German Shepherd dog, Franz. He also states that both Berto and Franz risked their lives many times together in efforts to save the lives of many citizens and children of Yuñeco and neighboring communities.

The reporter on the radio is in a van touring the City. Everywhere he goes, he sees and reports on people crying and hugging each other. Many others have gone to their knees in prayer no matter where they are, on lawns, on sidewalks, on porches, on balconies, and in churches of many denominations.

Back in the hospital room, Chief Medina walks over to Pablo Castillo and says, "I assume the responsibility for planning the funeral lands on your shoulders now Pablo. I'll help if I can, maybe the media announcements."

Pablo beckons his sister, María, to join them. He puts his arm around her as she wipes tears from her eyes.

"Sis, we need to announce the funeral. A lot of people will want to come. Chief Medina has offered to handle the media announcements. What do you think?"

"Well, today is Tuesday. I think we should have the body embalmed and the funeral on Saturday. That would permit a number of the other chiefs in the nation to attend as well as other people who couldn't get off work during the week. But what church can handle such a large group?"

Chef Medina observes, "Would you like me to phone the Army Base Chaplain and ask him if we can use the base chapel and have him conduct. That way the chapel can handle the crowd and the chaplain is non-denominational."

María says, "That's a good idea, and Berto often worked with the Army."

Pablo adds, "I agree. How about the service at 11:00 a.m. with family and special guests invited into the new conference room for a prayer meeting at 10:30 a.m.?"

Everyone agrees with the basic schedule.

Pablo says, "Chief if you can get this word out, we'd appreciate it. And if you and your secretary who knew Berto so well could meet at our motel room tonight at 7:30 p.m., we can plan the agenda for the service, who will speak, who will not speak, who will give the prayers, etc.?"

"Of course." responds the Chief. "Let's go into the hallway where I can phone the base about using their chapel."

The three who loved Berto so much leave the room where there is crying and go to the phone in the hall.

Chief Medina makes the call and receives strong support for the idea of the funeral service for Berto Saturday morning at the base chapel. The Chaplain also offers the use of the base choir to provide special musical numbers. That idea is well received by Berto's brother and sister.

The Chief then calls the local newspaper and radio station, giving them the basic information about the funeral. The receptionists at both agencies thank the Chief for keeping them informed.

The rest of the week is very sad for all those who worked with Berto and knew Franz, the great trailing dog. Various civic groups want to name a variety of monuments and special days after the police duo. The Police Commission is overwhelmed with the response in the city concerning the death of Berto and Franz. They never imagined that a member of their police force could be so well known and loved by so many citizens in the community.

They plan a special meeting for Thursday night to honor the two dedicated members of the department. People whose lives were touched directly by the two are permitted to speak. The Commission had no idea that Berto and Franz had been so active over the years saving lives and training others to do the same.

#

At the Police Commission's meeting, stories are heard about mountain climbing, cave searching, protecting others by killing charging wild beasts, saving spouses and children from kidnappers, both Berto and Franz parachuting together to save someone, etc.

The Chairman of the Police Commission says, "I imagine we have many other members of the Police

Department who are serving in the same manner now. We must remember to appreciate these other men and women who protect us and keep us safe."

When the meeting ends, there is a reminder of the 11:00 a.m. funeral Saturday morning.

#

Finally Saturday morning dawns with a beautiful blue sky and bright sunlight. Those people who were special in the life of Berto are invited to a prayer meeting at 10:30 a.m. in the newly constructed conference room next to the chapel. It has beautiful wood paneling on the walls, soft carpeting, windows with drapes that match the carpeting, and many soft chairs around a conference table.

The people start arriving in the chapel at 10:00 a.m. The ushers are already in place helping guests and friends of Berto find their seats. Rafael and Paco from the Cartel are dressed in new, dark blue suits helping as ushers. They have never been happier knowing now that Berto has forgiven them. They realize they have a job to do back in the jungle, but they willingly accept the challenge.

In the special conference room, Berto's brother, Pablo Castillo, will be conducting the prayer session. Those special guests are Pablo's wife, Sra. Cármen Castillo; Berto's sister, María Castillo Rodríguez and her husband, Humberto; Police Chief Luis Medina and his secretary, Blanca Hernández; Nurse Alicia Alvarez; the "young lady" Vera and Dos Brazos; and Dr. González.

At exactly 10:30 a.m., Pablo Castillo stands and thanks everyone for coming to this special meeting. He announces that he will give the opening prayer.

In this prayer, he remembers his childhood days with Berto as his big brother always looking out for him as he later looked out for the citizens of La Vista.

When he finishes his prayer, a marvelous event occurs. Berto and Franz appear in the room, coming directly through the wall standing about two feet above the conference table. The guests are overwhelmed at this spiritual event.

Chief Medina says, "Look at Berto's face. He appears 20 years younger. Even Franz appears younger. They are in their prime."

Berto communicates with the group, but not in regular speech from his mouth but more from his mind to the minds of the others in the room.

He says, "Don't worry about me. It's just like I recently read. I've been to Paradise and will return there. I'm happier than I've ever been before. All the pain I suffered these past years is gone."

Then Berto lifts his hand and welcomes into the room on the same level as he is, dressed in white like he is, his two former wives, Pilar and Susana. They both appear in the beauty of their prime and enter the room walking through the wall. And as if those aren't enough astounding occurrences, Berto lifts his hand again and welcomes his beautiful children, Bobbie, Miguel, and Elizabeth also walking through the wall into the room. Everyone appears as happy as can be. Throughout all this, Franz stands at Berto's side with his tail wagging occasionally.

Berto expresses to all in the room his affection for them.

Berto then lifts his hand and welcomes coming through the wall Betty, the Cartel woman who was assigned to kill Berto but was not able to kill another human being. She ended up in love with Berto and he with her. She was killed in the jungle by a curare tipped arrow to the neck.

Berto communicates with the group again expressing his love for each and everyone. He wishes them the best in their lives and tells them not to worry about him as he has never been happier, having his children and wives around him as well as his faithful dog, Franz.

He says the only sad thing about leaving is that he will miss other women whom he loves and other associates who have supported him over the years. Mentioning them by name, he communicates the names of Blanca, Nurse Alicia, and Vera. They are overwhelmed by this special concern on the part of Berto.

Everyone is astounded at this marvelous manifestation, to see Berto and Franz after they died. What a blessed occasion. But Berto informs them that they are not to discuss his return to them after he died. It is too sacred, he informs them, to be discussed around the community.

He next thanks Dr. González for trying to save his life and for the attention the hospital staff gave him these past few months. He thanks Police Chief Luis Medina for all the support he gave him over the years. He hopes that together they made a positive difference in the lives of many people.

He informs the group that he must now leave with his loved ones. Then Berto walks through the wall with Franz at his left side as usual followed by the others. They are gone.

Everyone sites quietly for a while completely overwhelmed at the marvelous spiritual manifestation they have been privileged to witness.

Pablo looks at his watch and says, "We'd better move into the chapel. Please remember Berto's request for confidentiality on this wonderful blessing we have been given. Berto lives on. Franz lives on. They all live on in the prime of their lives. Surely, if we too live the kind of life that Berto did, we'll someday join him. And Berto said he has never been happier. Remember Berto's words as you live your lives.

"Okay, please follow me and Cármen as we lead the way to the platform. Those who speak, please don't push the microphone away, use it so that everyone can hear you."

Pablo begins to walk slowly as he leads the small procession to the platform in the chapel. Each one radiates a smile like never before. Their understanding of spiritual things has increased many fold thanks to the visitation of Berto and his companions. The crowd in the chapel realizes that something special, something sacred, has happened to this small group.

#

That afternoon following the funeral, the citizens of La Vista listen as the radio reporter says, "This will be a day that will live on in the minds of the citizens of Yuñeco. It is very sad to see the end of the dedicated lives of Captain Berto Castillo and his great dog, Franz. But it is historic to see the termination of the drug activities of the nation's most feared drug Cartel. It is also historic to see the transition of this Cartel to a life-giving memorial as the members of the Cartel spend their waking hours searching for and harvesting the lifesaving drugs hidden in the plants of the Amazon Rainforest.

"It takes a very special people who can live in the Amazon Rainforest with its many dangers. The people of the Cartel have learned to live and survive in this environment. They are perhaps the only humans who could stay in the jungle and conduct an organized search for and the later cultivation of specific plants whose life saving ingredients haven't even been explored yet.

"This great pharmaceutical burst of knowledge will be the constant and permanent contribution of those who work on the trains and in the scientific labs that bring the drugs that will ease pain and prevent death around the world. Yes, to name that day 'The National Day of Forgiveness' is appropriate for the likes of Captain Berto Castillo and his great German Shepherd dog, Franz."

The End

Made in the USA
Columbia, SC
22 January 2021